PENGUIN BOOKS

YOU HAVE TO BE CAREFUL
IN THE LAND OF THE

James Kelman was born in Glasgow in 1946. His books include *A Greyhound for Breakfast*, winner of the 1987 Cheltenham Prize, *The Burn*, recipient of a Scottish Arts Council book award, and *A Disaffection*, which won the James Tait Black Memorial Prize and was shortlisted for the Booker Prize. *How Late it Was, How Late* won the 1994 Booker Prize. His recent work includes *The Good Times*, a new collection of stories for which he won Scottish Writer of the Year, *Translated Accounts*, a novel, and a collection of essays, *And the Judges Said . . .*

You Have to be Careful in the Land of the Free

JAMES KELMAN

PENGUIN BOOKS

PENGUIN BOOKS

Published by the Penguin Group
Penguin Books Ltd, 80 Strand, London WC2R ORL, England
Penguin Group (USA) Inc., 375 Hudson Street, New York, New York 10014, USA
Penguin Group (Canada), 10 Alcorn Avenue, Toronto, Ontario, Canada M4V 3B2
(a division of Pearson Penguin Canada Inc.)
Penguin Ireland, 25 St Stephen's Green, Dublin 2, Ireland
(a division of Penguin Books Ltd)
Penguin Group (Australia), 250 Camberwell Road, Camberwell, Victoria 3124, Australia
(a division of Pearson Australia Group Pty Ltd)
Penguin Books India Pvt Ltd, 11 Community Centre, Panchsheel Park, New Delhi – 110 017, India
Penguin Group (NZ), cnr Airborne and Rosedale Roads, Albany, Auckland 1310, New Zealand
(a division of Pearson New Zealand Ltd)
Penguin Books (South Africa) (Pty) Ltd, 24 Sturdee Avenue, Rosebank 2196, South Africa

Penguin Books Ltd, Registered Offices: 80 Strand, London WC2R ORL, England

www.penguin.com

First published by Hamish Hamilton 2004
Published in Penguin Books 2005
2

Copyright © M & J Kelman Limited, 2004

The moral right of the author has been asserted

The publisher is grateful for permission to reproduce from the following:
'Oooh Love' by Blaze Foley, used courtesy of Blaze Foley Songs,
PO Box 120185, Nashville, TN 37212, USA.
'Save a Bread' by Justin Hinds, used courtesy of Tropic Entertainment Ltd.

Set by Rowland Phototypesetting Ltd, Bury St Edmunds, Suffolk
Printed in England by Clays Ltd, St Ives plc

ISBN-13: 978-0-14-101411-1

Acknowledgements:
Simon, Drenka and Melanie came in with confidence,
and I appreciate that.

for my family in USA,
those I know and those I don't know,
and also for my friends there

blue eyes
she said, pretty blue eyes
she said I had pretty blue eyes . . .

(*from 'Oooh Love', a song by Blaze Foley,*
from the album Live at the Austin Outhouse)

I had been living abroad for twelve years and I was gaun hame, maybe forever, maybe a month. Once there it would sort itself out. In the meantime I fancied seeing my faimly again; my mother was still alive, and I had a sister and brother. The plane out of here was scheduled for one o'clock tomorrow afternoon. I was in a room at an Away Inn, out in the middle of nowhere, miles from the airport and miles from downtown, but it was cheap as fuck so there we are and there I was. The woman on reception gied me a look when I asked if there was a bar within crawling distance. Then she thought a moment and told me if I walked a mile or so there was a place. She had a twinkle in her eye at the idea of the mile or so walk. Then she said she never used the place herself but reckoned they might do some food

I hadnay asked about food in the first place so how come she threw that in? I think I know why. I just cannay put it into words. But it turned my slow move to the door into a bolt for freedom. I had the anorak zipped right to the top, pulled the cap down low on my heid. Outside a freezing wind was blowing. Ye were expecting tumbleweed to appear but when it did it would be in the form of a gigantic snowball. While I walked I wondered why I was walking and why outside. Why the hell could I no just have stayed in the room, strolled up and down the motel corridor if I felt energetic. Better still, I could have read a book. Or even allowed myself to watch some television. Who could grumble about that; I was entitled to relax. Yet still I left the place and walked a mile in subArctic conditions. Mine was a compulsive, obsessive, addictive personality, the usual – plus I felt like a beer and the company of human beings; human beings, not tubes in a box or words on a page, and masturbation enters into that. In other words I was sick of myself and scunnered with my company, physically and mentally. And why was I gaun hame! I didnay even want to go hame. Yes I did.

No I didnay.

Yes I did.

No I didnay. No I fucking didnay. It was an obligation. Bonné Skallin man it can only be an obligation. The faimly were there and one had to say hullo now and again. Posterity demands it of us. Once I am deid the descendants will be discussing departed ancestors: Who was that auld shite that lived in the States? Which one? Him that didnay come hame to visit his poor auld maw! Aw that bastard!

This is the obligation I am talking about.

Jesus christ.

But the reality was that my mother wasnay keeping too well. Let us put an end to the frivolity: if I wantit to see her again this seemed the time. I spoke to my brother on the phone. What an arsehole. Never mind, the point was taken, I had bought le billet with return scheduled a month from now and here I was. Yeh, the wind, and polar bears on the street. I like polar bears. And I like this part of the world. The auld ears, nevertheless, were being nipped at by icy spears. I settled into a catatonic march. Blocks of low-level factories and warehouses were on baith sides of the road, disused, some derelict. Maybe a cab would pass. I should have phoned one from the motel, I know that. But I didnay. Okay?

The wind whistled between buildings, rattling the roofs. Can the wind rattle the roofs? It did sound like that. This land was good land. But these capitalist fuckers and their money-grabbing politico sidekicks had turned it into a horror. I had an urge to write down my thoughts but where was my notebook? In my room at the Inn. And so what if it had been with me, in this gale it would have blown away or else my fingers would have froze and fell aff. I bought the notebook yesterday in a decent wee bookshop no too far from the bus station. It was a real surprise. But that can happen, ye enter a town in the middle of nowhere and discover some enthusiast has opened a bookshop. In this case a middle-aged couple who had grabbed their dough and skipped out of Denver or somewhere. So they opened a pure nirvana of a place. These folks were good folks. Although no doubt they were million-aires and the shop was a hobby. If their bookshop was in the vicinity and open I would have gone. I am convinced of that. But now it was evening and it surely would have been closed and how far away was I from the bus station? I had seen the day where I might have thought fuck it and tried to hitch a ride but buddy, no just now.

The cheery neon sign blinking a welcome to weary travelers had nothing whatsoever to do with my decision. I saw it ahead, its fissures of light streaming upwards to the moon. Jeremiah Brown, grunted the sign – for such was my name – rest ye here oh weary one.

Sure, I replied. Show me yer fine food, yer fine beer, yer wine, yer spirits; and what about an Isla malt at an affordable price?

Walk straight ahead oh venerable one oh wise one, the gravelly voice intoned.

I was either hallucinating or a god had collared me for his ayn.

The place was huge and empty, built for stagecoachloads of customers who never arrived. There was something about it, like it had been abstracted from a 1940s movie, made for

3

hotdogs and hamburgers and all kinds of similar fastfood sustenance. It was like it wasnay a bar at all it was really something else, a fucking what do you call it, a restaurant.

A restaurant! It wasnay a bar at all, it was a goddam restaurant. There was a little bar right enough, set into a corner in the style of a rock and roll obsessed backwoodsman's den, Jim Bridger goes electric. You entered the den you entered the bar. There were ossified wee creatures and paintings of such; toads, squirrels, foxes and beavers, mink, a huge bear, game birds and big fucking brown trout and carp; fishing rods and single barrel shotguns. Some interesting auld signs; one read PIKE'S PEAK OR BUST and another CALAMITY JANE'S ROCK N ROLL. Stuck alongside on the wall were 78 rpm records with sleeves, and LP and EP covers showing Little Richard, Jerry Lee Lewis, Fats Domino, Elvis Presley, Chuck Berry, Buddy Holly, Franco Corelli and Eddie Cochrane. The bar was done in the image of a redwood tree trunk and the barstools looked like sawn-off portions of thinner trunks. Naybody here. I was about to vamoose but a guy had spotted me, poked his head out from behind a door and was across immediately. Yes sir how are you sir?

I'm fine, how's yerself in this here jungle?

Okay okay. He attempted a smile, it became a question.

I didnay bother explaining. Just a lite beer, I said, I dont care which brand, nor its state, nor yet its country of origin.

The guy attempted another smile. I rubbed my hands together. It's damn cauld tonight.

Yeh, gonna be snow later, maybe sooner.

Aye, it's in the air. Time for Santa Claus eh!

Yes sir.

That bottle of beer later I skedaddled. To leave a bar on one such item isnay exactly typical. Maybe I had turned over a new leaf. If so naybody had telt me. Naybody never tells me fucking nothing but so that is okay. If they did one might prepare.

I was gauny call a fare-thee-well to the bartender but he was out of sight, no doubt blethering to a lassie in the kitchen, if he was lucky enough to have a lassie in the kitchen. I worked in bars much of the time and I never had nay lassie in nay kitchen. It was just the usual sentimental fucking shite man it came pouring out my brains. The reality is the guy in this bar was living a boring nightmare. What chance did he have? What life lay ahead? What

fuck.

Right, on we go. And so did I, out the door. In the lobby I phoned a cab which is what I should have considered back in the Away Inn. Never mind. Ten minutes later I was in the backseat of an elderly Lincoln, just about my favourite jalopy, that yin with the unEuropean lines, which is what I liked about it, it was just so fucking unEuropean. Times have changed for the better when the taxis are elderly Lincolns. Yes sir. There was a large sign pinned to the rear window.

'S YORE RIGHT TO SMOKE IN HERE,
'S MA RIGHT TO SHOOT YA.

I must not smoke I must not smoke I must not smoke. The guy himself wasnay smoking although his side window was a quarter way open. He had a woollen hat on his napper and a thick scarf wound round his neck. All the heaters were blowing warm and his music playing softly, a solo clarinet. Yeh, it was snug. Where was his flask of coffee and the nip of brandy? At certain periods ye could envy taxi drivers. I called to him, It's a miserable cauld night outside but warm in here!

Yes, very cold, the snow is coming.

What time do you finish?

I saw his eyes in the rearview mirror, studying me. There was a chance he was a writer. I finish at four, he said, maybe five.

He was from Africa but from what part. You from Ghana originally?

Ghana . . .

Yer accent is familiar.

He nodded, but noncommittally; was I right or wrong, who could say. His nod was to my idea about the accent and how I had arrived at the "Ghana" deduction, no about whether the guess was accurate which was irrelevant. He kept his eyes on the road. To hell with it, I leaned forwards and called: Nowadays we do not ask people personal questions. But once upon a time that was okay, that was civilized behaviour. I would have tried my guess out on ye without a moment's consideration but nowadays that is asking for trouble and the likelihood is you think I am some nefarious undercover Security agent from the anti unPatriotic Front, masquerading as whatever, a down-at-heel Skatchman. I'm no, I'm just an ordinary guy, I'm just an immigrant. I shrugged.

I didnay say "an immigrant like you" or "unlike you I am an immigrant" or "I am not an immigrant, like yourself, or unlike yourself". Nayn of that stuff. I didnay say fucking nothing. Ah but conversations are fraught, deadly dangerous. Then too the poor guy, the driver, just out for his 12- or 14-hour shift trying to earn a dollar and he gets hit by me.

The chat was now at an end.

The feller no longer watched me in his mirror, only drove to the appropriate area, one with a choice of bars. Okay. And the district we were in now, it had that familiarity about it, like I had been through this way in the past. It was funny how ye got these sensations. I was gauny mention it to the driver but

6

naw, I had blown it, and when I got out the cab he avoided looking at me. I hoped he had grasped that I wasnay a right-wing racist bastard and I wasnay an undercover member of some counter-insurgency agency whose specialty lay in perceiving the alien threat. I tipped him a typical sum and said, Have a good night.

There was a sign for the local community college and I saw a little river, and there were some no bad-looking bars, and farther on there was a leisure place, 10 pin bowling. Neat. As burgs go it was a small yin but here it had its ayn wee downtown area and all kinds of people should have been out walking, all kinds of people. Nayn of them was so walking, no tonight. It was just too cauld.

But at least there was nay snaw. I checked the first bar; busy enough and a young crowd; and the music, though dull and boring, was very loud and rhythmic. Could I cope, that was the question. There were a couple of beautiful girls; the boys with them seemed too young to buy a drink never mind act as escorts. I was inside the lobby and about to push open the door and saunter in but my arm locked and I was unable to fulfill the operation. But my legs were fine and they did a march on the spot while my upper body conducted a reverse manoeuvre. Next thing I know I am out the door thank god. When in doubt trust yer physicality.

Next along was a joint called the Shooters and Horses Sports Bar. This was the last place I should have gone, should ever have gone.

Thank you for the warning fates, now it was up to me.

In the bright interior I could see baseball on a few large screens, yep, Corey Parker. He was everywhere ye went. It was reaching the end of the season and everything had stopped to see if the new boy wonder could set an all-time record. I didnay think he could and would have taken bets all day. I reckoned it was down to his name. If the feller had been christened some less macho moniker – e.g. Herbert Summerbottom III – he would have remained in obscurity. Mind you the auld timers were saying the guy was special.

Never trust an auld timer but, no when ye want to lay down yer dough. Ever met a rich auld timer? There are a few rich ones but you will never meet them. The ones ye meet for daily communion are either skint or else do not gie a fuck about the dollar, almighty or no.

But I wasnay gaun to no fucking bar to sit and stare at the tube. There were five of them thar screens in this here joint, probably they even had one in the pisshouse. What a dive. But my feet led the way, I pushed open the door. It got worse. In this bar a man could hit the Oregon Trail without leaving his stool. Not only was Corey Parker a feature so too were the ladies, and a large poster screamed to lascivious boozers that come midnite adult entertainment was scheduled, sit back and relax: here come the Wicked Women from the Wild West. Then I saw the poster was dated 1872.

One feller was seated on a stool at the bar, he was doing a crossword puzzle. Six others were sitting below the main screens, their occasional comments no doubt concerning the league of all-time bat-swinging immortals. Fine, what is wrang with that? Nothing at all except I had to leave, leave, right at that moment man I couldnay fucking stand it. Stay!

Go!

Stay!

Go!

Fuck. How come I aye insisted on tempting the fates? It isnay as if I had never been warned. Once upon a time I wound up with a knife in the gut. Of course that was in fucking Glasgow, coming out a chip shop.

The bartender frowned. Had I paused by the exit just to

annoy him? How come I had done that? Or was I wondering what to drink? What else could it be? Surely I couldnay have paused there just to annoy him? Really? Yeh. Fuck him. Needless to say I returned, stepped to the bar and ordered a beer in blasé fashion, tethering my anorak to a nearby stool. The bartender nodded like what else. He was an aulder guy and I sensed he was a frustrated intellectual. No matter the deviant politics here was a feller that enjoyed whatever mentally stimulating data life tossed at him. I caught him examining me, gauging what I was, who I was, why the hell I had come to his bar. I resisted winking when he knew I had caught him in the act. Make that a lite beer, I said.

A lite beer?

Yeh.

You bet, he said. His brow had furrowed then frowned; now relaxed, now frowned again and yeh, I knew he was placing bets with himself: 8 to 5 this guy with the funny voice is a conman, evens he is on the run, 4s an unfrocked priest. But I warnt no christian never mind no catholic christian. And if he read my mind I would get accused of blasphemy and he would fill me full of holes and be awarded the congressional medal for services to the almighty while I would be buried at the crossroads, a lonesome coyote growling.

Now he nodded to himself. It was okay, it was just I was an unintegratit furnir, a member of the alienigenae, all was explained.

Why the fuck had I left the goddam motel room? why could I not have been satisfied with a relaxing night in front of el tele, instead of the baseball I could have bought into the porn and chastised myself mightily.

I should have known the evening would go wrang from the first pub I entered. This was the kind of town where the barstaff are aye depressed out their skulls, where the customers are forced to stay on for an extra couple of hours just to cheer them up. This is done no by overtipping but by getting them to tell ye about their life to date and dreams for the future. This guy was one of them, I knew the signs. And he looked about fifty years of age unfortunately, so was gauny need a week to tell it all. I sighed but the drink was set down in front of me, I squared the shoodirs and reached out my right haun, accepting the challenge. But my god it was damn tasty. It was just lite beer but what a flavour what a flavour. Nice beer, I said.

The bartender nodded, wondering if I was being sarcastic. He was hovering by me. I was obviously mair interesting than Corey Parker, ergo he wasnay a baseball fan, ergo he was on the outlook for displaced persons.

Of course he had that cigarette smouldering in the adjacent ashtray. The first time he left to serve another customer I was gauny steal a puff, a lungful of blue air is what I needit. I had gien up smoking six months previously. It was proving the biggest mistake of my short but doleful existence. I wished I was the psalmist. Only the psalmist ever spoke for me. One day I would speak on my ayn behalf. Until then

no sir, it was best to leave. Immediately.

But I have never been good at extricating myself from awkward situations. Usually I just resign myself, unable to make the decisive move that might allow my liberation. If I did make a decision it was guaranteed the wrang yin. Often I made such a decision on purpose. I enjoyed testing myself. Was my resolve steely? 12 gets you 5 I would fall by the wayside

Strange how the lite beer was so enjoyable. At this rate I would be here all night. Still the bartender hovered. I thought I would craïc a joke. It was like he read my mind. He grabbed a quick drag on his smoke and settled himself to listen. If ye dont mind, I said, I would like to tell ye a joke. A sort of a joke, it is predicated on a knowledge of international politics, reinforced by a punchline that assumes a radical audience.

Oh yeh.

Tricky to declaim in an ordinary bar.

The bartender stared at me, no with outright hostility, just quizzically. He already knew I wasnay from these parts but now suspected the difference was planetary. Or else I was having some fun at his expense. Dangerous. But he rose to the challenge. This aint no ordinary bar, he said, then he winked. And you aint from Colorado.

Where ye from yerself? I said.

Me? He inhaled on his cigarette.

Forget it, I said, I dont really care where ye're from. See it from my point of view.

Pardon me?

This next part of the conversation is aye tricky for somebody of my status. How to say I am no from this part of the world at all. I am no even an Uhmerkin and then have to go on from there. It is difficult.

Just tell the truth son.

Okay, I aint an Uhmerkin. But the faimly of one of my ancestors was. My great-great-great-granddaddy. He passed along this way once, a long time ago. He was a fairly conscientious auld feller; he startit out as a prospector but soon hit the harder stuff. I'm called eftir him. So it's possible I've got roots that arenay too far from here, and maybe long lost cousins. Aint that something?

He nodded, stubbed out the cigarette, pointed to a notice on the wall. It was that federal one with the blue borders advising customers they were required to display appropriate ID on request, in the case of visitors from abroad this meant displaying their alien status. I held up my hands in a gesture of surrender. I got it here, I said, patting my chest and keeping my hands in view at all times, lest he brought out the shotgun from beneath the counter. Do ye want to see it? I said.

I surely do, nothing personal.

Yeh it's personal.

Not for me, he said, it aint personal for me.

I sighed and brought out my wallet to show him. It's always personal for me, I said.

Oh you got a Red Card? He pretended no to look too closely. Who did he think he was kidding. He reached for his cigarette pack while squinting again at my photograph. He called to the guy doing the crossword puzzle: Hey Barney, this guy's got a Red Card.

Aye, I said, no just any auld alien.

Right . . . The bartender smiled, still squinting at it. You an atheist and a socialist?

Yeh, well, mair an anarchist I suppose, I'm opposed to authority on principle. Mind you, I'll negotiate on particulars. They aint deportit me yet.

Right . . . He grinned, studying my fizzog. Hey you've aged a bit since this was taken? He squinted at it again. What's that, Jeremiah?

Jeremiah, yeh.

Nice name. Bible name, he said returning me the ID.

Correct, I said. I stuck the wallet back into my hip pocket then drank some beer and gestured with the bottle. Could I have another?

Sure you can. He reached below, opened one and placed it before me. You a Swede?

Naw.

German?

Nope.

Dutch?

No.

Irish?

Nah.

English?

Not at all, I'm Skarrisch.

Skarrisch? Neat. Ever since I was a kid my dream is to go to your country, I mean from childhood.

What like to emigrate?

Huh?

To go and live there?

To go and live there, no sir.

Aw ye mean as a tourist?

Naah, like the kids do, backpacking.

You talking about rambling across the country, the islands and the highlands, gaun where ye like and doing what ye like? That kind of thing?

Yeh.

Mm.

Something wrong in that?

Naw. The whole world's yer oyster.

The bartender glanced to the side where the blokes were gawping up at the screens. It occurred to me he had been speaking quietly. Maybe he didnay want them to eavesdrop the conversation. It would have embarrassed him. He was discussing a childish fancy and wantit it kept secret. It so happened the crossword-puzzle guy *was* eavesdropping so he was right to be cautious. Listen, I said, your dream is shared by thousands of people, tens of thousands of people.

Yeh?

Bet money on it. What essentially it is: ye all want to go to the motherland in the off chance ye bump into one of yer ancestors' descendants, a long-lost cousin. What ye hope to discover is if ye are related to a clan chieftain, if ye are descended from royal blood and maybe own a mountain or something, if ye have any cheap servants at yer disposal, with luck they'll be wearing a kilt and sing praise songs for yer wife and faimly; bodies like me, we'll call ye sir, hump yer suitcases and dedicate pibroch airs and fiddle tunes to this race of which you are a leading member if not the central progenitor.

The bartender sniffed and stared at my forehead, then he smiled.

The chieftain of a clan is like a king, I said, although no too much like a king because in the auld days the clans practised a form of democracy.

I read history.

Aw right, okay, yeh, anyway, it was a communal experience, that is what I am saying.

I heard that, yeh.

Like an early form of communism, I whispered, sshh, keep it quiet.

He smiled, shook his heid, reached for his cigarette.

I expected ye to go pale there at the very use of the word.

How long you been in my country?

Twelve years.

Not long enough.

I know. What was I saying – like the clan chieftain was mair of a big brother kind of figure, paternal, ye might say presidential. Of course in the latter days he wound up stealing the clan property, just like the yoorpeen aristocracies, whatever, like the mafeeeaa.

Oh yeh?

Yeh, I said, loudly and clearly, the mafeeeaa.

He chuckled. I got you figured: you can discuss the mafia in public places, speak out loud with your voice, right? But you cant discuss politics? The words like "communist", you got to say them in a quiet voice, you got to whisper, yeh?

Now I chuckled. This guy was mair devious than me. I felt

like shaking his hand. He took a quick drag on his cigarette, returned it to the ashtray. He crossed to the other end of the bar where the crossword guy was seated on the stool, murmured to him.

Smoke from the cigarette drifted towards me, it smelled good. The guy had got up from his stool, was returning with him, but left his money and the crossword at his place. We exchanged nods.

This is Barney.

Hi.

Hi, I said.

Barney aint a big baseball fan.

Okay.

So what about your kings and queens? are they the same? like you were saying there, you spoke about the mafia.

Yeh.

You want to say it to him . . . The bartender nodded at Barney then went off to get an order for one of the baseball customers. He called back: Keep on talking.

Kings and queens, I said, basically what they did was they stole the wealth held in trust for their faimly, they transformed it all into assets, their assets. Just like governments do, they steal the people's wealth and make assets out of it, then they fucking sell it off to their sidekicks and get themselves whatever, penthouse suites in Manhattan, luxurious trappings in benign climates, acres of land in Calabria and Montana, Guerrero, Andalusia or back in Skallin they purchase the purple mountains, the beautiful wee islands and the deep mysterious lochs, the shebang – all of that belonged to the clan chieftains, who were the big brothers and the fathers, first in the male line, and they selt it to the highest bidder.

Barney pursed his lips, took a sip of beer. Then he said, So that reminds you of – what did you say, the mafia?

I closed my mouth to resist replying, noting the bottle of beer in my hand and the other on the table. Baith were empty. How else could I speak such shite. And if I was carrying on like that the now, how was it gauny be once I stepped onto the plane tomorrow, or once I got into Glasgow Airport and then hame. The booze had gone right to my heid. Unless maybe there was an oxygen deficiency somewhere.

Hey, did I say "hame" there? Yeh. My faimly was my faimly and that land was my birthplace. This was undeniable. Being away for so long it just went out my mind. How long had it been since I considered the word "hame" in regard to myself? Other exiles think about hame much of the time, they get together and talk about the guid auld days and all that stuff. I could chat about the dear auld motherland as well but it was aye with an uncommon sense of relief at no being there. I pretended otherwise to my mother whom I phoned every blue moon to apologize for the lengthy gap in communication.

I never spoke to my brother or sister unless they happened to be in my mother's house. Me apologizing, that was about all that went on in these conversations. Baith were a few years aulder than me and we didnay have too much in common, no that I could figure.

I noticed Barney still standing there, probably wondering if I was gauny continue talking or if he should return to the crossword puzzle. But how come he didnay talk to me? How come the social onus lies with the stranger! Twas ever thus. Hey Barney, I said, ye're no Irish are ye?

No.

It's an Irish name. See what I've noticed, Skarrisch folk I meet in various places, English folk, they go to bars and reminisce. But Irish folk I meet, they dont bother reminiscing, they want to sit there in the company of one another but they dont talk, they just like to be there and every now and then they turn around and nod their head and maybe later on they sing a song.

Yeh?

But if they do talk they talk about the here and now, what is the actual material substance, baseball and horses, boxing and football, the weather, what's on the tube.

About the mafia? You want to know about the mafia? You a newspaper reporter?

Pardon me?

You want to know about the mafia?

No.

You dont want to know about the mafia?

I dont, naw.

I thought you did.

Naw.

Italian people?

What about Italian people?

I guess you dont like them?

Yeh I like them, what ye talking about?

Italian people aint the mafia.

I know that.

No sir, said Barney. You think that but they aint, you got too much propaganda nowadays, this is the problem, this is why things go so bad for people. He sniffed then returned to his beer and his newspaper. The bartender was now wiping the counter close to where I was propped. What happened to the conversation? he said, glancing at Barney as well as myself.

What d'ye mean like highlands and islands?

You guys were talking, now you aint.

Barney said, The guy has ideas about Italian people.

Naw I dont, I said, the world's just full of misunderstandings.

Barney gied a wry smile. We watched the bartender lift a solid-looking, spotlessly clean ashtray from close by my empty beer bottle. He winked at us and flipped the ashtray into the air. I had to appreciate the way he got it to ground by a form of sleight of hand like he had performed a telekinetic feat or something. Barney made a show of applauding. I grinned and said to Barney, I would be wary of playing cards with him.

Oh you play cards? said the bartender.

Now where had that come from? I stared at him. Barney was smiling. But I didnay smile in response. My real opinion was that the bartender would have made a fine pickpocket. But in furin parts the sense of humour is a fragile entity and I didnay risk saying it aloud. Maybe he was a genuine villain, and this bar stuff was a diversion; during the night he crept stealthily off to rob banks but was always hame in time for breakfast and naybody was any the wiser. Unless he had retired to here, following his life of crime. He had got fed up with grumpy victims and the constant hassle with the cops, used the last of his ill-gotten gains to invest in this wee sports bar. It was either that or a bookshop. Maybe he spun a coin. If it had been me I would have opened a betting parlour.

One of these days . . .

The bartender had gien the ashtray a wipe, it glistened. Dont worry about it, I said, I stopped smoking ages ago. This is my sixth month down the lonesome trail and the coyotes are wailing. Getting worse by the hour but, I have to confess.

Yeh? The bartender nodded and reached for his cigarette pack. This set Barney off, he went into his pocket and came out with a fresh ceegar.

I stared about the pub. At the other end the baseball fellers were angry about something, gesticulating at the screens. One was onto his feet and swallowing the dregs of his beer, lifting his change from the counter and muttering to himself as he headed for the door. When he got to abreast of myself he paused then threw a mean look in my direction, raised his eyebrows; he strode on. When I frowned at the bartender he said, Having a good time?

Yeh, thanks.

You like our country?

I've been here twelve years.

Some people dont like it, they been here all their life.

No me.

Tomorrow you're flying home? called Barney.

Yeh, I said, it's too long to walk.

Barney looked at the bartender who was reaching for a bottle of beer. And I was thinking fuck it, what a stupit thing to say, let us get back to the motel immediately, watch a movie or something. Then the beer arrived in front of me. The bartender nodded, but less a positive gesture than a tricky self-consciousness. I gied a smile. Thanks, I said. But my smile was one of surprise. I hadnay ordered the beer, no that I could remember. So it was on the house. But I didnay see any fresh bottle in front of Barney, nor in front of the baseball fans. It was just me getting the present. I didnay like that. If I saw somebody getting free beer I would definitely wonder what was gaun on, especially a stranger. How come I was being excluded, that was what I would want to know. Now it was surely time to leave.

I had nay option. In situations like this I just cannay trust myself; life is too short. Also I was hungry. I had noticed an all-night convenience store and they would have a sandwich of some description. Grub grub, I needit grub.

I would drink the beer before leaving.

But there is a time when everything becomes significant. That is the time to watch yerself, in particular yer back. And drinkers are a strange damn breed anyway, especially solitaries, given that I too fit that description. I wouldnay dispute the label "strange" if applied to myself but I would dispute that it has to be negative. Strange characters may be mysterious characters, no just people who exhibit unnatural behaviour, no necessarily. Anywey, it depends on what we mean by "unnatural behaviour".

Some might argue that a Celtic male with pink skin, fair hair (receding) and blue eyes (watery) should have been empowered to travel the world where ere he chose and didnay need no colour-coded federal authorization never mind the okay from stray true-born persons he met in bars. How can Aryans be Aliens, is what they would argue. It is a contradiction. This feller's physicality and language are passport and visa. And then add to the tally that I was an ex Security operative, how Uhmerkin can ye get! Okay, failed Security operative. No really a failure, I just didnay make a career out it. But add to that failed husband and failed parent, failed father, general no fucking hoper. And now I was gaun hame, gaun hame! I was a failed fucking immigrant!

And tobacco smoke being puffed in my direction.

But once hame, if I got scunnered of the entire country in a matter of moments all would not be lost, I would just come back here, it would be fine, I would just fucking hop a plane.

How many fucking beers had I had? Couldnay be mair than – what? four? three? five!

So, what next? What was gauny happen? The usual, he grinned, sidling towards the exit.

No, only joking, I stood where I was, I was minding my ayn business and I was gauny continue minding my ayn business. No matter the pressure. And what business was I minding, what business did I know anything about. I knew nothing about business, I knew nothing about nothing. The truth is that I was a failure. That was the primary reason it had taken so long to book the flight. Failures do not fucking go fucking hame.

But I wasnay a failure. I was a guy that occasionally did crazy things, one who had lost his wife and daughter.

The bleakness of spirit descendeth, a simple bleakness of spirit. It derives from one's shortcomings. One is hopeless, no just at business matters, at everything that matters. I recently accrued ten thousand dollars. Ten thousand dollars. Imagine it. Then it was gone. Ten grand, fucking blown! I do not understand how that happened. Yes I do, it was just nonsense, the usual. I had just eh

Fuck.

Baith of them were looking at me. Maybe I said "fuck" out loud or else I sighed heavily; one isnay supposed to sigh heavily. I nodded, pointed at the television screens: What about Corey Parker? Is he as good as they say?

Who gives a shit, said Barney. He took off his glasses and smiled, sat back on his stool.

He was waiting for me to speak, but I wouldnay. There is a veil, one may draw it. The veil is drawn.

So you play cards? said the bartender.

Sometimes, yeh, I've played cards.

You got gambling buddies?

I smiled.

You got gambling buddies?

There is nay such thing as "gambling buddies", I said, if ye're a gambler ye should know that.

So you're a gambler? said the bartender.

What I'm saying is "gambling buddy" is a contradiction in terms. These guys slit each other's throat on a regular basis.

You a shooter or a horseman? said the bartender.

What?

He grinned.

I dont know that one, I said.

Barney also grinned, shook his heid, puffed on the bold ceegar. What happened to the ten thou, did you lose it?

Ten thou?

You had ten thou, then it went, what did you blow it on the tables?

On the slots? said the bartender.

Pool.

Pool!

You blew ten grand on pool? said Barney.

Yeh, there was a couple of guys I knew.

Gambling buddies, said the bartender with a wink of his right eye.

Winking right back at ye, I said and did so. Naw, they were nay buddies of mine; they owned a bar I used to visit. At the rear they built on a lounge room and installed two pool tables, good yins, then they organized regular tournaments, private tournaments, eftir hours. I was playing no a bad game at that time. They earned a few bucks off me in side-bets. At first they backed me against my opponents, until they realized that although I was a fine and subtle player I was a born loser. Show me the biggest dumpling in the hall and he is guaranteed to take money out my pockets. Ye want to bet me on that? Show me the dough. I shall bet ye my whole fucking wad. I shall bet ye my whole fucking wad that I cannay win one damn bet, not one damn bet. Bang bang fucking bang.

Seven letters ends in x, said Barney.

What?

Bang bang fucking bang, said the bartender.

Yeh, I said and lifted the bottle, paused and raised it to him in a salute. Sláinte, thanks for the beer.

It was Barney bought it.

Aw, aw thanks, thanks eh . . .

Barney shrugged.

Yeh. I nodded. In some places people dont talk to a stranger never mind buy him a drink, I said. But in other places these wee sparks do so occur. One can hit the skids, all things appear bleak, then along comes an act of human kindness. Never mind the "human kindness", an act of ordinary humanity. But some such acts are born out of desperation. This here is a bar that dulls the brain and quells all passion. Ye have yer dreams of better conversation but yer real dream is escape.

Close, said Barney, I did escape; I escaped to here. This is where I headed, this is my refuge.

Aye okay, fair enough.

So what about you?

Me? I smiled, then noticed the bartender was staring at me. In fact he was fucking glaring at me. Me, I said, I telt ye about me.

So what did you say?

What?

Barney smiled to the bartender.

I said I was gaun hame tomorrow. I havenay been hame for eight years and only twice in twelve. And just now I'm gaun to the room for gentlemen, the lavatory.

So it's a big deal for you?

Eh?

Your family, your wife and daughter?

What?

It must be a big deal, going home, see your wife and daughter. What did you leave them to come here?

What?

You came here. You ran out on them?

What ye fucking talking about?

Hey! the bartender held up his right hand.

Sorry. Naw, I said. I dont understand what ye're talking about. Tomorrow I'm flying hame and I mean by that back to

Skallin. My wife and daughter, ex wife and daughter, they live on the east coast.

Oh they do?

I havenay gied ye any reason to think otherwise.

You left them on the east coast? said Barney.

Naw I didnay leave them on the east coast, fuck sake, I'm getting divorced, she's divorcing me.

Hey I told you now your language is a bit too rich.

Sorry.

The bartender nodded. I shook my heid, stared at the bar. He had another puff on his cigarette. Barney was looking at me. I returned him a look. You aint a gambler, he said.

I didnay say I was a gambler. What I said was I gambled badly.

Oh.

Hang on a minute, I've got to go to the lavatory.

Sure, said the bartender, but why d'you insult my place?

I'm no insulting yer place. What d'you mean?

The bartender reached for his cigarette.

All I says was I was wanting to go to the lavatory. And I'll be back in a minute, carry on the conversation. Excuse me, I said and I backed off a step, still watching them. Then I turned, walked down to the side of the television screens where the fir sign signaled the way.

What was that all about, insulting his place? Ye cannay get gaun for a piss in some companies, even that gets misconstrued. There were mirrors round the side and rear walls and I tried to get a look back to the bar, to see what the other two were doing. Yeh, please dont talk about me when I'm gone. I wouldnay say they were. But at the same time, things change in weird ways, nothing would have surprised me.

It was a wee bit of a quandary though, I have to confess. I aint keen on these bars where ye have to walk miles for a piss and the only escape route is back the way ye came. The signs pointed on down a short corridor then round a bend, where there were arrows pointing ye along to another corner where the toilets were side by side, and if ye turned the wrang corner ye landed in some god-forsaken end staircase or else in a dark and dusty storeroom, and when ye push open the door there is a group of bodies in white hoods and robes, armed with fiery crosses. No sir, I aint keen on these kind of bars. Funny how in tricky situations this is how it works, you finish in a labyrinth. And a quick exit is the only saviour, if ye can find one, because it isnay guaranteed. Fucking hell, it was gauny be one of those nights. I felt like making an escape there and then, except the anorak, the fucking anorak, it was lying across a barstool.

Yeh, weird, weird how things happen. Inside the men's room there was a urinal and a w.c. cubicle. The urinal was overflowing man it was horrible. I was about to enter the cubicle but that seemed a likely trap. At times like these I could have done with something; my Security operative stick for instance, it would have been ideal. But I wasnay wanting to get my shoes drenched so I chose the cubicle. Then oh jesus christ I might have known, the outside door opened suddenly and my back to them. I rushed to finish the piss and managed it just as the inside door was closing. I zipped the trousers, took time to rinse my hands and use the drier, shifting side on so any sudden move was covered, then to the first door and out, and I kept walking, checking the arrows, making it back along the corridor. The bartender was down by the television screens, serving one of the baseball fans and didnay acknowledge me when I passed. Barney had returned to his former place and kept his head ower the crossword.

I lifted the bottle. I would have preferred to swally down the beer and just fuck off. Naw. The guy had bought me a drink. Besides, could I get out alive? Ha ha. But this type of hassle does one's brains in. One usually associates it with small towns but it happens in major cities as well: stray into a new district and ye discover it is a homogeneous hotbed of poisonous fuckers all staring at ye because ye are the wrang "thing": religion, race, class, nationality, politics; they know ye as soon as look at ye, boy, you is alien.

Even in places where it isnay obvious and ye think it is okay, suddenly the atmosphere shifts. It can even be your fault, you say something out of turn and the fucking roof caves in, ye wake up in Accident & Emergency with a guy in a grey suit staring at ye and naw, he isnay a doctor, he is a snooping bastard from the indigenous aliens' section of the Federal Bureau of Immigration and Assimilation.

The subtleties of social behaviour can alter in drastic ways and one never knows what other people are fucking talking about. Maybe that was at the heart of the breakdown of my relationship, just something as basic as that. We were supposed to speak the same language but did we did we fuck. Much of it was my ayn fault and I would never have denied that. I stopped trying to write my private-eye story about the same time I stopped trying to be a good father, good husband as well. Coinciding with that was another breakdown, the breakdown of my concentration. Thoughts drifted in and out my mind. Where the fuck did they come from, where did they go, what happened when they lodged there, and was havoc wreaked? Similarly in conversation, I forgot if I was talking, who I was talking to. I came in and out of perception like I was on dope. Yeh, I needit to get hame and see my mother, and the fucking cat of course, it had been a mere kitten when I left, now it was a proud castrated male. If I had been there at the time I wouldnay have allowed it.

But I needit to get back to something. It had nothing to

do with homesickness or notions of a motherland. Fuck the motherland, blood and guts and soil and shite, it didnay matter a fuck to me, it was just

Christ almighty I needit to get out right now. Hey, I said to Barney, can I buy ye a drink?

Pardon me?

Hey, I said, can I buy ye a drink? I need to leave. I need to go back to my motel and have some food, a bit of a sleep. Yeh, I have a long day's traveling tomorrow. I lifted my anorak from the stool and pulled it on. Yeh, I said, pointing at the bartender. Him tae, I'd like to buy yez baith a drink afore I go. It was hospitable you buying me one and I'd just like to return it. Well I mean ye buy a guy a beer and he drinks it down then bids ye a swift farewell! I shrugged.

I dont do that, said Barney.

Naw neither do I. It's no what I do either. I'm talking about the opposite. I would like to buy ye one afore I go. I would just like to return the compliment. I'm gauny go back to my motel, grab a sandwich.

Okay.

So: want a beer?

You talking about me? Do I want a beer?

Well I'd like to buy ye one.

Yeh, I'll take a beer.

The bartender was standing at the opposite end of the bar, his back to us, gazing up at the television screens. I walked down to him. When he turned to me he just was not friendly. Could I have a beer, I said, for Barney, whatever he's drinking.

He nodded.

Could I buy you one as well?

Right now I'm working.

Yeh, I know.

He shook his head, then stared at me.

27

I didnay say Fuck you to the guy: I said, Okay, two beers; whatever Barney's drinking and one for myself.

There had been mair misunderstandings in the past half hour than I had had in the past month. Everything was getting fankled. And the order itself, I had only meant to get Barney a beer originally, nothing for myself, I was just wanting to fuck off. But now I had bought myself another yin. Because of this huffy bartender bastard. So okay, when he brought them to me I would pay the money and leave. I had nothing to say. I wouldnay even drink the fucking beer, I would leave it there for whoever, it didnay matter; him, Barney or whoever, Corey fucking Parker, I just needit to get away.

I was back at my stool when he brought them. I pushed the money across the counter. He lifted it. I dont know why ye thought I insulted ye earlier on, I said, obviously it was a misunderstanding.

Obviously, yeh.

Yeh well it was.

You think this is a boring place, he said, that's your pre-rogative.

I dont think this is a boring place.

You said it.

I said it? I never said it. I know boring places man this isnay one of them.

He shrugged. That's what you said.

Naw I didnay.

Now he sighed in a vaguely amused way, and he looked me straight in the eye. I aint going to argue with you feller.

Of course for him to look me straight in the eye means I was already looking straight at him. It was all fucking male fucking keech but at the same time I wasnay gauny back down, no unless I had to. Barney had been spectating. Now he said, Hey ah, Jeremiah . . .

What?

Plenty bars around here, why dont you test them out.

The bartender smiled. He had lifted a bottle of uisghé and a glass and was set to pour, but no for me no for me. Easy boy easy, yeh, and time to leave time to leave. There was a pay-phone on the wall nearby the exit. I put my hand in my pocket, checked the coins. Then I checked my breathing. I was okay. I left the beer on the counter, strolled towards it. I glanced behind. Baith were watching me. I gied them a wave and continued on through the exit.

There would be a pay-phone in the convenience store. I could call a cab from there. It was my ayn fault for losing my last cell phone. It had been in a diner. An elderly woman was waiting table, red lipstick and expressionless countenance. Every time I got a new yin I fucking lost the goddam thing, and I wasnay buying nay other, no until my brains settled down.

The couple of beers had been worthwhile. Now I would sleep. And with a sandwich for my room, if I could maybe get a sandwich. And a late-night movie on the tube, yeh, I was looking forward to it.

It really was time to disappear. And no just back to the motel room. Fuck. I couldnay be in denial any longer. I needit to get out of here. This was urgent man this was urgent business. It was like only now I was recognizing what it was about: survival. It was to disappear, I needit to disappear. If I didnay disappear I wasnay gauny make it. Fucking hell man it was survival. Nothing mair nothing less. If I didnay make the jump from here then who knows, who knows what would happen.

I hadnay thought of it like that before so it was good, I was working through things. The last couple of years had been a nightmare. My life had gone to pot. But I was coming out of it. I hadnay quite realized how much of a nightmare it had been but now, yeh, I could see the reality. Fucking hell man!

But light existed, ahead, the end of the tunnel, ye could see the wee circle.

The convenience store lay two blocks away and the wind was still biting, blowing down from the north, the icy wastes of auld Canaday.

I turned up my hood and huddled along. Across the street I saw a couple of vehicles pulled up outside a bar; interesting-looking bodies emerged; they were carrying musical instruments. It was a music venue. But I had had enough of pubs for one evening and I kept walking. In the store I meandered around the aisles, seeing all the possible items for sale. They also had stuff for campers and hunters and the outdoor life in general; plenty weapons, efficient rifles. And some fine-looking blades were on display. I had a fondness for blades and there was one here I thought very fine indeed. But the problem is I would have had to stash it at the airport terminal for future reference because these Security fuckers wouldnay let me board the dang airplane with it. I would swear on my daughter's life it was for ornamental purposes only. But it wouldnay matter, nay exceptions existed to that rule. No for ordinary folks. Maybe if I had been a pentagon fucker or some multibillionaire businessman a rule would have got bent. Otherwise

but yeh, it was a fine-looking knife. One wantit just to hold it and check out the balance. Of course I hadnay enough money with me anyway, even if I did want to buy it. The vast bulk of my wad I had stashed in the customers' strongbox at the motel.

And the cigarettes, the cigarettes were all in front of my face. I looked at the different brands and multifold designs. They were fucking great. My throat got itchy just looking at them. From the cold counter I selected a salad sandwich and a mega muffin. Then, as I stuffed them into my pocket, I did something entirely out of character: I paid for a lottery ticket.

A fucking national fucking lottery ticket. What was that about? The woman behind the counter gied me a weary smile. I'm gaun crazy, I said, gambling on this kind of nonsense.

You dont bet you dont win, she said.

Aw I know the arguments.

She shrugged and glanced up at the video screen. Yeh, she could relax, I was being televisually recorded. Christ but I was a weird-looking fucker from this angle. Ahhhhhh, was that a bald patch!!!!!!!

Do you take a ticket yerself? I said, getting out the dough.

Yeh, she said, picking a tissue out of her cardigan sleeve. She wiped her nose.

Ever win?

Yeh.

You do?

Sure.

Okay, I nodded, added two packs of chewing gum to the bill. She returned my change and directed me to the pay-phone and the local cab advertisements tacked to the wall. A fast ride to the motel.

I stepped once towards the telephone to call that cab but I couldnay step twice; instead I about-turned. My feet took me right out the door. Jesus christ I was being borne along. Now I was hurled across the street in the direction of the likely-looking music venue. From here I gazed across at the faraway entrance to the Shooters and Horses Sports Bar. For some reason I didnay want the bodies there knowing where I was.

One beer, that was all; one last beer then back to the motel. I fancied hearing the music, no matter the kind. Fuck. I did hope it wasnay jazz. Jazz was aye too cool for the likes of me. My ex sang jazz. She occasionally earned dough by singing and jazz is what she sang, mainly. It was her preference and her manager's preference, so-called manager. In my opinion he was a slime-bag but so what man what do I know.

Yeh, I could enjoy jazz in its proper setting but for me there was a time and there was a place. Yes sir. And also there was the company, nayn or some, who that might be. And then the crucial question: if nayn, whose absence we talking about?

So I was coming out of a relationship for christ sake, aint we all, I had been coming out of relationships for years. This one was a marriage but and there were weans involved: one; mine, my wee lassie. So there ye are.

To hell with it.

Gie me blues, blues electric; what I found with blues electric, I could just stand there or sit there; I did not need nay other person and I did not want nay other person, just gie me the music, and loud, play it loud, I would get up close and take it from there.

So that is the kind of music I was wanting.

This was a long, L-shaped bar with booths and at the big end the musicians had their spot. The roadie was setting up the drums; the amps and some instruments were already out. There would be about the same number of customers as in the last joint. Nowadays people seem to stay indoors, no just in this town. Maybe it was the weather, gie them the benefit of the doubt. Anyway, it was so much mair comfortable here than in the sports bar. Even the shape of the room was a help. There ye felt on display because it was open plan, like a lot of pubs are. But some folk prefer other scenes, they want to just sit or chat or otherwise exist in a semi-private setting. That is the nature of the human beast. Okay, so I approached the bar. Naybody was behind it. Taped music. Jazz. Dear god no! no! Aaargh! Then at the other end I saw a guy leaning on the bar but from inside, he was chatting to the roadies. I signaled to him and he ignored me. Fine. Where's my smokes? I do not smoke. I do not smoke I do not smoke I do not smoke.

Fine.

Some of these barstaff bastards but they really need a lesson in manners.

It distinguished this from the last joint. No matter the criticisms I couldnay have condemned the bartender the way he ran that sports bar. He knew the game. But this yin here was younger; a few years aulder than myself, maybe forty, with a stupit thin ceegar poking out the corner of his mouth. He looked like he wantit to be mistaken for a jazz musician. I had seen a million of these cunts. But I wouldnay under-estimate this yin. He struck me as one of these mean fuckers, the type that brook no niceties. Often the only answer is to storm out, to leave: go from that place my son, pick up thy tab and walk. Then there was a woman at my side. I must have smiled because she was beautiful and totally luscious. She was pointing to the booths down the side of the room. I have to say what she wore, it was a long flowing skirt in a clingy material that certainly did what one asks of such a garment. And one of these blouses with the tied ends and the navel just about showing and her nipples as well just the way fucking hell man, and she had short hair, noticeable earrings, good style christ almighty in fact she looked absolutely brilliant. Sally, her name was Sally. Imagine that. It was written in a wee label stuck to one of the lapels on her blouse. I saw her smile at another customer. What a smile! It was a smile and a half. Before too long she would gie me that selfsame smile, I was a customer too. But how on earth could somebody be called Sally in this day and age? And wearing that blouse into el bargeño. What are ye my grannie, I thought to say as a kind of funny line about the name Sally and how the hell could she be my grannie with that blouse and skirt.

But oh christ what an extraordinary relief from the last place, I felt like spreading myself out on the floor and asking for a pillow and blanket and please could somebody tickle my belly please.

Then was the most weird sensation, and in succession a strong déjà vu followed by a sudden revelation concerning the course of the night, that I would wind up in good company and fuck it, maybe I wouldnay be gaun hame eftir all. I wouldnay even make the plane. I was gauny stay, maybe even here in this town. What was I gauny be offered a job in this actual bar! fuck sake! But something was up. I knew it, I knew it because me and Sally had already, had already,

already what? We hadnay met before. We hadnay done nothing before. Fuck all man. That is the problem with déjà vu, it promises so much yet leaves ye with nothing. At the same time but, at the same time; a phone call to the airline and I would try for my money back. In fact I wouldnay even wait to wind up in good company, I was gauny take the pledge now, I would stay in this town now, yeh, if no happily ever eftir, at least till I got myself sortit. I could worry about the formalities later. That was that. I would phone the airline and get my money back, and then there was my mother.

That brother and sister of mine, they would be puzzled, no to say hurt, no to say annoyed, no to say

To hell with it.

Any telephones in this dump!

My mind was made up. Here in this beautifully smoky bar. With all its photographs and fancy auld posters. I wouldnay even

finish the sentence, christ, what time is it? Where are my running shoes, have I time for a beer eftir all! Naw but if only the airline ticket was in one's hand, I would have ripped the fucker to shreds, but it wasnay, it was lying on the dressing table in the motel room. If I could just have got my hands on the damn thing! I would have ripped it up and flung it out the window. Who needs to go hame! Hame is for imbeciles!

The times I have wasted pondering the whys and wherefores on exile. I maybe was a selfish shite for staying away from the dear auld blood and soil but it had kept me sane. Sane! he screamed, a loathsome drip dropping from the corner of his mouth. Something wrang with that? Si señor you eez selfeesh. Sheeit.

The lassie had come for my order, she was smiling at me! But I know why she was smiling at me, she was smiling at me because she couldnay help but smile at me, having looked upon my countenance. I witnessed this and it was good. It relaxed me immediately and reminded me

Ye know that film with Laurel and Hardy?

Pardon me?

Have ye got a lite beer? Something mild, a beer.

Hey, what did you say before that? Laurel and Hardy?

Yeh.

I guess you did. She smiled.

Amazing how people even smile when their names get mentioned. Talk about fame as a deserved quality! I said, That is real immortality. I mention their name and you start laughing. But needless to say I cannay remember the name of the movie. It's that one where they have a wee business selling fish, then they decide to cut out the middleman. The middleman in this instance, as far as the bold twosome can deduce, is the guy that collects the fish from the sea, in other words the fisherman, he's the man that stands between them and their business product, the fish. So what if they could supply their ayn product, what if they could catch the fish themselves? That is the question. Right, so what they do is call in their entire capital, all their hard-earned savings, they go out and buy an auld boat. Then one thing and another and the boat rolls down a wee slope and gets all smashed up. Ye might say the Uhmerkin Revolution began from a variation on that, the East India Tea Company wanting a direct link between themself and yer tea-drinking public, in other words cutting out the middleman, as they thought, only of course they were the actual middleman, it was just merchant versus merchant.

She nodded politely.

Dont worry, I'm no gauny tell ye the whole goddam story. I think I ruined it anyway. Even the language I used. I could never be a stand-up. Some people fantasize about stand-up routines, how they would be astounding at it, how the audience would collapse with laughter. They would be so astounded they would be beyond laughter, just their eyes gawking, the mouth gaping open. No me. I just cannay tell the damn story. I have to embellish.

A lite beer?

Yeh, thanks. Thanks.

She smiled and left me. I had overwhelmed her. What a fucking fool. I had to talk though, otherwise I was just another cretin, a single cretin, an ordinary cretin. My hand went to my pocket but one does not smoke. I was getting her attention. What else? Winning her attention. Auld Laurel and Hardy and the East India Tea Company. I was embellishing the story and I lost it. In certain circumstances that is what happens and we have to do it, we have to interfere. But why interfere with the best storytellers? How presumptuous. I interfered with Laurel and Hardy. What next, rewriting *War and Peace*? At the same time it won me the lassie's attention.

It did.

Well well.

I stared eftir her. I know I was staring although at first it didnay register. But see yersel as ithers see ye. Some guy was sitting on a stool at the bar and he was in my line of vision, a big guy, dressed in pentagon clothes. I didnay register it for approximately twenty seconds. He was looking at me, it became a question. I moved my heid keeping my eyes focused in the same way, so he would know that I hadnay been staring at him deliberately.

I become psychotic, neurotic, hypnotic, parafuckingnoctic, paranotic, noctic. Was he wondering if I thought he was a suspicious character? Well aye, and so he fucking was a suspicious character but what was the nature of my suspicion, what behaviour nourished such a reaction? The behaviour was obvious, he was studying me. He thought I was studying him. He was in my line of vision so I couldnay help but look at him, but he assumed it was intentional, that I was attempting to intimidate him. What the hell would I do that for? And at what risk: here was I in a strange bar in a strange town and as soon as I open my mouth I am an unassimilatit alien fucker. And with the Red Card to prove it man this guy is walking the deportation tightrope; hey, where is the nearest Patriot Holding Center; lock him up and fling away the key.

The very idea I would try to intimidate a local in such a way. Laughable!

Unless I had the death wish.

I am not unfamiliar with said wish but I know when it fucking happens. Or do I? What goes on in the mind? Do we ever know everything? I tend to the opinion that such a thing is a logical contradiction.

Fuck him.

Unless if he had some kind of personal claim on Sally and resented my prolonged chat to her? But it wasnay as if she had distanced herself from me in the ordinary female servant to male customer as master routine. An objective bystander might have supposed she wasnay 100 per cent antagonistic.

37

I waited for her to bring me the beer. I could work out something to say. A spiel on Laurel and Hardy and the Keystone Cops or something. She would think I was a movie buff, or a guy connected with the business end of it – line management; checking out possible venues, wee out-of-the-way towns for interesting thingwies, what the hell is the word? first nights, the thing where all the rich and famous

festivals. Cannes, Vienna, Berlin. Or Sundance, that wasnay a million miles from here. So this is what I was doing in town, advance-planning and general line production for an independent film company, I had just dropped in for a reconnoitre, before heading back ower the mountains first thing in the morning.

What had I drunk? Three bottles of very low alcohol. Naw, five. Or was it four? And another ordered.

It was so unalcoholic but. All it did was bag one up, fill one full of wind. Then also it was so damn boring. What about taste, flavour, enjoyment; that kick, the boost, the intoxication. Who mentioned uisghé? gie me a uisghé. I want uisghé. Naw, make it a whiskey, a glass of genyooooine Uhmerkana. If I cannay have a smoke and smokes are barred then

What would I say when she came with the next beer? And if I ordered a whiskey what would she think of me, a fucking drunkard. I could argue the patriotic case, skatch or rye, I can argue baith. But it is too bad when I go from there to yapping about my daughter. In my wallet I carried a couple of photos of the wean; even one of the ex, just because well I mean I was with her for two years, mair than two years; two years is a long time. And the wee yin, with that beautiful smile.

I like photographs of people. Ye can look at them when ye sit on the subway, bus, plane or train. Even driving a motor, ye can leave them on yer dashboard and snatch wee perusals of the loved one, long perusals during traffic jams. The main use connects to social situations, some awkward. Ye open the wallet and show the photo to ward off unwantit attention from keen individuals, as evidence of prior commitments, also to show how trustworthy ye are. For all kinds of misunderstandings that would be ideal. Thinking how my life had been to date, proper photographs would have helped on numerous occasions. Never mind the uisghé, another couple of beers and I would be dragging them out to show Sally. It is easy done. Especially the wean, I usually throw her photo in so women know they can trust me: a reliable faimly man. Oh yeh? So how come he is separated? And here he is out on the prowl. Is that the action of a faimly man? Cheating skunk that he is, nay wonder his wife flung him to fuck.

Heh wait a minute, she didnay fling me to fuck.

And there are two sides to every story, remember that.

Out on the prowl! Glorious sounding, it makes me feel like one of those authentic hunter males, one of the shooters, the punchers, the sportsmen; the cops, the boxers, the Security operatives and of course the good auld military; big hitters one and all; the individyouells that made this country what it is today, I am an auld cowpoke etcetera.

I wasnay gauny talk to Sally about failed fucking relationships, given her hips swung when she set off walking from my table. Obviously it was unintentional. I know some guys, they would have thought she was doing it for their benefit but that was a lie sir, an uttah fabrication sir, you shame ma famly sir, yasm.

Was she wearing highheels? If not, then . . .

The lassie had only met me ten minutes ago in the name of god.

Highheels make the bum wiggle. If she wasnay wearing highheels maybe she was wiggling for me, for me! Aarrggh. Then the stranger collapsed and died yer honor, we checked the corpse but bullet holes there were nayn.

But there was nay question about Sally! I needit to tell somebody! Here I wis in that selfsame situation like when I met the ex and she was a musician as well for christ sake. Synchronicity. That déjà vu – here lay its grounding.

But how come I thought Sally was a musician? She had gien no indication except that here in this music bar was where she worked. What about hunches, do hunches count? Me and the ex had been close. I myself developed a very educated intuitary base pertaining to 1-to-1 bonding, and I entrusted to this major decisions of that nature; this base derived from my knowledge of that woman; intimate knowledge, carnal knowledge, intellectually pure knowledge, moral sharing and fucking hell everything one can think of sharing, gambling losses, and mair besides. It is incredible we ever split up with the amount of sharing we done, ergo there is mair to a marriage than sharing. I call it a marriage, and it was a marriage, though we didnay tie the bows in the formal manner. Nay authorities witnessed it. Oh no! Fuck the authorities. As far as I was concerned she was my wife and I was her husband.

I want, however, not to dredge through all that shite. My first meeting with the ex hadnay been like this one with Sally. The ex had been working as a cleaner during the day. She was singing at night and barely earning a cent from it. I had moved back to the east coast. I needit away from the sun and clement weather, back to good auld icy storms and torrential downpours; forced to stay indoors, having to be stuck there so what was there to do apart from pass the time. I had nay money, nay possessions, nay false hopes saturating one's napper. It was ideal. I was gauny have to amuse myself. So why no sit down and tell myself a story. Only my way of telling the story would be to write it down, yeh, so I would end up with a book. That was how I planned it.

I spent time here when I first landit in the country. I didnay know the big city too well but my voice and background aye got me a bar job. There were plenty Irish and English bars around. I couldnay find a Skarrisch yin but I never tried too hard. If I had found one I would have bypassed the street.

Then my thinking led me to avoid the Irish and English bars as well. I aye ended up in arguments. It was better to go Uhmerkin, the arguments were mair constructive. I tramped around for a couple of days then was taken on in a joint up between 70th and 80th. During the day the pub was lively with suits and office-workers and gallery people and mental shoppers and stuff but I wasnay hired for the lively hours; they hired me for twilight time. On Thursdays and Fridays it was busy until 11 p.m. but eftir then and out of hours people were away hame or onto mair exciting pastures. A busy night was half empty. Clientele consisted of elderly solitaries, aulder gay couples, adulterous hetero couples and tourists who had blundered. Obviously these bodies were all of interest. Once I got into their confidence some spoke of long-lost kiltit ancestors and highland chieftains. Two or three bemoaned the loss of their city and the degeneration of the species. The gays were mair sociable, they joked and laughed and had friends about town. They heard about better accommodation, other jobs and prospects. A couple did gie me looks but nothing new in that. Males could find me attractive, so could females – though maybe no so much, or if they did they didnay show it. But the adulterous hetero couples were just too jittery. Conversation was out the question. They veered between oblivion if I was standing in their face to acute sensitivity to the remotest of data. Sometimes I brought a book to read and it was apparent they thought it a subterfuge, that I was scrutinizing their every move. Occasionally I got into the fantasy and did do that, they all had their stories and I had made a start on one myself, it was gauny be a novel about a scabrous private eye. My hero – or anti-hero –

was a youthful but disillusioned cool dude of Skarrisch extraction who is at hame in all scenarios and well able to handle firearms, throwing knives, sophisticated women, corrupt practices, femmes fatales and sultry beauties; unarmed combat, corporate consignieri, wiseguy cops and shady financiers, corrupt politicians, racist immigration policies; in short, miscellaneous hoodlums and a host of luscious lassies. It would be a readable yarn but a fucking ripsnorter of a movie, guaranteed. Actors would fight for the role of central character and

Fuck off.

So, the boring pub. Yeh, and the other main group during these twilight hours was the tourists who blundered down the stairs and would wait an hour then realize it wasnay gauny get any better. I saw them look at each other then avoid each other, look at me, look at the decor and other customers, look at each other again, avoid each other again, and so on and so forth. Sometimes it worked in my favour and they left major tips out of guilt. They didnay want me to think that my personality was inadequate. Apart from hurting the feelings of a poor exile far from hame I might have been overly sensitive and lost the fucking temper, pulled the shillelagh baseball bat out from under the counter and whacked them ower the goddam napper: take that ya furin fucker!

The tourists didnay ask me if I knew mair interesting bars or districts but thought it was alright to ask the customers. I knew that mentality but still found it bizarre. People assume if ye are a customer in a boring bar ye are a local and there by choice. Fair enough but no in all cases. A bar is just a bar; bricks and mortar. It are the folk inside the bar makes it boring ma friend, or exciting. Hardly an onerous concept. I never saw the locals react with animosity to the tourists when asked stupit questions. Sure it was peaceful and boring but it suited the clientele. Sometimes it suited me, theoretically at least. A too interesting work environment would have been detrimental to my chance of fame and fortune. I would be as well out enjoying myself all the time. Naw, I needit boredom and unedifying experiential data on a constant basis. The writing itself becomes the thing. My story would transform my life in an exciting way. Not only was writing a serious affair but it could be a very exciting occupation. So "they" said anyway, these cunts that know everything.

On my days off and from lunchtime before I startit work I did the typical rambling around in the hunt for better accommodation, better used furniture stores, secondhand bookstores, better coffee bars, better cheap restaurants, better places to meet women, good places, relaxed places, non-fucking-demanding fucking places where one doesnay have to be on one's best behaviour. I didnay have best behaviour man that was the fucking problem, and was ever thus. I was aye a chap of two sides, baith extreme.

Nor does time stand still. I had my wee room six flights up and it was okay, cramped as fuck but I wasnay gauny grumble; I was a skinny poverty-stricken bastard, so living in a high-up cupboard was aye an option. Mind you, it was en suite. Nay elevators of course but who needs convenience. There were kids and faimlies in the neighborhood and a wee sense of community. I cut some interesting pictures out colour-supplement magazines and tacked them to the wall for decoration. Some were fine, mighty fine. I was no bad at interior rearranging, I could shift things about so it gied an idea of

of what? Beauty, space? I dont know. Something was gaun on but. I had the trusty auld laptop aboard the table, and the chair I had wasnay too fucking uncomfortable. So, so

So what it amounted to was I was making myself at hame.

The neighbourhood convenience store was a 24-hour operation run by a faimly and me and the eldest son used to pass the time gabbing about cards, horses, women, art and revolution; the usual kind of thing. Ranjit was his name. Him and his cousin worked the nightshift and I usually went in on my way hame. Somebody he knew was dumping an auld television set so I got that. It was fucking prehistoric man it weighed a ton, but it worked. And then another couple of bits and pieces came my way. I heard about choice domestic machinery that fell off passing trucks. I put an order in for a microwave oven but it never materialized. Such strokes of good fortune are aye for others. Once a month on Friday evenings Ranjit got the night off and played poker with his mates. He invited me along. He was thirty-eighth-generation Indian and had lived in the neighborhood all his life so he knew the ins and outs. His auld man's great-great-granddaddy had fled from the subcontinent to escape some of the excesses of briscch imperialism but landed in the Caribbean. Eventually his son fuckt off to the Gulf of Mexico to escape mair of the same. He wound up working on the Texan oilrigs where he got into trouble with the bosses for trying to improve working conditions, in particular the attempt to safeguard himself and workmates from certain accident, injury or death. To avoid a bullet in the heid he and other trade unionists fled north with their faimlies. He died before his son was born. The son was Ranjit's granddaddy who managed to borrow dough from a local loanshark to open a store. And then he lost the store but eventually reopened it although he couldnay walk properly or use his right hand ever again. The details surrounding this remained mysterious. I asked Ranjit to elaborate but he couldnay; he didnay know any mair because his auld man didnay know any mair. What do ye mean, I says, yer grand-daddy never telt him? That's it, he says, yeh.

So yer dad didnay ask?

I guess. His father didnt tell him so he didnt ask.

I'm no being critical, I says, but did you no ask him either?

Like who, he says, my granddaddy?

Yeh.

He was an old man, I wasnt going to bother him.

You is too polite.

No, it was too late, my father should have discovered all such information, him and my uncles, they should have discovered it.

Maybe they did, I says, maybe they did. They just havenay telt ye.

Nah, he says, they are cowards man they dont want to know.

Ranjit had the dream of getting enough money together to head off to India and see how things were, maybe discover something of his past. But some of his past was in Texas and some was in the Caribbean and some was here on the east coast of Uhmerka. But India was where he was gaun. These Indian people were freedom fighters, he says. My people are fucking fools man, how else to say it, my dad is a fucking fool and my uncles man, my cousins. We are all fools, indigenous aliens man we eat shit.

But we all eat shit, I says, my faimly's worse than yours, my entire country man it is much worse, we are all cretinous fucking goddam servants, arselicking bastards.

That's your business. You think that's something to do with me?

Sure, I says, of course it is; one of my ancestors might have been out there in the subcontinent employed by the imperialist Brit fuckers, executing women, weans and men to keep the wolf from the door, a soldier, an ordinary feller.

GI working class. I heard of them! Yeh! Ranjit shook his head. Zombies man they aint got a thought between them.

Ye're wrong! Who knows what he was, this hypothetical

ancestor of mine, maybe he was a political kind of guy, a subversive for fuck sake how the hell do I know, maybe he helped the locals fight the raj bastards.

You should know.

How, how should I know?

Because you got to know your own goddam history.

Working-class people, we dont have history.

Bullshit.

Well I dont have any apart from this auld ancestor of mine went to the gold fields and converted to some fucking religion or other. I think he was a fundamentalist christian cunt, auld Jeremiah was his name, he's the one my line's called eftir, I take my name off of him.

Change it man!

Naw!

Ranjit laughed.

He became a pillar of the dang community. Naw but fucking hell he was an interesting auld feller. One of these days I'm gauny try and discover where his hame was. According to faimly gossip he became a citizen of note, a kind of local hero. I think it was somewhere in Utah or Wyoming, maybe farther north; one these states with the far-right strongholds.

You should find out.

Yeh.

Go to Oregon, pick up his trail, get a covered wagon.

I might just do that.

Yeh, give us a break.

Meanwhile the issue of the monthly card game with Ranjit's squad became a major gripe for me with my immediate superior, the manager of the bar. She wasnay gieing me any Fridays at all. Not one. She gied me Monday nights and I should consider myself lucky because she threw in an occasional Tuesday from the week eftir, so that it made a long weekend.

A fucking beauty that yin.

I explained to her I didnay know what she was talking about, that Mondays and Tuesdays werenay classifiable as long weekends in any of the world's cultures; forget IMF dictats. She shrugged and gied a shake of her locks, which signified go or stay, who gies a shit. It was funny how she took a dislike to me. At first I had a wee hunch she fancied me, she had a certain twinkle in her eye. She was in her forties but a very sort of smartly-dressed woman, and shapely. No my style, she was too eh sophisticated I suppose ye would call it. Christ it was only a pub she managed, no a theatre or art gallery. One of the bodies telt me she had Parisien antecedents and that she dressed the part. She joked about putting me in a kilt to attract the tourists.

I smiled at her joke.

I did manage to get into the poker game with Ranjit and friends two or three times but I had to lie to her about sickness, diarrhoea and headaches, that I had become subject to acute spasms of vomitary ejaculatory spouting.

The poker games were enjoyable but for the wrang reasons. They were hell of a rowdy, much shouting and bawling. And I found it hard to win. Maybe I didnay play often enough with the company. I needit mair Friday nights. One a month would have been ideal.

Another job would have been ideal! Ranjit telt me there were plenty restaurants in the vicinity that would be glad to employ pink Skarrisch fuckers, and he knew a couple. Why the hell I endured the hassle traveling into the heavy downtown area six days a week was beyond him. Yeh, and occasionally beyond me also. On the other hand there were times it was peaceful and the unsocial hours helped me steer clear of trouble. Besides, I had worked in restaurants before and hated it. I was too jittery, kept dropping the plates man these fucking customer bastards, sometimes they got on one's nerves. The booze trade was bad enough.

But I quite enjoyed being in my wee cupboard of a room with the laptop, the coffee and a couple of packs of cigarettes. Other people were away to their dayjobs and there was me, okay an anti-social loner cunt but aye an individual, reminding me of these auld-time private eyes. And I had made a beginning with the yarn, except it kept getting bogged down in long meandering conversations. The hero would go into the apartment building to rescue a dame and then meet up with the caretaker and they would start chatting about politics and philosophy, art and revolution, women and life in general. I found it good craïc but when I read the stuff the day eftir it wasnay good craïc, it was boring shite. And it was hard to sustain. Then one time the hero guy had to start running cause the fucking gangsters and crookit politicians were eftir him and that was tricky, it came out sounding hopeless. He was aye gauny be in situations where he had to take to his heels and I couldnay get it to come out in a natural way, it aye sounded stupit: "he went flying down the stairs three steps at a time", "flying down the steps at three rows at a time". All that kind of keech. Then I went through a period when I kept writing "teeth" instead of "feet". He was running so fast his teeth could not touch the ground.

Agh but my energy wasnay that great. And my concentration was desperate. I am talking about very very desperate. As soon as I switched on the laptop I had to light a smoke. Then I needit a coffee. Another smoke. Sometimes I had to have a wank. Then I dozed off with my heid ower the machine. For fuck sake! I knew ye had to build the concentration up but this was like fucking hell I had to get into training. I startit running up the stairs as far as I could, running down them as fast as I could. And I aye jogged round to Ranjit's store. I thought of joining a gym. But I needit money for the gym. I tried exercising in the room, press-ups and that kind of shite. It just seemed so contrived. There were nay mirrors on the wall thank fuck. Imagine seeing yer face when ye were doing these self-improvement-style physicks. One would have to fucking chortle man and chortle is the only word. It was even worse if I tried writing when I came hame eftir the shift. By the time I had a sandwich and a cup of tea and sat down for a smoke I was done in completely. I would manage to switch on the laptop but by then I was asleep on my feet, all I was good for was the tube. I would sit for ten minutes watching an auld movie then blink myself awake an hour later, and crawl into bed.

At times like these I thought the best thing was to gie up the pub job and find something with better hours. Then I thought if I could involve myself in Ranjit's game properly, nay stupidity, I would just play quietly, win off their mistakes man because they fucking made plenty. I just wantit to get ahead of the game, build myself a stake. Then I could chuck the bar job, get another yin later; I would take a month's vacation. That would sort me out, I would get on with the writing and also maybe who knows meet up with somebody. There was a club I knew on the south side that ran an Irish night once a week. It was full of single lassies, single lassies that by all accounts were luscious. The trouble was it was a Friday night.

Fucking hell, everything was a goddam Friday. So okay, if it was card night I could go and play cards first and then move on to the club later. But what happened if I went broke at the cards and couldnay afford to go to the club. So okay, I could go to the club first. And if I didnay get off with naybody I could just go and play poker. Or maybe I could go to the Irish club one week and the card game the next, depending on how it all worked, depending on how many Friday nights the manager of the pub allowed me.

Problems problems. It was a load of hypothetical nonsense and yet I spent mucho tempuso worrying about it.

Then I met the ex. How did I meet her? I met her in a bar. What did she teach me? She taught me everything. Did she gie me anything? She gied me a daughter. Did she gie me anything else? Plenty, she gied me plenty. She gied me everything.

There is nothing to add.

But that is why I had to get hame to Skallin.

I had nay choice. It was driving me fucking crazy.

I never thought it would end this way.

Of course my father aye says I was for the chop, from when I was a boy. You'll die young, he says.

Thank you da, I says.

Naw but ye will, he says, you mark my words.

He was right, but what did he know, he was guessing, he was ignorant and he was prejudiced and all he knew was what my mother telt him and she only knew what I told her long distance, or wrote down on a postcard par avion. He didnay even come to the phone when I called. From 6000 miles away? He doesnay even come to the phone? Gie us a fucking break.

Strange auld bastard right enough. He died before I met the ex. It was a genuine regret of mine that I missed his funeral. In some ways he was okay. I think I would have tried hard to get hame if I had known he was dying. I was on the west coast at the time. The trouble is my maw didnay know how to contact me and when I finally phoned he had been deid for weeks, and I wasnay gauny exhume the body for a blast of the last post.

My maw hadnay met my ex either, never saw my daughter, her granddaughter. How come?

Because life is unfair, life is unfair.

What distinguishes one life from another? What makes a life so different?

Nothing and everything.

My mother couldnay reveal to me the desire to see her granddaughter. Why? Because I would let her down.

Pardon me?

Yeh, because this was my life. I let my faimly down and I let my daughter down. The ex, I let her down as well. How the fuck I dont know but I did. I must have. She never said it but that was what she thought. She thought I did, she thought I fucking let her down. No in ordinary ways. In what ways then? Aw fuck knows man ye cannay aye think about these things, life is too short, it is my life, I only have one, I have to make the best of it.

That is how people exile themselves, to avoid hurting their faimlies and friends. I had two faimlies; one here and one back in the UK. I now was exiting here. Where the fuck else was I gauny go?

I could sit in this booth and listen to music, gaze at the surroundings, gaze at the lassie as she served her customers, do whatever. I could do whatever, any damn thing, I could stare at the wall, I could

I closed my eyes.

The plane left tomorrow eftirnoon. I would be on it. Maybe I would get off in Edinburgh. I had never been to Edinburgh and I didnay need no fucking visa or work permit, nay Red Card, Green Card or fucking Blue Card.

I could even get off in Iceland. I heard they cooked a nice pot of fish broth in Reykjavik. Then I could stowaway on a fishing boat ower to Kirkwall, then a chopper down to Aberdeen.

Aw fuck I could just get off the plane in Seattle. I had been to Seattle, there was good and there was bad. Plus they had a decent bookshop and served healthy salad and a nice pint of stout on the side, and all these great wee islands. Or I could stay where I was and quit moaning, quit the self-pitying whine.

I even whined when I was thinking. It wasnay just me talking man I listened to myself thinking and yeh, that too was a whine, it was fucking terrible.

The breakdown of a relationship is one of the mair traumatic experiences. I was suffering post-traumatic-relationship-break-up-stress-syndrome and it manifested itself in this fucking self-pitying whine. Nay wonder people got sick of me. Who wants to listen to some girning-faced furnir prick constantly moaning. Why dont ya fuck off hame to yer ayn country and moan. Yeh, precisely, le billet is booked monsieur. So gie us a smoke to celebrate. And le bier, où est le bier? Donde está la señorita! Eh hombre, gie us el brekko.

Naybody gies ye a fucking el brekko. Ye have to grab this world by the coat-tails. Ye have to dive right in man heid fucking first; where is that place down Mexico where the guys plunge all the way down off the cliff, timing it to perfection with the tides, otherwise splatter splatter.

I was aye a loner but I did make the attempt to start conversations. Ye heard the psychology experts on these crazy talkshows. Dont let life pass ye by! Grab the bull by the horns! Dont be a wilting flower!

Aw, right, okay.

So how does one order a beer in this joint?

Judging by the taped music the ex would have fitted into this music bar better than me. She sang jazz in a bluesy style. Jazz isnay my primary area of musical interest. I have to admit this frequently. Maybe my ignorance of the music was in at the root of my attraction for her. Naw, that is nonsense. Mind you, given that in many ways I am a pretentious fucking cretin in regard to music,

naw, I remain ignorant of music and shall remain so: that is the truth so help me gahd, gahd! he sobbed, gahd! boo hoo.

(What the fuck was that about!)

I met the ex in a music bar on 3rd Street. The session was an open mic come-all-ye and began from 1 or 2 in the morning. It took place on a Monday. A quiet night in the booze trade and my regular day-off from the alcoholic hellhole wherein I earned my crusts. I went with a pal of mine that first occasion. Haydar was his name. He had come ower from the west coast on a cut-price deal with a cheapo airline. This outfit averaged something like 5.37 crashes a month nationwide. Maybe it was 3.57. Surely no 7.53. But for a period life insurance was out the question unless ye were a millionaire thrice ower. Nay frills but plenty spills and plenty thrills. It didnay worry Haydar. He was a fourth-generation mountain man of Mesopotamian lineage, mair at hame with mule trains than fucking airplanes but he loved women, jazz and gambling, and like myself he enjoyed the odd game of poker – the people *v.* people variety. When I knew him he was hooked on the livepoker.com sites on the net. We were good buddies for a long while, it began from us playing the weekly pool tournament in the local club. Nay mellow cornets on this jukebox, a bunch of auld timers hogged the music machine and it was either Albert Collins, Doug Sahm or Roberto Pulido; side-bets included how many pitchers of beer ye could swally at a sitting

Eftir I vamoosed east we kept in touch for a short period. Then one Sunday night I was serving booze and he was my next customer. He had jumped a flight for a three-day trip. It was great to see him. I felt like downing tools immediately. Instead I waited until the next night and we went for a few beers and to hear some music.

So it was through him. He is the guy one could blame, if one were of a mind. I wouldnay have bothered gaun to that 3rd Street joint unless he was there. But he wasnay responsible for me meeting her, it was me that spoke to her and me that sat down beside her. It was me that done these things, it wasnay him.

Christ, it was a decisive time. Ye look back and ye see these things. Naybody could condemn me for indecision. I grabbed the bull by the horns. I didnay wait for the fucking fates, fuck the fates, I just jettisoned the cargo and went for it. Nothing mattered. That was the auld-style me, ye fancy that bet! well go for it, re-raise the cunt, get yer money on the table.

Christ.

One has to sigh. One raises one's bottle to one's mouth, one sips. One is aware of a sourness in the pit of one's belly.

One is a father. One should not be separated from one's child. One does one's best. One's best is not good enough.

One's best is not good enough: that is fucking that.

Who knows what she wantit. No fucking me anyway.

Hell with it.

I needit another beer, otherwise I wouldnay get maudlin. My last night in lil ol mean ol US of A, I was entitled to get – no maudlin, just pissed. But I wasnay gauny get pissed. To hell with the stereotype. I was sitting myself down for a relaxing couple of beers and then it was home james dont spare the horses.

It is strange the way barstaff vanish. Ye think of the Shooters and Horses, what a dump, but the guy ran a good bar, he ran a good fucking bar, and I aint speaking here as a dang customer, no sir. I wear baith hats when I go for a drink.

My sensibility aint a jazz sensibility. I was forever explaining that to strangers and acquaintances. It was funny; the folk I knew and friends I got to know, maist of them liked jazz; they said they did anyway. Haydar wondered how the fuck I went to Sacramento where they are big on the auld-time stuff, the Dixieland stuff. It was the gold rush man that was why I went. The ex was one of the few that understood. She appreciated that there was some psychological shenanigan gaun on inside my nut that curtailed the very possibility. I put it down to the same kind of thing that once produced the comment from my primary schoolteacher that I wasnay "mathematically inclined".

Of course if the 3rd Street bar hadnay been oriented towards jazz Haydar wouldnay have went. They called it a blues bar but it was jazz jazz jazz and maist of it done my fucking heid in plankle twankle little star. I remember it was late when we arrived and we had to wedge wurselves in at the back of the space. But nay question the atmosphere itself was okay, the occasional excitement, albeit suppressed. Plenty of people; the young and the auld, the male and the female, the lookers and the non-lookers.

And then she moved onto the stage and I was smiling.

How do we say it about people, the ones that bring a smile to the face. We get a gift from them. It connects to vulnerability and it maybe happens mair with women than men because we expect their vulnerability to be less visible. Women will disagree.

The ex wasnay especially thin and I cannay say I was attracted to thin women but who knows, just if ye get the chance, we dont always have a choice. In my ayn bar ye didnay get available women, no the right age; sometimes at weekends ye got a few in town for shops and galleries and they came down the stairs to wur place for a quick gin & tonic and a couple were what ye might call "available", except no for me, being honest. I didnay even qualify under the "rough trade" label. Nay question they would have bought and sold me but also like what do they call it man sophistication, they were looking for these rich pink cunts ye get in hollywood soaps, those west-coast guys with faces like space puppets, plus they all have these weird square heids.

It would be wrang to say she took the venue by storm. It wasnay that kind of place. There were a lot of jazz buffs there and their kind of excitement can cast a shadow on the world. They would applaud in a knowing way and some gied a nod of the heid to their friends but generally it wasnay that enthusiastic. Nay fervour man nay fervour. But it was the wrang place for fervour, that was what I thought and I said it to her. We all like jazz, I says, I love jazz. But . . .

You dont love jazz, she says.

Naw, she was correct, correct. Amo amas amat amamus amatis amant. But what I thought was these bodies man, them sitting about listening and sipping their drinks, they werenay the right kind of folk to be listening and watching and I thought a lot of them were doing mair watching than listening the wey Yazzie aye stood at the mic, she was a hip-swiveler, and she moved her hands mair from the elbows down, yeh, and one has to say it man it was damn sexy, no that she intended it that wey I dont think, it was just the wey her music came out, and sometimes she did that wee smoothing movement with the haun down her belly and I waited for that. When it happened ye felt like applauding, like one of these okay solo passages ye get.

It was a 20-minute set, with one guy on bass and one on drums, kind of "house" musicians. They gied her big smiles and a good shake of the haun at the end.

Christ, just gazing round the walls inside this joint, ye couldnay help thinking about her; there were photographs and auld posters everywhere. And everybody; from John MacCormack to Victoria Spivey, by way of Howling Wolf.

But where was the beer? Had I ordered one? I saw the lassie at the end of the bar talking to one of the band. Sally! Sally oh Sally, Sally who has won my heart, Sally of the flowers, down by the gardens we go. There was something truly luscious about her shape and the way that long skirt of hers flowed yet somehow clung to her hips and thighs, a swirling process, it was just beautiful my god man ye got the erectile message now man christ almighty it is good to be alive.

But the beer, I needit a beer. I tried to signal her attention but she didnay notice me.

Let me repeat that.

Nah, Sally hadnay not noticed me, she had just, well ye know, a girl has things on her mind, males gain no entry. 'Twas ever thus. One is closed off.

What else is death?

Peace unto you brother.

Peace, peace.

Ye find yer way in the world. In the past dozen years I had undertaken some hopeless jobs. Tending bar wasnay the worst. What was the worst? Waiting table! In the name of god man that fucking drove ye fucking crackers man these fucking arrogant customer cunts.

I trust my gut reaction. So it wasnay the Security job was the worst, it was waiting table. Fair enough. One time I was an attendant in an art gallery; boring as fuck but nay complaints except the weather, the weather exacerbated matters. They tried to block out the sunlight, a phenomenon that effected a certain movement in my brains. The owner used to come in during the late mornings; an elderly millionaire lady, she was ensuring us attendants werenay sitting about. I didnay know who she was at first. She keeked her heid round pillars to watch us. At first I used to shout: I see ye! figuring she was some poor auld biddy reverting to childhood.

I lifted the exbottle of beer. How could Sally no have noticed me signaling? Unless it was just my signal she hadnay noticed. It wasnay the fact it was me signaling, it was the signal itself. So it wasnay that I was a dull and uninteresting feller? Of course no. How could it have been? She couldnay have known that. She had barely spoken to me. She didnay realize I was a wondrous feller, an inventive and imaginative feller, one who

Fucking hell man. I again lifted the exbottle of beer, looked about for nonexistent smokes.

Funny how my life had gone. Funny is the wrang word.

Ach well. At least the music was good. Some auld blues singer. The ex would have loved it. The ex. How come my heid still went to her? And what did it matter if she would have loved it? Ye dont have to be a musician to appreciate music. Ye dont get a bonus because a musician shares yer musical tastes.

Her and that mental Security job went the gether. One was the fire and one was the frying pan, ye straddled the fuckers, a foot in each, losing yer balance.

Ach man I was aye a fucking

a fucking what?

Tales from the Lonesome Pine. The Braggadocio Kid rides again. Maybe I should have been trying a cowboy story.

Where do thoughts originate?

Zoom zoom. Sally had walked past, trays of empty glasses and bottles and shit. She came from nowhere. Then she had vanished. That girl was a witch. And definitely a singer. I could imagine her up close to the mic, her lips purring, one hand smoothing down her waist, down her hip, eyes closed much of the time and then when she opens them she is looking at you man she is looking right at you and that little smile curling there.

It was this place. There was something about it. All these ghosts stuck up on the walls. Good times and bad times. Pain and struggle. I appreciated the atmosphere. Except for this big keech at the bar who was observing everything, including me, especially me. White shirt and grey suit, the stereotypical trimmings, like he had walked out a government office. Fuck him. Big guy! Oh dear I am a-quaking in the shoes! I am a worried man, I shall leave immediately, tail between the legs.

Maybe when the music began so too would Sally, mic in one hand, tray of drinks in the other. If there was any individual in the whole world who could perform such doughty deeds this here was the lady, she was the one, the lassie who hadnay noticed me signaling my order. Unless she had noticed and was taking her time. I was in the queue. She wasnay gauny rush. Why should she? Life is short. Her heid was probably full of other business. Nay doubt she wrote her ayn songs. The ex also wrote her ayn songs, composed them on her auld geetar. A couple were beautiful. I broke the cds later on. I couldnay listen to them. When she practised at hame I offered to help if I could, hold the songbook, turn the pages for her, if that was what she wantit, I would have done it. I would have helped her. When I wasnay helping her I would be writing the auld private-eye ditty and between the two of us we were bound to strike it lucky; maybe the book would hit the right note and earn some dough. The first thing I would do is buy a beautiful house for the three of us. It would be an arty style place out in the country, and we would flourish, we would surely flourish. And some hollywood mogul cunt would offer me a few hunner k to make a movie of the book. A stack of amazing actors would queue up for the parts – cool white dudes, stalwartly loyal black yins, impressionable luscious lassies, upper-class English servants with a detached ironic air. And they would all need a guid Skarrisch tongue in their heid. The fucking lot of them. How would they get it? I would fucking coach them! And nayn of that shite where they tone it down for worldwide bourgeois language markets. Fuck the bourgeois language fucking markets buddy we are talking truth, natooral reality, nayn of yer fucking hypocrisy shite, gie me a bastarn smoke man a hit, a hit, gie me a hit.

Ach I didnay need a smoke, just a beer.

How come persons I was close to had such a hankering for jazz? I fucking never experienced nay such hankering. Very peculiar. Me and Haydar used to trundle round Nevada for the occasional game of cards. We went other places as well; no for the gambling so much as the craïc. We reached ower the Utah border but I thought nah, my heid willnay cope with that religion right-wing stuff, so we turned back although I had been wanting to dig a wee bit on the Jeremiah Brown phenomenon. How come he ever landit in that place! Surely he never turned, surely he never fell for that fucking christian patter? The guy was a Chartist man a fucking socialist. Any ancestor of mine! And he wasnay gauny renege on his principles. Unless he wasnay as strong as I thought. Yeh, one of these days I was gauny go digging. Jeremiah was contemporary to a host of great people, for all we know he corresponded with Eugene Debs or maybe Frederick Douglas with the auld Skarrisch connection. Maybe my maw knew mair than she let on. That was a wee thing too, if she was up to it, I wantit to ask her about history, my ayn history. It wasnay a big deal, just if she was up to it, there were a couple of minor details. How come I was me! That was the main question! A fucking flummoxer.

Agh but I was looking forward to seeing her, how she was keeping. She was a good woman. It was time to see her. Maybe take her for a sail down the Clyde. Boats are great. I aye got excited by boats, even as a boy. These wee islands down the Clyde coast. Brilliant! The only drawback was I couldnay swim, so if the boat capsized it was Davy Jones's Locker for me for me, Davy Jones's Locker for me.

My auld man used to laugh at me about that. He would have been better fucking teaching me to fucking swim. I aye regretted I couldnay swim. Okay, it wasnay a priority. But it was something for the future, the near future. And Yasmin as well, she would have to take the wee lassie, get her some coaching, it would gie her confidence. Weans should have that confidence. Confidence in yer body. Weans should have that. All weans, send them swimming. I was gauny nag the ex about that. There were these wee aspects about fatherhood; if she thought I was gauny no bother she was very much mistaken. If she thought I was just gauny fucking disappear out her life man, if she fucking thought that for one fucking minute boy she didnay fucking know me, she just did not know me, no sir.

Never mind. When was I last on a boat? Floating casinos down Louisiana. Me and Haydar had spoken about it many a time but I could never get past Arizona. There was something about that place. I wouldnay say I fell in love with it. But it gied me ideas. Maybe that happens to everybody; ye hit certain places and they stick in yer heid, and if ye want to write books about them then ye want to write books about them. It isnay that I wantit to write a book about Arizona but it seemed a place where "things happen". Ye could imagine all sorts of plots and adventures, murky deeds and corruption, crookit deals, and very fine landscapes. Mind you, when me and Haydar went a-roving wur sole preoccupation was a decent music bar or club venue, and women who would gaze benevolently upon music-loving strangers.

Except we aye landit in joints where jazz was the sound. Jazz and women dont mix. That was my belief. The odd thing was not only did Haydar land us in jazz joints, he landit us in jazz joints where women were present. Single women in bars where jazz was the main music? Such phenomena did exist and Haydar found them. He could find anything. He had never been lost in his life, especially if there were mountains in the vicinity. His ancestors were nomads. One of his great-greats had been a trapper in the Union Army, a scout for the fucking bluecoats. So he said but I never believed him. He only startit the yarn eftir he heard about my namesake ancestor.

We baith liked getting into a car and driving, avoiding interstates and main highways where possible. It was some auld dirt track with geese a-flapping and ducks a-quacking that we were seeking; life-altering experiences; auld guys with wizened chops on the porch playing the geetar, mandolin or harmonica; fresh-faced lassies with torn blouses and shy smiles of welcome.

But quite often it was boring. I did the driving. He said he could drive but I never saw him do it. We had these stupit wagers to pass the time. We would bet on the first woman we see is she wearing trousers or a skirt? is her blouse grey or blue? what age is she, ower thirty below thirty? what colour is her hair? Or on passing cars, the next along between a chev or a ford, name yer bet, buick or beamer? The first animal ye see is a rabbit or a dog, a cat or a horse; road squash dont count. He tempted me with crazy gambles. I thought that was what they were. It turned out he had researched and manufactured the damn things. So we would take the back roads and maybe land in some wee town by what I thought was a fluke. We would park the jalopy and get out, wander around yawning, then he would say, Ten dollars we find a bar with a five-piece jazz band and the sax player has the name Joe Sanchez and there is many single women present.

Fuck off, all sax players have the name Joe Sanchez.

No, I'll lay you 5s.

Fuck off.

10s? 16s?

16s . . . Mmm. Well now, how do we spell this Joe, is it with an "e" or what? Is it Jo Sanchez or Joe Sanchez?

Pardon me?

Nay pardon meez, ye want to bet ye have to be precise: Joe Sanchez; ye spelling it jay oh or jay oh ee? And what about Sanchez, how do you want to spell it, spaneesh or yohhhroooba, you want it in the frenchee style, serb or croat or ancient portogeese; is it "ch" or is it "ç"? So let us wager on the guy's antecedents is he 3rd-, 4th-, 5th-generation, what is his fucking politics is he a fascist bastard, pink liberal jerk-off, is he one of you muslim fuckers or is he a smooth-talking anarchist fucking socialist free-thinking fucking atheist all-round good guy man you tell me?

One time the thieving conman bastard had two cigarette lighters exactly the same colour and design and kept it a secret. After one long bout of driving even the mental mad bets were beginning to pall then we were approaching a little town and looking forward to some grub in the local restaurant, final bets had been on the available pie fillings: blueberry, pecan or lemon.

Haydar had brought out the cigarettes, he passed me one, and when he flicked the lighter, he stopped and he goes: Hey man last bet. Crazeee, something crazeee. And he looks about the dashboard and the glove compartments, everyplace, then at last he holds up his lighter and goes: Another cigarette lighter like this, I shall find one somewhere, in a bar, restaurant, in the street, the parking lot. Exactly the same, colour, all of that, exactly. See, we will find a lighter same as this one. Maybe not exactly man but you know what I mean, same colour and so on, same style. You listening to me here? We will find one someplace.

Naw fuck I wasnay listening I was relaxing, I had been driving four hours and switched off the engine, opened the door, I had one leg out, enjoying the breeze. The usual five-dollar bet. I cannay remember how suspicious I was but it went out my heid. A few hours later we came out a bar, heading to a motel and I saw something glitter on the street, and he saw me see it and I stepped across and lo and behold . . . Obviously the cunt conned me and I knew he had conned me but I couldnay get my heid round it. I knew he must have had a duplicate lighter and somehow palmed it and got it there; maybe he came in advance, maybe the week preceding, or else maybe he knew somebody in the town and sent it by fucking fedex how the fuck do I know, except he took the five dollars and never confessed, never ever. There are things in this life Jerry boy. Yeh, and that wasnay one of them.

The gambling was always unlucky when he was there. No just for me, for him. He was real unlucky on the tables, mair unlucky than me. He denied it. When he was gambling alone he was a success story. It was me, I was the problem. Unlucky in love unlucky at cards. Naybody would accuse life of being fair. I was never lucky at fuck all. Haydar was the opposite, where women were concerned, that lucky in love palaver, that was this cunt to a tee. Gambling with him I went skint umpteen times but through him I landed in some unmissable experiences, occasionally of the Keystone Cops variety.

The women he favoured were no skeenee cheeks my frenn no sir these were women females with the curves and the soft places; and if there was one of each oftimes it was me for the less slender of the duo, and I wasnay grumbling and wouldnay have grumbled; either was fine, mighty fine, although they were always a bit aulder than me.

He wasnay even handsome; a heavyset feller with a big heid and then the fucking lip growth. I thought the mountain man muslim background was all just an excuse for the moostachayo that draped its way ower his fizzog. How in tarnation he got off with women wearing one of them I dont know. He insisted on wearing it but and it was just goddam ludicrous. Like maist of us he had a tremendous regard for Pancho Villa but so what, it doesnay mean ye stop shaving.

How women go for moostachayoed males beats me. Another yin was the ex's uncle, auld fucking slugface, Mister

Moostach. His growth went tripping down from his nose like a big slug perched across his upper lip. Maybe it was a big slug, perched there to keep warm and moist at the same time, catching the spray out the auld yin's nostrils. Maybe it had crawled there for a rest when he was lying out the game with the drink. He loved that rum, his house was full of it; all with picturesque labels; he was a rum collector. In his younger days he was a bootlegger, doing the Demerara run, top hand on a speedy schooner, yoh yoh yoh me hearties.

No sir. Me and moostachayos dont mix. My auld man had one too and when he was drunk he insisted on kissing all sorts of bodies, including his younger son. It was worse than meeting my Auntie Meg at one of those faimly events. Aw daddy daddy fucking hell man what is that a fucking mop! soaking wet with a repulsive mix of porridge, slabbers and stout; totally disgusting me hearties.

I wondered about the physical mechanics of sex when I was a boy. Inherent was a calvinist medieval christian element. It came before the pleasures. I lay in bed in premasturbatory mode, sturdily postponing the carnal for the sake of diverse mental peregrinations concerning theoretical physics and the advancement of humankind as a whole viz I wonder what happens with skinny wee females and big huge males? How can a wee woman support such a guy! Some of them are just fucking monsters and then ye see them with their wives who are just so wee and skinny and delicately beautiful man in these frilly pantie outfits ye see in these glossy magazines with beautiful tits it is fucking extraordinary! Ah well, if only I could figure that one out. Sigh. Then I settled back for the business in hand. And now here I was a fully-fledged male and solving the matter empirically, only from another slant: medium-sized skinny males and medium-sized huge females. We were across the Nevada border again and Haydar had got us involved with

65

two females and they were baith not at all slender. The one I accompanied was the largest lassie I had ever been with. But she was sharp as fuck man what a fucking tongue she had on her. She reminded me of my Auntie Meg, one minute she was skelping my ear and gieing me a row and the next it was slobbering kisses and me getting clutched to the big bosom with all these erective textures and odours and luscious handfuls. In the first place it exacerbated matters that Haydar and her pal were in the adjacent bed. I didnay like when that happened. I was into romance and various male-to-female chatting stuff where privacy is essential. The idea of people eavesdropping the romantic patter was a turn-off, hey blue eyes, let yore hair down, dispense with the off-putting spectacles, I just couldnay have done it in front of an audience.

I heard them sniggering a wee bit but mainly they were getting on with the job in quite a peaceable manner. With me and the one I was with it was all grunts and groans and minor squabbles and one thing was me sliding out or how I aye seemed to be on the outside and having to start again christ one time the dick nearly bent in two. I got the hang of it although I will say she didnay lack patience in that direction and eventually the best way was me climbing ower her. Once back inside I stuck to her like a crab or is it a scorpion, my legs on top of her legs and pinning her down by prolonged flexing of the upper thighs. I was gauny wind up with arthritic hip joints in my auld age.

I only knew her three days and two nights yet it took off like a fully developed relationship. She was blaming me for stuff that had nothing to do with me. The word "grateful", she had "grateful" on the brain. Am I supposed to be grateful? Did I expect her to be grateful? Who the hell did I think I was, arrogant ungrateful arsehole, who the hell did I think she was, with these expectations. What expectations? I didnay have expectations, no apart from the usual male-to-female business, I wasnay gauny be grateful and I wasnay expecting her to be grateful christ I was only there to relax and enjoy myself, that was what I thought she was wanting as well.

But this lassie worked in real estate and had a lot of pressures and tensions, fair enough: and she also was wanting to write a book, christ, who didnay. Only her book was gauny be about serious things, the world and all that fucking keech, it wasnay gauny be about something so *crass* as private eyes having to solve political mysteries in Arizona or wherever the hell.

Crass! What the fucking hell was crass about that? My hero wasnay the usual apolitical right-wing hollywood prick, his sympathies went to the underdog, he was anti-cops and anti-robbers, anti-authoritarian, he was also a good anarchist; anti-sexist, anti-homophobic, anti-racist, pro-justice, pro-truth, pro-asylum seeker, pro-immigration, pro-equality – christ I could go on forever. And the place to do it was the book. And I was gauny. I definitely hadnay gied up the project. Only sometimes it depressed me because for all kinds of reasons I wasnay able to get on with it.

But I would. Whether I came back to this place or no. Maybe I would just stay at hame for a spell, with ma mammy. In a couple of days' time I would be stepping onto the hallowed tarmac at Glasgow Airport! My fuck that was scary business; it scared the living wits out me anyway. What the fuck are living wits? I dont even know what they are! Living daylights?

Nay wonder we reach for the beer, my beer having just arrived. Sally had appeared from naywhere, she dumped it in front of my nose. I saw the manager guy gazing in my direction. Maybe he didnay like folk fraternizing with the staff. So why run a bar?

Aw fuck, I would be glad to get hame. It was eight years since I had been there. I would probably get lost on the way,

I was passing through 38 cities to get there. It was my ayn fault for carrying the economic factor to that extent. It was a deal I got, saving $130. Rapid City, Seattle, Montreal, Gander, Reykjavik, Amsterdam, Edinburgh then the final flight to Glasgow. Maybe they would let me parachute down between Reykjavik and Amsterdam.

The lady I dealt with at the local flightsaver office took it as her ayn wee personal project to get me a good deal and with proper all-round international insurance. Fuck the international insurance, I says, just get me the deal! Well, I didnay swear. I rather appreciated that lady. She was a few years aulder than me and having quite a hard time of it, a grown-up faimly and problems; her man had damaged his spine in a fluke accident while driving a fork-lift truck and she had three teenaged daughters who drove her crazy.

But what a cheapskate I was! Always was, always will be. A saving of $130; at the time I thought it was worth it. What do I mean "worth it"?

What do I mean "hame"?

What do I mean "mother"? My daughter has a mother, she also had a father, I had a father, I had a home, I had another home, maybe homes are ten a penny, I have had fucking millions of them. Except in the land of my birth.

Of course one's mummy had a spare room wherein one might doss. I might even settle back down in the place, good ol sunny Skallin.

Oh for fuck sake naw.

I take that back. What a way to talk about the motherland!

She wasnay nay motherland to me pardner, no sirree, that is how come I hit the lonesome trail.

I didnay have to go hame, naybody was forcing me. I could spend a couple of days right here and check it out for future temporary residence. I could invent some tale for the airline.

Official bodies would surely listen if a tale was mete, given that discretionary practices were allowed. But in my experience they were suspicious of any judgment that wasnay thrust upon them by verifiable inference. If I phoned now I was inside the stipulated refund period and that made a difference. But why make the call to the airport just now? Why get embroiled in such immediacy. It was bound to be a digital recording anyway. There was always tomorrow morning. And if the worst came to the worst, and I wasnay allowed a refund, so what, I would just have lost the fare money. I didnay have to leave. Naybody was gauny drag me screaming and kicking onto the plane. If I didnay want to go that was fine. I would lose the money. I wasnay exactly a stranger to the concept.

And if I got the refund I would return it to the bank account or else mosey along to the nearest track. Any greyhounds in this here state? Naw, no the track. Better off heading to some unknown casino and walking in blindfolded, asking a waitress to point yer hand to the first even money call. But even money calls and me dont mix.

And then what do ye do if ye back a winner? We know what happens if ye lose but what if ye win? The same again maam thank you maam, only this time with mair money. Why no get out of there immediately. Buy a new computer. Look for a good apartment, a decent apartment, get settled in and find a proper job, fuck the booze trade and the Security industry, maybe go driving again.

Yeh, or head south, get out the states altogether, head to where a guy could breathe, breathe, a land where people cared.

Ah fuck, when I first met Yasmin I was a relaxed guy, just glad to be back on the east coast. Even the booze trade had its positive aspects. Sure the hours were long but it didnay destroy me intellectually; if I was gauny try something like writing a book then now was the time. My boring job was a plus. I only had to be there. Fine. I had to talk occasionally. Fine. Although it was mainly listening. A few of the solitaries who used the pub were "eccentric", or is that the wrang word. José and partner called them "eccentric" but they would have been called that by other folk. They lived closeby and knew everybody, especially who was rich and who wasnay. According to them it was the auld story about the one ye least expect: take auld Charlie there in the corner, him with the nay socks and the torn-arse trousers, he was the man, he was the multibillionaire.

A load of fucking sentimental hogwash.

No sir, Jerree, amigo, who is the most raggedy-looking bum comes into your bar? Customer I am talking about . . . ! Ha ha.

Yeh ha ha to you too.

I would glance at the appropriate party and shrug. José would wink to his partner. Oh yeh! You think Charlie! Let me tell you about Charlie, Charlie is the richest man in town, he is beyond a doubt Meester Super-Rich Charlie, Meester Super-Duper-Rich Charlie, he is the man.

I feigned astonishment. Auld fucking Charlie! A multi-damnbillionaire, jumping jehosaphat. José grinned at his partner who shook his heid at me. And what about the toty wee elderly woman! Her with the pins fastening her overcoat, the stockings trailing round her ankles. She had come walking in from the local Spar with her bags of groceries, having hitched her cart to the nearest parking lot. I was the only bartender in the entire art gallery district that let her in the door. She liked her ouzo. I liked ouzo as well, I tried it out eftir witnessing her relish: whenever she smacked her lips she just about swallied her nose. Yeh, said José, you know who she is? she is auld Annie Mae Morgan, she is J. P.'s great-great-granddaughter, she is worth a fucking treelyon twice over man, there is statues of her on Broad Street, she is a First Lady.

Well well, says I, would ye credit that.

Such sentimental fucking el turderro. But they were serious. Of course if it came to money it was this pair, they were rich as fuck, or so they acted. They were artists or maybe designers, one or the other or baith, and they were fashionable, and they liked a drink. Maist nights they came into the bar they sat until closing time and I would have to gie them heavy hints so I could lock up. They were fine as long as they didnay get onto the subject of politics. Once they had two or three margaritas all that amazing procapitalist shite would hurtle out their gubs.

Eftir my first visit to the 3rd Street bar I mentioned it to them. Of course they knew all about it, they were goddam regulars, they went there all the goddam time. Even when I thought they were in my bar they werenay, it was all an illusion, they were someplace else.

Okay, but they did know the joint and they did know various people and the couple of times I went with them there was always company. Some nights when I locked up my ayn place the three of us got a cab downtown but she was never there. It turned out it was only Mondays she went because that was the open mic session. Monday was still my night off. I asked Ranjit from my local store but he couldnay come. I traveled ower myself, but José and partner were there and I was glad to see them. Then they knew somebody who knew somebody and later on Yasmin and her cousin were part of the company. She had finished her set and when she came to the table I quickly created space by shifting to the side as much as I could, irritating the prick on my left who tried to shift back again and I had to use force so no to be pushed off, at the same time I was trying to point out the space to Yasmin, plus gie a nonchalant shrug.

So that was us squashed in the gether; that was how we got talking. We had to do something, or I had to, she was just knackered, nay communication for christ sake she had done it all at the mic. I shouldnay have expected a single goddam thing from her, except I did, the same as everybody, expecting her to be the life and soul of the party. Eftir she had done a gig. How naive can ye get. Yet that was the expectation held by people. I was nay different. At the same time we were squeezed in the gether, tight in and I was so aware of her, she was so hot, her body temperature, christ and it would have been the maist natural thing to put my arm round her shoodir. She had just done the set. A friend of José and partner was yapping on with an anecdote relating to famous persons. It was funny and everybody laughed. And I noticed she smiled although she hadnay heard a word. I knew she hadnay because I was paying complete attention to her and I was just so aware of her, and her body, wur thighs and all the way up, and it was like these scenes in a movie where boy meets girl and suddenly all the music stops, all the sound, it is a silent moment for them alone. That was how it was. I spoke to her, I made some comment. What did I say to her? Shite. Fortunate was I that she didnay understand a word. Thank fuck because I was my usual know-all self, arsehole cretin man I was a presumptuous fucking fool. The usual.

She just nodded then gied me a wee sideways look. And I had this peculiar sensation that I was now able to relax and that if I went to the men's room she would make space for me to squeeze back in beside her. That was what I felt. What a weird encounter this was, almost like we were now a couple. And christ almighty my life did change. It was a genuine life-change experience.

Now José's partner was a quiet feller and wary of me and I think it was because he thought José fancied me. I just played it ordinary and relaxed, no picking up the signals. On this same night but what I remember was José spinning one of his yarns and I caught sight of his partner. And I saw him just staring at

José with this smile on his face and it was like fucking hell man he couldnay take his eyes off him!

It wasnay that me and her loved each other, I wouldnay go as far as that, that I loved her. I want to be honest about that. What love is, who the hell knows. But I was finding it hard to let go, I admit that; that was my problem. I wasnay hiding it from myself. Sure I can be a fucking hypocritical cunt but no with myself; any time of the day or night I can tell lies, but no looking into the mirror.

But being with her, it was a peculiar experience, it was like I relaxed in some unique way, like I had been exhausted, taken a few deep breaths, and now come to rest.

I didnay feel it was arrogance on my part to speak to her. Maybe it was. How the hell did I think I could land a woman like her? I didnay. I just heard her sing and thought she was great. What is wrang with that? I knew I was nothing, a naybody, stupit dreams maybe but nothing else. I had fuck all man the usual, nay prospects. I was never gauny be one of these immigrant Carnegie fuckers who finish up hurting millions and making billions. But this shithole of a world, who knows, about the writing, if I stuck at it. Sometimes I felt that it wasnay total garbage. Maybe I could do it.

Art and politics and fucking life man that was what I blethered about to her; making yer life and doing yer best and no letting the pentagon fuckers do ye in. Her cousin heard some of it and gied me a good response. What did Yasmin say? Fuck all. She listened. But it wasnay critical. Okay I was just a guy she met in a pub, a guy with a funny accent who was talking about being a writer. But for her it wasnay crap. She was a musician herself and wrote her ayn stuff, lyrics and music. It wasnay hard for her to imagine somebody like me wanting to have a go at writing

And I aye talked a good book. I could aye talk.

73

But it wasnay all talk. If possible I wrote something before I went to work. By the time I got hame from a shift and into bed it was 4 or 5 in the morning, midday before I was fit to rise. Other mornings I just sat on and on in front of the tube, sucked into these stupit fucking chat shows, didnay crawl into my kip till maybe 8 or 9 o'clock, and didnay get up till late in the eftirnoon. And I left to go to work at 4.30 p.m. It was even worse when I got the Security job, fucking nightshift, five nights one week six the next. Ye werenay fit for fuck all eftir that.

Then sometimes it just depressed ye and it was just like impossible to see the stuff on the computer screen ever making it to the page of a book. The words didnay seem right, there were too many wee yins or something. It sounds stupit but that was how it appeared. Other times I thought it was alright – no to sound boastful – I thought it was good. Once we startit gaun the gether I showed some of it to her but she never said nothing. I would have been as well tossing it out the window. Then I read an article in a magazine that says never show those closest to ye anything ye write, ye would be better gieing it to a stranger in the street, because what ye were seeking was an objective report and close friends and faimly could never offer that.

There was aye cunts offering ye advice. Then ye read articles where writers plowed a lonely furrow for years till suddenly it happened for them, red carpets from hollywood. But who wantit red carpets from hollywood. I just wantit to earn a couple of dollars. All it needit was one book to hit, just one.

Ah fuck man nay point fooling yerself: I would have been better taking out a patent on some new form of cludgé paper. In twelve years in this country I had had many a good shite but never a good fucking wipe man they didnay know how to make toilet paper. Imagine that! supreme destroyer of the planet; leader in world exploitation, in the destruction of all human endeavour; supporter of the tyrant and genocidal murderer, yet they couldnay wipe their dowp without sticking a finger through the paper, dear oh dear. Unless it was intentional. That hadnay occurred to me. It was a dastardly plot! These fuckers deliberately manufactured unsafe toilet paper, as a method of controling the domestic population. That could be a plot for one of these right-wing secret-service novels that always get to the top of the media book buyers' charts and earn the writers big bucks, big big bucks, big big big big big big bucks, the fucking biggest of fucking big bucks, billions of the bastards, countless billions, countless goddam agh forget it. Forget it. But naw, ye could see how

fuck off

The ex's cousin and me got on okay. At that time she went to maist of the gigs. Neither her nor the ex had met anybody from Skallin before but they had heard of it. Their grasp of geography was a wee bit better than the usual Uhmerkin deal. Even so they thought Skallin was somewhere in Germany which they guessed was to "the left hand side" of Australia, up above the Arctic fucking Pole. Okay.

When I startit gaun regularly the cousin looked out for me and I sat beside her. I think she liked my company. Sometimes I made her laugh. She looked at me and guffawed. Her and Yasmin were good pals as well as cousins and they shared a wee apartment.

There was aye a build-up inside me before the performance. I got nervy. The same went for the cousin. She went fucking giggly, eyes wide. I was worse. She said I was worse. It was true! My teeth literally startit fucking chattering the gether! And if I was standing my knees would be knocking and that second before she sang I thought the world was gauny have to end or else I would collapse onto the floor in a withering heap.

She didnay have a big outgoing style of personality and when she stood her upper body swayed to one side, away from the mic, and ye thought she might keel ower. It was also the way she had of looking at everybody; and this was to the fore if she was introducing her songs. It was mair than shyness, in fact it wasnay shyness. Maybe it was extreme caution. Her singing was strong on her main influences who seemed from a different generation and mair bluesy than jazz to my mind but that was just to my mind, and I would never have made such a statement to her. She loved a lot of these auld singers – Nina Simone was her hero – and a lot of why she loved them was political. She knew it was but wouldnay talk about it. And definitely no with me would she talk about it. How come? I asked her a few times but never got a real answer, no a satisfactory one. She didnay want to talk to me about people that stand up for their rights as human beings. Naw, how come? I have to ask. Do aliens no get included in this? What is the fucking issue here! I could never get to grips with that yin, how come bodies like me were excluded from the debate.

Plenty other musicians were there for these open mic nights but only one played regularly with her; a keyboard player whose machine had all the wee knobbly bits that meant ye could hear drums and guitars and sax and trombones and whatever. He was okay I think. Except on occasion he hit the keys too hard which gied a preponderance, a heaviness, to the front of the note, it being too loud, an artificial way to gain significance. But speaking like that makes my hair stand on end. He was fine and what do I know I know fuck all, although obviously it was better when he didnay use all the knobbly bits: a keyboard is best just as a keyboard. The open mic sessions gied her the space to slip in a song of her ayn then she accompanied herself on geetar. That was what I liked. Otherwise if it was an ordinary gig she would be along with other musicians. Then it was mair jazzy, it gied them the chance to do their ayn thing. And they took the chance. I dont blame them, except sometimes a pause doesnay need filled in. That used to grate on me. She would let a note hang there or just like be silent for a wee minute but then in comes a big-sounding instrument, blasting through it. The guy that acted as her manager came to a couple of gigs. He was a pal of the keyboard player, but a nasty cunt, a bit of a gangster.

Once her performance was ower I said I would like to see her hame. She lived way nor-nor-west, and was maybe too tired to argue but that is too easy an answer. I reckon she did fancy me and that is that, who is gauny deny it? She looked to her cousin for support but her cousin just grinned. She thought the situation hilarious, that I was hilarious; the idea of me and Yasmin, it just knocked her out. She was one of these females who keep slapping ye on the wrist, apropos of fuck all. The equivalent in males are the shoodir punchers, these cunts who keep punching ye on the shoodir in supposed gestures of affection.

But she was fine, Yasmin's cousin, mighty fine, and I loved her.

The manager had a jalopy and when he showed up for a gig he did the driving. He wasnay too pleased having me tag along. I tried to be sociable but to hell with it. When we reached their place Yasmin took pity on me and no only brought me in for a coffee she took me into her bed, we wound up sleeping the gether. An explanation is vital: I often wondered about it myself and sometimes it kind of worried me about her other away performances. Maybe she was exhausted. Her eyes aye went that sleepy way, like a wee wean's. I knew she was tired but didnay take it in properly. Right under my nose the lassie was falling asleep. I was blethering on about some nonsense or other. She could barely keep her eyelids open. She had her elbow on the arm of the sofa and had startit tilting ower. What was I blethering about? fuck knows; all kinds of choice items: art and revolution, untypical private-eye heroes battling mysterious political forces in out-of-the-way environments. The usual nonsense one is wont to blether christ almighty I was a youthful cunt, it was five years ago, a long five years. Her cousin had been sitting on the sofa beside her. I sat on the floor, on a cushion, my legs crossed at the knees like I was into yoga but it was just weanish behaviour, I was just showing off in some foolish manner. Eventually her cousin yawned and went to bed. Yasmin had her eyes closed. I rubbed my back, lighted another cigarette.

My arse was numb. I got up and walked to the window for exercise. It was a wee two-bedroom apartment six stories up but eftir the en suite cupboard I was living in it was like fucking I dont know what. The windows overlooked a back alley; but a scenic back alley, stuffed full of choicer items some of whom I got to know during the next couple of years. I stood until the cigarette was finished, enjoying those mighty fine inhalations of tobacco smoke and all its weighty constityooent flavourings or toxins. When I returned to my cushion she looked at me and sighed, she had to go to bed. She opened the door to her room and showed me inside. It was just big enough for the double mattress; she pointed to the edge of it and gied me a look, a look. You wait in there, she says, for twenty minutes; okay? then you come in, twenty minutes.

Yeh, sure. I pointed to the sofa. I could sleep there if ye want? I shrugged. She also shrugged. She was in the bathroom for three hours. I thought she had gone in to chat to her cousin or crawled out the window to escape my presence but she hadnay. It was getting to the stage I was gauny bang the door if she didnay return in one second flat. But the woman was a witch man she definitely was. Just as I raised my clenched knuckles to gie the bathroom door a bang what happened but it opened and out she came indicating her wristwatch and she continued on into her bedroom, leaving the door unshut.

So that was that and it was my decision. Well let me tell ye I was definitely going in after her. First I would do what she asked, bide my time for twenty minutes. Already it was becoming light; 0622 hundred hours capn and the high seas were rising. Yasmin was a shape on the far side of the mattress. I undressed to my shorts and crept under the quilt onto the edge of the opposite side, and onto my back and lay there with a heart gone mad fucking crazy yelp yelp yelp. I never knew hearts could yelp until that moment. There was nay sheet between me and the quilt, I was lying on one but there was only the quilt above and there was something in its touch on my body. It was peculiar because I was lying at attention, on my back with my feet and legs the gether, arms straight down my sides, fucking shoodirs hunched and a total extraordinary hardon, like it was in its most natural condition, it wasnay like an erection at all, it was just another limb, or a bone or something; it was like it didnay even haud a pulse. How could I sleep it was impossible. I was exhausted but so what. Eftir I settled down I tried to discover if she was awake. Ages I spent listening to her breathing, attempting to spot changes to the rhythm that might indicate a state of tension, but she wasnay awake, she was asleep, fast asleep. Once we were living the gether I became accustomed to her post-performance. All she wantit was a kip. Ye hear about musicians and they want to party and screw all night long. No the ex. What she wantit was a kip. Kip is the wrang word, it means a kind of shortened sleep. Yasmin needit a real sleep. The kind of sleep only a woman seems capable. Being a double mattress wur bodies didnay have to make contact so I couldnay pretend there was nay option but to touch her legs or feet occasionally.

My ayn feet were yon cauld damp way and if they had touched her legs she surely would have shot into the air. I startit dozing. Later I was awake with that same unbreakable hardon and this time she was backed into me; she was still sleeping but it was body to body and the most natural thing in the world to poke it between her thighs, get it nestled beneath her vagina, then wiggle a wee bit and wait, another wee wiggle. It was just a beautiful damn thing and that is that, I can feel it in my toes. We done a few that morning. It is etched into my brain. Eftir we got up and done the appropriate ablution stuff we went out for something to eat.

She was also starving and a diner near her place looked spectacular with its Low Cost!! All-Action!! All-Day Breakfasts!! So that had to be wur first stop. A slap-up no-nonsense polateful of grub. Mayple syruple drippiling down the chin et cetera et cetera, runny yolks and whatever else, slabs of thick ham. I shall show ye beautiful, if ye want to know beautiful, get them rashers on the table. And the diner was only two blocks down the street and it was a fine morning my god at the end of my first couple of months back on the east coast with this luscious lassie whom I had just slept with for the first time, a lassie who was so so special.

She was christ let us be honest about it, if something is the case then confess, confess.

But we never made it to the spectacular breakfast joint, even although it was by nature of a celebration, shampanya to follow, big ceegars, whatever the lassie wantit. It never happened. Nor the next times she brought me hame. Something aye seemed to get in the way. She had her ayn ideas. I wondered sometimes maybe she didnay want to be seen with me because I was a pink fucker but naw, that was wrang.

Her last guy never took her anywhere. She liked the movies. I took her to the movies. Just fucking ordinary hollywood shite, the usual turgid sentimentality; how a bunch of staid & stuffy upper-class Englishwomen come to know and respect a plucky but headstrong Uhmerkin lassie who winds up saving their lives from a fucking megalomaniac pagan or some goddam keech, plus the usual hollywood adverts on behalf of the roman catholic and jewish religions. Jumping fuck man I was sick to the teeth of it. The extraordinary thing was that Yasmin liked it. She sat there and grinned. Grinned! D'ye want some pop-corn? I says with an ironic twitch of the lips. Yeh, she says, and a pepsi. So off I went and had a smoke outside, then a coffee in the foyer to calm masel down. Twenty minutes I stayed away. Why take things so seriously. Okay the movie was a load of right-wing tosh but so what? why make her suffer?

I wasnay making her suffer.

Aye I was, I delayed her popcorn and pepsi by twenty minutes.

Wur first quarrel?

Naw, no quite, it just gied an edge to the rest of the evening. But she still came back to my place. I took her into Ranjit's store to say hullo. Okay I was bragging. Ranjit kept smiling but gied me respectful looks.

Next morning I was wanting to take her for breakfast. She would have preferred to stay and eat in my apartment. My apartment! That was what she called it! But it didnay matter because I had nay food anyway. I had to show her the "nay food", its nonexistence, because she didnay believe me. I was then existing on fastfood, sandwiches and whatever; pre-packed meals I could fling into the oven for a quarter of an hour's bake; that tasty stuff with the cellophane sleeves that ye puncture or stab or whatever and then pap into the oven and wait twenty minutes – enough time to swally a beer and grab a smoke in a relaxed fashion. I couldnay be bothered cooking, no for myself, no when I came hame eftir a day's graft. I didnay have the energy. It isnay that I couldnay cook, I could fucking cook and earned a living at the game on one ever-to-be-forgotten occasion in the town of Sweet Elizabeth when the silly prick who owned the diner stationed me at the pie compartments. This was a useless fucker who pretended to be Oirisch, that his people were from Connemara. A long story.

Eftir me and her startit living the gether I cooked all the time. If I hadnay I wouldnay have fucking ate; the ex wasnay what one would call a domesticated person. Even eftir the wean was born. Then I was working in the Security racket and falling ower the doorway at half past seven in the morning, staggering into the bed just as she staggered out. But it was me heated the baby food and made the boiled eggs. She smiled.

She had a good smile.

But in those early days something was gaun on that I knew nothing about. I sensed it. There were obvious things like how she needit advance notice if I was gauny call on her. Twice I made the mistake of traveling out to her place without prearranging it and she wasnay home. It could take me an hour and a half to get there. Then when I phoned her cell phone number I couldnay get through.

It was up to her what she did. I had nay claims on her. Sometimes her cousin looked at me in a funny way, like she was surprised by something, maybe how seriously I took life, or because I didnay take certain matters seriously enough. But what were these "certain matters"?

The thing about me but at that time, I was breaking clear of a fucking what is another word for horrible – terrible, fucking terrible, fucking horrible fucking terrible – it was dreadful, my life was dreadful. Things had happened on the west coast and I was blamed for them. They had nothing to do with me but still I carried the can. It was unjust man and it was shite. But I couldnay get it sortit. I tried. So then it was time to move on, swiftly, before the ceiling collapsed. Thank fuck for the Greyhound bus is about all I can say. It is like sometimes man you are fucking running on the same spot – one of these nightmares – and the bus driver switches on the engine and the last passenger is climbing aboard, 1.30 a.m., dark, the yellow lights, that door is about to shut and inch by inch ye get there and ye just make the lower step as the door is closing but one last gasp and ye manage to push it open; up ye go, whhhoohh fuck made it, the driver gies ye a nod, ye show him a ticket, then along the aisle ye walk, a corner seat down at the back, ye stick the backpack on the rack then climb in, whohoohh, next thing the bus is heading out onto the interstate and ten minutes later the city lights are falling behind and ye can afford to breathe properly, ye have made it, ye have made it, oh for fuck sake man ye have made it.

The truth is that before I met the ex my life was out of control. It happens. There comes a build-up. It isnay a sudden phenomenon. I know the signs. In gambling everything ye touch has been crumbling. Ye feel apologetic when ye make a bet. This is because other people will have bet the same thing and ye know ye will have jinxed the fucker. Because that is what ye are, a jinx, a fucking hex, a jonah, ye have stuck the kibosh on the bastard. It doesnay matter what ye bet ye are fukt. Even if ye dont bet.

This was something completely new and fucking completely unique. She was different from other women I had been with. She was even about the first lassie of my ayn age, size and fit – yeh, we fitted. And she had her ayn take on the world, and her ayn goddam point of view, her ayn wee smile and curl of the mouth and shake of the heid, shake of her curls and that smile, she smiled with her eyes, it was just beautiful and I held her chin in my right hand, my fingers onto her cheek and she just studied me. I should have been one of these guys, sculptors.

We had that plasticine, putty substance when I was a boy and we moulded faces and figures.

Nay point thinking about it.

Sometimes the way she gazed at me, like she couldnay understand what I saw in her. Or the other way about, she didnay know what she saw in me, if she saw anything in me, how come she had let me land her?

Fucking hell man she wasnay a fish. In gambling things go like they go and ye do yer best but with her my life was changing. But it was me making it change. Naybody was doing it for me.

Yet she didnay think of me as serious. I wasnay like other guys she went with. She said that to me and couldnay explain it, didnay know what to make of me. I was the only alien she ever knew never mind got in tow with. She couldnay remember ever meeting an un-Uhmerkin activity in the flesh before. In her entire life? What about all the Spanish-speaking peoples, all the different folks from South-East Asia, from Africa, Pakistan and all these countries of the world . . . ? What about all of them? ye cannay walk anywhere in any major city without meeting somebody. Yasmin, I says, ye're meeting aliens every day of the week. How can ye say I'm the first one ye've ever met?

Spoke to, she says, slept with, she says, you know what I'm talking about, you are the first one, ever.

Other bodies had faimly and friends. All I had was myself. Other bodies had clothes and possessions. All I had was – what the hell did I have? I skipped out from the west coast by the skin of my teeth, fuck knows how I got through man getting through it was the worst condition I had been in for a while. I was rebuilding my life. I had nothing when I met her except a jacket and a pair of jeans, a couple of tee-shirts, insufficient underwear. I was all set to replenish the wardrobe. Nay mair of that west-coast slack, henceforth it was east-coast cool; fashion and style and all that shite. There was this clothing store I kept meaning to visit. José telt me about it. I was definitely gauny go. I just hadnay got round to it. It wasnay laziness or lack of interest, mair a question of time. Also money of course because although the clothes were secondhand they were the best of threads and expensive as fuck. Apparently some had never been worn at all, no even once. "Secondhand" is the wrang word. Them clothes were extra-special, pre-owned stuff, good labels or whatever. The people that designed it were known names, famous cunts. I telt her mair details. She stopped and looked at me. She hadnay quite realized when I said secondhand I meant secondhand, pre-owned. This a joke? she says. You want to buy pre-owned clothing?

It's different to what you think. It's a high-class operation.

A charity store!

It's no a charity store. It only gets called a charity store.

You want to buy old men's clothes like for yourself? She was gaping at me.

It isnay auld men's clothes christ this is a place for the skint man-about-town, somebody who is no so much down-at-heel as in the process of getting back on his uppers.

Funny.

Honest, this is personally made stuff, it's got the fashionable-style labels, designer bodies and aw that.

So how come it aint famous?

But it is famous. It's a secret but, one of the best-kept secrets in town. Even me, I am duty bound to keep its identity and location a mystery. I swore a holy oath of sacred secrecy. The guys that gied me the information insisted on confidentiality. The buying of clothes is a competitive affair among males ye know.

Yasmin laughed.

What I shall say is that the store is situated in a toty wee back street in what one calls a chic district. When I say chic I mean sshheek. The guys that telt me about the place were amazed I knew the street. How come they were amazed? Because I am a furnir. Because I am a member of the alien-igenae. All yous indigenous folks wonder how come furnirs know their way around the highways and byways of this city. It is because we walk, we walk, everywhere we go we walk. It took me nine fucking months to get my driver's licence and during that nine months I walked right across your entire fucking country Yasmin excuse the language, from the east coast to the west and nay interstates, there and back and on we go. I spent the night in wigwams, under trees and under bridges, under roads and in trenches and caves and ditches, beneath aqueducts, chuckalucks and pipe ducts; tree huts, riverbanks and various shady groves and leafy hollows. One night I slept near to a small loch

Pardon me?

Like a wee lake, a wide stretch of water, and an auld feller came along and took me back to where him and his wife were camping. They had been out before dawn, they were fishing. I was quite into fishing at one time masel. They loaned me a rod and I caught a sizeable brown trout – so did they, and we cooked them and ate them. No as tasty as catfish but with spices and hot sauce, a lick of good bread, it sure does the business when one is in the throes of malnutrition. Ah but it was memorable.

She smiled, smiled, smiled.

Of course all of that had nothing to do with not-so-knackered clothing stores in chic urban districts. This pre-owned designer place was a three-generational faimly concern. Father and sons were the salespersons and front-of-house workers while the auld granddaddy was stuck out of harm's way in the alterations room – him and his 19th-century tobacco pipe, ye could see the smoke belching out the doorway. He used a 200-year-auld brand of thick black tobacco twist – hoicht clear yer throat, speedaddle into the spittoon – and everybody listened for the clink. The father and sons all worked alone and had perfected a system of facial gesture, nods and grunts that allowed them to communicate in secret. And nary a smile atween them.

These very special secondhand clothes all come from good hames. Nay fleas nor lice nor nothing. It be rich parties that donated them, celebrity personages.

What happened was a lot of rock stars, movie stars and sports stars spent fortunes on their wardrobes. They threw their dough at every upmarket designer outfitter they found, all the fashionable yins. Then they went back to their three-floor penthouse apartments and waited for the delivery boys to bring the stuff ower. Then they saw it and boked on their caviare, Oh for fuck sake we have bought too much as per usual, and they got all guilty about it. There they were being radical musicians and radical movie stars and radical sports stars, all cool as fuck and fans of Che Guevara and plenty other deid revolutionaries with or without beards, plus certain religious personalities and other harbingers of a vigorous but pacifist solution to the problems of eternity.

So how do they reconcile their public dreams of justice for all humanity and nay suffering throughout the universe ever eftir when there they are with wardrobes fit for Catherine the Great, the Queen of Inklin and the Emperors Nero and Caligula all fucking rolled into one? Yes sir. So their wives and lovers, agents and managers say to them: Look, ye should donate this to a worthy charity and help feed loaves and fishes to the god-fearing galaxy; safeguard the rainforests, unite the universe and cure the disease-ridden multitudes, bringing water to the dustbowl refugees. Good idea, say the embarrassed multi-billionaire heroes of young people the wide world o'er and they order the delivery boys who are standing there scratching themselves in their holey trousers, bare feet and tattered togas, with nary a crust between them, to go cart all them brand-new threads across to the charity stores. But then at the last minute they change their mind and tell the boys to take them to the danged pre-owned store instead and see if they can earn a couple of dollars, and keep the change, that will do next month's wages. Get yer camels, they shout, form an orderly queue outside the elevator door.

I was surprised the ex hadnay heard of this place before; she was in the company of male musicians much of the time. Surely they knew about it. Apparently no. The guys she played with hardly changed their socks never mind their shirts and between them there was little communication. I find that disappointing, I says. I would have expected a generosity among performers, exchanges of information, that bodies would tell one another about all the good deals going down; there would be a real solidarity between them, all the rich yins would inform their workaday, sessional compadres of the good things that life renders to them if only they work very very hard and play their musical instruments in mete fashion. Or oh me miserum am I just a sentimental fool?

What do you know about performers? says she.

A lot, says I.

She chuckled.

You think because I'm a furnir I know nothing? How come absolute true-born Uhmerkins need to assume us aliens are a bunch of naive bumpkins!

Bumpkins?

Yeh, bumpkins, it's a word. Probably Charlie I'm a bum comes from it, or how ye use the word bum for a vagrant or hobo: bum, it's just an abbreviation for bumpkins.

What you dont know Jerry!

Yeh.

So why dont you write it down?

Write what down, a dictionary?

She was laughing. When I see somebody on the street I'm gonna say that to them, Hey bumpkins! You should write it down. You got any paper? You got a notepad? Writers I know, that's what they do.

You talking about songwriters? I dont see songwriters as writers; when I'm talking about writers I dont mean songwriters.

They aint good enough?

It's just different, what they do is different.

Why dont you write me a song?

You write them yerself.

Yeh but you could also.

Maybe, if the thought comes, if the thought comes I could gie it a go. Yeh, ye're right.

And she was. Occasionally in a subway or somewhere a good line came into my heid and then I got it rhyming with something else. The last time I saw my daughter I played a wee game with her based on rhyme endings. I heard about it on a radio talkshow and it worked, the wee yin thought it was great fun. Me and her had a real good laugh.

Sometimes it was as if she forgot that – the ex – she seemed to forget the wee yin liked me. No just because I was her dad but because I made her I dont know just fucking laugh, have a wee laugh, she liked me for christ sake.

Yeh, I should have carried the notebook. A few times I thought of something that made me laugh but I didnay have a pen and paper. And then relying on memory fucking hell man mine was so bad I had a cheek using the word.

Once I got a few dollars the gether I was gauny upgrade the technology. The auld laptop was heavy and slow; about ten or twenty steps behind the average human brain, two or three behind mine. I bought it out a pawnshop for a few dollars. Later I tried to pawn it back and they declined, dirty bastards. No, says the guy, and he couldnay look me in the eye. I felt like buying a gun and sticking them up.

So that was me stuck with it.

But it was fine for present purposes. It wasnay as if I was a fast typer. I found a book in a Sunday market that dealt with improving one's typing speeds but I hadnay made a start on it. Eventually I would and eventually I would upgrade and eventually this and eventually that.

Fine, fuck all wrang with eventually.

Nay cigarettes either.

Why is the guy no smoking? Because he gied it up six bastarn month ago. He is clean, clean; lungs like the new-driven snow.

Usually the smoking business didnay bother me but tonight, for some reason, it was affecting me maist dreadfully. Sitting here in this music bar, maybe it was the atmosphere, all that jazz scene, it is so damnably cool one desires to vomit,

or a click of the fingers to the bartender: yeh yeh yeh, pour me treh fingerz of bourbon por favor speedily and fucking hurry up.

Somebody had switched albums on the sound system. A woman was singing. She was good. It had altered the atmosphere.

There are times when the world changes.

Ah fuck.

What was gauny happen to me? It was like I had had everything and then lost it, like I had built it patiently, so patiently, in a game where ye spend hours accruing a decent pile and then va va voom, you is busted man, you is busted. But that is how it goes, ye take such pains to build it and in one haun it is gone, the past and the present lie the gether, it is gone – paradox, seven letter word ending in "x", jesus christ.

What is life? What are we fucking talking about here? I can get so fucking angry, just angry. Gie us a beer, why cant I fucking smoke, gie me a pack of fucking Luckies, and a large Glenmorangie, and let us go for a dip in the ocean or is zabranjeno kupanje in this yere boozer. Why is there a fucker observing me from his stool at the bar? Does the fucker think because he is large he is safe? Does this fucker know that I may wield this bottle in such fashion that his fucking nose fucking busts wide open man and the blood ruins his sharp white shirt except he aint got no blood, just milk, just milk, in them thar veins

and what is wrang with milk? Without it weans would-nay survive, wouldnay thrive, wouldnay grow up, my ayn daughter. I had a child, he said, elbowing his way to the exit.

Peace.

Peace.

Okay, I was still sitting there, still gazing at the table, at my haun on the table, at my haun holding the bottle on the table. I too was a wean.

When had I finished growing?

Aha, a trip fucking question.

Where is Sally, oh she of the long skirt, the tied blouse and nipples revealed. In the name of fuck a body is having a breakdown in booth number four, call the Security operatives, there is slabbers and snotters gushing out his orifices, plus he is in confessional mode. What a typical scenario: lonely man is to go hame, lonely man enters bar, lonely man has a drink; lonely man has another drink; lonely man ponders a third drink; lonely man has that third drink; lonely man mulls over his present in terms of his past, then blows out his fucking brains. Spare seat on the plane to bonné Skallin! Read all about it! His aged mother hirples to the door to receive her express delivery; Dear momma I'm writing to tell you, I was happy I was having a ball, but if now ye are reading this letter I aint a-coming home at all. Yore pore son maam he done have gone. Si señora maam I done bit the dust. He done bit the dust, pore sinner.

But the taped music was okay now; in fact it was good, a woman singing blues; a familiarity about her voice. Some auld singer had died recently. Maybe it was her singing. Yasmin would have known.

She knew everything.

I fucking knew nothing, that was my claim to fame.

Such were my dreams.

I wasnay getting any younger. Other guys were successful careerists at my age. E.g. Corey Parker. That bastard was only 23. This was what made the media frenzy so absurd. Needless to report, since the start of the baseball season the suicide rate among young Uhmerkin males had risen. Quite a few of them either shared wee Corey's birthday or were a few days aulder. His sort of success was predicated on the failure of the rest of the male population. Even I was affected. Promotion! Gie me it! Yea, in the quest for career glory not the totiest of details would I leave unattended. My attitude would be fitting. My brain would be up to the task. And I mean each and every portion of my brain, all sides and bits in between, including the big middle bit that tries to go to sleep every time a social difficulty arises let alone the need for direct political action. Nor would I seek to place one single solitary awkward question in front of my immediate superiors and bosses. They werenay gauny fling me on the plane hame man I was keeping the nose clean. That was my strategy for the Security job. Yes sir and I would plow that probationary furrow with full flying colours. Simultaneously and thereon the domestic Defense industry would provide a fund of memorable incidents for my writing career, the which thought came from a deeper stratum of my brain, one used to decision-making at the executive level. Is stratum even a word?

Where was my fucking beer? I aint got no fucking beer.

This was a relaxing kind of bar and Sally had her ways but when it came to customer satisfaction I was absent from the frame, I was an also-ran. Sally may have been great but she wasnay perfect, naybody was. Me and the ex had fights about various things. In her opinion I buttit into her business. Some might have thought her business was my business, and vice versa, is that no what marriage-style relationships are about? Especially if ye see yer partner getting screwed by a fucking no-good fucking bastard man and that was what he was, her manager, so-called manager, a ratbag scabby fucking prick, that was what he was. Then he got her this gig in Cincinnati. The way he telt her, how it came to me, it was the break she should be dreaming about. I was wanting to go with her but he was taking her. What musicians are gaun with ye? I says.

Nayn, she says.

Nayn? They were picking them up at the gig. Aw aye, I says, how come ye're no flying or something, gaun by train? I says. She just looked at me then she goes: Jerry, I'll be home tomorrow, dont make things hard.

I'm no making things hard, I just think if life can be easy how come we dont go for it and just make it easy.

But the point is anyway I couldnay have got the time off the job. The manager of the bar was tough as auld boots, a whip-cracking bastard. That Cincinnati gig would have meant one and a half nights off the job. And besides that I couldnay offer Yasmin a drive. My vehicle was an absurd load of junk. I looked at it and sneered. A new yin was in the list of priorities. All I could offer was a shared train or bus; she wouldnay fly.

Part of the attraction of gaun to an away gig like that was the entire business of being away with her, just being away with her, in a whole new environment as well. We still couldnay get living the gether, and the job situation didnay help matters. But if she had agreed to me gaun I wouldnay have went with her and her manager, no in the same car. I wouldnay have survived, it would have been impossible; all it needit was him to look at me the wrang way and I would have got done for murder.

So off she went and done the damn gig.

Nayn of these bodies were keen on my presence. I exclude her faimly in that. I mean her manager and the musicians, even the roadies wantit to lay down the word. Yasmin was to perform how they all thought, sing what they thought she should sing. She just listened but I didnay I got fucking annoyed, I shouldnay have let them bother me but I did, and that was what annoyed her. It wasnay them that annoyed her it was me. Looking back on it now I know better man, what I think it was: they were there before I arrived and they were there eftir my departure. And that was what she knew.

Christ but I was very tempted to fly into that Cincinnati gig unannounced, very very tempted. Just walk into the venue: Aw hullo there Yasmin, just passing.

Just passing!

Bastards.

I went as far as checking the flights. It was straightforward. I hadnay much cash to spare but the "persian bet" story was in its infancy so there were still plenty of deals to be had. I didnay gie a fuck about the state of the airline and insurance industries. I hadnay been on a plane for years but the survive or perish issue wasnay a worry. I was one of these macho cunts. Fuck the fates. If yer plane comes down it comes down. Okay, so I was having to knit my ayn parachute. So what?

When Haydar visited me he managed to stuff it into his hand luggage.

Only kidding.

I heard the same airplane scare stories as everybody else; mair, because I worked in the booze trade. The auld salty dawgs that prop up the bar were aye telling ye stupit survival jokes. On the west coast especially I heard them. Ye had to draw laugh lines on yer cheeks with a marker pen before gaun to work. It was the same in the pool halls and the betting parlours. The jokes there hinged mair on probability. The east coast gets the reputation for the wisecrakks but that west-coast patter was sharper and fucking cooler. But that is an opinion.

A common theme had to do with the insurance problem and how ye would get a better deal if ye accessed a bookie offering odds on yer plane's survival. There were all sorts of variations. The feller that kick-startit the "persian bet" affair either was a gambler himself or else hung about the scene. I read about him and he had quite an interesting life. As a boy he was in advertising then got an entry into scriptwriting, including work on a few hollywood movies but one thing led to another and he was like one of these Pat Hobby characters and wound up he made a last-ditch return to the copywriting game before becoming a complete wreck. I think a Blonde Bombshell with a Heart of Gold had something to do with it.

The feller's early television advertisements were said to be classics but the stuff he was doing second time around was nondescript until finally one he did for an airline company hit the jackpot. This company's safety record was so fucking pitiable millionaires couldnay find an insurer. The advert was done in cartoon form and had a storyline spread ower two wee films. The first yin ends with a lil ol pink lady entering an illegal betting parlour in somewhere like Norfolk, Virginia. This is prior to her making an air trip to Portland to meet a host of golden-haired grandweans. Recent furnir disturbances have unsettled so-called "securities" and on one singularly difficult day the feisty ol lady's life savings are gobbled up. The very next day things return to normal and the big boys get their money back with interest. But due to the vagaries of fate the small-time players are left high and dry as usual. The lil ol feisty lady's dough is blown! Her entire life savings just upped and disappeared into thin air! How can she take care of her grandweans!

On her way hame from her Church next Sunday morning she bumps into a neighbor, a kindly big ol black guy – retired gangster or judge, we arenay quite sure – who is returning hame from his Church. He doffs his hat to her and they chat a moment. He has always admired her feistiness. Now he points her to the nearest betting parlor. It lies in a very rough neighborhood. We hear the sound of rattling wheels. A patrol car. She hides in the doorway of a barber shop clutching her cookie-jar coin-bank. The patrol car trundles past. Into the illegal betting parlour she skips but doesnay study the racing form. She just empties the dough onto the counter. The wisecrakking ceegar-chawing bookie counts it out and the auld yin returns hame with a spring in her step.

Now we see an electric storm and a toty wee airplane with a brave smile fighting to survive; flying this way and that dodging through a series of angry towering mountains. Next we see a host of golden-haired grandweans outside the airport terminal. The plate glass doors open to reveal the elderly heroine on crutches and covered with bandages. But behind her come porters pushing grocery carts full of boxes and boxes of treasure. The lil ol lady raises her crutch and points to a stretch automobile where the uniformed chauffeur gies her a salute. The host of golden-haired grandweans cheer and applaud their grannie. She turns and winks to the camera and out her mouth comes a bubble with the line, "I didn't perish, why should you!"

People spoke about the advert and had a laugh at it but irony is aye fucking dangerous to power structures and the authorities deemed the campaign "sick". The airline who had employed the marketing company was lambasted privately and publicly by indignant political and religious organizers, also media commentators and other spokespersons for the corporate finance industry who thought it reflected badly on ethical capitalism.

Another airline rapidly introduced national advertising based on the same model although it dumped the lil ol lady and introduced a young pink surfer couple whose life-long dream is to hit the highest waves round some beach in Hawaii. They are just hardworking but honest students who cannay afford to get there. But then all of a sudden they meet a bookie and then catch a plane or some fucking thing, I cannay remember the punchline, except they win money and make the trip of a lifetime. Now it was described as "the survive or perish" variation. Then folk called it "the perishing bet" and from there "the persian bet".

The bookies were yer insurers. Neat. But listen, hey, there had been a slight increase in flight figures for the last three-month period. This humorous take on public fears was proving a selling point for a market that had long been in the doldrums. Unfortunately for the guy that wrote the original cartoon his immediate superiors lost their nerve, they fucking sacked him and he vanished from the scene. Fuck knows what happened to him. In true hollywood fashion the joke rumbled on and memory of that lil ol lady lingered in the national consciousness.

Graveyard humour is cool in the underground scene and for a while it had been staple fodder on the alternative comedy circuit. Why not bet on survival? Place your bets ladies and gentlemen: survival in one piece, in two pieces; would travelers emerge with all limbs, one limb or no limb or would they enter a vegetative state, be paralysed from the neck down. A bit later less objectionable variations came from the anti-establishment and subversive talk-show hosts and comedians employed by the major television networks. The joke had just about run its course when came a surreal twist. Rumours circulated the gambling fraternity that if intending passengers did want to wager on the survival *v.* perish question there were bodies willing to take their money. Yeh, you name it we'll lay it. Where air travel was concerned there were bodies in the deeper bookmaking recesses willing to lay odds on any damn thing ye liked.

A majority of males had regarded plane-crash probability as a gender test anyway and there was aye a macho quality to certain cheap flight options. These were courageous fellers who werenay gauny kowtow to the fates under any circumstances. Who did these fucking fates think they were? They werenay even Uhmerkin, they were fucking non-national furnirs, unassimilatit non-christians! Let them do their worst or get the hell hame to goddam ancient Greece or whatever pagan hell it was they came from. If they wantit to put their hex on the Uhmerkin people then Uhmerkin males werenay gauny step aside. Come hell or high water red-blooded males were boarding that dang plane, every last one of them, yes sir, and they were gauny sit on that dang seat, even a window seat, yes sir. And if they perished then so be it, so fucking be it, so fucking

Yes sir.

So now their nearest and dearest would earn out the deal. Flight became a moral and social obligation for down-the-line male fellers. For traveling gamblers it was a dream come true. Either way ye were a winner. If ye survived ye lost the bet but if ye perished yer faimly collected the cash. Now the more formidable apparatuses were cranked up and set rolling. The money men instructed the hollywood studios to instruct their writers and directors to deliver positive images on behalf of the airline and gambling industries. Several television dramas and two major movies were quickly produced wherein cool WASP male dudes and their staunchly patriotic lieutenants battled the fates in the continuing war against evil. These staunchly patriotic lieutenants – e.g. humorous black dudes, loveable senior citizens, feisty females, eccentric upper-class English males – came to an unfortunate but inevitable end while saving the lives of the cool WASP male dudes for the benefit of humankind as a whole. If perishing aboard a plane the staunchly patriotic lieutenants bequeathed a clutch of valid betting receipts, the proceeds of which allowed their weans to purchase a high-up groove on the educational pyramid. Boys and girls the wide world o'er now pondered whether one of those fine days, all things being equal, and race, religion, gender, class or ethnicity notwithstanding, if they too might become cool WASP male dudes when they grew up.

It took a wee while for the stunt to catch on where it mattered, the purses of Middle Uhmerka. The workings of the gambling and bookmaking fraternity lie beyond the ken of many travelers and their relatives, some of whom required to ask the more basic questions: Mom, what is odds? Hey pop how do I make a bet? Is there a bookie on any auld street corner? How many combinations can a guy have? Hey mom when does pop's flight lift off? Why aint ya flying this month ya cowardly auld fuck? Is it a prop or a jet? How many engines? How auld are the nuts and bolts? Hey granddad, what is a spread bet?

Eftir me and Yasmin hooked up it was discovered I knew a bit about the business and my stock rose within her faimly. For a while she had taken me with her to these events ye get in domestic circles; births, deaths and marriages. In many there was a gender divide and ye would find all the men in one room and the women in another. Gradually her uncles and cousins realized I had a grasp of the parlance and could expand on a couple of finer points. Sometimes it became a story if I used characters to illustrate a bet or brought in past gambling experiences. On baseball and basketball I was fukt. But I knew a wee bit about football and something about sakyr. But once the conversation moved to cards, horses, greyhounds and "persian bet" variables then hey ho Jeremiah was the man.

It was nice being deferred to, almost like I was a member of the wider faimly. Ye notice how bodies have their functions in such settings. I wasnay a husband, uncle, cousin or brother and naybody ever called me Yasmin's boyfriend or Yasmin's man. So this gied me a place. By the time the wean was born I was Yasmin's baby's daddy. I was persona grata man I was winning my spurs.

They were too big for my boots but and soon fell aff during the christening controversy. Yasmin had agreed to this ceremony by default. Fine. But I didnay see why I couldnay hold some kind of atheist alternative. I was tolerating them and their fucking beliefs why could they no tolerate mine? Yasmin's baby's alien Red-Carded daddy. I remember one row that broke out. It was a horror and involved aged aunties and irate moostachayoed uncles. I thought I was gauny get fucking lynched. All to do with religion as well! Unbelievable shite. Yasmin's cousin saved me. They had problems with me. I had problems with them.

But no with her, not at all.

But this is why I was needing to clear my heid properly. This is why I was gaun fucking hame. Too long I had spent dwelling on the issue and the problem and the fucking whatever the fuck and about messing my life up completely let alone the wee yin's life. Yeh, she had a life as well and I wasnay allowing her to get on with it. Cause of this crap: me, me me me. So the wean suffers.

That bar I worked in, sometimes it was so fucking boring, but it didnay work in favour of the writing. I didnay rush hame to my room and switch on the laptop. It was like an intellectual numbness had set in. My brains were like fucking minced beef. My body wasnay but my body was great. No great, the fucking usual. When she was around man I just had to breathe the same air, it was wherever whenever. We were having sex all the time. Nay wonder I laughed a lot. Ach but so did she, we were fine. Sometimes halfway through the shift I would make the decision to go to her place. As soon as I made the decision it produced a physical reaction and it was like I had the shakes man I was all shudders and fucking twitches and if I was having to do some daft pair of cocktails for a couple of lost tourists it was a surprise if they escaped without getting hit in the eye by a flying object, a lump of ice or whatever. It was an amazing thing. Ye have that auld saying "I couldnay get there quick enough". That was how it was for me. As soon as I locked the doors and bolted the shutters my legs seemed to hurl me towards the subway but I would never make it man cause there goes a cab and I am out there flagging it down and in there on the seat and my chest is heaving though I havenay even been running, fucking hell.

And bang goes another few dollars.

Having these two places, hers and mine, it was a waste of money and a waste of time. I would have moved into hers in a minute but her cousin was there and didnay have another place. But I knew she was looking. Especially eftir Yasmin got pregnant. But the money the money the money man I was fukt christ almighty.

Really, I just needit some dough, that was all. Some nights

tips were good but maist nights they werenay. Maist nights were just dreich elongated affairs. It would have helped greatly if I could have brought in my ayn music but there was a set list I had to play in keeping with the theme of the pub which was just too shameful to mention. I was a fucking zombie at the end of these shifts, I didnay have two thoughts to run the gether, exhausted, incapable of gaun to my ayn place, locking up the doors, the bolts, trying to yawn to stay awake, forgetting to watch for gangster cunts. The thought of journeying ower to my place, that horrible wee room man if I had had the energy to commit suicide . . . It was just so tempting to head north, collapse into a cab. Three in the morning. Her staggering to the door in her nightdress, staggering back to bed eftir gieing me a cuddle. I would sit there listening to music, the volume turned low; there were fire-escape steps outside and when the weather was nice I moved out onto there and sometimes she sat with me for an hour – longer; faire taire monsieur, silenso, recuperato, the muscles, the sinew, the gristle, the varicose fucking veins, all of the body and all its entire functioning, just recovering, sipping coffee or for special treats there could be some rum or who knows, a drop of beer; even just a coffee, a smoke on the side – dont tell me life is a drag, life is just a beautiful thing.

Before she went to her part-time job we would go for a slap-up breakfast at a diner no too far away. Her cousin still poked fun at my material possessions. Yasmin just smiled. However, I decided to replenish the wardrobe.

This was the third time me and her set off in pursuit of the most sophisticated pre-owned menswear store on the entire eastern seaboard, that legendary byword in sartorial splendour, the joint that dealt in job lots of not-so-knackered exquisite garments; interesting sexy velveteen and all sorts of suedes and sexy leathers and

excuse me while I learn to tango. The best I knew was

a variation on the Texas two-step developed someplace in southeast Oklahoma apparently, a kind of fast waltz where ye skip a beat and the male gets pushed by the female. She birls you about! I learned it at a club in LA that had instructor-led dancing nights every Tuesday. It was full of salsy southern gals, gents in tayyin-gallon hats who had accountancy jobs during the day, and a few of us alienigenae doing wur best to meet an ordinary woman.

I enjoyed it but. It was relaxed, naybody had too much to drink. Yeh, real good natured! And ye learned something. How to coordinate yer feet, how to place one in front of the other deftly and with style boy style, nay malice aforethought. It was kind of fucking cool to be honest. The woman that led the sessions was an ex ballet dancer and she had that way of standing, the splay-fittit thing, toes to the east toes to the west, and ye felt like hoisting her right up off the floor, holding her up by the waist with her feet fluttering, stretching with her in that arced movement, pushing up from the ankles, to the very end of yer fucking finger tips.

Maist women seemed to appreciate the singular activity I liked to think of as "my dance", all but an influential handful of whom the ex was one. She was on her ayn anyway, even when she danced with other women; highly individualistic is an appropriate phrase. But anything that smacked of southern shite was out the question for her. I thought it had to do with slavery and the Civil War but she said no, it had nothing to do with the Civil War, it was politics. I thought the Civil War was politics but apparently no.

So what politics my love?

The kind of politics she wouldnay discuss with me is what politics. There were taboo subjects of discussion and politics was up at the top of the list. But fair enough and I didnay want to be presumptuous.

The not-so-knackered pre-owned menswear store was a distance from her neighborhood and would take us a week to get there unless a miracle happened. The journey needit a bus and a subway and a long walk. Yasmin thought it would have closed down, they would have demolished the building, turned it into an apartment block; they would have shot the auld granddaddy and buried his fucking pipe on yon bonné banks of Boot hill. If it wasnay that then it would be something else.

Off we went arm in arm, shaking wur way sou-by-sou-east on a ramshackle subway which had standing room only. Next to us was this skinny body with a block of wood for a heid, reading a Spanish-language newspaper. It wasnay just Spanish-language it was Spanish, a Spanish newspaper. I had my arm round Yasmin, no especially trying to see ower the guy's shoodir but it was a large advertisement – Visit Historic Spain!

Fucking hell! My heart jumped. I hadnay seen my faimly for years and here I was with my new-found love, my one true love, soon-to-be-mother of my child – she was three or four months pregnant at the time. It was these feelings mixed in. I was gauny be with her all my life, I was gauny set up hame with her, no matter what, and nay cunt was gauny steal her away. Although nay doubt they would try it, these bastards, somebody would, somebody would try it because what I realize now was that I had some other thing in my heid like maybe a presentiment, I dont know what it was but I just had a feeling, and my reflex action was to hold her more tightly. Yasmin just smiled and I smiled also but seeing that newspaper advert made me think of hame and life and faimly. Spain wasnay that far from Skallin and a common destination for Skarrisch folk.

I noticed the guy reading the newspaper, he looked like Franco's politics would have been okay by him. A right creepy-looking cunt, these horror right-wing fascist fuckers ye some-times see creeping out from behind middens. He had the type of face ye wantit to christ I dont know, I wouldnay have trusted him as far as I could throw him, ye just imagined things about him, secret police, anti-freedom squads, dangerous bastards, evil, on a lucrative retainer by the pentagon greysuits. They get by on fear; vicious, malicious, ruthless fucking terrors, torturers man the lowest of the low, and their fucking arrogance! Incredible! They think they can just go anywhere do anything and nay cunt will fight back, as if we are all too scared man too scared of these bastards, evil bastards, bullying thugs, paid torturers, the scum of the earth, all on their ayn wee career structure. And it is me they want to deport! Nay wonder ye get angry. I did get angry, angry a lot man these cunts getting paid from state agencies, it is just fucking appalling.

Yasmin was gripping my arm. I was close to the guy's shoodir. He was aware of me and getting edgy, maybe wondering if I was making a fool of him. Unless he was just annoyed I was reading his newspaper. I wasnay even reading the fucking thing but so what if I had been? It was in Spanish and I didnay read Spanish except for words here and there. But if I did read Spanish then sure I would have been reading his newspaper of course I would have been reading his newspaper. But I didnay read the language. No yet anyway although I positively wantit to. Spanish was one of the languages I often tried to learn, like Gaelic – if only because every time I had the bad luck to find myself in a stage-oirisch bar I bumped into these stage-oirisch pricks who got very blood and soil and linguistically pure and I wantit to confound them to the very marrow of their traditionalist beings. St Patrick was a fucking Skatchman anywey from the town of Dumbarton. Of course us Browns originated from oillin, the MacDiumhns, and we had wur ayn business with St Patrick, no to mention the auld Fenians and yer man Connal Gulban. That is the trouble with heritage, ye can do anything ye like with it; one late offspring of the

MacDiumhns was the Dirmaid, Dhairmaid or Dhairmid, which makes us Browns responsible for the Campbells never mind William the Conqueror, the Siol Dirmaid, lord save us all. Imagine being responsible for the Campbells! A wee sip of the Campbell blood is within me, probably in ma ragged toenails, all the better for ripping a heid aff. Self-defence is no offence, like the army generals and pentagon fuckers tell us. All that blood and soil stuff is a joke, it is a fucking joke.

The guy with the newspaper was reading away, holding the thing very tightly like he was feart I would grab it off him. His wrists were just about trembling with the pressure he was applying. How come he was so goddam edgy? Because I was reading his paper ower his shoodir. How lacking in generosity some people are, getting all excited by something so petty and so minor. What did he want me to pay him a percentage of the price? I felt like asking him, fucking tapping him on the shoodir: Excuse me ya fucking halfwit bastard.

But why bother. Except that they annoy ye, the way they act like one is a fucking cretin man it is a crack on the skull they require, fascist or no fucking fascist. Yasmin was looking at me. I smiled. I put my arm round her waist, but a certain flinching occurred such that I disengaged immediately. Her sigh of relief might have been heard on the platform of the next subway station. I definitely had done something. Maybe I stared at the guy with ill-concealed hatred! Unless she just didnay want me touching her in public. Funny how women resist physical contact in social settings. Men are show-off bastards and displays of affection in public do not worry them one ifuckingota, me included. But there were elements of my character that could irritate the ex. She admitted it.

Never mind.

All this because of viva la république, Visit Historic Spain!!

Strange how these little incidents throw us back on wurselves, into wur ayn heids, the last place we want to be and then on the subway aisle across from us was the usual plainclothes guy staring straight at me. Maybe he wasnay. But maybe he was. Nothing surprises me. One just cannot get fucking walking. It was beginning to do my nut. The lovat gaberdine overcoat and the dark greysuit, the guy was masonic government. He must have heard me speak to Yasmin and picked up on the accent, then his wee check on the mobile technology. Yeh, a non-assimilatit alien, Jeremiah Brown, nothing to worry about, Class III Redneck Card carrier, aryan caucasian atheist, born loser, keeps nose clean, big debts, nay brains, big heid.

The blue-bordered ID notice was on either wall of the subway. He could have exercised occupational rights and asked me to produce the documentation. I avoided gieing him the finger. Ye could see also how he gazed at Yasmin. Yeh man it is me walking with her, no fucking you. A guy about six three tall, looked like he had a good build and nay doubt could fight like fuck. It was a relief when we arrived at wur stop. We walked up the stairs in silence, and right to the exit. Outside the station we crossed the street and here she applied pressure to my haun and I realized I must have taken hers in an absent-minded way and squeezed it quite hard. Hey, she said.

What?

Dont worry.

I sighed and put my arms round her.

Come on, we'll go for a coffee.

Yeh.

Oh but the clothes, what about the clothes?

Fuck the clothes.

Jerry.

Later.

You got to get some clothes.

Yeh but Yazzie see the now, a coffee is paramount, it is what I need, right at this point in existence, the fates have decreed: let there be coffee . . . And I sank onto my knees right there on the goddam pavement so help me gahd I spread open my arms and opened out my lungs and I praised the very concrete she trod o'er, yes sir I sang, I sang: Long and slender, a real big spender, the girl from Ipanema goes walking, baby, lead me on. She laughed, tightening her grip on my hand. I made her laugh, that kind of daft patter.

Although also, sure, it grated on her. Eventually I grated on her. My very presence. Nay doubt she boked when she looked at the photograph album. Or else she had cut me out the photographs. My sister used to do that, she chopped up the faimly photograph albums, excising bodies here and there. I could imagine the ex with the pair of scissors, cut-throat blades, snip snip snip, there goes his heid, snip snip, snip, his dick, snip snip, there go the bollocks, snip snip, the smelly feet, snip snip.

So how do ye get to here from there? from where us two were. Irreconcilable differences, the proximity of hate to love, from love into hate. If she ever did love me anyway man what the fuck does "love" mean, what does it mean?

Forget it.

Also the wean. That wasnay fair. It just wasnay justice. Yer baby is yer baby.

We can all sing the blues

or smoke like fuck. In five minutes time, now aint that a man, I was gauny buy me a pack of cigarettes.

It was the perfume, what a perfume! Sally, she was at the next table!

The auld nose had been twitching. I was gauny wind up with a hooter like W. C. Fields. I blame perfume and smelly feet. Smelly feet is one of the drawbacks to tending bar. Dont tell me ye have clean feet if ye work in a bar, I dont fucking believe ye. The best guys I ever worked for were the same guys that robbed me out my wages week in week out on their bastarn fucking pool table that they installed merely to conduct highway robbery upon their employees. Jereee, buddeee, here is your cue, here is a beer, relax man, shift is over, here is good music, here is big money, you want to bet on this game, you want to bet money with us Jereee, buddeee. The sharks from Sacramento. But what they did install was a foot-jacuzzi and it was great. Ye could gie the feet a soak during the shift. All us bartenders, we sprang about with a spring in wur step, jolly as fuck.

Whereas Sally swirled, Sally swoooossshhed oh man. There definitely was something beautiful about her, and especially her long skirt. It wasnay just me and my bias, this was a verifiable thing. Ye could see she was appreciated by the bodies at the bar, even that cheapskate thieving manager bastard.

Why is it we see that wee bit of midriff? Aint it a wondrous thing, aint it just a wondrous thing. All you preacher men now come on out of these yere shadows, that aint no place to be a-lurrrking for god-fearing honest young fellers. Here is this woman and she is like out there, she is out there.

Christ she wasnay coming to me!

I thought I had asked her for a beer ages ago. Maybe I was dreaming. If I didnay get something to drink in 90 seconds I was buying a pack of smokes and that was that. 90 and counting.

She was back behind the bar. But now looking anywhere except in my direction. So what did that mean it meant she was coming.

Yippee!

One bottle on the tray. Mine, all mine! I smiled. She also smiled. Hey can I run a tab? I said.

I thought you were, she said.

Aw am I?

Yeh.

Sorry.

Alright, she smiled, lifting the two empties from my table. Bravo! Bravo! I exclaimed, applauding profusely. Aint this lady a wonder to behold! What time does the music start? I said.

In a little while. She checked her watch and shrugged.

Heh you got cigarettes here?

She gestured behind with a slow movement of her shoodir. A machine back there, she said.

Okay.

She turned to leave.

Hey what kind of music is it they play, the band?

Depends who turns up.

Okay, yeh. Well, if it's the usual, what if it's the usual?

That'll be kind of swing, jazzy . . . Bluesy.

Sounds good.

She hesitated. I smiled again. But that was that. It is a cliché to say "pert nipples". What does "pert" mean? Pert; fucking stupit word. Now she was leaving. Nay wonder. She was tired. She had smiled again, but only politely. It isnay that nice to discuss somebody's bodily parts but what else can we do. I was attracted to nipples. There were clothes women wore seemed to enhance their presence. Of course they didnay wear them on purpose. Maybe some did. No Sally but she wasnay that kind of dame. What kind of dame?

Fuck knows.

A woman once telt me she couldnay stop looking at men's crotches. What a flummoxer. Even walking along the street, she says, if you were coming towards me, she says. What, I says, what? Then she startit laughing. Only kidding. I didnay know whether to be happy or sad. Or what else to think. Could she have been telling the truth? What a thought! Some women are amazing.

She wasnay a bad-looking lassie, no bad figure, quite good style. She had a loud laugh and talked nineteen to the dozen. But we got on okay. I drove a van and she worked in the dispatch office.

I could never explain myself about women, I knew nothing about them and never would. And them that worked in bars man they were a total mystery, and I am talking as customer and colleague. The ones in managerial positions were aye the worst. But males in managerial positions were every bit as bad so what does that prove? The only decent thing about the booze trade is

what?

Ye make a few tips. Ye go in skint to yer work but at the end of a shift ye have a few dollars in yer pocket. That didnay happen in the Security industry. If there was any graft, bribery and corruption available I never found it. No sir, nay matter how quiet a bar was ye aye made a few cents.

It all helped. The actual wage I earned went straight into my state-savings account. The only money account I could hold was under the state-savings plan and of course as an alien I wasnay allowed a credit card. From that account maist of my savings exited into the personal accounts of sundry others. Yes sir. I wasnay a feller that skipped out on a loan, he said bravely. No unless I was desperate, no unless I was willing to risk getting stretched out on a slab. Desperation meant flight. I knew about loans and flight and desperation. And the time I am talking about wasnay a time of desperation.

Or was it?

I lifted the bottle. I would have preferred a glass. Bottles got dirty. Mice had a crap in bottles. But this here was an escape, me gaun hame to Skallin, and it is from desperation escape derives.

I needit a cigarette. But I wasnay gauny have one. Nay point being a failure all my life. The past years had not been good. By nay stretch of the imagination had they been good. But the last couple of months had improved, even just slightly, I felt mair positive. Otherwise I would never have booked the flight hame. Never.

Fucking hell, I mind seeing this mental auld Disney cartoon where one of the characters is trying to chuck the smoking, goes to hell and back and then at the end he caves in and starts puffing, and ye see the poor cunt, he is sitting there, at least four cigarettes in each haun, all burning.

And did the cartoon end in a puff of smoke? or am I just inventing that bit. Ye wonder who wrote the script. Because there has to be a script. Even a cartoon gets a writer. I could have written some good scripts. Adult cartoons. Ye see these ones from eastern Europe late at night, cannay make fucking head nor tail of them but they haud the interest. Concept cartoons. Musical soundtracks. Even the fucking adverts, they need writers too; somebody has to do the words, the copywriting. I was never a proud cunt, anything would do me, just to get away from the fucking service industry, to where I could make use of my strengths.

That was what I fucking hated, there was never a job I done that took up everything, my strengths is what I am talking about. Gambling punditry, that would have suited me to a tee.

Nevertheless, and apropos of fuck all, it is my opinion there is nay such thing as a ludicrous bet. But ludicrous odds? Yeh. If ye are gauny bet on something that is pure mental fucking crazy then at least make sure the odds are appropriate. Whereas ye might stake dough on whether it will rain between 6 p.m. and midnight ye would never bet real money on a star falling out the sky. Or would ye? I am no saying dont make such a bet but at least get the correct fucking odds – e.g. a dime to a Boeing 737.

A dime to a Boeing 737 says a star is gauny fall out the sky.

If a million bodies make the bet then you the bookmaker have earned $100,000. If a star falls out the sky and does so in such a way that complies with the pages and pages of rules and regulations that yer legal team has drawn up pertaining to said wager then ye owe the million punters a million Boeing 737 airplanes. So what do ye do? Easy! Ye keep the money and tell them to fuck off.

Because it is a goddam conspiracy against bookmakers!

Somebody has had a hotline to a high and mighty being and heard and spread the word re forthcoming miracles. Dont ye know there are laws against that? If not we shall frame the fuckers forthwith! But if all else fails ye just enter liquidation, sequestration, all that stuff, sign yerself bankrupt. That is what these business financiers do and small-time bookies also know the ropes. If the very very worst comes to the very very very worst then ye kiss yer wife and weans goodbye, make a fistful of "persian bets", book a few flights and pray for a faulty engine.

I would have taken the dime to a Boeing 737 wager myself and enjoyed a year's worth of glorious imaginings, being at the helm of a great jet plane and flying above the clouds in that expanse of blue, espying a sister plane a couple of miles away, sending yer wee radio signals, hullo there pal, how is it going?

Even attendant worries about refueling and shite: it is all well and good winning a Boeing 737 but what about the fuel, is the fuel part of the prize? Or have ye got to buy yer ayn? How could ye afford to buy enough barrels to fly the fucker?

But I would have luxuriated in such worries. And all for a dime! What a deal. I had a host of related fantasies. I lay in my en suite cupboard and dreamt about hijacking a wee propeller plane from the outskirts of the airport terminal where I worked, flying to a remote desert island; a tropical paradise, beautiful girls with garlands of flowers greeting me with trays of spicy burritos, cauliflower pakora and coconut shells filled with single malt uisghé. And some of these single malt uisghés do have that tang of coconut. Of course I would want a smoke. But abracadabra and lo and behold, says a lassie with a lingering smile and nay claes; on this here desert island cures for tobacco-related cancers are in abundance and I just happen to have a pack of Luckies concealed about my person.

Aw darling, darling.

Yeh.

Except if I was the bookie the punters would get a fucking miracle, and I would go skint as usual. I was a hopeless gambler and I dont mean by that compulsive I just mean somebody whose bets were goddam useless.

There is a passivity about gambling. Then ye have to act. But ye cannay force the issue too often. Them that force the issue too often man, their arms will get tired reaching for their wallet. At the same time but if ye are too passive, that can be a worse crime. Ye cannay aye wait, hoping the "cards will fall". Ye see players like that, especially auld yins who have borne too many failures, witnessed too many so-called "bolts from the blue". It inclines them toward letting their opponents call the shots, they go along with whatever, ye rarely see them on a re-raise, even with an ace king suited. Mind you there was one memorable occasion in a game ower in Reno, and poor auld Haydar got guttit with an ace king suited and the fates landing him two kings on the flop. It turned out he was in against a cunt with two aces in the hole and the river tossed him a third. Now that is like a major fucking I dont know man ye would need one of these ancient Greek dramatist fuckers to describe it. With that kind of haun auld Zeus is trying to tell ye something and you better listen man you better listen.

Sometimes I couldnay sleep for thinking about gambling and games of cards and extraordinary winning sequences of even-money bets, beginning from a straight dollar and pool also, unusual angles with enormous stakes and small crowds of spectators watching and wondering how the fuck I was gauny play the shot, what was I gauny do and just slap bang in ye go mister 9-ball, in ye go. And all the time what I needit to think about was the fucking private eye and what he was doing, what he was up to, instead of cards cards cards, all kinds of deals, stupit deals but good yins too; them where the cards fall for ye just right, ye just play it right, where ye are chip-leader in the final of a "no limit" tournament and one by one ye just push them off, pull them in and push them off, never mind Binions, fucking Jo Smith's would have done me, it wasnay the glory, or the cash, it was just the craïc.

Sentimental shite.

The best cards I ever saw were cards that fukt me. Ye can take pleasure in that. The fates consider ye so important they dream up these incredible hands just to gain their victories.

If I spent half as much time on my stories. I tried to think about it deliberately but my mind always wandered. Even like in ten seconds it wandered. I would force myself. It just didnay work. I needit that notebook, pen and paper. They say people's faces gie ye ideas as well and it made sense to me. Sometimes I couldnay help attaching stories to them. Ye saw some ugly fucker on the subway or train, maybe sitting staring at ye, some totally mad cunt; eyes wider open than the average, eyebrows raised that wee bit and his mouth wide open as well, his lower lip drooping – dribbling – and a kind of an aghast look, that is what he is gieing ye. I mean what the fuck is that about? Ye feel like calling a transport Security operative but nayn of them are ever about when ye need them and for christ sake man he is carrying a carving knife, and needless to say there are women and weans in the immediate vicinity, so just as well ye are carrying yer ayn wee concealed weapon, a fucking shillelagh baseball bat with a knuckle-duster handle. Go on ya prick! Ye can feel yerself quaking with excitement man suppressed smiles and shit all ready to set about the bastard if he so much as looks at ye the wrang way man fucking dribbling man he soon will be fucking dribbling.

Yeh.

The ex. She changed. Nay point talking about her.

On the absence of a notebook and poised pencil, she thought this indicated a lack of serious intent, as if I wasnay trying, as if I was being lazy. She just assumed it. It was so presumptuous. Funny how people have the nerve to think they fucking know ye inside out man that does my fucking heid in. She thought she knew me. She knew me fuck all man she didnay know me. She thought she did. She didnay.

Nay point talking. Later on I did, I talked. So did she.

Nah she didnay, that isnay true. She thought plenty but she didnay say it. That wasnay her style. It would have been better if she had said it.

But ye never know what ye want, no at the time. Then it is too late.

Even that isnay true. I knew what I wantit, I wantit her, and then she was pregnant, and I wantit her even mair, and the wean, and then she had the wean for christ sake it was beautiful.

So I did know what I wantit. I just messed it up. Quite straightforward, quite ordinary, quite fucking ordinary, when I was out with her, I would forget what I was doing, what I was thinking, and just be mentally lost just suddenly there in the heat of the moment and standing there or else walking and just like whatever, talking the gether – ye could have felt like kissing the pavement ye were so glad to be alive and just doing that, what ye were doing, going along the street having a conversation, it was amazing, and putting yer arm round her when she wasnay wearing a coat or a jacket or a jumper, just a blouse maybe, how ye feel a lassie's body that way it is just like yer arm is round her and sometimes ye know she isnay that strong or tough, no like yerself, and ye feel like ye could just sometimes ye have to be careful or else ye might no know yer ayn strength, and then too if she is pregnant.

The way she looked at me; I saw her watching me with this wee smile on her face. Other times I saw something else, and I couldnay reach it; she didnay let me.

We used to talk; anything and everything. Name a subject. We discussed it. All except politics, politics and related topics, these were taboo. I had theories or opinions on everything under the sun, in particular the domestic political set-up of this ma host country and I loved getting my teeth into such discussions. But she seldom allowed it, and found ways of finishing the subject if I was doing it in other company, especially with the musicians, following on from a gig. I telt her I had to do it somewhere, if I did it in public they would fling me out the country. She just pinched my arm in answer, up by the upper muscle. And she had powerful fingers, carpenter's fingers; maybe because she played the guitar, they were like fucking steel clamps man. She didnay know her ayn strength. She chortled when I told her that. Aye, her laugh was a chortle. D'ye mind if I wax lyrical, I says, yer laugh is like a wee mountain burn flowing ower toty wee chucky stanes. D'ye know what chucky stanes are lassie?

Yeh, she says.

Ye do? I says

You told me already. She smiled and blew gently into my ear. I had been about to launch into a full explanation of the merits of an auld Skarrisch comic singer I heard once who spoke, sang and telt yarns, funny wee ditties whose titles I cannay remember. I first heard him courtesy of an elderly couple who had an astonishing collection of hard vinyl records, the ones ye pick up at yard sales, they crack and snap in two.

They had me in for a meal a couple of times, barbequed brockwurst and garlic sausage and the wildest chillies in lil ol mean ol, pickled habañeros, special delivery from some German town in the Texas hill country. They played all these records and had these good nights in the backyard. The Skarrisch comic singer took a bit of getting used to, just like the habañeros, but the best things aye take time.

Hans was one of these early football – I refer to sakyr – players based in California. He played with a German team way back years ago. At that time in the LA region there were eyetalian teams and mehican teams and joymin teams and skarrisch, inkliz, velch and oirisch teams. I asked him if it was an all-oirisch team but he didnay know what I was talking about.

He earned a part-time wage at football and drove buses on the side. One time he found a batch of these Skarrisch records on the rearmost seat. It was a mystery because at that time it was uncommon to see a pink face on the rearmost seat of an LA bus and he had assumed the Skarrisch owner of the records was a pink cunt which, on a balance of probability, was a stonewall racing certainty.

But I had an answer to the mystery: here we had a Skarrisch guy recently arrived in the country getting a bus hame with his pride and joy vintage record collection and no knowing nothing about colour-bars and racist stuff, especially if he had had a wee tipple or three afore boarding the bus, and being a smoker he was wanting a smoke, and so naturally he headed to the rear which is where all decent folks go back hame if they feel like a smoke. So then he dozed off, nice and relaxed, and then nearly missed his stop, raced down the aisle and jumped off the bus, and the next morning discovered he had lost the fucking pride and joy record collection.

Then it was a case of whereabouts unknown. He had nay recollection of leaving whatever pub he had last visited in whatever part of downtown LA he had been, maybe round-about the auld bus station. In which case he might even have purchased said records from a pawnshop. So it wasnay him that brought the records from Skallin in the first place! He had just been browsing the pawnshop and spotted them piled in a corner! It was some other poor cunt had brought them, down on his luck, and been forced to sell them, the usual fucking shite.

Cultural difference is interesting. One time I done a course in sociology at a community college. I enjoyed it apart from the cunt that took the class, he was an elitist prick. He came from ol Youropey and dressed like the fucking Whitehall diplomatic service, ye were expecting spats and a bowler hat. The bodies there were mainly from Central Uhmerka; El Salvador and places, Columbia, Nicaragua man escaping the US death squads and then they have to cope with this elitist shite, fucking make ye puke, ye wantit to get a grip of him. I thought of sending him an anonymous letter, just to explain it to him, maybe he had a short fucking memory, treating people like that man.

Ye breathe out ye breathe in.

In the auld days I didnay, I lit a smoke, ingested poisonous fumes and lived happily ever eftir.

We aye seem to be jumping about, us human beings. Never any fucking peace. If I had had peace me and her would still have been the gether. Now I was a visitor. And she wouldnay see me. Classic. I was talking to a guy about it, he was in the same boat. Sure, he says, and you got to put up with it, step out of line and you reap the consequences. The law dont favour the male, that is for certain.

The man from Jupiter. I swooshed in to see my daughter then swooshed back out. How many forms of alienation are there. Mair than there are exclusions?

I enjoyed being an alien. Fuck them. The invisible man. Fine. It would have been better no being pink, it would have suited me. I could have settled in this town, worked for the guy from Ghana, I would have done his nightshift. I would have

fuck all, bastards.

breathe, breathe,

People forget to breathe. Boxers dont. I did a wee bit of training in my teens and the auld coach spent his time teaching me to breathe. Forget the gloves, he says, ye're no putting on nay gloves.

I just want to hit people, I says.

Naw, he says, first ye have to learn to breathe.

And I didnay. I never did learn to breathe. Nay wonder people climb mountains. At the time I thought he was talking shite, similar to these auld-style football coaches who dont gie ye a ball, they tell ye to run for long distances and do a lot of skipping and exercising whereas all ye want is a ball at yer feet and to run like Maradona. Imagine if it was sex, there ye are dying for yer first shag and some stupit auld feller tells ye to go for a run round the block or else eat a bowl of broth. Or else writing, ye want to write a book, a novel, and some prick down the library says, Okay, first ye have to

what?

Nah, I was wrong and the auld boxing guy was right. Part of my problem as a human being was that I didnay know how to do it properly, how to be it properly, be a human being.

What the fuck do ye do? What are the appropriate actions? When is it wiser to say nothing, to do nothing; to let the world roll past ye, let it go, forget about everything, faimly and the rest of it.

Ye go days without thinking of people then suddenly they are in yer heid and ye cannay get them out. Ye get fucking sick of it.

I didnay even know how to smile! How to lift yer wean, and hold her, hoist her up onto yer shoodir, these things, ye forget how to do them man how do ye hold a wean.

With a song in my heart,
a lump of steel in my fist
if we're a-gauny part
I'm a-gauny get pissed

Where is my notebook, where is my notebook.

The mair ye live with somebody the mair ye discover about them. Even before she got pregnant the ex would lie in her kip listening to music and scribbling hieroglyphical notes to herself on sheets of lined paper. I thought she was writing new songs but she wasnay. She sat hunched ower in bed with the blankets drawn up and the music blasting, or else no blasting, no even turned on. With her knees up and her chin resting there I got this vision of her vagina because of the way her thighs were up from the bed and I thought christ that must be sair. She wore this scabby dressing gown with wee twiddly bits hanging off the collar. It had come down through the generations; a gift from an auld grannie whose death had occasioned prior to the advent of oneself.

I liked that comment. Maybe I could write it down, borrow a slip of paper from Sally

whose death had occasioned prior to the advent of oneself
Lines from an auld ska number were in my heid

the greatest thing is to know
what you dont know you dont know

I get these mood shifts, I am moody, overpowered by moodiness.

Sometimes listening to music it is the instrument I am hearing, no what is produced on it. If it is fiddle music then any style fiddle music is okay, from Cajun to Portree, from Brittany to Galway, Lerwick to Lafayette, Gallup to Albuquerque, the Ozarks to wherever, Tbilisi, if it is the fiddle then the fiddle; or maybe trombone, ska music or dixieland music, brass bands; maybe if accordion then conjunto music, zydeco music, Skarrisch highland dance music.

The ex sang in a bluesy style. She didnay deny that but wasnay appreciative of me saying it and didnay take it as a compliment.

Okay.

Whatever happened in Cincinnati, I dont know if anything happened. I just thought she went silent for longer periods. I watched her.

I regretted no jumping a plane. It would have been an embarrassment for her with me turning up unannounced but so what? Sometimes ye have to take the plunge.

Money hadnay been an issue. I would have paid it.

The days of the bargain-basement deals had gaun. That was because the bookies had moved in with their survive-or-perish options. Folk figured out the new-deal insurance betting thing and the airline industry had a further economic upsurge. The words "boom time" were being whispered.

I heard stories in the bar where I worked. People gossip and tell tales and generally pretend to have an ear to the higher workings. I just listened. Apparently The Mob had entered the proceedings. Oh The Mob! Oh dear, let's run for cover!

But that was what they were saying: enter The Mob where they hadnay already penetrated. So now corporate interests were irritated, in particular those with large holdings in the airline and insurance industries. Nay wonder. This was supposed to be their action and had been legally legitimized by order to the democratic powers for that very purpose. Why in hell were maist of these new profits passing them by? Questions were asked at the most senior levels. The money men swiftly instructed their legal teams to swiftly instruct the state and federal politicos to move swiftly; procedural rulings and all kinds of legislations were swiftly enacted to ensure the bulk of these profits were assigned to their righteous owners, swiftly and absolutely at once and fucking immediately.

So now The Mob were getting squeezed. Maybe they were entitled to grumble but those who fought to retain all profits as opposed to a vastly reduced percentage were dealt with summarily. Some tried a rearguard action using the old 14th amendment ploy but that was doomed to failure even before reaching the Supreme Court. It was the wee non-aligned bookie who wound up with the public's sympathy. How come the little guy aye gets it in the neck, that was what good Uhmerkins were wanting to know. To hell with the soul and the finer points of religiosity, these smaller fellers were just out to keep life and limb the gether; simultaneously they were providing a service.

Cunts discussed these topics constantly and if ye worked in a pub ye got sick of it. It was like baseball or jazz or darning socks or something, if ye arenay into it and folk keep yapping on about it. Ye could be playing a pool tournament and yer opponent would stop the game and ask ye what weather conditions have to be in place for the odds on "whole-body survival" being reduced by a quantifiable margin.

Even before I left the west coast, I remember me and Haydar

were ower in Reno and this body kept fucking blabbing on about "the last vest roll".

What the fuck is the "last vest roll"?

I thought it maybe had to do with craps. It didnay. Although atheists arenay nonexistent in the gambling community agnostics are rife and the "last vest roll" was a "persian bet" variation created especially for them. It had to do with the "last vestiges" of humanity and christian living, designed in a non-sectarian manner so that the countless sects could have a bet. Haydar was a muslim and said the subtleties were beyond him. Well I was never an agnostic so the subtleties were never anything but lost on me. But it appears to have been similar to "perishing" descending to "persian", "vestiges" got mixed up with the plural for "vest", a sleeveless item of clothing worn ower a plaid shirt. Cowpokes and pioneering settlers wear vests made of animal hide; they pin their US marshal badge onto 'em then go out and blast pesky indigenous varmints. In mair than one pub where I worked I was obliged to don said garment and a bow tie. It appealed to me. It reminded me of the auld-time snooker players. As a boy back in Skallin I liked playing that game. I used to assume it gied me an edge at 9-ball. How wrang can a body be.

Eventually people got fucking sick of all the talk about combinations and odds fractions and functional probability and arbitrary variables and oh man it was like being back in school on a hot summer day, the swimming pool is beckoning and there ye are stuck in the fucking classroom having to study these arithmetic exercises about Misters A, B and C and their movements to and fro the village well with empty buckets, full buckets and fucking holey fucking buckets. Gie us a break! shout the weans.

The fact is that any gambling system or lottery-style speculation is a novelty and boredom aye sets in. Uncle Joe public gets bored with hula hoops and these wee plastic shapes ye twist one way or another. The corporate bodies were well aware that the demise of "survive or perish" insurance betting was inevitable. Even a budding entrepreneurial genius knows no to hold novelty stock beyond a month. Eftir that ye send in the clowns, ye invest other people's savings; especially people who arenay feisty.

But it was already a class issue. Where money and existence are primary ye expect that anyway. And if class is the issue then the media and the establishment will want to drop it, get it out of the national consciousness. Stop all these stupit fucking hollywood movies about WASP heroes and their staunchly patriotic lieutenants in the war against evil. Audiences are wanting to know how come these WASP fuckers aye live happily ever eftir. Near where the ex lived I heard a couple of good debates around that issue, presided ower by a feller at a street-corner newsstand. These debates appear to spring out of naywhere until ye notice the guy selling the newspapers has a certain grin on his face.

But analysts employed by the airline marketing and public relations departments did notice a shift in the client base. A significant number of those flying on regular cheapo deals were individuals in straitened circumstances. It included bankrupts who saw the scheme as a virtuous end to the whole goddam mess, i.e. life. When word of this leaked out to the public their sympathy veered towards these bankrupts. They were seen as true patriots, bodies whose fiscal errors had caused friends and neighbor investors dear. Now here they were selecting the responsible way out while still exercising freedom of choice.

Other would-be suicides cottoned on to the deal. Soon the bookies, media commentators and society leaders strove to find a non-evaluative term or phrase to describe a suicide, e.g.

"a wannabe-dead", something that wasnay too positive but at the same time wouldnay alienate the air-traveling public.

I enjoyed all this discussion and controversy. It livened things up and gied humour to a lot of dull evenings. There is nay question it brought a solidarity. Ye saw strangers in bars and ten minutes later they were in company and enjoying a conversation. 24 hours a day on radio or television ye were guaranteed a talk-in on the arguments for and against "self-murder"; first principles of the inviolable freedom of the individual were invoked and revoked, differing constitutional points were put forth. And later, when I was a Security operative, I couldnay always sleep eftir working a nightshift so it was good tuning in to a debate. And obviously as an alien I breathed the usual sigh of relief whenever the political spotlight was focused elsewhere.

Yes sir. Was it a man's right to be dead? Could such a "right" be assumed by a god-fearing minority let alone a godless majority? No sir. A weighty question sir. What is the Lord's position sir? He it was set us down in this vale of tears to suffer for three score and ten. And no a day less ya pesky libertine varmints.

Was it a woman's right to be dead? No sir, no if she had weans to bring up. No if she had a man to look eftir. It was selfish behaviour and nay god-fearing christian would countenance such a thing, no from their womenfolk, no in this man's army.

Talkshows were full of baptists, methodists, presbyterians, coptics, quakers, roman catholics, muslims, buddhists, parsees, jews, sikhs, taoists, shintoists, hindus, wee frees, jehova's witnesses, mormons, episcopalians, zoroastrians, quakers and sorry if I have left any out; there are numerous religions and religious groups and bodies that I havenay heard of at all never mind forgotten about and each and every last one of them is a valid enterprise and a credit to its Maker so help me, so I pledge.

But it has to be said that by the time the credits rolled at the end of some of these daytime talkshows maist of the audience were pondering suicide themselves, including the fucking atheists who had escaped through the vetting that allows people into these debates. Everybody else was stoned or drunk.

There was a tricky finding courtesy of a PBS special. This showed a significant proportion of those who speculated on the "persian bet" were poverty-stricken bodies on an income so far below what official government experts reckoned it took to stay alive that the term "income" was dropped. These included young folks and asylum-seekers, immigrants, refugees; war vets, down-and-outs, alcoholics, addicts; unwantitorphans and homeless people; people with mental and psychological disorders; people with long histories of abuse, disabilities and deficiencies. It was like a majority of the population: the millions of daily would-be suicides, those who spend three-fifths of their waking hours dreaming of how to accomplish death in as unobtrusive, unselfish and unirresponsible a manner as possible.

The panel of specialists wantit to know, What do we mean by "stay alive"? What do poverty-stricken folks mean by "stay alive"? Do "we" have the right to assume that "the wish to stay alive" even exists let alone as a universal?

Of course contradictions abounded. Without contradictions was survival of the species possible? Is "alien" a valid inference from a concept such as "species"? What do we mean by "species"? Do poverty-stricken folks have such a concept? What is the nature of "have"? Can we ever "have" anything? What about poverty-stricken folks, can they ever "have" anything? And if it comes down to it, is the multibillionaire a "have", a "have-not" or is he a "have-in-trust"? And so on. There was a music bar Yasmin played and on occasion they had stand-up comedy shows. Me and her went along and they could reel off that stuff verbatim and get a laugh.

It was a fucking eye-opener man I enjoyed it.

Some of these poverty-stricken folks booking flights on these cheapo airlines appeared to have nay income and nay capital whatsoever. What a goddam cheek. How in tarnation were they enabled to go by air travel in the first dang place? Surely this was a welfare issue? If not why not?

Yet once the marketing hype had run its course it was plain for all to see that it was from the ranks of the desperate but righteous poor that the bulk of would-be travelers now appeared. When the airlines increased the fares these folks formed same-interest groups to buy up tickets then raffled them amongst themselves. It was great! Auld forms of combination were being rediscovered. At this rate the great Uhmerkin people were gauny create their ayn wee Enlightenment! But nay wonder diverse capital interests were irritated. They thought to have stymied all such communal practice by federal order, discriminate low-key policing and increased funding of the domestic Defense industry.

What is more these poverty-stricken folks were holding their pitiful air-ticket raffles in the carpark zones of the actual airports. Initially they did it in the fucking airport lobbies! Can ye believe it! How brazen can ye get! The airport terminals were hoaching with ragged persons bearing blankets or pushing grocery carts. Even so-called "safe" areas were clogged full of folk, including reverends and other fervent worthies hoping to nab these manifold souls of the wretched; also came vendors of religious icons and bric-a-brac, saintly knick-knacks, body bits, and garlic-coated good-luck charms.

And these good folks couldnay all be ejected or pushed out to the carpark zones, let alone the Patriot Holding Centers, no without good cause. These were fucking bona fide natural true-born Uhmerkins man these folks werenay fucking aliens, no sir, not at all.

For the hundreds of thousands of low-paid workers employed in the air-travel industry, it began as an enjoyable diversion from the daily grind. Ultimately it palled. For some it was a bad dream in unexpected ways; numbered among the crowds thronging the terminals were some friends and acquaintances. That was my ayn experience on three occasions; two guys I knew from the tables and the other was a woman who worked beside me the first time I landed in the States. It was an embarrassment for the two guys but it was the sort of licks a gambler gets used to and ye just have to take them; next time round it might be you for the money. That sort of embarrassing experience is a common occurrence in Nevada diners when the feller washing yer dirty plate is somebody ye last saw having a rush of blood in a hold 'em game, re-raising on a pair of sixes or some fucking thing.

For the cops and Security agencies linked to the airline industry it was exciting times ahead, and expansion was rapid. Airport employees were working all sorts of mad overtime and agencies were gieing starts to all sorts of mad bodies. I was one of them. And I confess most vigorously that it was through this that I hoped to obtain a Green Card.

Two factors gied me a chance: 1) this Security job, 2) being the daddy of an Uhmerkin-born wean. She was just about born when I landed the job.

Before any of that a Red Card wasnay the next best thing for the likes of myself, it was the only thing, one move up from a deportation order.

And who knows what lies in front of us? Working diligently as a Security operative ower a period of time I might turn into a right-wing fascist bastard. If so I could skip the Green Card and apply for a Blue Card. After that I was en route for fast-track naturalization.

Is this guy disillusioned or what!

Unless I kept failing on these slippery grammatical queries, e.g. what happens if and when a lassie lies with an alien male on the marital mattress? Is she engaging in, or with, an unUhmerkin activity? These and other irrationalities confound a feller. Calm down my boy.

But now I was the father of an Uhmerkin daughter surely they couldnay call me an alien furnir fucker? Can alien furnir fuckers father Uhmerkins?

And what about becoming the President? So okay, no having citizenship I cannay do it myself and neither can my daughter as a first-generation wean and nor yet her daughter as a second-generation wean and nor yet and so on but at what point could the nth-generation wee lassie become the President? Presidentess la bella, Señorita la Presidentia, whatever they call it.

I asked the ex about all this but she never took me on. Anything touching on politics done her heid in, so she said, but it was only if I was involved. I noticed that at these faimly domestic events. I would walk into a room and find the ex talking. With me there she shut up. Maybe it was a male/female thing and I shouldnay have taken it too personally.

In maist companies she tended to be quiet, she just sang, it brought a smile to yer face, ye just shut up and listened.

Every day of the week ye see women ye want who are out yer league. The ex had been out my league.

Just like the lassie in this music bar in the middle of nowhere man she too was out my league.

Agh.

Fortunately there was breath left in my body.

If somebody put a cigarette into my hand I would calm

down, a nice Isla malt, that I may be led e'en to an appreciation of existence.

All women were out my league. I didnay have a fucking league.

Sally was her name.

She wore her clothes well.

What a fucking weird thing to say.

What was noticeable about her – and patently obvious to all – was that she had that central element, that what else can ye call it except grace. Grace. Grace in a woman. Men do not have this quality. Graceful men do not have this grace it is strictly and elementally female. Graceful men who are transvestites do not have it. But is that true? And what about transsexuals? That could be possible.

So my whole "grace" thesis is fukt? Okay. Transsexuals can have this grace, fair enough, male to female.

So what about female to male? What about female-to-male transsexuals, do they have this grace?

Are we gauny deny bodies grace because of some nature versus nurture fucking prejudice keech! Fuck that.

Life is complicated enough man what are we discussing here at all?

Mind you, the concept schizophrenia; there is definitely an aspect of one's personality, of my personality, an aspect that caves in for no one.

Okay the ex was out my league but I tried for her. I was aye a bit arrogant. I needit the relationship. She didnay.

Maybe it wasnay a marriage-type relationship so much, just something with a bit of a permanent feel. I was a rootless footless cunt, shuttling back and forwards across the country. Man I was a mean sucker, a no-good fucking bum man I was a

It is true but let us face the facts, that particular fact, hoc hoc certo auctore comperi, that I was a no-gooder.

An acquaintance suggested it was to do with beating the immigration rap, me getting hooked up with Yasmin in the first place like for me it was a marriage prospect. He said: Jeremiah, God bless you and God bless these bastards who can beat the Federal Bureau of Immigration and Assimilation. If you are on the run it remains a day at a time for the rest of your life sweet Jesus I know it and so does everybody else, and if you can find yourself a good Uhmerkin lady why then there be hope for you, you and your children, and your children's children.

This guy was speaking from an unstable background himself. He had been an addict and that was him now clean except he was heavy into gambling and considering checking in with Gamblers Anonymous. Except he was a born poker player. He hadnay discovered he was a born poker player until whatever age he was, quite auld, 50 or 60 or something.

But he was wrang to impugn my motivation. I didnay gie a fuck about beating any immigration rap. It was just Yasmin I was eftir. I was an Inkliz-spaking pink-face caucasian frae a blood-and-soil motherland heil hitler hail mary hullo to king billy. And I had my Social Security card. And I had my Driver's Licence

although only a few months were left on the meter and one hesitated to update the fucker lest the authorities took it and withdrew it on the grounds of whatever the hell man these shites made it up as they go along. There was aye some fucking new legislation designed to hoist yet another damocles sword ower one's fucking neck.

So okay, if I got my Green Card, so okay.

But I wasnay gauny fucking creep and crawl about it. How could ye creep and crawl to a right-wing load of keech like the US State? If it wasnay for the individual population naybody would stey in the dump, we would leave it to the greysuits and gangsters, we would jump into the long ships and row like fuck to another hemisphere. Naw, I wantit to marry her because I was an honest young healthy male person and she was a just extraordinary kind of human being and she made me laugh and clap my hands and because if I didnay marry her I would pine away and dissolve into a pint of strange-smelling liquid of a deucedly slimy nature. That is what happens to young people in such a situation, the distillation of a passion thwarted on too many occasions.

Nearly five years since we met, I was a kid myself. No like now, a prematurely aged body who

Food! I could smell it! I was fucking starving! Instead I sipped the beer. But a cigarette, of course, was not the thing for me, for me, for me

A cigarette, of course, was not the thing for me, for me, for me

A cigarette, of course . . . and so on, sung to the tune of "Mine Eyes Have Seen the Glory".

The period immediately eftir we met was especially disastrous. Some of that had to do with unwieldy, untimely and just fucking stupit fucking crazy stuff. The upshot was I needit to sort out my cash soon sooner soonest. But I was in that boring bastarn bar job. How was I to get out of that? I didnay want into an exciting bar job that left me physically drained and satiated from life's pleasures. I was wanting to do something else with my life so boredom was what I was wanting, so I couldnay really grumble, I just had to concentrate on things, I was needing space, I was

Fuck off.

Alongside the ID a practice of mine was to carry essential paperwork and employment details on my person. If I was tramping the mean streets in search of work and chanced into a bar or café and met somebody hiring help then whoosh,

Here are ma papers sir. You need someone to pour a proper glass of stout sir? carry bricks and mortar sir, wear a kilt and wait table sir, wield a claymore sir, push a pen, pick a pocket, deal the cards, construct a database, settle a bet, perform minor heart surgery, sell ma body, write a screenplay, scramble up the rone pipe and enter that toty wee window and rob the Inkliz crown jewels?

And so then what happened?

Weird, even for me: I went out to play poker and later next morning I signed a job contract with a national Security agency. I was down casino town with John Wong, a player in Ranjit's game. Me and John werenay really pals, mair comrades of convenience. Plus we recognized each other as – no so much deadly serious about gambling, we just werenay flippant about it. The problem with Ranjit's game was it was just too friendly. For all its good points the standard of play was wild and variable. Sometimes it was fucking impossible and one was left scratching one's heid at the vagaries of the human intellect.

That can be another excuse for failure. Folk have to change their style of play and I wasnay as capable of that as I should have been. These guys never knew when they were beat because they never knew the cards. So they won. They didnay know what hand ye represented because they didnay know what was possible. Fuck knows why they gambled but they did. And they won.

I heard John muttering about it one night. The baith of us had been knocked out the game and were reduced to making sandwiches. He fancied trying his luck at casino town and so did I. We wantit into a proper game where we knew what was what and so did everybody else. We nominated the following month. Ranjit was coming, him and John worked in faimly businesses so it was easy for them. But I couldnay make it for a few weeks because of different things and couldnay use up my one and only day off. So I cheated the system, I phoned in sick and "stole" a day.

For some reason Ranjit never made the trip. We went in John's car. I had one but it was a heap of wasted junk.

At the casino we gied wur names in for the evening tournament, ate some grub then sat in the lounge to wait. John was too edgy, the money burning a hole in his pocket, he said he was gaun for a walk. Other players were in the lounge. I sat drinking fruit juice and coffee, listening to the conversation; mainly sport and gambling, including the latest on the "persian bet" with one guy saying how he made a spread bet on his next six trips. One of the auld fellers didnay approve of it all and he spoke about the airports and the bad effect all this insurance suicide stuff was having on them. I hadnay heard it from that perspective before. It was especially bad for airports located in or near to gambling towns. He had come in at the local regional a couple of days ago and it was havoc. Hordes of bodies were wandering about the place with naywhere to go. These werenay the usual traveling gamblers, stranded gamblers or plain down-at-heel losers waiting for something to turn up. These folks were ordinary Uhmerkins, maistly true-borns, many without adequate social skills. Nor could they cope with the disciplinary treatment to which regular domestic travelers were accustomed, they didnay do what the authorities telt them to do and were ignoring all the rules and regulations. They didnay seem to fucking grasp that orders were orders. These bodies were clogging up corridors, reception and gate waiting areas and were even finding their way onto the goddam airfields themselves. One minute they were there the next they werenay. How the hell were they managing it? It was like they were phantom apparitions or something. Different branches of the domestic Security forces, including the cops and assorted immigration officers, were forced to clear reception lobbies and dump ticketless people into the Patriot Holding Centers.

But that brought an outcry. These Centers had been designed for asylum-seeking furnir suspects, no for Uhmerkin true-borns. This was a rights issue; human, democratic and civil. But one thing was clear, the airport authorities were crying out for additional Security workers and hoped the federal government would step in to help. But it wasnay a federal problem apparently, and local militias should be put on alert. Meanwhile scores mair airport cops and immigration officers were recruited and sub-contracting agents attached to the Security and Defense industries tried to handle the demand for new employees. Latterly they were gieing starts to any mad bastard. If yer papers were in order ye could sign a contract on the premises and receive a travel voucher and expenses. Ye just walked in the door and they gied ye a start. Many of the losers traveling out from casino airports had done just that. This same auld yin was saying how when he came through the regional airport he recognized a buddy wearing a uniform, with gun holsters, who telt him that even he could get a job. And he was 67 years of age. I listened but I found it hard to believe. It wasnay so much the auld yin's age I found the drawback, it was the origin issue. He looked like he hailed from the Middle East, or maybe east North Africa so ye wouldnay have expected him to get employed by nay damn Security agency, even if he had been young, fit and healthy, no unless they hired him as a hollywood-style furnir villain for target practice. But I was wrang. Another guy immediately says how he personally had witnessed airport Security agents dressed in turbans and fehzeeezehz.

Fehzeeezehz? What the fuck is "fehzeeezehz"?

The plural of "fez" ya fokin eejit.

I paid attention to this pre-gambling discussion about

airports but the longer it went the mair jittery I was getting. It was aye like that before a game. I found external concentration very difficult. "External" meaning outside of myself, a concentration from inside myself that might have extended to things on the outside, outside of my body; I was having difficulty with it.

'Twas ever thus, although somewhere inside my brain "jobs going a-begging" had logged in and was causing minor electrical kerplunks. But beyond that

it looked like the draw for the tables had been made.

For many weeks I had saved for this night. And that wasnay a good omen. It was a fucking terrible omen. I should never have went in the first place. Ye should never put too much into one game. It gies ye too much to lose. And a part of the brain goes to that when ye are playing, and it isnay a time for shite and shite is what it is, anything that draws yer attention from the business.

Players were drifting across to card tables and a certain nervous chuckle was abroad; it belongs to all players and signifies a game is about to begin. Now John was at my shoulder, returned from his walk, a walk round the blackjack and roulette tables. He hadnay spoken but I guessed he was down a few. We were drawn at different tables which suited us both. We had a quick shake of the hands for luck. See ye in the final, I said and regretted it immediately. But worse if I had apologized because then the fates would have come down on us like a ton of bricks. John gied a slight shake of the heid and avoided looking at me and we went to the tables.

The truth is I was the wrang guy for poker. My psychology was so straight-down-the-line it was fucking haywire. I know that nowadays. Then I fucking didnay. My heid was just eh I think I was just fucking I dont know man Yasmin was about to gie birth and the pressures were on, the pressures were on, ye think yer life isnay gauny improve and it needs to improve, ye have to fucking make it improve and there ye are stuck in some shithole of a job. Things are changing roundabout ye and there isnay much ye can do, ye have lost control. The thing with gambling, there was aye that wee chance like ye could do something, change something, just fucking if ye got in front man, just a wee bit, then ye could I dont know, just fucking depends

I saved for that night, and I needit to, otherwise I would have been knocked out the tournament in the first ten minutes. It was buy-in eftir buy-in. I managed to hold on but and then startit winning, and finished with no a bad stake to take through to the next round. Late on I was odds-on to get through to the final and I got caught once and caught twice, then fucking guttit. It wasnay really my fault, stupit thing to say, but it wasnay, just incredible cards. I was all in on a flush with an A and Q in the flop. Unfortunate was I that the opposition held a J, 4 in the hole to my 10, 9. It depressed me mair than usual. It was so goddam fucking predictable. Nay point discussing it. But how the hell he had stayed in with a J, 4 in the first place I shall never know. It was extraordinary nonsense. Before the flop there had been two re-raises. I done well with that 10, 9 but it wasnay bad play at all, but his! Jesus christ man what was that all about? a J fucking 4, that is crazy cards at that kind of level. Or am I a fucking dumpling? Technical infantilism man, it is what sickens ye about cards. It happened all the time in Ranjit's game.

What is the point in talking. There is nayn. Poker doesnay get played with the clear, pristine purity it deserves. Obviously it is only a game. Why could I never understand that basic point. As soon as I saw myself winning early on I should have known, it was obvious, I should have held back, bided my time, let the bad luck run its course.

But ye see even saying that, what the fuck am I talking about? This is like setting out to lose as a long-term strategy? Crazy.

And that was that.

And I was broke.

And with a new woman in my life. New woman? Christ she was pregnant, she was gauny gie birth to a fucking beautiful wee fucking lassie who was just christ beautiful man and here I was.

What the hell was going on with me? How come I was back on this track?

Because I needit money. I needit money and I needit to change my life. That was why I had left the west coast. That was why I was back here. That was fucking why I had fucking fukt up yet again. My job was lousy fucking boring fucking shit fucking crap, and the wage was lousy, and the fucking tips were fucking man twilight time I was lucky if I made ten bucks a night and prospects there were nayn, fuck all. If and when I got time to try writing my story I was aye knackered, just wanting to sleep or watch that fucking goddam fucking goggle-box television tube load of fucking masturbatory keech man fuck john logie baird and mister macafuckingroni, I just couldnay cope with it.

When I left the table I left the casino and stepped along the boardwalk. It was good being outside, it wasnay warm. But it was alright being cold. And my blood was thick christ thick as fuck, just like my heid. But my heart was sound, and my politics were left and my spirits were as good as the next man. I had my ayn ideas but they werenay bad ideas. Okay, here was I back on the auld fucking – the auld eh

what was the opposite of gravy train?

But so what, so what, I had met a woman, that was the difference. I had met a woman and she was great, really just great and beyond what I could hope for, and here I was destroying it man just at this time, about to become a father it was pathetic what I was doing, how mental crazy can ye get! I was aye an unlucky bastard but this, this was fucking

jesus christ, I was such a tawdry fucker, my life had just been fucking tawdry, and then there she was, she was just like everything man in a way, with her music. She was the fucking real thing and it drew me on. I got serious about things like if she could do it so could I. It tied in with how I left the west coast, making a new start – it had been strangling me there, fucking choking the breath out me. Ye felt like ye were on yer knees. Life does that, drags ye down. All ye can do is rise above it, or else get to fuck, which is what I usually did.

One thing about the ex, she put up with the nonsense. She just gied me a look and a shake of the heid. That was what she did. She could handle me. Who the fuck else ever could handle me man nay cunt, no even my fucking maw. She was the only one. She had let me into her life. Why had she no telt me to eff off. She allowed me to hold her, and I held her and it was like how the hell did she fit me so snugly! I knew we were right because of that. Some women ye meet, if ye gie them a cuddle, ye bump into all their bits, their bones and whatever, but no her, we fitted the gether. I have to gie her that.

Nay point talking about "bad luck". It was me had blown it, luck had nothing to do with it. If I wasnay careful I was gauny blow the lot.

Even that stupit fucking bar job, when I phoned in sick it was like ye werenay supposed to get sick, people didnay get sick, the manager never got sick, she always went to her work; rain, hail or shine man I was gauny end up gieing her a mouthful and then that would be me on the fucking tramp again. I couldnay handle it man, these mental jobs, I needit something else, something different, especially now.

Imagine being a father, I couldnay imagine it at all. I walked the boardwalk and smoked a couple of cigarettes, and the second one didnay taste good at all, there was a bitterness, or sourness, if these can be distinguished. I dropped it onto the spars, snatched it up and went to the fenced-off area, flicked it to a spot beyond the electric lighting system. I stayed there for a spell, leaning the elbows. That ol devil moon. It was sinking fast, fast. I was having fanciful notions about swimming hame. I never mastered swimming so I would have to learn as I went, but if I just charged into the water as far as I could and then lifted up my legs and lurched forwards the sea would carry me, it would carry me, eddies and currents and gahd knows what lurking there, dragging a body out. If I sank to the bottom I would grab an auld tea chest or something and float my way across. There were ships on the horizon. One might toss me a lifeline capn. Three thousand miles from here a boat was going up the Clyde. A hundred years ago boats left for the States from the Broomielaw in Glasgow all the way to Ellis Island or farther south. James Connolly startit from there on the first stage of one trip, his auld Glasgow comrades at the quayside to wish him bon voyage. Every day of the week ye could jump aboard. There were nay Red Cards in those days, ye wouldnay have allowed nay ornery sidewinding right-wing scabby prick bastard to put ye under that kind of pressure. No sir.

And at the end of the ocean there was light. Dawn approached. It was moving to the end of the summer season. But heavy clouds like rain was imminent, no doubt torrential, journeying from the east, the hame of torrential rains, looming and threatening and fucking hell, what happened if John disappeared? I had been with people before and they disappeared. Genuine, no just avoiding me. That is what happens. Mainly gamblers. Half the time they dont know if they are coming or going, and if going, who with, did they come with anybody?

They cannay get their heids round day-to-day information, or if they make a real killing on the table and head immediately for an airport, fast-track it down to Cancun without telling nay cunt, or if they lose and sicken themselves, or sometimes

In the name of fuck! I would have to walk it back to the city!

Did persons ever have to do such a walk? Sure, frequently. It was close to three hundred miles, the side of the road was paved with dem bones and dry bones. Calcium highway the losers called it, no just the losers. Many's the time I had walked it hame from disastrous evenings myself, but no that sort of distance. No sir.

I lighted a cigarette and leaned my elbows on the barrier. At least this one tasted okay. I smoked it and then went to check out the table but I met John coming from the doorway, broke, completely down and out.

So that was that, the two of us. He was taking defeat badly, in an emotional state and hardly audible, muttering on about the hand that done him in. From what I gathered the damage happened before the flop; he had been holding a pair of good 10s, they just werenay good enough. Overall he lost very heavily and very personally by which I mean that his losses were no solely his own. But it wasnay only the poker to blame, he was at the roulette and blackjack beforehand and received a major doing. Why was he still playing these stupit fucking house-games! Surely he knew better than that, house-games! I said it to him. What a bad habit man, what a bad habit.

He gied me a look and walked along in silence. I followed. He stopped walking and stood still. His teeth were chittering, he gripped baith his elbows, startit mumbling again. It sounded like he was gauny gie up the ghost. I said that to him as well. Whereas me, I says, I dont think I've even got a ghost. He ignored me. Look, I says, I've been gambling badly since I was two years of age, the first bet I lost was with my maw on a diaper change, an even-money shot I had shit myself but I hadnay, and it wasnay evens anyway, it should have been odds on. That maw of mine was a hard taskmaster, mistress I should say . . .

I should have folded on the re-raise, he said.

Naw, ye went on the 10s and it was proper ye went on the 10s I mean fuck all wrang with it, ye were third man, is that right? 10s are good cards John the kind of fucking cards that eh know what I mean, good cards. How much was in the pot by the way?

He didnay answer.

Rain definitely imminent. He was wearing sandals. I wasnay wearing sandals but I was wearing thin trousers; thin jacket and thin shirt and if we didnay get out of here soon . . . I realized then about John that I should never trust him too much. I get these feelings about people, I would say maist people, ye just learn no to trust them. Ye have to impress that on yer kids. Some people are good but maist arenay, maist are selfish bastards. About his demeanour there was an inference lurking and it was so easy to read. Not only did he want money he wantit my money. I knew it and I said it. By the way John, I do not have any cash, I wish I did but I aint got a fucking penny.

He nodded. You got any credit cards?

Ye joking?

No I aint joking, I aint joking. You got a Visa or something?

Have I fuck.

You got no credit card?

That's right, yeh.

He nodded, smiled.

I dont have no fucking credit card, right?

Yeh, he said, right.

Yeh, fucking right, I dont have nay credit card because they wont fucking gie me nay fucking credit card. I'm an alien furnir bastard John the only card I got is a Red Card, it's a Class III. Do ye know what I'm talking about? My worry isnay credit cards man it's fucking deportation.

He frowned and I felt like grabbing him by the lapels. Listen to me, I says, they have my card marked. I am a registerrred fucking non-integratit cunt with the wrang fucking politics, the wrang philosophy of life man, the wrang this and the wrang that. The Red Card is a marked card. If I aint got cash in hand I aint got cash. That is how it is. All I have is money. Or else no money. I can go into a bank and gie in my dough or else I can take it out, but that's that.

He studied me now. So you an alien?

Did ye no notice I had a funny voice?

Yeh.

Anyhow, even if I could access cash, the game's finished. It's a final they're playing. Unless ye're talking house-games, ye're no wanting to play house-games, surely?

I guess that's my business.

Yeh, I said.

He stared at me, prepared for anything. I wasnay gauny lose my temper with him. I didnay know him well enough. Maybe he was a weapons expert, karate champeen of the world. I shrugged. Ye've lost, I says, tough, I says, you've lost I've lost.

He turned on me. How much you lost?

A hundred per cent.

A hundred per cent? He frowned.

Yeh, ye know what that is, a hundred per cent?

I know what that is.

So okay, I says, so dont fall out with me. Plus you've got the transport.

Yeh. He smiled.

So ye gauny drive me to the airport?

Huh?

Could ye drive me to the airport? I'm gauny go for a job. The guys were talking about it before the game. Ye can sign the contract there and then. The bosses gie ye travel vouchers and expenses money.

Expenses money?

Yeh.

They give you expenses money?

Yeh, ye have to sign the dotted line first but.

How much expenses money?

I dont know. Try it with me and see.

John frowned, then he said, I got a job.

So have I. Mine's in a bar, yours is in a restaurant.

Family restaurant, mine is a family restaurant.

Yeh.

My family restaurant man. It is a different thing.

Yeh. So will ye take me to the airport?

Fuck the airport man.

Thanks.

Where is the airport?

I dont know.

Two blocks from here, why dont you take a walk? John pointed to the side, smiling at his ayn joke. Then reality returned and he sighed and closed his eyes.

All I'm asking is a drive.

He shook his heid slowly, staring out to sea. I aint going to no airport Jerry.

I heard ye.

Your wife is pregnant; so is mine, she is five fucking months; so what do you know, you aint a father, I have two kids already, one year old, three years old. So now another. My wife is tired, fucking tired man you dont know about that you are like a single guy, you dont know nothing.

That's true, I said. She isnay my wife by the way, she's my girlfriend.

Oh she is?

Yeh. I gied him a cigarette, flicked the lighter. We stood smoking for a minute, then John frowned:

So you guys cant marry? he said.

What?

Like if you're immigrants?

Sure we can marry. We just cannay have sex but, we got to get the operation.

Huh?

Only kidding.

So you can marry who you want to marry?

Sure. If she'll fucking have ye, ye can marry her if she says yes. The trouble is if ye fuck up. I've fukt up.

Yeh. John smiled, exhaled smoke. Hey, he said, you get nightmares?

Yeh I get nightmares. The trouble is I enjoy them, maybe I should book a flight, make a few bets, maybe I should take a walk, go for the long swim.

I get nightmares, said John. I tell my wife. She fucking worries about them, she always fucking worries, some women man they just worry all the time. Yours worry like that?

I couldnay answer this one. He was waiting for me. I says, I'll have to be honest with ye John, I dont even know if she worries about me. I dont think so. Maybe I should phone her and ask.

So why dont she live with you? John was watching me, chewing on the edge of his thumbnail.

Live with me? How the fuck could she live with me, I've no got fuck all, nothing, nay money, nay place, nothing. My apartment isnay an apartment it is one big cupboard and a couple of wee closets. One window in the whole fucking space;

one table, it is the size of a newspaper; one laptop, one cup, ashtray. Shower-cubicle, toilet bowl – weeist toilet bowl ye've ever seen, it is so fucking wee ye cannay aim into it it is a joke. Then the bedroom closet, walk-in, one single mattress, it takes up the floor, and nay window. I throw a sleeping bag down and climb inside, shut the door and it is pitch black, you cannay see in front of yer nose, nothing. Then I think what happens if some maniac psycho enters when I am asleep and shuts the door on me? I'm serious man it only locks from the outside, that is me fukt.

So why you dont live with her?

It isnay possible, no the now, her cousin's there as well, just nay space. We have to get things sortit properly. I have to make some money, I just need to make some money, then when the baby comes . . . Heh! Look . . . I pointed out to sea. My country is three thousand miles east of here, go down the beach and start swimming, ye cannay miss it, just plunge in and start swimming.

You start swimming.

I cannay swim.

Yeh you can!

I cannay.

You cant swim?

Naw.

John grinned.

But I wouldnay go hame even if I could. Why? Because I am a fucking failure. The only way I'll get hame is if they deport me. Or else I hit the lottery. Then I would get a good place, me and her would get merrit.

More kids?

I shrugged.

You like kids?

Yeh, I suppose so.

They know things we dont. We have forgotten them, the kids remember them. Kids look at you man, they know.

What do they know?

What I'm saying man is they know, they know things.

Aw mysticism, sorry.

John smiled.

So, ye gauny drive me to the airport? If it was close enough I'd walk it. It's the cops but, they would pick me up on a vagrancy charge, they would check me out and hang me up on a fast-track deportation order, probably dump me in the wrang fucking continent, these immigration fascist fuckers, they cannay differentiate.

Okay.

Thanks.

You got the gas?

Fuck you. I'll no get the goddam job anyway, it's 20s against.

You'll get it; white fuck.

Aye but they dont like my politics.

Who cares.

It's mair complicated than that.

John shrugged. The doormen gied us a nod when we returned through the casino entrance. The parking area could be reached along past the slots and the house-games, upstairs and across the walkway, on around the other side of the building. We stopped off for a coffee and a sandwich; on the house man aint we the lucky ones. About half an hour later he set me down outside the terminal building. I split my cigarettes with him and gied him a wave when he drove off.

It was weird seeing all the bodies around the airport. Maist of them were in poor condition, a lot were down-and-outs. Inside seats and benches were occupied and I stopped a couple of times to rest against vacant walls but the Security operatives were a wee bit sensitive and gied me to understand pedestrian mobility was preferable. That included me, buddy. But I took the first opportunity to get onto a seat, then I dozed. The Security outfit that gied me the job is still operative although times have changed. They opened their recruitment office at 8 a.m. It was entered via the secured section of Immigration and Assimilation. I showed my identity materials and explained my goal, they paused on the Red Card but accepted it and kept it and allowed my entry. There was naybody else waiting.

Some of the agency's marketing material and business plans of the past and present lay on a table in orderly piles. Fortunate was I there was a free coffee and hot chocolate dispensing machine. The next forty-five minyooets were most agreeably spent though rauchen verboten, I would have had to leave the building. A few other journals and PR materials were there and I browsed through them. Their basic philosophic position was of interest. True change could take place in society if the entire world were true believers and evil cast asunder. Until then folks would just get on with things, assisted by a variety of humane structures; some freshly created; others passed down through the generations whether by common assent, divine support or state intervention by either peaceable decree or the democratically-enabled force of arms. It all made sense to me though I began from a different premiss and was wont to continue in that vein.

The interview office was located in an upstairs room. It was there I received my ayn wee personal interrogation by two males and a female. It wasnay the first time I had been involved in tricky job interviews and this was only slightly different. Certain classes of employment were beyond the alien or such as the alien and until presently this particular area of the Security industry had been one such class. The woman wished me good morning and returned my Red Card. She asked if I would say something about my life and times.

This line of approach wasnay unfamiliar to me. I was sitting facing them, and facing the back of a computer and monitor. She would have been about 35 years old but had a nice manner and it relaxed me. I explained my background and why I had emigrated.

The younger male sat in the middle; he nodded occasionally but said nothing. He was operating the computer. He would have logged into my file and would be displaying relevant matters. The usual. This sort of stuff could irritate a feller. One had to avoid the daft smiles, the loss of one's temper. But the bodily behaviour telt its tale. The elder male said, Hey Jeremiah, we know all about you so why dont you relax. You are the problem that we address. Once we have you figured we decide the areas best suited to your particular weaknesses. In the Security industry people's weaknesses should be high-lighted, they can be more crucial than strengths. In this agency we go further; the way we see it these weaknesses are the true strengths. For some this is a complicated concept but our agency is a successful agency and this has been our way forward.

I nodded. They noticed this and exchanged glances. Do you wish to make a comment? he said.

Okay. I dont want to be presumptuous; it is just that I do have my ayn beliefs. I see it from a non-aligned religious perspective, as ye know, but I can also see it from the other side, in keeping with what you are saying, there are more weaknesses than strengths in this vale of misery and with the help of our Lord we may defeat them. I understand also from the business perspective that the more weaknesses an operation such as this may harness the more outlets become available to them.

Excuse me, said the younger male. He gestured to the screen and the other two gazed at it for a few moments. Nay doubt he was displaying my faimly tree. Great, maybe he would gie me a swatch at it, I aye got stuck in class relations at the time of William the Conqueror.

The woman looked at me. Would you care to speak further?

About anything in particular? I says.

About whatever you feel is important.

Well okay, I says, in an interview like this it pays to be honest because ultimately you know everything anyway. Right? So ye know my beliefs have been agnostic with occasional shifts to an atheist position.

You describe yourself as a libertarian socialist atheist? She frowned but only to indicate a possible ignorance. Whereas the elder male had smiled.

I smiled back at them. Well, I said, that's it, why beat about the bush? I am a non-integratit unassimilatit member of the alienigenae. That to me is important. Also I am a man, a human man. Frailty is inherent in me. But what do we mean by "frailty" in a context that is utterly and only human? I do confess that I hold many weaknesses of a personal nature. Daily I could ask that strength be gien me that I might fight temptation but if an agency such as this can harness such weaknesses then it becomes in a stronger position to confront those with similar weaknesses.

But personally I've changed. We all want to settle down and that includes me. Why should I be different. I want kids and I want a nice home and I want a decent job. Ye know my wife is pregnant? Well she isnay my wife yet she's my girlfriend, although we are gauny name the date soon, if the authorities allow it.

I should say I do have strengths, positive strengths. Being from a slightly different culture I see things that wee bit differently from you. My ayn personal experiences and inner singularity are a potential strength as well. Not only in a domestic capacity but also in the international one, should the opportunity arise. The Security enterprise is both business and moral. Crusade is perhaps too strong a word, although who knows, in this present climate of fear and horror, perhaps it is; at least partly, partly a crusade.

The younger male gestured to the monitor and the other two studied it for at least half a minute.

The woman glanced at me. I smiled and was about to speak when the elder male said, Well now Jeremiah, do you sometimes consider that fate deals a hand in life and that you are left to pick up the pieces?

Pardon me?

Do you consider that fate deals a hand in life and that we are left to pick up the pieces?

Okay, yeh, well, sometimes I might have considered that but although I am a young man my memory aint great. Neither was my father's and it probably runs in the faimly, through the male line that is. But the folks that stay behind arenay as prone to risk-taking as we who need to move abroad. Luck does come into play whether we like it or no. And the poor auld fates, I wouldnay blame the fates; if ye get dealt a hand ye have to play it, ye play it to its proper value.

They were listening to me with frequent glances at the monitor. I gied them a wee poker analogy; once ye have seen the flop the way ahead exists, whether we like it or no. All ye do is shrug and get on with it. What is for ye willnay go by ye as my auld mother used to say. If they had wantit me to recount some of the causal factors and picky details by way of explanation of certain of the events that had occurred since my arrival in their country then I was prepared to try it.

The woman telt me no to worry. Bodies like myself might appear unlikely candidates from the more typical vantage point but here was different. Casino airports were central to staff recruitment and the habits of gamblers were nay secret. This town thrived on chance and while our particular Security operation was a national affair its headquarters were at the heart of this community. She spoke of the situation in their industry in which the state of the world also had a role. There was a crucial need for peace-keeping forces at hame and abroad and these should be marshaled.

I attended to what she was saying in case she sprung a trip question but gradually became aware of a pong emanating from somewhere and it was nay metaphor. It was myself for fuck sake, having spent mair than twenty-four hours in these same clothes, sitting about in smoke-filled sweaty rooms, snoozing in congested areas. I was a fucking mawkit clatty bastard.

I was! When had I last washed! I had worked in the pub till late last night and when I got up yesterday morning I just fukt about watching some stupit auld movie on television. I needit a shower fast, fast. As soon as the interview was ower I would head straight for the bus station. I would sleep on the bus and be hame for mid eftirnoon at the latest. I would be into my work for 5.30 p.m. Well, not for much longer. Incredible as it seemed it looked like they were gauny offer me a job. A Security agent! What a fucking joke.

The section of which I would become a member was consigned to the outer arenas of conflict; the highway roundabouts and carparks, the grounds of the Patriot Holding Centers. Did I find that disheartening? Of course I didnay. One had to start somewhere. What about constant nightshift, was that a problem? No maam, it was a way to save money: with nay social life there was nothing to spend it on.

The elder male had pulled out a drawer while she was talking and he passed me a training manual, flicking through the pages as he did so. It was an out-of-date copy but remained pertinent overall. Even if you were never to work for us, he said, you would find it of value.

Thanks, I said, putting it to one side.

It is like this Jeremiah: we existed prior to the insurance crisis and likeways we shall survive this boom, and post-boom. Our agency succeeds by adapting. The air-travel industry will get its act together, level-headed folks will refrain from survive-or-perish gambling. God knows it aint a healthy thing. I look at you and I think, Here is a feller can succeed with us. He is not afraid of the world that lies outside these shores. In this line of business there are many afraid to open an atlas or engage in geographical matters. They wont have a map in the house; even the sight of our country in outline causes tension because it posits the existence of the *beyond*.

He continued talking about related stuff, about me doing office-work and maybe handling a computer and carrying messages and doing these wee sort of extra chores that all added up to – promotion! What was it promotion he was talking about? I hadnay even signed the dotted line and here I was being hoisted up the ladder. It sure pleased the ego. Mind you, I was personable and I had them smouldering blue-eyed blond-haired Celtic good looks that can pass for Anglo-Saxon and thus appeal to every conceivable gender, race and ethnic group, and include the planets in that, the ol outer solar system and galaxy, why they would a-favour me also. And as for my ancestral lineage, well boy let me say that this lil ol ancestral lineage didnay just include William Wallace, the KKK and the Therty-Three and a Third Masonic Skarrisch Rite, but it also included

for fuck sake!!!

Listen, I said.

The elder male stopped talking.

Sorry for interrupting ye but I just thought I should tell ye

– and I dont mean it to sound like a boast or as though I am trying to disguise what essentially is a boast but I am just reminded that my great-granddaddy's granddaddy used to work for the Pinkertons.

Huh?

The Pinkerton Detective Agency. Yeh, the ancestor I personally am called after. He came to this country midway through the 19th century and landed in the Colorado gold mines. But he grew tired of men's avarice and took the road on out of there, thinking to head south on the Santa Fe trail and maybe onwards to find farm work in the vineyards of California. But then something unusual happened, and this is part of the faimly myth and history, auld Jeremiah blundered and found himself heading west on the Oregon Trail and it was while passing through Utah he discovered his true worth as a human being, yes sir, and he threw away his gold-prospector tools and became both a devout christian and a god-fearing body involved in the detective profession, primarily the custodian of pioneering business interests. This may serve to indicate that a feller like myself can do well in this line of work. Okay I am an alien but so was he, and so was Allan Pinkerton, him that my great-granddaddy's granddaddy worked for, he too was a Glasgow man and he too began as a Chartist and an eh democrat and or what do ye call it, certainly he was involved with the auld Chartists and I suppose, being honest, well what I mean is well ye would have to say I suppose socialist, that he

The younger male who operated the computer paused to smile. He was an annoying little bastard and I wantit to smash him one on the chops.

Look, I says, I'm one step from deportation, all I seek is an honest day's toil for an honest day's return. From what I can figure it is a question of hard work, and hard work doesnay scare me, and never has scared me.

The woman smiled but no ironically.

Nowadays people arenay hard workers, I said, that is my opinion. Us aliens have to work that wee bit harder than the average. In my travels I've seen folk reject an honest day's toil for an honest day's return. Sure they work their 3 score and 10 but the passionate personality can reach beyond that. It's a question of attitude. Some would say it is no attitude, some would call it an ethic, call it a core value. But without it success in any career is unlikely. I've moved back to the east coast for good. I just want to get merrit to my girlfriend and settle down, raise a faimly.

The woman was studying me.

Although in saying that I dont want to tempt the fates.

Right, said the elder male, glancing at the screen as the younger male drew both his attention and that of the woman to the data there. The elder male nodded to the woman who looked at me and said:

Do you have a question?

No so much a question, I was just wanting to say that I'm prepared for the work proving shabbier than citizens might anticipate. I would argue that the word "anticipate" is of dubious value anyway; history is history. But I just want it on record that although I would never knowingly or wilfully advocate, abet, advise or teach the duty, necessity, desirability or propriety of overthrowing this or any other government by force or violence, whether verbal, physical or psychological I positively cannot vouch for the rest of the population and when I work as a Security operative I shall think as a Security operative. Ye know I'm a gambler. But I wouldnay call myself a real gambler, no insofar as I meet real gamblers, those who are a stone's throw from perdition which I look upon as a halfway stage in the process of enlightenment: perhaps a step prior to revelation. I see bodies in casinos who are poor souls,

I see bodies in casinos who are not poor souls. I see grown men on their knees praying, right at the tables when the cards are being dealt, they get down on their knees. These folks are engaged in a life-surviving process. They are just ordinary individuals scratching to get by. Me personally, what I shall say is that I dream a lot. And I have opinions, everybody has opinions, maist people anyway. I speak as one myself, a person. I am aware that some folks are executed or not executed, tortured or not tortured, deported or whatnot. I can only say what I feel and I feel that nowadays there is very little escape, naybody can be outside the system, there is nay room for hermits in the 21st century, the days of the mystical stargazers are so to speak o'er. There are singular liberties to which folks arenay privy in this world but liberty is one thing, security another. Would I wield the executioner's sword myself appears to be the question. But does the executioner still use a sword? or does it depend on the state? I admit that I'm never a hundred per cent sure how to handle my life, especially in situations rife with risk or intimidation. Also, I know that yez know maist everything about me.

I shifted on my chair. For the past few minutes I had been getting twinges in the erectile region. I couldnay think what they were. Maybe it was linked to thoughts of the Security industry. I was never into uniforms and implements relating to warfare, punishment and bondage. At the same time, there was a pub I once blundered into. It was in LA and I was with a lassie, on wur second date. What a look she gied me! She thought it was intentional but it had been a complete blunder. Maybe it wasnay a blunder and I was fulfilling a subliminal desire, or else if it was a presentiment. Maybe the S & M side of life was gauny happen to me later on! Christ, it wasnay something to look forward to.

Mind you, I liked weapons as a boy. I dreamt about finding

a gun stashed away in rubbish bins or behind a bush and now I was a member of the domestic Security forces and lawfully entitled to crunch a wrongdoer's skull. I have to confess that I was never a timid guy. I wasnay even timid with women. But, in essence, in essence

in aysons misoor it was just braggadocio, I was baith braggart and blawhard. Once I stopped blethering I was fukt.

Or do I do myself a disservice? he yawned, reaching for a bottle of beer, but the bottle of beer was an exbottle of beer, dregs of a bottle of beer. I refrained from swallying these dregs.

Fuck! Sally had appeared suddenly, from a doorway to the rear of the bar, balancing large platefuls of grub on both arms and wrists.

And I was starving too! Some kind of meat stuff and fries. She headed along to where the musicians were joking about something, laughing the gether. But the grub looked beautiful – barbequed or fried chicken, sausages and ribs, and piles of french fries. A dream dish! I was in a greasy-spoon music bar! I had stumbled into heaven. Packets of aspirins hung between the nuts and nachos. You could do anything in this joint, cure a heart attack or get drunk on a full stomach.

She disappeared and reappeared with three more platefuls. Nay wonder there have been so many songs about women called Sally. It wasnay quite in the Maria class but baby, baby.

Maybe I could write one myself. Sally, long-legged lassie from the uplands, woman of the hot fries/lady of the warm thighs

a pencil a pencil a kingdom for a pencil. My notebook?

The drums had been set up, the instruments were in place, and the band was ready to eat. Yes sir. One of them had been hauding a cornet in his hand, hauding onto it while he listened to the guy in charge of the bar yapping away. Now he laid the cornet down and took some napkins from a holder and arranged them beside his plate. Fuck the music, he cried to the awe-struck audience, let the munching begin. Then out the vest pockets came the wee salt and pepper condiments, the pickled beetroot and onions, good bread, Texas chilli sauce.

On her way back to the bar I gied Sally a wave and signaled I wantit another beer. She nodded. Maybe I should have ordered some grub as well, I was so fucking hungry man! And too long without eating aint the best behaviour. How many beers had I swallied! My trouble was I didnay get hangovers.

Ach.

What is "ach" in pictish?

Mair folk had drifted in. Nay doubt this bar would prove the musical artery of the entire downtown area. It was a surprise me and Haydar hadnay made it here. Maybe we did, there was a familiar something about the place. Naw. It was me aye done the driving and I wouldnay have drove across Utah man I would have detoured farther north then taken a right, bypassed the place aw the gether.

But my memory just aint good. Nayn of that side of the brain. So what about the other side, or sides, the lobes or whatever ye call them? No savvy hombré, I dont fokking know, everyting ees concealed.

Maybe he would come in later. Nothing would have surprised me. No about Haydar but about life. In life anything was possible. Folk enter into yer world, then they vamoose. If I was dealt a straight flush lightning would strike the roof and the game would have to be abandoned.

One wondered where Sally had vanished. Her boss was back behind the bar serving bodies. I didnay like him. I didnay like the way he goofed off and left her to do the graft. That to me was out of order. I got up and walked to there. He gazed at me with that strange expression used by bartenders everywhere. I was invisible to him. I smiled, a seemingly fatuous smile but it wasnay, it was deadly cool, if he so much as blinked the wrang way I was gauny batter him one on the mouth. What was his best uisghé? I studied the gantry for two seconds, a musty auld Glenmorangie. How much was left in it? About a quarter-bottle. How much was that? Whatever. I would buy the lot to sicken the cunt, leave him without a drop of skatch in his entire hostelry. That would teach him a lesson. Cheeky bastard.

Him and the pentagon spy were having a conversation about politics and xenophobia, art and revolution. I eavesdropped. What a conversation! I heard the noise of plates clacking together. Yes sir, Sally would be washing the dishes. Now I did something silly; on a table to the end of the bar I saw some fliers, re forthcoming cultural events in town, so I walked to them and lifted a couple, then glanced at my wristwatch and at the large clock on the gantry, as though comparing notes; then I yawned and returned to my table, pretended to be engrossed in reading the fliers. The manager prick got the message; before long Sally arrived with a fresh bottle.

Hi, I said.

Lite?

Yeh.

She put it down on my table and left without further comment.

Oh dear, fukt again.

But what was I supposed to do? die of thirst? It wasnay a tacit complaint against her I made by gaun to the bar, I just needit another drink. If anything it was a tacit complaint against him.

Me and women just didnay mix. I would be better involved with a cat or a canary or a fucking one-leggit parrot. Months it took me even to speak to a woman, I am talking about properly, in the male-to-female sense. An ordinary conversation as between the genders. I aint talking about gaun to a restaurant or the movies here, never mind full sexual relations of a delicious nature. I am talking about an ordinary conversation as between the genders. But what the fuck is an ordinary conversation as between the genders. There is no such thing. All is fraught between us. Even talking to yer auntie subtleties abound. At the age of 34 I was obliged to accept I would never again sleep with a woman except where entry is a function of an economic contract, if I saved my cash to visit a prostitute. I had gien up gambling. Gambling was bad for ye. Gambling ruined yer teeth and caused deafness.

There had to be a pool table somewhere in town. Nevertheless, I wasnay gauny find it. I would get beat anyway.

Women are never 100% convinced by gambling successes. How can anything be 100% if it concerns a man? Men arenay 100% beings. Women know they never get the whole story. My ex never found out how I got the Security job. The last she heard I was tending bar. She didnay know I enjoyed a game of chance, never mind I was down at casino town in the perennial but doomed attempt to win copious bundles of dollar bills. No sir she did not sir god strike me if I should so much as move from this spot sir, flagellation is all I deserve, put me outside the garden for the eternal duration your lordship for I shall not want.

And she didnay like me talking like that either; the irreligious stuff, the radical chatter. When I launched into a tirade she gied off a frisson that meant she wasnay listening any longer which was no in itself strange, but what was strange was how some bodies have this precise kind of energy, this what-d'ye-call-it, I dont know. Even stranger was the way people gied up listening to their associate human beings. There is an additional strangeness or strangeity about talking to somebody when they have made that as a premeditated decision: either no to listen to their partner or no to reply when spoken to. A curt nod or some vaguely relevant facial movement would have sufficed.

There was an interiority about the ex. She had a secret life. Sorcery was involved. One time she disappeared for an hour and a half. She did. We were lying the gether in bed. It wasnay long since we had uncoupled and I was on my back. She had turned away from me. I wasnay so much dozing as in a trance, in some never-never-land that had me dressed in uniform and pushing grocery carts with buckled wheels, searching for suspicious packages in the midst of great conflagrations. I woke and she wasnay there. I assumed she was in the bathroom or maybe gieing the wean a feed. Time passed. Then I had to go for a piss myself and the bathroom door was ajar, inside was darkness. So then I checked the baby. The baby was sound, her wee face poking out the blankets. She looked like she had had a feed.

So where the hell was the ex! How the fuck do I know. I was only her man, she wouldnay discuss it with me. These disappearances happened a few times and she never gied me one explanation. Was sorcery the answer?

No sir. I needit to change my circumstances: such was the bottom line.

But that was precisely what I had done! Fucking hell man it was me effecting change here. I had to gie myself some credit.

Mind you, I wouldnay have went for the Security job in the first place if some stupit geek bastard hadnay held on to a mental crazy J, 4. Against a re-raise? No one re-raise, two of the bastards. These things prey on a feller's mind.

Ower at the airport they gied me a nice wee uniform to wear. It was supplied on credit by the agency, cost deductible from immediate salaries. Great bosses, effficient bosses; through such benevolence they summoned a special loyalty in the workforce. Me and the compadrés werenay used to these dollops of largesse. Credit! Fuck sake, the next thing they would be dishing us out with genyoooine credit facilities and los swipe cardos.

The uniform consisted of a pair of very pale blue trousers with a light greyish stripe, and light watery blue top with faded pink and white logos; the cap was faded pink and white with a wee greeny-grey symbol that awakened an ancient folk memory inside my skull. It concerned the auld Hittite culture. So there ye are; in a former life I was either fighting with or against the Hittite Empire! Do we never get peace from these fucking scabby prick misanthropic fucking imperialist bastards?

Even Security operatives get rendered speechless.

But these uniforms! When I first got the dang outfit from the company stores it didnay occur to me how come the colours were so actually eh well they were colourless, lacking in differentiation: then by the light of the lord understanding was mineth. Nay self-respecting liberation group in the universe could have sported these hues. Thus when we went on duty we wouldnay have to arrest each other for terrorist-colour crimes, lending support to advocates of a new world order. A committee of senior advisors to the democratically-instructed political parties had discovered that all colours singly or severally sported might denote adherence or association to every conceivable organization or assembly of persons whose base existence was structured in subversion, subversion your Honor! The jury sighed.

Seriously but. Even the rainbow was barred. I guarantee these authoritative bosses of mine were nay fly-by-night politicians, these were permanent players who had studied the manual, manual upon manual.

But for myself it was for the new weapons I awaited; my stun gun plus my beating stick, the shillelagh baseball bat. My thoughts soared: but would they gie me the weapons to take hame? Life was following fantasy! My private-eye hero carried a pistol. He traveled on buses and subways and was aye engaged in menacing life-threatening scenarios that arose unexpectedly. Other males would sit there pretending to mind their ayn business; no so much cowards as unheroic individuals. But the private-eye feller, he would calmly yawn and take out his pistol, gie it a brief wiggle, and save the lives of sundry auld ladies and infirm gents who wuz being robbed, tortured, vilified and generally castigated by teams of cauld-blooded druggies of unknown extraction – barbarian furnirs, swarthy barbarian furnirs, savage swarthy barbarian furnirs, ones with beards, ones who had forfeited the right to breathe in this man's army.

Then I discovered my section wasnay allowed weapons of serious destruction lest we seriously destructed wur hosts.

Agh but in my rational moments I knew it was better no to have a gun. I would probably just use it. It was alright for relaxed private eyes, a different story for the likes of me. I couldnay rely on my temper so why appeal to fate. It was bad enough with the stick they supplied. I was adept with the stick. I liked having it. If I was to come out of that job with anything that is what it would be, the goddam shillelagh baseball bat. With such an implement a body might be firm, firm but gentle. In fact these were the watchwords of the agency and in Latin provided not only the business logo but a slogan for the squad. A few of my compadré operatives used to tap the side of their nose and call it to each other as they passed on patrol: Solidus sed clemens buddy.

I hoped those in the section who didnay gie a fuck for authority would recognize in me a comrade. At the same time who was I kidding. For bodies like us options were restricted severely. We knew it and the immediate superiors knew it. The authorities saw my status as an agency strength, it enfeebled me but it didnay enfeeble them. I knew better than to conceal certain matters from the authorities. Either they knew it already or had access to the knowledge; all my habits and proclivities, everything. Even eftir I got the goddam job I continued to browse the manual, and the regular journals that arrived from different areas of the industry. I was keeping abreast of stuff. I couldnay afford to take chances but nor could I hide from reality, I just wantit to know the facts. I might no have been able to dispute them but I wantit to know what they amounted to.

Ye cannay dispute the facts. No unless ye are in a position of power, and the poor auld Security comrade is employed to bear the message which is the fucking opposite of power.

Apropos of fuck all, if ye have to start apologizing for honesty then buddy can ye spare a hundred bucks.

A group of us alien operatives was bussed in and out daily. Lucky for us we didnay have to don the embarrassing uniform until we arrived at the airport. I felt sorry for two sikh guys on the bus; the turbans they had been supplied with were especially nondescript. We men can also be colourful, albeit in an unambiguous manner. In recent weeks there had been a spate of suspect parcels and clothing bundles left unattended on the upper carpark floors. These were whisked away by Security and destroyed by a powerful technical process akin to burning but which left no trace of matter behind. People were wary of getting their hands too close. One feller left his cell phone someplace and that was snatched and obliterated in moments. When we discovered that the original owners of the suspect parcels and clothing bundles were down-and-out folks they had wur sympathy.

Bodies complained about the wage we were on to start. It was particularly fucking stingy, and eftir the plethora of tax, insurance and compulsory charitable deductions there came the company stores payback on travel expenses, uniform and other essential sundries. In another life I would have sought an interview with my shop steward immediately. But here in Uhmerka naybody confessed to knowing what a shop steward was. We were encouraged to see Miss Liu Lee if we had problems. She was a state-registered nurse employed on a part-time basis who impressed me with the regularity of her breathing. I attended her clinic not only on account of the specks of grit in my eye. No sir. One time I had a bloodied and swollen nose which might have been fractured. Luckily it wasnay fractured. Miss Liu Lee had the typically calm demeanour of a nurse but with a prodigal ability to hypnotize patients, which was especially good for the Alien Section where paranoias were rife. The last I remember was breathing her perfume and being suffused by the cleanliness of her skin while her breasts ebbed onto my cheeks, causing me to giggle at a crucial moment. I woke up on that mobile bed thing they use to transport corpses. A truly memorable experience. And my nose was cured!

The injury followed a skirmish with intending lottery participants, one of whom wielded his feet in skilful, Thai-boxer-like fashion. Unfortunate was I that he wasnay wearing shoes and his toenails were jaggy; he caught me on the upper cheek bone, tearing into the corner of the socket and I was lucky no to lose the eye. This was one of those preposterous incidents that derive from a misunderstanding. The feller had been lying spread-eagled in a corner with his heid someplace in the clouds, hardly breathing as I thought. I bent to check his pulse lest he was deid but far from deid up he leaps in a backward somersault and launches straight at me with one superb kick but then he falls back on the strike and cracks his skull on the concrete flair. The thump! Christ I thought he had halved his skull in two. We got him an ambulance immediately. I never found out what happened to him. We werenay encouraged to pursue an interest in folks hospitalized in the line of duty.

I nearly lost the eye but it was enough to attend Miss Liu Lee's clinic. She gied me the needle for lockjaw and assorted death-inducing blood disorders all of which seem to have been preempted by her prompt action.

She was very good but nay substitute for a trade union.

In my lifetime there have been many good people and quite a few are women. I cannay include my sister in that. Instead take Sally, the luscious lassie who served at the bar. I watched her continue in the company of the musicians. I had a smile on my face. My hand cradled the empty beer bottle and upon my fizzog was an indicator of a guy not only relaxed but at home in the world. I didnay care if she had forgotten all about me. She had to work in a dire situation, the manager of the place was a fucking terror of a guy. The managers of maist places I worked were terrors. All bosses and immediate superiors are terrors; fucking shites man that be what they are. I have never met one of these bastards who

well, that isnay quite true cause for a time I was one myself; a boss, and I didnay hate myself, no at that time anyway, and no for that reason.

But one thing is true, carpark patrol was the lowest rung of the ladder.

Naw, even that isnay true. What the hell is true? Nay fucking beer, empty bottles, a lassie serving behind the bar who spends her time addressing issues that have nothing to do with the needs of her customers and who is, without doubt, luscious.

But carpark patrol was close to the lowest rung of the ladder. Behind the outermost carpark lay the secured areas and for operatives like myself those were viewed as a step up. All airports had these barricaded compounds nowadays; they were known as Patriot Holding Centers. Behind the barbed and electrified wire, and the steeply-angled high walls were tens of hundreds of furnir varmints. Some compadrés hoped to gain promotion to the Centers and expected to find long lost faimly members incarcerated therein. And did they truly believe such promotion possible? Who knows.

During my probationary period the operative delegated to show me around the place was Riçard Osoba. I was wary and wondered if he might be a management stooge. The thought was unworthy, but valid. We were four floors up and having a quiet smoke when we noticed an immediate superior stroll out from the rear of a suspicious-looking staircase. He's on his way up, says Riçard.

What's his name? says I.

You call him boss.

Moments later he appeared from the elevator and came towards us, whistling a piece of classical music. If this feller had a weakness it was probably historical. How come he had been promoted to that position in the first place?

Maybe it was demotion. Maybe he hadnay startit at the bottom and worked his way up. Maybe he had startit at the top and was on his way down, reduced to having little pricks like me look him in the eye. Riçard made the introductions and the boss said: How do you teach the lord in your part of the world?

I nodded to acknowledge the question. It was a pure flummoxer.

You from Ingaling?

Skallin.

Skallin, yeh. He nodded. How do you teach the lord in your part of the world Mister Brown?

I looked at him. His blue eyes gazed back at me with nary a blink between them. What answer could I gie? "With Great Gusto sir" sprang to mind but I managed to hold off with that because he might have thought it referred to a medicine-show magician or else to a biblical body pertaining to an antichrist context.

He smiled a smile of artless friendliness; but his eyelids had narrowed. This guy was a shooter. I racked my brains. Well sir, I said, the truth is that I've no been hame for a long couple of years now, no since my poor auld daddy died. He was a mean-spirited man but in his later years he mellowed a lot and I only wish I had been there with him at the end, but it was good that my mom was there for him. I ask daily that strength be gien my faimly that we may fight temptation and win understanding.

You bet. But son, the lord is a just lord. We ourselves are a fortunate people and should be grateful that his bounty has fallen into our gardens and orchards. The boss gestured in the direction of the Patriot Holding Center. Our agency is one of a few that deal here with many poor unfortunates, furin folks, folks of diverse genetic and ethnic strain.

Yes sir, I said, and I am one of them.

Indeed you are Mister Brown.

I shrugged. Nayn of it is anybody's fault, says I, no as far as I can see. I glanced at Riçard who was watching me: It is the way of the world and the nature of society's operations. Ye would be as well blaming South-East Asian moms and pops who chop off their kids' limbs to fit them for a career of beggary instead of pornography, also their grandparents and their uncles and aunties and the whole thing that gies rise to the very concept "extraction". Neither is there any yardage in blaming the elected representatives to federal or state office. Ultimately we are all in the arms of the Saviour, whether richman, poorman, beggarman or thief; plus all their female counterparts. What I wondered also, I says, entering my stride, ye see I've been a bit surprised by news of the salary, and what I wondered was about the scale and promotion and how these most important considerations function in temporal terms. This is the all-important domestic Defense industry yet the salary we are to receive amounts to the wage of a youth. I was gauny ask that I be granted an interview in this connection but now I am meeting ye personally I figure I may as well come clean.

Nothing wrong in coming clean son, my ancestors came from your part of the world and they were unpolluted.

Yes sir.

You a Red Card?

Yes sir.

What class?

Class III sir.

The boss smiled. His hand moved towards the top pocket of his shirt where the heads of three spruce cigars poked out. Well son, he said, the time for negotiation passed at the time of interview. And now, let me see, you are only two weeks into this situation, is that correct?

Yes sir. Ye see I wasnay sure when I signed on, I was dazzled by what was happening: here am I a non-integratit unassimilatit alien cratur being welcomed into the embrace of the host country's protectors. So I confess I was a wee bit under pressure, and furthermore

The boss had stepped his weight onto his left foot, he breathed lightly through his nostrils and squinted sideways. I was having to look up at him. Fuck sake I hadnay even noticed he was a foot taller than me. I imagined a belt on the ear from the feller. It would have catapultit me into the middle of next week or at least across the floor and maybe ower the fucking wall. But I reprimanded myself sharply: The bigger they are man, come on, pull yerself the gether.

Yes sir, I said, I know that I am a rookie and rookies are at the lower end of the hierarchical strata. Mind you, I have never understood the concept "strata", is it a Latin root or what? but for the crucial work we do here the wages are, I would say, fairly low; mair akin to the wage of an adolescent, homo summo officio praedatus or is it praeditus. Also, I said, I have la muchacha hermosa to look eftir, one's girlfriend, and a wee baby about to be born sir I am about to become a daddy ergo the relationship has that feel of permanency. My girlfriend is a musician; an artist, impoverished.

You bet son, mine too.

Pardon me?

My own lady, she is a sculptor. What's yours?

I telt ye, she's a musician.

Oh yeh. Well, invite her round to see me. Is she looking for employment opportunities? We always got room for females in this neck of the woods. What d'you say Riçard?

Not a thing boss not a thing.

The boss smiled and gied a jerk of the skull to signify the end of this part of the interview.

Skull is the wrang word; he had the head of a brangus bull only much softer and the flesh was all droopy. As well as that he had one of these very thick necks and very red faces. I knew it was a prejudice but I was always suspicious of very red faces and very thick necks; size 24-inch collar for his fucking shirts. It seemed to signify "one who exploits the other" and at the same time gorges himself on meatpies, grits and catfish chowder or any other tasty foodsicle that happens to be available, including that of god-fearing passers-by minding their ayn business, eheu vir, pardonais moi m'sieur, je ne comprend, el guerro por favor, these red-neck cunts steal their french fries and chips, lettuce leaves with barbeque sauce or these wee red vegetable things – horseradishes – fucking anything, gie me it they cry, I'll fucking eat it.

The boss shifted his heid to study me from a different angle and the expression on his face altered to one of predicted relish like maybe he was gauny throw ketchup on ma heid and take a knife and fork to it. He glanced at Riçard then turned to me again. Okay, he said, you got two more free weeks in this Security operation, let us see what you make of it first and what we make of you second. Then come to me and we shall powwow some more.

Yes sir.

Mister Brown, you call me boss, okay?

I nodded.

You call me boss. Okay?

Yeh boss.

I aint no authoritarian brutal bastard but we got some formalities. This area of business contains sinful goings on and we got to keep them formalities intact else all is lost. This means you got to see the proper authorities, in this case fiscal authorities, you need more salary you got to ask it from these folks. Okay son, two more weeks like I say and we'll see what you make of it first, and what we make of you second. If you dont hear nothing dont worry about it. You know what I am saying here, no news aint bad news.

Yeh boss.

But I wasnay about to make anything of it first, nor had I the slightest bit of interest in what the "we" made of me whether second, third or fourth. One thing I did know, by hook or by crook I was gauny survive this job. That was one wager I knew I would win. I felt like phoning a bookie. What odds me avoiding the chop? Would I still be around in the event of airplane-insurance recovery and the consequent demise of the bookmaking enterprise, the manifold staffing cuts and redundancy takeower bids? You bet yer goddam sweet goddam

I was a survivor. I had had that understanding thrust upon me years ago. It wasnay entirely to my credit.

We followed the boss to the elevator and saluted him aboard. I gied his underling a cheery wee additional wave for future reference but he ignored me and who could blame him.

Certain questions did arise for new operatives. Did one fit one's uniform or did it hang on one like an ill-fitting boilersuit or kimono? It was a crucial issue for many from my section who were a malnourished bunch of fuckers, skinny wee guys and gals. And what about the boss? Although he was one mair exploiter, it wouldnay have done to blame him too much. If he had been too thoughtful in regard to lower-end staff he would have got the heave years ago. There is a definite price on morality. Any Security agent would be up on such detail. One has to know one's opponent's strengths, one's partner's weaknesses. Those who hire Security operatives may be engaged in selfish practices ergo watch yer back. Nay doubt me and the comrades were expected to perform the work of formations such as MI6, KGB, CIA, UNITAS, MOSSAD and the various sub-sections of Immigration and Assimilation, and the Department of Social Security all rolled into one and ye must take it as an honor and a compliment, as great a compliment as anyone in the WASP Team of Nations could ever pay ye, gien that ye arenay a member of the upper classes cum ruling elites. That was why one accepted the wage of an adolescent, even at the age of 29. Plus of course the obvious reprisals from one's former associates back in all the places I called hame, including dear auld the west coast no to mention lijep Shkotsk. Once they found out I was a full-time paid employee of the internal Defense industry they would go in the huff. Here I was an erstwhile discusser of the fomenting of political disquiet across this wise and wonderful planet who had sold out to el capitalistas.

Little did they all know I would salvage my reputation with ease. This private-eye ditty I was writing would blow said el capitalistas sky-high. Corruption in high places, debauchees, a debased media, runaway heiresses who lose their memory and wind up in a down-and-out condition, trusting only to fortune and the advent of a bold but intrepid adventurer. This book had everything. Also, I was a goody and would always be a goody, even if I became a baddy for it was predestined I would succeed; it was all part of a greater plan and so was I, being central to it, I couldnay do nothing wrong. That was the way I felt. I wasnay positioned in this world to be a fellow-traveler.

Escaping from the booze trade and the service industry was a major bonus for any alien. Of course I would have preferred a mair particular type of job but that would have entailed the purchase of study certificates, qualifications, special visas and authority-friendly IDs. In future I did want to have a bash at the study. I could even apply myself while working at the airport. Whenever I went off duty or perhaps during smoke-breaks I could bring out the academic textbooks and set to with a will. And I wouldnay let wisecrakking comrades put me off. I would be resolute. Fuck the gambling. Nor would I waste time thinking about cards. I had the habit of mulling ower potential hands at poker while engaged in boring jobs but henceforth I would reflect upon graver matters. When I had accrued enough dough I would enter nightschool or maybe one of these early-bird morning programs at my local community college. Them institutions were aye chokablok with non-national persons cramming their minds full of educational and other assimilatory junk in the off chance that by engaging in such practice they might improve their lot or otherwise lessen the risk of violent racial assault and other life-denying harass-ments. Now that I was a daddy I wantit to settle down and fulfill my early promise, enter a career, build a house and call it hame. Yasmin would back me to the hilt. I had ambitions and she supported me. Whenever I stayed ower in her place

I did my share of the baby business. I enjoyed it, the feeding and the rest of it, patting the wind out the wee thing, gently, gently, christ. But it was all brilliant.

And if promotion came my way I might apply for a transfer. I fancied overseas work in the new Europe. Yasmin would jump at the chance. Musicians got employment abroad. Jazz, blues and latino stuff were all popular. Paris appealed; those Montmartre clubs where you found bodies like the Hot Shots, Django Reinhart, Grappelli, Bill Broonzy, Dizzy Gillespie; and then there was auld Nina herself, she even lived in the country. That area of cultural history was unknown to me but the ex telt me all about it. She could have joined that squad in exile. They were all furin performers who had been made welcome. Unfortunately maist of them were deid, and had been for decades. Then too there were the writers; Paris was full of them; Sartre, Genet and De Beauvoir, Camus, all sipping their cognac et café solo, ehspressoh misoo, merci and bon appétit, you will do for me. Of course they too were deid. I was aye out my time; half a fucking century too late. The same when I was a wee boy, I aye missed out because I was a late child.

Och aye, he sighed, reaching for a warm and tender empty bottle. Times is tough and I'm a-gaun hame.

Why did I use these sentimental expressions? Hame! I mean what the fuck is hame! I tried to set up a hame. I tried to set up a hame.

I did.

So did she, okay, I aint gauny fucking deny it. The two of us were the gether on that. Sure. Yazzie was goddam good man, no sir, I wasnay gauny deny it, I wasnay gauny fucking deny that! No sir. What I would then be denying was my true self and my true self

was a smoker. How come I wasnay smoking? I had been

playing games with myself for six months. No having smoked for how long? Six months! Unbelievable.

Time to wise up.

Ma heid was a fucking mishmash. I had the reputation for being surly and uncommunicative. But see if ye had examined inside my nut? Ye would have found a veritable

I dont know, something.

On the other hand I could be communicative as fuck. Eftir I finished the probationary period I became Riçard's shift changeover so I rarely saw him. He was coming on duty when I was going off. It was a pity because we shared a laugh and were a pair of blethering bastards. He told me I had an honest face. He hoped I wouldnay take it the wrang way. Not at all, I says, the odd thing is that it is entirely vice a versa. I think you've got an honest face and I hope you willnay take it the wrang way.

Touché mein herr, says he.

Thanks very much, says I.

He wasnay a feller to underestimate and I preferred to think of myself in that light. One time I saw him go into action with two guys and he gied a good performance. The rest of us stood back and applauded. That was what we were encouraged to do in such circumstances. If he needed help fair enough but on that occasion he was acquitting himself readily and we were enjoying the show. He was a ju-jitsu expert and exponent of other forms of hand-to-hand combat. The two baddy guys couldnay cope. If me and him had worked the same shifts I reckon we would have swallied a beer the gether. But maybe no, on other occasions when in paranoiac mood I might have charged him with being too good to be true. Underneath the uniform he wore these crazy chequered shirts with musical emblems, plus fancy patterned boots in fawn leather, not an ill-advised choice in my opinion although ye were expecting him to don a John B then come out with some mournful dirge concerning the auld folks on the range. I says to him quietly, What's that cowboy shirt and boots all about?

I'm from West Virgiña, he whispered, it's my mountain home; my people and my people's people.

Okay, I whispered, but ye wouldnay be working in this goddam section unless ye were an alien.

It was my daddy was the alien, and his daddy before him; both were registered Blue Card carriers. No citizenship but generous allowances were made to the filial offspring.

You sure that daddy of yours wasnay a denaturalized communist fucker?

What! Riçard glanced up to the CCTV then grinned and whispered. My daddy wasnt no denaturalized communist fucker man what you talking about, he was from West Virgiña; it was his mountain home. Dont you know there aint never been no goldarn communist fuckers in this here country, no, and nor ever shall there be, sure as the lord is my saviour and I shall not want.

What about yer ma?

She was the great-granddaughter of a naturalized lady, minor French aristocracy, she hailed from a chateau in the beaujolais region and called her dogs Marcel, the whole goldarn host of them.

Wow.

She surely did.

That is so fanciful it has to be the mccoy.

Thank you.

And so we shook hands. But was he trustworthy? And what grounds did I have for thinking otherwise? I had plenty of grounds. He was a jittery bastard and generally speaking I slap the burden of proof on jittery bastards. I knew the different agencies employed at the airport reported on one another.

There were strategically-placed mics and cameras saturating the entire area, especially nearby the secured arena and where the new Halls of Retribution were scheduled for construction. What about the Blue Card stuff? I says, Ye only get one of them if ye start yer ayn wee protestant church. Not only that, I says, ye've got to hold the inaugural service on primetime television dressed in top hat and tails, with a pair of army surplus jackboots.

Yeh, whispers Riçard, but what about the men? He laughed sotto voce. What's your name?

Jeremiah Brown.

A convenient anglo-saxon disguise.

Maybe, I says, but I was born with it.

Where you really from, the Ukraine?

No sir, you are thinking of little ol Uncle Joe.

Riçard winked. You make me smile but it aint in a wholesome way. I think I know what's the matter with you Jeremiah; you got a problem with authority-figures, it's an unusual concept on this side of the world. Perhaps you got a problem with authority itself, as a thing in itself. Yeh?

I've no heard that yin before, maybe ye're right.

I think I am. He tapped himself on the chest. I got the same problem. It's you and me both. We just got different strategies for covering it up. I hide mine under layers and layers of fucking smarmy shit, sickening hypocrisy and doomed attempts to integrate whereas you dont, you are out there, you are like fucking out there.

Naw I'm no, it's all interior. When ye say sickening hypocrisy ye've got me to a tee, ye're summing it up with great exactitude, and by "it" I mean me. I am an interiorizing bastard. I may be an anathema to the great Inklo-Uhmerkin tradition that continues to build and render unto Caesar this miraculous world in all its empirical and verifiable splendour but naybody knows I'm one, I keep my anathemaness a secret. If I dont they'll send me hame. Tell me this Riçard, were you a devious wee fucker as a boy?

What you read my biography? Devious devious devious. People thought I was insane, I was Mister Devious I was Doctor Devious I was Professor fucking devious Devious I was from another planet man, why see my temper y'all, I lost control forever, them red-neck bitches man but that loss of control was a cover up, it was *the* cover up. It warnt no genuine loss of control, it was deceitful. But unfortunately being so devious and deceitful was stressful to me, it surely was; I was drained, I was exhausted, I was a no-gooder; I dropped behind in my math and English studies. How far would I have gone if all them fucking things were equal Jeremiah, equal and in my favour. If I could have channeled all my energies, that is what I am talking about, instead of this, instead of what I've become, what now I am man . . . He shook his head sadly.

Ye're no a bum, says I, looking him squarely in baith eyes with baith of mine.

No sir.

But ye might have been a multibillionaire chicken farmer.

Yes sir.

Champeen chicken farmer of the world.

Damn right, yeh.

Me too, I whispered, knee deep in poultry shite and brown-stained feathers, you in dear auld Kenya and me in le bonné Skallin.

I aint from Kenya man, I told you, I'm from West Virgiña, it's my mountain home.

Sorry.

Where you from?

I telt ye.

So how is Kiev today, is it hot on the Black Sea?

Nemas pravdu pane.

Si, ja, da!

What about yer grandpappy, was he one of the anti Mau Mau brigade?

Hey you are fucking too much man. You want to wrestle?

I dont, naw, no unless I can use my shillelagh baseball bat.

You know they have a name for it in this country, what we have, it is a recognized deficiency order. People get medication for it. That is why we sing, Georgia, Georgia the whole night through, and I aint talking about no state.

Sir, you still checking on me?

Boy you aint dull-witted, you are sharp, you are dangerous.

Well I dont take no medication, no from naybody. If there be music playing then I'll drink a glass of wine, I'll sink a beer, or if there's any uisghé then yeh, I'll imbibe, I'll smoke some weed, sure I will, I aint fussy – so go tell that to their highness the boss class, I'm an International Working Feller of the World sir and I aint fussy.

Sure you are and I shall do that little thing but Jeremiah, if that indeed be your name, so what is wrong with my country you go to such lengths of ironic savagery? You got something against this country where you have sought refuge? You dont think it is a good country that has taken you into its warm and tender bosom and will provide succour for your family and family's family? What dont you admire about it?

There aint a thing I dont admire about it so help me gahd.

Your woman is a musician?

Pardon me?

So you listen to music?

Why surely, I telt you so.

In this country?

Any country.

You listen to this country's music?

Sure.

So what do you listen to country and western music? Big band music? You dont listen to big band? What about funk music, hip hop? House or rap music? Jazz music? What about zydeco? The rock and roll? You listen to them? You aint talking Jeremiah. What kind of music do you listen to?

All sorts.

Classical European?

Naw.

Tell me. Riçard grinned and shook his head. Why dont you tell me? You dont know me well enough?

I sure dont.

You are a trainee operative. Take me into your confidence. You a moody person? Me also. You think my culture is alien from yours? You think I am a fool working here?

I work here also.

You are a pink-face Skarrisch masculine male Jeremiah you are an Aryan champeen. These superior-hierarchy Uncle Sam folks man they want you, it is you they are pointing the finger at. They dont want to deport you they want to promote you. I am your teacher and you are my trainee. Ye shall be promoted. Ye shall be taken off pooch patrol. Ye shall be a clerk in the office. Henceforth ye shall carry messages, be allowed entry to the airport terminal building and Patriot Holding Centers. Ye shall step where no non-integrated unassimilated alien has before stepped. Ye shall be a top-dog bona fide body brother they shall withdraw your Class III Red Card for Naughty Strangers and bestow unto you a Blue Card for Fascist Familiars; there shall be neither wailing nor gnashing of teeth. Jeremiah, henceforth ye shall father Uhmerkin children and be upstanding in the presence of glory. Let me shake you by the hand.

Thank you, I whispered and he did so.

What Riçard foretold might well have come to pass in a world other than the present, in circumstances differing from mine own. But the world as encountered by its present-day spirited occupants is a dark and fusty arena where fearsome shadows are encountered. We rarely know what is true.

The Security job became my life. Eleven nights a fortnight. One thinks back to these shrouded clouded times, these shrouded clouded mental times, mental mental mental times.

I should have got myself a doctor.

No sir, Miss Liu Lee was all the doctor I wantit, she was the finest healer this side of Smith Mountain.

You need real dough for doctors. Occasionally I had real dough but it was aye a stake, and ye never touch yer stake. A proper doctor would have gien me a proper check-up; the full medical works. He would examine insides, outsides, all sides, he would need a third dimension for me.

Maybe I needit counseling. Nay doubt there was an identifiable condition I was suffering and it was just naybody had telt me, no apart from Riçard. One has to go to a doctor to get telt properly; and I hadnay been near a doctor since some cunt stole my appendix. When was that fuck? years ago.

Why bother.

It is important.

Okay.

But why would the ex no even talk to me? Was that no a strange thing between a couple. No just certain topics were taboo it was every goddam topic. She hated hearing about my new job. She acted pleased on my behalf but was she? I fucking doubt it. She didnay appreciate its significance for a cunt like me. Also I think it bored her. But a partner has to put up with the boring as well as the exciting. Ye cannay just switch off and tell yer man no to talk to ye unless it be something that interests ya.

Time for a piss.

But that was how it was. Eftir my first month in the job she closed up her ears. Jobs in the Security industry joined the list of taboo subjects, following politics, religion, art, revolution, private-eye novels – naw, that isnay quite true. Sometimes I blethered onto her about my private-eye story and she enjoyed it, she enjoyed stories. She did. In the early days she smiled a certain smile when she knew I was about to begin. It was like my ayn childhood when the storyteller gathers in the weans by saying, Right yous coorie in, I'm gauny tell yez a story. And all the weans' teeth start chattering man they are so fucking excited! Yeh and Yasmin shivered.

Christ am I inventing that? Naw, I am fucking sure that lassie shivered when she knew I was about to tell her a story! It was the one thing I could do. It was how I fucking snared her man I just telt her stories, I fucking blethered on. It was just me and her that first time we met. We were crowded in the gether and the company was noisy and the music was mellow and fucking bla bla bla but she just kept smiling at me and my fucking yarns and that is the fucking entire truth so help me god, your god any god, the god of the atheists man I dont gie a fuck.

Maybe it is a male–female thing. I dont know. Or else it is just two people as close as can be when there is nay physical penetration. She lay in the classic heid on chest position. Is that no the finest position ever invented. The two of yez are lying there in bed, the wean is asleep and ye have a wee nightlight on in yer room because ye are enjoying each other's company and dont want to turn out the lights and go to sleep, no yet, so ye just lie there. Then one of yez starts gabbing, maybe something from childhood; an auld tale about aged aunties and uncles, the eccentric behaviour of yer elderly faimly members, their peculiar characteristics; these choicer items that set your faimly aside from all others.

These are fucking praise songs man!

In the time eftir the wean was born I went straight to her apartment at the end of the nightshift. Once she was fit again she resumed her late-morning cleaning job and sometimes I watched the baby. Usually her sister-in-law did so; she had three of her ayn. But I enjoyed watching the baby, I was good at watching the baby. I was good at feeding her and changing her and so on. And I liked the time it gied me just to think, just to actually fucking think about things. And the wean enjoyed her time with me. There is nay question about that, no matter what the ex might have said. Ach she wouldnay have said anything. She never said anything. She stopped fucking talking to me. I went down to see her no long ago. She wouldnay talk to me then either. Nine hours there and nine hours back. She wouldnay speak. Christ. I saw my daughter, I was with her for the eftirnoon. She had this wee nonsense thing about saying jokes and then she would yell: Only kidding! and laugh the house down.

Only kidding!

All weans are beautiful.

Time to visit the men's room. But I couldnay visit the men's room. No until Sally brought me my beer. And for some reason, for some reason. Yes sir, no doubt about it, she truly had forgotten this handsome-looking body with the interesting accent. And if I didnay have a drink to leave behind on the table then it probably wouldnay be my table when I came back from the dang men's room, a crowd of jazz-loving strangers would have moseyed their way in.

My trusty anorak was draped ower the back of a chair, pockets gaping to tempt even the godliest of passers-by. Hardly an exercise in personal security although my passport and maist other official stuff were planked in the safe back at the motel. And maist of my money, I had shoved that into the safe as well. And it wasnay because I couldnay trust myself no to find a money-game at pool, or even a wee hand of poker. Naw, it was in case I got robbed, or it fell out my fucking pocket. Okay, I was being cautious. The ex had accused me of a lack of said quality in the past and she was right, I erred on the side of foolhardy magnanimity. Without the fucking money there would be nayn of that nonsense, I would be a niggardly besom, the soul of parsimony. Fuck you and yer fucking generosity son, that would be me.

Okay, re the anorak and visiting the cludgé: were I to don this outer anorakical garment for Security purposes then customers would suppose I was exiting. They would see an almost empty beer bottle and presume the table had fallen vacant, that they were at liberty to seat themselves around said furnichoor.

What a quandary!

It wasnay an emergency but so why all the panic? Because things enter my napper and become affixed.

That auld anorak was a good piece of clothing and I didnay want to lose it. Where the hell had I purchased the damn thing. It wasnay a faimly heirloom. I hadnay brought it with me from the auld country, a relic of bygone etceteras; as far as I knew it hadnay been worn by le bonné Prance de Charlee when he crossed ower the sea from Skye in 1745 to route the anglo-armies. Naw, there was nay story attached to it. But there fucking should have been. And I was the boy to write the bastard. For a start, how do we know he rowed the boat himself, it was probably the young servant lassie who did it, what do ye call her? Flora MacDonald; Charlie was a fucking monarcquik lazy cunt man he would have needit a servant to do the physical work. So how come wee Flora didnay scupper the boat and swim ashore, leave the lazy fucking arsehole to drown in his tartan hose. Unless, of course

But the goddam notebook!

What chance did I have of writing a single solitary word if I forgot to carry my notebook? Maybe I could borrow a piece of paper from the lassie behind the bar, just to write down "anorak", just that one word. I would remember what it signified, that there was a tight wee swashbuckling adventure story linked to it that would make an obvious motion picture. Maybe I could make something out of it for the private eye. Private eyes dont wear anoraks. Christ, mine would. Maybe that was the missing link, the key into the hero's psyche. He wasnay so much a hero as a kind of realistic, morally-sound young feller, a bit auld fashioned insofar as he hates seeing bullies terrorizing the weak and then getting away with it, getting lauded for it, getting praised and prized by society. That makes him sick. He hates that kind of shite, lopsided social values, outright hypocrisy. It makes him sick. But he isnay self-righteous about it, he

Heh wait a fucking minute! That big pentagon feller at the bar was glancing in my direction. Not only that, he was pointing me out to what appeared to be an acquaintance, a bruiser, a trucker, plaid shirt and five bellies. One could only smile. Their attention returned to the gantry and the mirror mirror on the wall where they could observe me at leisure.

Christ almighty when did one get to relax in this country.

Never ma boy never.

This was no unusual scenario, no for folks in my situation. Suddenly there is a body staring at ye. Nay wonder we get parafuckingthingy, whatever ye call it. Maybe I had spoken aloud. Occasionally I did. It used to happen when I was at a gig with the ex. I met such fucking fools but, what else could ye do except talk to yerself. And in public, ye talk to yerself in public.

Nay big deal.

To hell with bursting bladders. I lifted the exbottle of beer and pretended to sip it. No for long but. I placed the bottle into a likely spot on the table, edged the chair holding my anorak into a likely position on the floor, nonchalantly raised maself to ma feet and started walking, making a hesitatory play of looking for the men's room sign so that eagle-eyed spies wouldnay miss that I wasnay exiting, that I was off on a routine urinatory assignment. The pentagon immigration guy would have detailed my every movement. It is likely that he followed me from the Shooters and Horses. These bodies could be so obvious ye wondered if it was intentional.

I paused at the bar and managed to resist gieing him a wink. He would be using one of those micro-mindatexts that fitted behind the eyelid and made a word transcription of yer thoughts. His contact was Barney the crossword guy, him with the soft spot for the mafia.

Yet there was something familiar about the big guy and his trucker pardner. Maybe they came from Arizona. Real life may resemble reality.

Real life is reality.

No necessarily. It is a debatable point.

Naw it isnay. Real life has to be reality, what the hell else could it be! Even if it is a fucking nightmare, it is still reality.

Ma brains is twisted sir. And nay wonder: Sally had reappeared and was standing at the far end of the room with arms folded, and her right hip thrust a little to the side, her left leg concealed beneath the slinky long skirt and certainly bent slightly at the knee because hers was that classic pose of a woman at hame in her body.

She was, she surely was. Now she fiddled with a thin chain round her neck and my god touched it to her lips. Two of the musicians were there and chatting with the manager; the scabby arsehole who nay doubt owned the bar and who nay doubt had inherited it from his father and had never done a proper day's work in his entire miserable silver-spoon existence. Which is why presumptuous pricks like him think they can score with every lassie with the bad luck to enter their employ. But he wasnay fooling Sally, she wasnay paying attention to him, she was just standing there kidding on she was. Then he seemed to nod to her. Then she turned and looked towards me, as I moved on towards the men's room. She didnay notice it was me until I smiled and gied her a sort of wave, while pushing open the door.

Christ she would think me a total fool.

The men's room was along another corridor. And it was fucking freezing! Snell winds were blawing down the goddam corridors man icicles, icicles; stalactites off the ceiling. The place was full of these corridors man it was like one of these auld-fashioned hotels or else these tunnel networks ye find deep in the very bowels of the earth. My god and the smell of cooking! coming from somewhere. I could have done with a big fucking plate of barbequed chicken legs, with good salsa, hot salsa, piping hot salsa man fucking habañero fucking salsa, and a wee bit of guacamolé señor, gracias, christ! Food. There aint nothing like food. Food is fucking incredeebleh! So is drink right enough. But food and drink are complementary, one need not choose between the two. Many have made the error, few have survived to tell the tale. Because they have nay fucking notebooks man they always forget their fucking notebooks.

Och aye one has to sigh.

There was nay automatic haun-drier in el cludgero. One had to purloin the toilet paper for said purpose. And what can one say about Uhmerkin toilet paper that hasnay been said elsewhere. But is it no a joke? a total joke: one look and it is rent asunder, they just dont know how to manufacture the goddam stuff. One wipes one's hands down one's trousers. It is a problem but, when ye cannay dry them and ye come out and ye meet some cunt ye know and yer hauns are soaking wet. What you been up to? dipping them in the toilet bowl? You got some perverted sexual thing going on there? So ye have to attempt the polite thing, and at the same time do yer best to avoid the friendly handshake. It aye ends in embarrassment.

Never mind. I came back into the bar and scabby prick the manager was lurking behind the door. I was sniffing. Cauld through there, I says. He nodded like he hadnay understood my accent. I returned the nod.

Hey, he says with suspicious bonhomie. Hey, he says. So you from Skallin?

Yeh.

He smiled, nodded slowly. You got your ID there? He gestured sideways to the blue-bordered federal notice. The pentagon fucker and the plaid-shirt trucker were staring at me quite blatantly.

I was the cabaret.

Down at the other end the musicians were watching, so-called musicians. Ah but it was aye interesting to see some poor refugee cunt getting dug up by a fascist bastard who wore the same uniform as yerself. How could ye be a genuine musician and watch such fucking shite, why did they no emigrate back in time to the Third fucking Reich.

Of course Sally was also watching. I didnay look at her because she wasnay in my line of vision. I just shrugged. What was there to do? Scabby prick was waiting. Sure he was. The main thing was to drop my britches and have a crap on his fucking floor. But instead I smiled boy I smiled, yesm and curtsied sir I surely did because I was feeling sooo good right there. Boy did I smile: sure I smiled, and I raised my goddam hauns in the surrender gesture, pointed along at my anorak although it should have been my fucking dick man suck on that a while. My coat, I says, the ID's in my coat, and I continued walking back to my table without waiting for an answer, allowing my hands to lower slowly as I walked. This manager bastard would have had me covered all the way. Guys like him ask questions later.

And fuck you anyway ha ha ha, the ID was on my person at that very moment.

The ID was inside my wallet and my wallet was inside the right pocket of my jeans. It wasnay in my anorak at all. I was telling lies, lies.

When he asked for it I could have handed him it there and then, I could have taken it out my pocket, I could have gien him it right at that moment, I could have done what I was telt.

So I was making life awkward for him. One of these days he would drop deid with a heart attack and I would have contributed to it. If I didnay drop deid myself.

My heart was pounding and I was taking these fighter-breaths; breaths ye take during a pause in a fight, no gulps, but making use of yer nostrils, aware of yer lungs, and focusing man focusing. And that wasnay bad that was not bad, no sir it warnt bad at all.

When I reached my table I kept side on to him, manoeuvring the wallet out from my jeans' pocket and when I reached to the anorak and stuck my left haun into the side pocket I pretended to draw the wallet out from there, instead slipping it from my right into my left sir, allez fucking oop sir, the Great Gusto rides again.

Why?

Because it let *me* see I didnay gie a fuck man, neither for them nor whatever, their Security my Security any fucking bastard's Security; this is war. As far as him and Sally and the big pentagon prick at the bar knew I had left my ID documents and stuff right there in the anorak when I went for a piss, that I had been so fully at ease in the place that it hadnay even occurred to me to worry about personal Security. Fuck you bastards, dirty fascist fuckers, that was what it also telt them, I hope. I returned to the bar and passed him the documentation. The shotguns were out of sight. Oh, says he, you got a Red Card?

Aye, says I, surprised?

He smiled, took it from me and studied it. He nodded, pursing his lips.

So ye interested in politics? I says.

He looked at me.

Politics is an interesting subject. I know quite a few jokes about politics.

You do?

Yeh.

He smiled to me and returned my ID. Nothing poisonal.

Sure, that's the motto.

Pardon me?

I smiled to him, me no unnastand you kind sir, begging pahdon of evbiddy. Then I turned to the big guy on the barstool while replacing the ID in my wallet, shoving it into my right hip pocket. How are ye? I said.

Yeh, he said.

Great, I said.

You bet, he said.

I turned to scabby prick: Hey sir, could I have a beer?

Sure can.

Great.

I'll bring it to ya.

That's okay, I'll take it masel.

He smiled. I waited while he reached for it. I nodded to the big guy's five bellies trucker pardner. Kind of cauld tonight, I said, eh?

He didnay respond. The manager placed the beer in front of me.

I'm running a tab, I said.

Yeh, he said.

I smiled sweetly and returned to the table, easing myself onto my seat in a smooth continuous movement so that in turning I would witness whatever situation was extant in the most natural manner.

But it made one smile. Did they no know it was always goddam poisonal. Did they no know that was precisely what it was, what it all was, them and their fucking armoury man, so why did they continue to lie and fuck knows what dissembling hypocritical bastarn

Ohhh yehhh

Never mind.

One simply sighs.

Nay blocked arteries the day.

I believe the good lord made me with two hearts, the extra one I keep in my mouth. And two souls also, the second one I keep in my socks.

At least the music was strong. I had a swig of the beer and gazed at the faces.

My back wasnay to a wall. Who was that cowboy again? Wild Bill Hickock; he used to sit with his back to the wall but the bastards still got him, they still shot the guy, filled him full of holes. The ace of spades had something to do with it.

Ah well. And I could smell the smell of fresh cigarette smoke, somebody had lit a new yin. Mighty fine. With a nice kind of blues playing, blues, blues, blues, blues – blues, blues, blues, blues.

So, okay.

Where was Sally? And during all the shite, no doubt she

went to the kitchen, couldnay bear it. Well, she didnay have my sympathy.

Strange but, it was utter arseholes like mister scabby prick the manager that sent folk back to smoking. Ye wound up getting change for the cigarette machine and buying a pack because of a total arsehole. Hey mister backlash, Immigration Issues Can Damage Yer Health.

But no me, I gied it up six months ago. And contented myself with an inward smile lord I would be rising to no bait, no today and no tomorrow, at which time I would be pie in the sky, flying away ower the ocean and away from this fucking place; leave them to their wallowing piggery practices, I was gaun hame to see ma mammy. I needed to get hame. I needed to get out of this place otherwise I would get fucking killed. These fuckers would drive a body insane. But here came Sally with another beer for me, with another beer for me.

She laid said beer on the table. Was this a joke? No sir. She smiled. But I didnay. I said, Thanks. She saw the two bottles I had already and reached for them. I indicated the empty yin, and then I smiled. I did smile. I liked her. I thought there was a hesitancy in her when she lifted it but maybe no. One relaxes into sentimentality, especially with women. I watched her walk away, stopping off at another table, collecting empties, changing an ashtray. It wasnay anger I felt.

But it had been anger. Now it had left my system. By the time Sally had come it was contempt I was feeling. And maybe she saw that in me and took it to herself. And she would have to take it to herself man she warnt no goddam hypocrite.

Scabby prick had returned to the musicians.

Okay this wasnay déjà vu but it was reminiscent of a few situations I had been in with the ex, especially in the early days when I went to every gig. I tried to get to maist of her sessions. Unfortunate was I that the inclination to lose one's temper remained constant. One's temper is a fragile entity. On occasion one may lose it inexplicably. It got too stressful. No for me so much as her. I could get it out my system but sometimes she was performing and spotted me in a corner with some dickhead arsehole bastard and she would worry about fights breaking out.

Ach but tonight I was pleased with myself. I hadnay succumbed. I took it off them. I did as I was telt. I gied them what they asked. I kowtowed. Then I grinned. And I fixed that grin. I was fine, relaxed. I was so damn fine and so damn fucking relaxed I could have took out my fucking tongue man and licked the cunt's upper lip and nostrils, I could have performed cunnilingus on the guy, I would have pleased him, I would have made a woman out of him. Yeh massa, here's the ID massa, thanks for asking massa. Let me bow let me scrape, you ees uhmereeekaan ameego, you ees meester heroeec figyoor, you ees meester cool meester magneefeecohh.

Come on, I handled it okay, I was entitled to be pleased with myself. Or was I? Maybe I wasnay. Maybe I hadnay handled it fine at all.

I had acted badly towards Sally. High and mighty, a self-righteous bastard. It wasnay her fault she worked for an arsehole.

But was he an arsehole? Maybe he wasnay. Maybe he was just – who knows, who knows.

I lifted the bottle, swigged a mouthful, smiled at the table. Everybody got the benefit of the doubt from me. Becoming a Security agent had helped in my struggle with spleneticism. Prior to getting the Security job I think I was losing the fight altogether. At the airport one developed the passive reproach. Yes sir, yes sir, yes sir. I dont think ye should park there sir, no sir. Or maam. Ye have yer raffle ticket there maam? That I might confirm ye have a seat wager on this afternoon's flight maam? Thank ye maam thank ye. Why sir just push yer cart on down by the mean ol concentration camp and them outer carparks sir you head for that nice ol terminal main building and take a left there, straight on past the shuttered occupation area, and you have a nice day also sir ees good for you sir meester señor, hvala.

They prohibited the grocery-cart pushers from the airport terminals. Why did they do that? They had to. And the other down-and-out bodies, they prohibited them as well. It was policy no to call them hobos or ramblers which was regarded as too positive. Before the prohibition they wandered the public areas and reception halls, the terminal diners, bars and bookjoints where they stood for hours staring at magazines and customers which I could understand; sometimes I had difficulty distinguishing between the two myself.

Panhandling was always proscribed and if any of them tried that they could be ejected by rights and without preamble. It happened, but no that often. There were charity points throughout the terminal and if they were caught they were frogmarched there and had to empty their pockets. Others were abject figures who would kiss yer arse for a drag of yer cigarette. A few were as arrogant as anybody. Or stubborn. They were all fucking stubborn. But all people are stubborn.

Even so the use of physical force by Security operatives was frowned upon. The consequences were unpredictable. Nor was the approach from theory to be encouraged. Individual operatives tried to bluff it but too often the down-and-out folks proved expert on the Constitution and caused much embarrassment in front of airline staff and the traveling classes.

It was a mess, the whole thing. These werenay illegal people. They werenay immigrants and they werenay refugees. They didnay carry nay colour-coded ID cards either. No sir. These were true-born Uhmerkin citizens, albeit unusual yins.

Some of these unusual true-born citizens rode their luck by trying to board planes without a ticket. Maist held lottery tickets or raffle tickets in the air gieing them a shake at the cabin crew like next time it would be them flying out. One guy used to stand there shouting: Jumbo jet, jumbo jet, jumbo jet!

Ye would spot bodies hanging about the Security checks, trying to shove their belongings through the xray machines at passport control. When they were caught their grocery carts were confiscated and they were dumped onto us. A three-man Security crew collected them in batches and drove them out of town. The instructions were to drive them south, no less than a hundred miles distant. Yet some of these folks returned, and kept on returning.

In themselves the grocery carts were suspect receptacles. We had to check through individual goods and chattels, much of which wasnay too wholesome. Some was beyond redemption; brown or yellow-stained clothing rags stuffed inside poly-bags; bundles of auld newspapers, and soiled paper goods like cups and plates. Security staff wondered if it was some new advertising stunt where bona fide tickets were exchanged for certain categories of garbage. I found a few interesting auld paperback books, medical dictionaries; a couple from a White House sponsored self-help welfare series with titles like *Spot the Symptom, Healthcare for the Hermit, Bidding Maladjustment Goodbye.* It struck me as an idea that we could turn one of the spare office cupboards into a wee lending library, just as a kind of public service.

People carried jars and bottles that werenay quite empty; a few had acquired quantities of empty plastic containers and aerosol canisters; squeezed toothpaste tubes were popular with some bodies. On one lanky big feller I found a large quantity of them and when I says something he gied me a very mean look. I cannay remember what I said and I hadnay intended it as sarcasm. For christ sake the guy looked like James Stewart man I wasnay gauny insult him. Honest.

The problem remained: how to deal with these unusual true-borns. A correct procedure had to be resolved. Airports were designed as down-and-out-free zones. These people were not even content with the ordinary public areas but were continually discovered in the plush leather lounges of the VIP executive suites. How embarrassing for leading financiers and pentagon bodies, having to conduct business with their VIP overseas visitors and discovering some cunt snoring beneath yer walnut dining table. Some found it disgraceful that the dregs of society were flaunting themselves publicly. The legal team entered discussions with the politicians to discover or create a ruling based on the nature of patriotism, whether it might be deemed unlawful to bring shame on the Uhmerkin people. Surely the "flaunting of one's poverty in public" by tiny minorities caused undue suffering and stress to the vast majority of folks who didnay *have* poverty, and was not only socially unacceptable but a breach of their civil rights?

During the time of the "persian bet" airline companies kept a limited number of lower-end one-way tickets for publicity purposes. Media folk bought these and disposed of them to make filler news items. Raffles and races were common, different stunts and competitions. The weird, wonderful and loathsome were filmed and photographed. Before the start of competitions me and my Security compañeros had to sort through the belongings of the entrants. But with the media involved it appeared like we were employed by them and were part of the stunt. This irritated the agency bosses because we werenay earning money by it. They compromised by selling advertising space on the uniforms. I had four logos pinned there like I was a racing driver. These things had to be accepted although some of the compañeros objected. I have to confess that I couldnay be fucking bothered getting annoyed. As though somehow that was the only exploitation we had to contend with.

For us non-naturalized Security operatives the media were aye a danger. We were at risk each and every occasion wur faces were revealed in newspaper or televisual image. I aint talking here about these upstanding far-right cowardly murdering bastards taking pot-shots at defenceless immigrants whose photograph they saw in a newspaper. No sir. Sections of wur Security industry comrades were employed purely "to patrol" the media and nayn of us expected demonstrations of solidarity. Part of the remit of wur brother agency operatives was to scour media organs not only for the alien or terrorist threat but on behalf of debt-collection agencies and them yins that deal with marital and other domestic conflicts.

In spite of increased Security operations sections of the airport were crowded and down-and-out folks often gathered at the arrivals lounge. Every day of the week there was hustle and bustle with new bodies coming in off planes. It was joyous to see all the waiting relatives, the tearful reunions and screams of joy at the safe return of full-bodied survivors. Some of these true-borns joined in the faimly occasions. They pushed their grocery carts alongside travelers and their luggage carts. Foreign tourists or business travelers would be courteous to them and occasionally mistook them for a gimmicky but official PR welcome party.

It was uncommon to hear tales of theft or robbery but there is nay point pretending it didnay happen although it wasnay as much of a problem as the airport legal teams said. They sought excuses wherever whenever. That was the nature of their jobs. Nevertheless, ye heard tales of tourists who discovered they were pushing grocery carts full of minging polybag parcels instead of pushcarts with expensive leather luggage. Somebody had pulled a switch on them. We watched for inauthentic individuals, tricksters who adopted a disheveled appearance and were up to nay good. Ye learned to spot them. There wasnay that much considered theft, no from legitimate down-and-out bodies. Twice there was some cunt stole my sand-wiches but I suspected a comrade operative by the name of Billy Zannu. Me and him didnay get along too well. I dont think he even ate my sandwiches, probably he fed them to the ducks out by the wee decorative lagoon.

Everything was a learning experience. Having a wean was a learning experience. We hear this sentimental nonsense about how weans have heightened intuitive powers. I dont believe it, that to me is fucking hogwash. Eftir the wee yin was born I didnay notice any superhuman qualities, she was just a wee lassie with big eyes and extra long lashes: amazing things, ye could have swept the flair with them. In the early photographs ye can see them quite clearly.

But it is true that when a relationship breaks up it is never any good because ye have the weans then ye have the parents, the ones that dont get to see the weans except on visits, fucking visits, oh aye, yawn yawn yawn, visits.

Bitterness Kills.

Yeh, but with a dog there is nay need for bitterness. Animals dont go through that sort of shite. Eftir a certain period in the Security job ye were gien a rota dog and every so often ye went on pooch patrol as we called it. Ye kept the same dogs for a while. Mine was a good ol boy kind of mongrel beast, near retiral age and no what ye would call a looker. It had an enormous heid. Its gub gaped so widely its cranium was at risk when it barked. I called it Buster although its registered name was Latin for Loyal to Jesus, *Fidelium ad Dominae Jesú* or something, I am guessing. I patted behind its ears and stroked its upper neck in the learned procedure, based upon no going against the grain lest it became disgruntled. Strangers werenay allowed to pat the guard dogs because they would get their haun bitten off. Us operatives had to watch out for pet-loving down-and-out folks who wished to curry favour and had set out to win the affections of wur canine craturs.

Maist of us thought pooch patrol was a good side of the job because it gied yer sentry stroll a side purpose. Me included. Except later on I stopped getting that work and was "promoted" for dispatches and messages. I was telt I had been earmarked for this but it followed a stupit wee misunderstanding I had with Sharifa, another operative. She was a wee bit aulder than me, no much. There was something about her I thought was courageous, quite courageous, so I respected her. What was wrang with that? Plus the way she handled dogs. That was where she excelled. She specialized in the kennel section and in her spare time helped out at a charitable concern for infirm rottweilers so that when they retired from active service they could finish their days in decent retirement. This is similar to what they do for senior-citizen greyhounds – the original four-legged friends, especially if ye are a fucking bookie.

But rottweilers were her favourite. According to her they were an under-rated beast. She named her special favourite Queenie. She assumed I would approve. I tried explaining the links between anti-monarquizm and republicanism and how for me it wasnay a tendency and it wasnay a label for certain managerial strategies, it was the very air I breathed. Sharifa belonged to a church whose beliefs included the one that humanity and all the various animal, insect and fish species have two lives per being and sometimes mair. Wow, says I.

I dont care for sarcasm nor ironic savagery, she says, but it dont bother me if you use it.

I wasnay being sarcastic, nor ironically savage, whether to you or yer church.

I guess you were, she says and gied me a smile.

She had one of these knowing smiles that can lead to misunderstandings, I am talking male to female. It also led guys into confessional mode. When she accused me of sarcasm I just went, Yeh, and I apologized. But a moment later I says, Usually I find religious people a source of irritation, particularly them that are into pretend religions and carry the occasional placard. They are nuisances who bring out the worst in people like me. I apologize though because you arenay like that.

She shook her head but didnay smile this time. Maybe she thought to have recognized a soul bereft of spiritual upliftedness, a heart heavy with the burdens of subliminally suppressed joy. Maybe she would see me as a caring-project.

Sharifa was from the south and had transferred here on a temporary basis to broaden her experience. Airport security was a growth area down there. The coastal region south of Marsh Island and on eastwards into swampland territory was now vying with the Bermuda Triangle as a tourist trap. Salty dawgs spoke of time getting *trapped*.

She had these beautiful looks ye get in people from that part of the country. One night I saw her in ordinary clothes and she was wearing some slinky diaphanous thing masquerading as a skirt. What an outfit! And a beautiful pair of upper damn thingwi tits man breasts, quite startlingly beautiful. Ye got the urge to take her in yer arms and charge her Cajun style across the floor.

According to reports in different parts of the south authorities cut running costs boldly. Air crews paid their ayn overnight accommodation and not only brought sandwiches, tea bags and coffee to work but their ayn electric kettles. Even so, they werenay allowed to make air-travel customers a hot drink as a sideline earner. In one southern town – I think in Louisiana – they used a local racetrack for emergency landings; they conscripted the back straight. Nearby the stables lived a hospitable auld couple in a lil ol 19th-century dilapidated structure. Whenever a plane made a successful crash-landing they turned their house into a soup kitchen for unlucky survivors. During the time of the "persian bet" they were revered throughout the south. Friends of Sharifa's faimly knew the hospitable auld couple. But I picked up a cautionary note in the way she telt me about them. I realized it was because they werenay bible thumpers. From the way she was talking they sounded mair like kindly and sensitive libertarian socialists, bodies ye could have a laugh with and an exciting conversation, play a haun of kaluki or sup a homebrew beer ower a game of "friendly" pool, where nay money was exchanged and everybody was content just to twang their harps and chaw corn on the cob. Apparently they knew the great Boozoo Chavis, that selfsame elderly couple.

But it was a double-edged sword being assigned Sharifa as a pooch-patrol comrade. She was one of these women men have difficulty walking beside. Except for loose-fitting trousers where would we be? I foolishly raised this subject with the ex. I thought it a regular gender insight. The two of us were lying in bed. We hadnay spoken for ten minutes. I began chuckling. She asked me what I was thinking and like a fucking dick I telt her.

Silence.

And I filled the silence! How naive. But I was aye experiencing the exact same thing with her, with Yasmin, christ, that was why I was chuckling! It wasnay like a macho boast. I was being open about my sexuality and how us males sometimes got a hardon walking down the street and how it made yer walking awkward. And if it wasnay such an ordinary occurrence when I was out with her I would never have raised the goddam topic. I wasnay making a big deal out of it. It was just a basic factor in masculinity. It had nothing to do with anything, nothing at all to do with "that other woman" for christ sake I could have raised it in connection with any number of lassies; there was nay "that other woman". The fact that I raised it in connection to Sharifa was foolish and I could see that, even later on and I am talking days later, it was very very foolish because with me and the ex, we werenay having any sex, because the wee wean was just born for christ sake it was one of these times it was out the question. But I knew it was out the question and it wasnay bothering me at all christ almighty I had lived as a single guy for fucking years.

Because that arousal took place it didnay mean males had an unquenchable lust for particular individuals or that I had had any particular lust for Sharifa, no for her no for naybody, not at all, it just didnay enter into it.

It didnay. It was hard to explain. Guys would know what I was talking about.

It wasnay that she was jealous

Aye she was, she was jealous.

It was me who should have been jealous: her out there singing to all these so-called male audience members. As soon as she was able to she resumed performing. I didnay think she should have returned so quickly. Her cousin agreed with me. But the ex did what she did. The money was important, it wasnay great but to her it was crucial.

I didnay get jealous in the way she thought. But I did get annoyed and it was the hypocrisy, it was the hypocrisy. That was nothing to do with her. It was the audience, some of them; and the rest of that wee isolated world, the musicians and them and okay it especially was the males. It was leering. That was what they did. I had to sit beside these bastards. It was my girlfriend up there singing. That includes these money-grabbing gangsters that hung on her coat-tails, these bastards. Even when she was pregnant and ye could see it quite distinctly. Naybody else seemed to. What did they just think she was fucking fat! Christ. And I had to sit there. Even later on and she was able to go back performing; it was rare for me to get to a gig then but when I did I still had to sit there, no matter what and it was like did anybody even realize she was an actual mother? Would it have made any difference to the bastards? I dont fucking think so. She said I didnay have to go. Of course I didnay have to go. She told me often enough to stay away, take her there and meet her there or just see her back in the apartment, but no at the gig, do not come to the fucking gig. She could not understand why I got so annoyed.

Okay.

Angry.

Naw angry isnay the word. Just sometimes I didnay know where my heid was.

But it was just about impossible to say good words about any lassie without her getting the wrang idea.

I admired Sharifa. The way she had come up north to seek her fortune. Okay, she was transferred by the agency but it still took guts to leave her hame.

Ye were never quite sure with women, whether ye were picking up the correct signals or involved in wishful thinking. I put it down to elderly parents and me being a late child. Even belly buttons were a mystery. One of the first lassies I slept with regularly I asked to keep the light on so I could study her body. I poked into her belly-button with my pinkie. It made me smile but she got nauseous.

This male–female unpredictability extended to the canine world. It was funny to see the dog I knew as Buster steering clear of Queenie. Males were liable to get their snout bit off if they got too close. I had a precipitate insight and broached it with Sharifa. What if female agents got male dogs and male agents got female dogs; then we might gain insights into the mysteries and habits of the opposite sex, the mysterious gender, the never-to-be-known gender. What if each pair of guard-duty operatives had a male canine and a female canine but these were mixed so that the male had the female and the female the male. Then the relationships could be observed, how the male human interacted with the female canine, the female human with the male canine, and it would surely be of value to us.

Also there was the weird albeit relevant nugget of infor-mation I overheard during one of these disjointed conver-sations we had on the bus hame eftir a shift: somebody was saying how the kennel operatives got loyalty from their dogs by paying what was called "sensitive attention to the genitalia". It was the kind of comment ye hear when ye arenay taking part in a conversation although ye are present during it, and ye wonder if ye have been dreaming or has somebody just flung it in to check if ye were asleep. I raised the information with Sharifa but no sooner had I begun than she drew me such a crakkerjack of a look that I thought oh fuck naw man this lady will chew ye up and fucking spit ye out. That became like a major misunderstanding between us and although it was never corroborated I believe she spoke about me to a couple of her female pals.

She was in her early thirties and no into younger men. So she telt me. But why tell me? People wouldnay say a word unless something tweaked inside their brain. Maybe I had gien off a scent near the end of a shift. If I was heading across to Yasmin's place the erective twinges were never far away, even towards the end of her pregnancy. In this life there are aye misunderstandings. That is another name for life, the Great

Misunderstanding. Of course sex strayed into my heid, who would deny that. As in any job these long shifts were tedious in the extreme, and it was left to yer brains to provide solace. Idle thoughts; these wee cupboards and back lobbies on every carpark level, the wee offices in the early hours: it wasnay difficult to construct a fantasy.

I was starting to get mair office and dispatch work some of which took me to the front gates at the Patriot Holding Center and into the airport terminal itself. I was glad of the work, anything to break the monotony. The Security staff inside these places aye seemed to have plenty of stuff on the go. There were frequent "scares" and "incidents". Us in the Alien Section never had that. There were nay incidents with dangerous desperados in the time I was there. I saw a few interesting things but mainly it was teenage car thieves, vandalism, feuding down-and-outs, occasional drug abuses, sexual hanky-panky. There was also suspicious behaviour by Security operatives from other agencies, some unknown to me, plainclothed or uniformed. There was nay point in getting upset. Some were high-powered bodies and ye would wonder which personages were passing through the airport. The human traffic in and out the Patriot Holding Centers was by armoured bus and we had nay dealings there apart from package delivery in or out.

The job itself was boring. When I was gien attendant duty on the inside office I could never work out if it was one rung up the promotional ladder, or one rung down. Ye sat there staring out a window at the front office and that front office was usually empty. I tried to read. Other times I thought about my ayn story and took notes with pencil and paper, but I found my fingers got sair quite easily. Maybe because I was so used to tapping letters out on a keyboard. Every ten minutes I rushed out for a smoke. I could reach a state of fatigue that bypassed debilitating exhaustion and left me on an unhealthy mental overdrive: I stopped leaving the inner office aw the gether and by the last of the six 12-hour shifts I was having to bind up my fingers to stop myself dialing freefone numbers at random. Who knows where my heid was. I think I was hoping to fluke my way onto a premium sexline by some techno-telekinetic marvel. The upper strata wouldnay have bothered. That *Pro-World Psychologies* journal was subscribed to by the agency, it ran a series of articles related to the proposition that succumbing to the seedier pursuits might be crucial for the stability of "the typically exploited labor force".

Part of the section's remit around the outer carpark areas was to sort out awkward situations before they reached the terminal building. Wee fires were a common hazard. Maist of the down-and-outs' possessions were combustible and some poor bastard's cart routinely exploded into flames. It wasnay too surprising. Besides their goods and chattels a couple of bodies collected auld raffle tickets, auld lottery tickets and auld scratch cards; masses upon masses of them.

Many of these folks had nay next of kin. They were leaving their worldly effects to each other, including all kinds of betting receipts.

But these auld raffle tickets were useless now they were "used", although they at least bore a relationship to the "persian bet". People had originally bought them to enter the draw for a seat on one of the lower-end airplanes, hoping to win an honorable exit from this vale of woes, or a fair return on a lost-limb wager. But used lottery tickets or scratch cards! They had fuck all to do with it. No even in the first place. So they were worse than useless. So how come they were being saved, unless it was just another neurosis.

Then we discovered some of the unusual true-born bodies had devised new forms of wagering. Me and a comrade were on pooch patrol one evening and turned a corner, spotted a group rummaging through a couple of carts piled high with them auld fucking tickets. We stepped back and kept the dogs quiet, watched from behind a wall, waiting for the right moment to step out.

Yes sir, these folks were trying to find a winner. But how would they know a winner if they found one? Ye dont get raffle tickets or betting receipts with the words "this is the winner" written on it, no unless it is a lie. Perhaps they were keeping note of the numbers of past winning tickets and were checking them all in the off chance somebody had ditched a winner by mistake. That soundit reasonable but with too big a reliance on faith. No that I had anything against "faith".

The rummaging continued. Then a feller leapt up punching the air, a ticket held aloft. A few examined it. A couple of them clapped their hauns and gied him a slap on the back. Yeh, the feller was a winner. Others shook their heids and went away, gieing the feller dirty looks. So it was true. Where there is a winner there is a loser. Some handle it and some dont; people are generous or they is mean boy they is mean. I could be generous, but I could be a miserable grudging sonofagun shite man, a disgrace not only to god's earth but the rest of the cosmos and the myriad almighties thereof.

We kept watching. In went the folks again. Now I saw they were running their ayn competitions. In one they were anteing up 50 cents a heid and were each gien certain numbers, and the first to get his or hers in sequence lifted the pot. There was a lot of laughter and backslapping, suppressed yells. I saw also how they might have moved the game on from there and ran it akin to craps, with various betting taking place on the margins. I felt like having a go myself, if just for the craïc. But it was impossible. As soon as somebody in uniform appeared the unusual true-borns disappeared into cracks in the concrete. Well, no quite. I did get on nodding terms with a couple of bodies and gied the occasional nod to individuals. It wasnay encouraged but and we were gien to understand that the bosses didnay approve of hobnobbing.

So what was supposed to happen when ye bumped into an auld acquaintance?

And ye would. Check out the feller with the soles flapping, the one bumming a smoke, the one raking through the garbage, the one comatose in the corner; maybe the last time ye saw him was face to face in a no-limit game and now here was he on the lower reaches of the downward spiral. Stories abounded of bearded scarecrows who turned out to be former dandies of the baize, still dreaming of putting a stake the gether, redeeming the silver plate and jewelry, calling up the ex to say hullo, how are the faimly, how y'all keeping, then the triumphant return to Binions, a late entry to the World Championships.

Auld habits are auld habits. Many of us in the Alien and Alien-Extraction Section enjoyed a wager. Off duty there was a group met for card nights. I never got involved in it properly. The two times I went it was fine, I won a few dollars, but the invitation wasnay repeated. Naybody said nothing but I knew they still played. I was just off the list. Ah well man it was up to them. I assumed it was my fault for winning. Then I thought naw, it was fucking stupit nonsense to do with me being who I was. I wouldnay have wasted my time challenging it. Except it was irritating. Why did they no open their minds to the wider world. It wasnay my fault I was the only pink furnir fucker in the section. If ye wantit another ye had to go to management level or take a walk inside the terminal buildings. There were hundreds of the fuckers in there, either true-borns or with an appropriate status, integratit, assimilatit, whatever man, something that wasnay fucking Class III Red Card.

Who cares. I didnay want to be one of these cunts anyway,

even if they offered me. I was happy with my status. Imagine being related to der pinker WASP königin ingilander and her barrel-load of kowtowing arselicking subject cunts. No sir, Ah am a republican, vive la république! Ah am a socialiste, vive le socialiste! Ah am a Worker of the World; vive le internationale; vive vive vive, emancipation, egalité and the rights of man, and woman and humanity, all humankind, which includes children. And also the cratur kingdom in its entirety; animal, insect and fish, whose existence forever should be treasured. Craturs also have rights and then too we have the sanctity of plant life, every wee leaf that flutters has a name and a wee soul and benefits from the guid lord's acquaintance; take away the heavenly breath and that wee leaf goes fluttering to the ground, deid as a fucking dodo man bring on the bulldozers, let us lay the concrete.

What a snarl!

And where is one's fucking beer?

But forget that. How many brains does a body have? Is it one, two, three or a thousand?

The bars where I worked were 90 per cent fucking pink; ye werenay gauny meet any underground revolutionaries in them.

Sally was not in view, she was maybe in the kitchen.

A glass of milk, she sure would have some in there.

A shot of rye with a milk chaser and a nice big beefburger, auld-fashioned style, yes maam, did you say with everything? And that is to include fried onions? Assorted pickle and chilli sauce and any damn extra you can dream up? roasted garlic, si señora, fire it in, a couple of wee habañeros – in fact maam just gie me a double hot tamale on the side.

Hey! a scabby prick was watching me! The good ol boy owner of the bar. He had come from the rear where the musicians had a table nearby the little stage. He gied me a studied look that might have been interpreted as a glare: it went on for several moments, then he retreated to a back room. Maybe it was something silly like he wished I would drink up and leave so the table would be freed for other customers.

The joint was getting busier and half the tables were full. In fact maist of them were full, I couldnay see any that were empty, apart from mine, if I wasnay here. Nay doubt it was a popular bar, and deservedly so, I enjoyed the portraits and photographs round the wall, and ye could sense the atmosphere. And one of these hours the music would begin.

Nah, nay sarcasm, there was a music tradition here. They began in their ayn sweet time. The ex would have enjoyed it as a venue; its intimacy and so on, she aye enjoyed intimacy and so on.

The next time I needit a piss I was heading back to the motel. I couldnay leave the table to return, they would just dump the anorak on the floor and sit themselves down. Fucking scabby prick would ensure it. He would probably get the big greysuit pentagon guy to come fill the space, or else a quick call to the Shooters and Horses: Hey fellers, the baseball finished? come on across y'all, we're having some fun tonight, we gonna whup that no-good furnir's arse.

Heh excuse me, I am a faimly man.

If I went for the piss I would have to resort to the anorak on the back of the chair routine; if I didnay they would snatch ma table and then where would I go? would I sit at somebody else's table, or else stand at the bar alongside Mister Mountain?

Aw dear, nay option, safeguard the bladder.

Naw! Fuck the "aw dear, nay option, safeguard the bladder" shite, I wasnay gauny be dictated to by any body, no even my ayn. I would exercise mind ower matter. Think of churches and once-upon-a-time scenarios, i.e. my story, my future stories.

I certainly had plans and potential developments. I was gauny befriend me a computer expert and get masel a website. I had heard musicians blethering to the ex about it. They were cutting their ayn albums and stuff, had created all sorts of websites, dvds and shit man it was the only way, and that ol world was yer oyster; all of Europe, Africa, Asia, freedomm comm comm freedomm comm comm.

But I did gie it some thought in regard to myself. I found the very man; he roamed the carpark zones nearest the terminal. He was a good feller, another yin wanting to win himself a lottery flight ticket and retire from existence after a fair but unequal struggle. So long cruel world I am flying outa here but he wouldnay gie me the background detail except for computers, he knew all there was to know about them motherboard fuckers, these beasts were his downfall. He wasnay keen on talking. When I was dispatched with messages ower to terminal Immigration I would see him lying on the floor at the entrance to the transfer section for international travelers. There was aye a large queue there so he was a nuisance.

Females were mair wary than males of Security bodies, as a rule. But some folk I met wantit to tell us their lifestory. As soon as ye approached they were gieing ye their faimly history. It began from the uniform and in my ayn case the auld skarrisch tongue put them at ease. They were wanting to identify no just with us but themselves to us, something like that, and I was required to acknowledge them in a certain spirit, as if their desire was to one day emulate wur achievements or reveal to us their acknowledgment of achievements they regarded as inimitable. I couldnay quite fathom what it was about although it appeared to centre on one-nation politics. These folk saw us as responsible big-brother figures and one day real soon maybe they could be allowed to enter wur ranks. Well they couldnay enter them particular ranks, they would have to join the Indigenous Sectors.

Two war vets hung about near the lower-ground carpark offices, they called themselves Homer and Jethro. We were supposed to monitor every move they made. They were trained killers, proper yins; unlike us who werenay allowed genuine weapons. We were like these oirisch regiments they had in jolly auld fucking 19th-century braindeid britane. The army generals didnay gie them a gun in case they turned round and shot the goddam officers. Quite right too. In any civilized society it would be a dereliction of duty if the boss generals failed to safeguard their officers from getting fucking shot by their underlings.

Me and Homer and Jethro had decent conversations when we were out the way of the mics and CCTVs. They drank very strange brews that seemed to have seaweed or some other stringy brown plant trapped inside the bottle. They kept offering me a sip. It was absolute death for Security operatives to do this but fuck sake man a couple of times I couldnay resist, they kept inveigling me so agh well fuck it, these long long shifts, I had a go. Dear oh dear! Obviously it was better the second time. Eftir a while it got quite tasty. No that I drank that much but it did have an effect. Christ man these guys had some stories to tell! They were wanting me to write down some of the worst yins, some of the terrors.

I thought why not. Maybe I could write them down. They said if I could only do that then people would be able to read them and know the truth. Fair enough. I had nay taboo subjects. I could write any damn thing I liked. How no? The yarns these guys telt me were saleable commodities. The supranatooral is always popular, especially with governments and other apparatuses of state. If I just wrote the yarns down with embellishments here and there, a wee bit sex and this and that; and then got them onto a suitable website with the help of yer man the computer feller then we could make it downloadable at a very very very minuscule fee.

Forget the wee bit sex let us just go for a big bit sex. No porn, just erotica, high erotica.

What is high erotica? Sexy erotica but in an arty way, obviously.

And then throw in a bit of music to make it the even 100 per cent. People love music, especially rock and roll. Even erotica writers. So I would enter that onto the thing. The computer feller telt me ye could rig up the music as a sound track to the story. Great. That was like radio. So some pure guitar stuff, maybe with an accordion and banjo or something. Nayn of that synthetic shite. Gie me an auld-fashioned blues band, maybe toss in a Celtic fiddle with a lick of Skatch mandolin and a powerful but relaxed trombone, and that was just for starters man telling ye, my heid was nippin, i.e. I had ideas in affiliated directions. What am I talking about. That website. Once I had it the sky was mine, mine, all mine, he drooled. Stop gloating. Okay. But I reckoned I was a certainty to earn a few dollars. Everything I wrote I would log it in and then bodies everywhere could download it at minimal costs. Even a lowly 50 cents a shot. Even 10 cents. How many computers are there in the States? How many are there in the inkliz-language speaking world? All ye need is a couple of million downloaders at a dime a go. Even a nickel! and that is you a millionaire, or close to it. And if I could get a couple of these translation programs, eg. inkliz-pampangan, inkliz-senga, inkliz-kirghitz, inkliz-ewe, inkliz-livonian, inkliz-kurdish, inkliz-gandi, inkliz-adamanese, inkliz-grabar, inkliz-khalkha, inkliz-zapotec, inkliz-n to the power-n.

The world was one's universe.

And while I was earning a wage through that I could do

anything I wantit, whatever that might be, taking care of my faimly and living the good life, correcting wrongs and hindering evil deeds.

I was quite into it but the mair excited Homer and Jethro became the mair their brains launched into these outer-cosmic tales of supranatooral magic, mystery and hobgoblins. Nay wonder with that 147-proof rotgut they drank. Baith liked wonderful books about inner-earth goodies and netherworld baddies and wee boys that outwitted baleful sorcerers. They were of the opinion that the world "as we know it" could never go forward until having returned to the true values of Lancelot, Guinevere and the Knights of the Round Table. They offered all manner of explanations for the iniquities they had witnessed on foreign shores, especially the Devil's right hand, which they believed wasnay severed from his body at all. They had seen the Devil. This wasnay a metaphor. They said he was "whole". As opposed to one-handed. I am always useless for verbatim accounts of religious arguments but Homer and Jethro were among those who believed that the Devil had a body and of his two arms one had a bad hand at the end of the right wrist and the other had one that wasnay bad, or no quite so bad, or its badness went into some unusual, unspecified area that wasnay transparently bad. Some said the right hand was severed from his ghoulish torso; others that the hand had thereupon reunited with the torso. Others said it had never been "severed" because there was nay need; this bad hand could leave the torso at its ayn convenience, and return at its ayn convenience. But no matter and whatever this hand was made for wielding weapons of destruction, mass or singular and therein lay the cause of "the world's woes".

They told me of a famous country song commemorating the event. These fellers believed that if we could do away with that malevolent ol son of a gun then the world would be a beautiful place. But surely if the Devil was indeed alive and returned to planet earth, why then, according to a song from the Skarrisch tradition, that selfsame Unearthly Being would have landed in Kirkcaldy, a wee town on the east coast of Skallin. All I could remember of this song was part of a line and a snatch of the tune, which I hummed to Homer and Jethro and they were mighty impressed.

I was wondering if the bookies maybe took a bet on the Devil's right hand turning up unannounced. I could see the bookies offering a host of likely wagers. I didnay raise it with Homer and Jethro. It was just me being sarcastic and although undernourished they could fight like fuck and kill ye with their bare hands. Unfortunately I telt my Security comrades on the bus hame next morning, gieing them all the details. What I wantit to know was why Homer and Jethro spent their time telling me all that supranatooral stuff and there was I an atheist! Anomalous behaviour, I says. Mind you, that malevolent auld Satan cunt doesnay even know I'm an atheist!

There was a sharp intake of breath from one, vague smiles from another, but naybody laughed. I then gied a wee bit of nonsense about ludicrous bets and logical absurdities. I expected thigh-slapping guffaws at the notion of the bookies offering odds on the manifestation of a one-handed Unearthly Being inside the airport terminal. Instead it produced an awkward silence. One woman didnay smile at all, she gazed out the window. Then I noticed she wasnay gazing out the window, she was studying my reflection in the glass. A few coughs followed, the silence continued. Apparently my compañeros had connected the Unearthly Being to the legendary grocery-cart pusher. There were tens of grocery-cart pushers but only one precise individual to whom we referred, of whom more anon, a character whose very existence lay shrouded in mystery. Not only had they made that connection, they thought

I was declaring it. Of course I wasnay. Trying to explain myself would have made matters worse.

One night eftir a lengthy conversation with Homer and Jethro I had a weird experience; well, it wasnay that weird. I dont think it was an effect of that fucking rocket juice they drank but who knows, I confess to having had a wee sip in the line of duty. We alien operatives had to show a certain solidarity with true-borns. That was an opinion rather than company policy. These long brown plants inside the bottles interested me. The pair of them just tapped their noses, Say nothing. I suspect it was a concoction they had brought back from furnir land.

These two guys were heroes but they werenay being treated as heroes. It seemed obvious that their gripes were justified, about the treatment meted out to them by military legal teams and here they were now with fuck all, nay pensions, medical aid and the rest of it. I had to pick out the threads of what they telt me and try for a coherence. Their heids were fukt up by that supernatural stuff but from what I gathered there were auld excomrades of theirs fighting cases against the military through the law courts.

I took them a coffee occasionally, watching for the mics and cameras. Vigilance was the watchword but Homer and Jethro were very knowledgeable. When they got themselves a wee niche someplace ye could just about guarantee seclusion. If they wantit they could have shut down electronic surveillance through the carparks and outer areas. So they said. When they spoke about Security they aye guffawed. I could never find out why exactly. Eftir a couple of slugs of the rocket juice I joined in with the guffaws. And a couple were plenty. Nay point deluding yerself. In my experience ye were better to act like yer immediate superiors knew everything. If any of the bosses charged me with hobnobbing with the down-and-outs I wasnay gauny deny it; instead I would have made a case for such hobnobbing.

The remainder of that night shift in particular I spent on office duty in the lower-ground office, where a few safes were located. I passed the time messing about with computer games in the back room. My obsession was solo patience. It was the first game I clocked into.

Basic cards. Me against the machine.

Okay you ornery fucker, get yer money down!

It is perhaps irrelevant to mention that I didnay win. When I say didnay win, I mean I never fucking won on any occasion in any game of patience in any shift on any goddam computer in all the time I was in that stupit crazy fucking mental job. That, I think, is remarkable and worthy of some fucking scientific interest from the authorities. I was in that Security job like for a fucking year – mair than that! And I never won one solitary fucking game. Aint that a bitch! No sir, it am a scandal, goldarn scandal, that is what it is. Them federal-licence fellers should not allow it, that such a game could be pedaled. One wantit to hurl the computer out the window. But the window in the back office just showed ye the front office. If ye had hurled the computer through it ye would have had to go clear up the mess yerself, the broken glass and computer remnants. So I was playing away at patience this night when I heard banging and scraping noises like carpets being peeled back, furniture being pushed on a shiny floor surface, a search for secret trapdoors or fuck knows what. Instead of Homer and Jethro there were two plainclothes heavies in the front office, studying me through the window. Then I saw another yin in my actual doorway! I hadnay even noticed him standing there, he must have crept in. Hullo, I says. What agency you guys with?

Sssh, he says and then he turned and spoke quietly to the

others. I couldnay hear a word. I got up off the chair. Hang on, I says, I shouldnay be getting sshhhed here. It's me that's the Security operative, it should be me telling yous what to do.

Then I experienced something intuitary but couldnay quite grasp what it was, but it concerned a strange, familiar factor about these bodies. It lay in their attitude, their behaviour, their demeanour. Their contempt? Naw, it was beyond that. Absolute authority. That was it, they assumed they had that. Heh, I says, yous guys are upper-echelon; so what's a team of upper-echelon fuckers doing in an outer parking area? Is this normal procedure?

One of them chuckled, nodding in my direction. I winked at him and he paused. Seriously, I says, what is this an internal psyops espionage job or what? Are yous guys members of MisteR MaJeStIc InVinCiBle's PlainCloThes PresidentiaL PlA-tooN of ImmiGrant wiZarDs? Or are yez just the usual? Who's taking precedence here? I'm an Uhmerkin Security employee remember, I've got a legit SSN and my ID's valid valid valid, pure Class III.

Sssh.

Dont fucking ssh me, I thought angrily but eloquently. Naw but there was something in the way this yin ssshhusshed me that was especially irritating. I moved to the doorway and the three of them gazed at me, waiting. I stepped back. So how can ye hold me prisoner in my ayn back office? I says.

One strode into the back office now, passing me, and he went to the night filing cabinet and pulled it open but inside was only irrelevant stuff to do with the freakier pooch patrols and infrequent rites that govern illegal intoxication in both furnir and indigenous cultures. I sat down at the computer again. Another body entered and he turned the machine round-about. He grinned when he saw the game of patience and he worked on that for a few minutes. Then the first feller was crouching on the floor with a handheld electronic device and was checking something out along the skirting board, now moving under my desk; and he was under it that long ye would have thought I was wearing a kilt. Maybe ye're wondering if I'm circumcised, I says: I did consider it once when I read a copy of *Healthcare and the Male Operative*; one of their medical experts was advocating the surgical blade for enhanced thrust! Fucking hell man, enhanced thrust! What does that mean? Who knows but I thought goodbye foreskin, small price to pay.

They ignored me. From the front office I heard other banging and thumping but couldnay see anything through the window.

Guys, I said, listen; there's nay entrances to tunnel-corridors on this floor if that's what ye're looking for: I've checked it out myself. And if ye want to know what's in that safe ower there, I'll tell ye: wage receipts. And nothing to worry about there, between you and me, welfare pays better. It's typical third-world furnir rates, and nay work conditions either man I've been thinking of forming a branch of the Wobblies, what do ye think? Let's fight for worker dignity and the politicization of wur common struggle.

Seriously fellers, know what we get paid for securing these outer carpark and Patriot Holding Center areas against encroaching malevolence? I am including all-night Saturday shifts and the complete Sunday 24-hour period. Pennies. That is what they pay us. Why dont we compare salaries? You tell me yours and I'll tell ye mine. It is a complete and utter disgrace to the capitalist system, especially a caring one in the enlightened christian tradition. And listen to this: we have to pay wur ayn fucking fares on the staff bus into the bargain! And see if we rip wur uniforms in the line of duty? we have to darn the fucking things wurselves. One of my compañeros was joking there, saying how one of these days new employees would be required to knit their entire goddam uniform outfits, including hats. We'll be woolly fuckers.

They ignored me.

Heh what yez really looking for? I says: Is it the legendary grocery-cart-pushing character of whom more anon? If so you are too late. That individual has disappeared completely and forever, having relocated down by the Louisiana bayous, or is it the Californian vineyards, returned to a long-suffering faimly.

They ignored me but manhandled my chair while I was sitting on it – fucking hell – to get at the supposedly secret safe secured behind the false bookcase. Somebody has talked, I growled menacingly to myself.

One held a cell phone near to the locks and combinations while another fiddled about and I could see him poke in a thin electronic tool with forked prongs, and he held another to the other lock. There came a fine purring sound. I hadnay seen nothing like this before. He laid another clamp-like instrument against the non-univocal dials and it was like they found their ayn way, sounding a high pinging note. While he did that another one re-examined the floor. They were definitely looking for uncharted trapdoors and concealed entrances. Yous guys know yer job, I says, ye trying to tell me ye arenay government sponsored?

One guy stopped and stared at me.

Sir, I says, yez are treating me with contempt. I'm a comrade operative remember. What yez looking for? Ask me and I'll tell ye. I aint got nothing to hide. Are yez here to find out the gist of life among the lower-ordered alienigenae members of this great nation's Domestic Security? or are yez looking to score? Cause I know a source and it's the best of veg. Nay sore heids, nay paranoia, nay fuck all, just a nice blaw to while the weary hours. Ideal for lengthy nightshifts, and this is a poisonal

recommendation. Heh by the way, says I, I have long har-
boured a fantasy. Ye know what it is? helping one of these
mass exoduses where all the asylum-seeking coalition allied
democracy-loving refugee forces led by Steve McQueen, Paul
Newman and Captain Kirk break down the gates of the Patriot
Holding Center and usher the inmates straight to the airport
terminal and onto flights for freedom. What say you? Ye in or
out? Dont worry, I says, it's a dream. I'm lunatic fringe, classi-
fied under the crypto-communist former trotskyist-anarchist-
workerist label, I'm a no-good evil horrorist; a rattlesnaking,
sidewinding sonofagun. Not only that, I dont believe in the
Prince of Darkness.

The feller now smiled and I knew it was time to sit in the
chair and say nothing. From then on, each time I made to open
my gub I punched myself on the side of the heid. It got fucking
sair but it was necessary. Eventually I sat there. I twiddled the
thumbs, I twiddled them again. But it was so dang frustrating
and verily verily I was getting irritated by this challenge to the
very core of integrity and civilization and all manner of righteous stuff, good stuff, humanitarian stuff and so I says – and very
very very politely – Heh guys, guys, ever go round the back of
the carpark for illicit favours? I'm talking sex, I'm talking dope,
I'm talking liquid refreshment of the alcohol variety, a wee
drink with yer buddies, I'm talking about a wee game of cards.

Every time I wander down there myself I get set about by
urban bumpkins wanting to tell me their life history and
maybe have a wee haun at blackjack. These bodies are gender
non-specifics, them and their grocery carts. They drink that
auld wine ye know, heid-banging stuff, I've tried it. And see
that dope they smoke man that is fucking beyond man that is
crushed dandelions and a strange kelp that floats down from
the Great Grand Banks of Newfoundland. Mind you, I fucking
recommend it man.

One confiscates the odd item in this section. In my opinion but and this is highly personal, ye are better off with a nice cup of peppermint tea and a slice of good auld toast and cheese. Plus a couple of painkillers if ye have a sore back; and face it, maist of us Security operatives do have back problems. Unless we are in the midst of a terrible post-traumatic-stress-syndrome on account of the essential but sadistic drudgery done on behalf of the indigenous slave trade, gentlemen, I gie you myself, ace clown, comic singer and gambler; scribbler in embryo: Jeremiah Brown sir, for such be my name. I proffered my right hand: Let us shake.

The feller stared at me.

Hey, I says, if yez want relevant missives I'll gie ye them. Class isnay an issue. Is it true that some of you advanced career fellers favour castration to keep the mind focused? And what d'ye mean by loyalty? ye want to define that for a Skarrisch revoloooshoshoneee warriorrrr. Honestly but, I admire you higher-up james bond grunts. And I speak as yer average pink operative fucker, a medium-sized medium-phizzziccued yin. Some of wur male spy comrades are complete brutes man total fucking physical grotesques like them Mister Universes that cannay even buy a shirt to fit their airms – a joke, they are just a joke. Or is that unfair, maybe they arenay a joke, maybe they are spot-on fellers who just happen to have good physiques and I be the joke for finding arguments to defeat their masculine beauty. What say you?

He said nothing till one of his mates returned then he stepped forward and slapped me twice across the bridge of the nose. It was an experienced assault, it didnay sting to fuck but nearly broke the bridge of my nose, numbing the nasal passages and blinding me for several moments but a peculiar effect also occasioned, like Homer and Jethro's rotgut booze had transmuted into steam and was issuing from one's orifices.

Also something on his knuckles or wrist caught my eyebrows, parting both sets of lashes and breaking the skin. If that hadnay happened the whole episode might have been a hallucination.

Defence was impossible, they carried all sorts of armoury and would have dumped me; these fuckers had no compunction. I was reduced to slapping myself on the cheek again to stop me talking. But what a struggle! Their necks were the same colour red as mine. Know where red necks got their name? I says. Fucking us! I says, us! Peely wally pink bastards, we dont tan brown we just go red. Take myself, an unashamed Class III Red neck Card carrier in this land of give and take, this land of hurry home, this land that for some is never furin while for others eternally remains so; now faced by four assailants on behalf of a secret federal agency staffed by lickspittle watchdogs whose masters have exercised ruling authority for the past thousand years. Am I right or wrong? Ruthless and cynical fuckers in regard to freeedom and genuine democracy and will stifle it in their ayn interests at our costs and any costs so help me gahd the case is rested citizens of the state, support Solon the Lawgiver, he's yer man for this election, meanwhile all you bastards

Ach, and on I ranted.

But here also is one weird thing and I have just now remembered it, there was an earlier point where the accents of these guys were unmistakable in a different way. I said to them: Where yez from?

Mind yoah oun fuckayng bihsiniss, they barked. Get! oun! yoah! fuckayng! feet! Naow!!

Well, by the good lord harry, these cunts were upper-class Inkliz persons adopting an ordinary accent! Hey! I says. What's a team of upper-class Inklixers doing in the upper echelons of US federal security? Is this normal procedure?

He's a bloody jock, barked one.

More like a bloody joke, barked the other, haw haw haw.

I like yer laugh, I says, rocking back on my chair and pointing at them.

Shut it.

Ah but lads, I says, it is a supreme pleasure to hear ye oldé upper-class Inkliz voaice mimicking a working-class east-coast accent; I cannay mind the last time I heard it in the flesh. This is a big occasion for me and I'll go hame and boast about it to my wife and kids. And I must also tell ye, see yer true accents – and I speak as a Skarrisch chap – see yer true accents, I says, I would agree with them media surveys that tell us that that selfsame accent is the one and only thing a true Brit misses while sunning himself in sunnier climes. I include myself in that and I think I can speak for the rest of the world.

Quiet! they barks.

Agh and I did that, as far as I remember, I kept the mouth shut from thereon. Who knows what they had been telt, who knows what they sought but I just sat in the chair, nursing a sair heid.

I didnay report this incident officially. There was nay point. What I did was enter a coded entry into the computer then emailed it to a convenience address. It was a way of getting something date-recorded. For the next few weeks I did mair pooch patrol than usual. I didnay mind. I quite liked pooch patrol. I had a good ol boy dawg whose temperament suited my ayn although he inclined towards doleful silences. But when the nights were warm I enjoyed the stroll. Except some-times yer patrol pardner was a pain in the arse.

When wur paths crossed with other compadrés we would stop for a smoke and a chat. We all smoked like fuck in the Alien Section, it was genetic, plus it meant ye could steal a lot of breaks. But naybody spoke about real things. If ye didnay begin with "Cold tonight" or "Warm tonight" it was always

"Quiet tonight!" or "Busy tonight" or such variations as "It was busy earlier but now it's quiet". If somebody said, "Tonight was baith quiet and busy" it would be a talking point for two entire cigarettes. If ye were gauny steal a third ye needit a new topic e.g. sport, fellow operatives, gambling, sex, television. Politics, religion and the meaning of life were outlawed.

There were times I wantit to blast through convention and get to some level of communality. Let us share the fucking burdens. Let us find a way ahead. Stop all this one-by-one-by-one stuff. If the animals came in by two by two then surely us human beings could perform the job team-handed?

No sir.

Yer comrades can make or break such employment. Some people are so aff their heid that the rest of the workforce pass the time by talking about them. If I ever became an employer I would look for two or three spectacular eccentrics and pay them a wage. That is how to keep yer workforce interested.

In the Alien and Alien-Extraction Section ye wantit to hear about each other's lives but without divulging yer ayn. Nayn of us spoke beyond the minimum. If somebody did it was noteworthy. Ye were wary. There was an obvious need for caution because of wur plural status. Let others do the talking. Sometimes I felt like blethering but a body that blethers is suspect in any society. My only decent conversation was with Riçard Osoba, the feller who showed me the ropes during my probationary period. Now he was my shift changeover I never saw him. But even if I had, what would I have done? I dont know. It aye nagged at me that it was with him the bosses put me to train.

In my section who could blame the compañeros for being wary about issues around immigration. The alien-extraction group should have had nay problems with authority but among the actual aliens quite a few would have been borderline cases, some earmarked for deportation, others worse than that.

For a long while the central topic for discussion was the legendary grocery-cart pusher of whom more anon. But it was weird how this fabulous fucker entered and exited the collective consciousness. Ye could be standing having a smoke on an upper carpark level and somebody would make a remark that could only relate to this person. I would realize my mind had been drifting on the same wavelength. Or even the rare occasion there might be a low growl from the dogs then a shuffling of feet and clearing of throats from us; and we knew we were each hearing the trundle of that singular cart's wheels which had a distinctive rattle. Were we dreaming or was the vision about to be sighted? Even playing a computer game in the back office ye could hear the trundle of these fucking wheels, the image close to overpowering, and ye would need to rise and get outside, clear the brains, go to the bathroom and gie the heid a good dousing of ice-cauld water.

Some of the gambling around the carparks and outer areas centred on the grocery-cart pusher. A couple of perceptive punters found ways to make a book and different wagers became possible. These included guessing the individual's age or even name – Charlie, Ahmed, Herman, Mick, Margaret. Supremely crazy but standard lottery-style ventures. Heavier players looked at the mair sensible bets, the ones with tighter odds but offering a fair chance of success. Was the individual male or female, ower forty or under forty, nay teeth or false teeth, blue eyes, green eyes or brown; pay yer dough and name another.

The gender issue might have seemed a straightforward even-money bet and the so-called "shrewd" money was on male. But I have had one or two shocks in my time and occasionally if the money had been down I would have lost; lost on a straightforward gender bet. Nothing surprised me. Especially so-called "even-money" bets. Any of them ye encounter on a day-to-day basis, they seem easy but they arenay. No for me. I aye lose. Is it gauny rain today. I lose. How come? Since boyhood I had been figuring that yin. A side of my so-called intellect knew I *must* lose these bets so I gambled on the opposite. On the "gender bet" I thought the grocery-cart pusher was female but if I bet female I knew I would lose so the answer was to bet male. Apparently. But I knew something would go wrang with that. The only escape was to bet *baith* as two even-money bets. In this way ye thought okay, I might no win but it is impossible to lose. Wrang. What if a third sex turns up? And then too what if there was a "fourth"? The fourth sex. There was a movie called that.

Apart from a pair of strange flip-flop footwear items and a heid of curly hair all reported sightings were in agreement that the person had only the one outer article of clothing. This was a coat that reached midway down the thighs, with a couple of buttons and pins to keep the modesty intact. Baith legs were bare from above the knees. It was the belief of many that but for the coat the character was naked. I hoped underclothing might be found. It was my conviction that the grocery-cart pusher was female. Obviously it was a hunch. There appeared nay outstanding mannerism nor gesture that indicated masculinity or femininity. Nayn that I heard about. My reason for betting "female" concerned the individual's legs but no to do with "hairiness". Nay disrespect and forget breast implants, it is the ankles that require surgical cosmetics. I thought it improbable I could make a mistake in that department. Only a hunch but a good hunch: reports attested that the individual had thinnish legs but naybody ever vouched for the ankles, were they thin as well? Naybody ever said, which to me meant they were maybe natural, i.e. okay to look at, ergo these ankles were female.

And, by way of consolation, a weird datum in regard to

one's personal psychology. I refer to the mental shenanigans that take place inside one's fucking heid, or "brain", as well-wishers describe it. That grocery-cart pusher reminded me of naybody so much as christ what was her name again? that auld fictional lady whose huis burns down and she vows never to change her wedding-day clothes eftir being left at the altar by her husband-to-be, but she makes the wee orphan boy suffer, she brings up the lassie – "her charge" – to treat all men with disdain.

Poor auld sowel. When she lifted the hem of that faded wedding gown she jumped straight into my mind. The scene I recall was from the movie. I couldnay remember reading the novel. But surely I must have. I was aye a reader. Wherever I went I searched out the secondhand bookstores. I liked especially these bumper short-story anthologies from all ower the world: *Brown Shoes for the Vicar*, William Percival, England; *Solace*, O. Johannson, Sweden; *The Genie Who Stole The Donkey's Emerald*, Anon., Arabia; *The Romantic Desperado*, E. D. Hollingsworth, USA; *The Wintry Journey*, Ivan Kannitsyn, Russia.

And yet, although the idea of the grocery-cart pusher put me in mind of the auld lady in the faded frock it wasnay because of age. The grocery-cart-pushing character might have been hitting forty but nay mair than that. Contrary to conventional opinion I figured her for younger, maybe if "she" was all spruced up, all washed, dried and cleaned, then powdered with sweet-smelling herbs, myrrhs and so on, if all that was to happen then

What I am saying is who knows.

It was difficult to find a name for this person. The phrase "grocery-cart pusher" was clumsy and ambiguous, as are maist singular references that arenay ordinary names. I thought if we tried we could do better and that it was important to try to do better, fuck sake, it was bad enough doing a job that forced us into a right-wing sensibility, where would we be if we failed to find a non-evaluative designation for an individual human being. Would that no sum up the whole load of keech we call life on earth?

I used the word "character" occasionally, e.g. there is a discomfiting "character" around the airport carparks such that this "character" pushes a grocery cart and is believed naked apart from a short coat. This "character" never responds to a greeting, nor to an order. This "character" appears from naywhere and vanishes back into there in the twinkling of an eye. Nayn has heard this "character" speak nor engage in daily human activities. This "character's" face is either expressionless or not to be gazed upon.

What does that mean, "not to be gazed upon"?

It has an otherworldly tone about it. I was aye an atheist. I never resorted to a belief in any supranatural presence, animate or not, touch wood.

But naybody was ever able to say a word about the grocery-cart pusher's face, was the chin cleanshaven etc. Folks of a mair impressionable nature awarded the individual apparitional status, a goddam ghost is what they called her. Or him. At first I thought "spook" mair apposite; "spook" as underground surveillance terminology for a fucking stool pigeon spy bastard. It struck me as great cover for an immigration pentagon cunt. The mair I thought about it, naw, it was just so unlikely. This figure was such a lost soul s/he brought attention down upon his/herself and that wasnay what was wantit by undercover agents, no unless something very very very devious was gaun on.

Some of the Security comrades used "it" to refer to the person which I thought demeaned everybody. Others referred to "the It" which was beyond even that. "Character" wasnay appropriate in my ayn estimation because of its veiled meaning that the subject was an imagined entity. Eventually we did find a nomenclature, it wasnay a big deal, but seemed to fit and was quickly adopted by my comrade compadrés.

It was one night me and three others had stopped for a smoke, on the top floor of the outer carpark nearest the secondary retribution camp. If somebody had lobbed a grenade it could have landed within their communal exercise garden. The conversation had moved from grocery carts to a wee blether about mathematical terms, value-free reference and generality. A new trainee in the job was third-generation Arabian and I assumed, erroneously, that he would have an interest in algebra and maybe we could work out a mathematical sign that might be used to denote individual individuals, and an extension of that to bestow upon such as the grocery-cart-pushing individual. But the feller accused me of racism. About to offer a tricky nature/nurture defence based on topographical heritage that utilized algebraic v. geometric reasoning $>< - ><$ shifting sands $\wedge$ desert landscapes $\wedge$ pale blue horizons $< - >$ mountains $\wedge$ lochs $\wedge$ clouded skies, I instead accepted the racist verdict and hung my heid. I forgive you, he says, and shook my haun.

But *then* it was I coined "being". It derived from the brief statement I made in mitigation re my ayn heritage, being from bonné Skallin where landsakes we also had that dang mathematical genetic thing, 'twas our tradition gied rise to the invention of logarithms for mercy's sake that was how together I thought we might figure a referent for a single being, an extant being, a being such that

heh! and there we had it. "The being".

I got the same satisfaction from deriving that appendage as I got as a schoolboy solving a tricky moral dilemma, e.g. if a wee Skarrisch laddie lost money while gambling with his buddies and borrowed a ten spot off his feyther and he lost that ten spot also gambling with his buddies: and then one dark and wintry evening eftir his auld man had had a few uisghés too many and passed out on his chair and was snoring fit to wake the neighbours, and that selfsame aforementioned wee Skarrisch laddie was to rifle through his feyther's sporran and find not one ten spot but a few of them and he grabbed three, plus one squashed cigarette . . . And then . . . And then . . .

At the end of that shift on the long drive hame from the airport I was either dozing or staring into space. There came the low murmur of a conversation from up front, the driver blethering to the guy on the passenger seat. And I heard the word "being". I kept listening. Sure enough. It was the driver, he used the phrase again, "the being". There was nay question to whom he was referring.

Before me I never heard a single solitary individual use the term. So, for what it is worth, I believe it was me gied the being her name. The only person to whom I confided was the ex. And she didnay want to listen! She fucking hated hearing about the being, and my job with Security. She hated me working at the airport, she wished I had stayed in the bar. Sometimes I wished I had stayed in the bar. But so what? Ye cannay move back in time. The cards get dealt and ye make yer move. How else do we survive?

The being had been unsighted for a few weeks now and the bus driver was discussing how he expected a return very soon and had backed his prediction with a spread bet on the number of days beyond a week. To my mind it was one of the madder bets a body gets trapped into making. It is a bet that derives from obsession. It fills yer nut till ye cannay think of fuck all else, ye must hit that bookie now now now or else what might happen? these bastards the government might introduce some new decree to outlaw the bet, to outlaw you, to outlaw yer bookie man you have to make that bet now now now, and get the dough into yer haun as ye rush into that betting parlour, whhwww, made it! The guy takes yer dough and gies a wink to his buddy. Aw naw, fukt again.

Just the way that driver spoke about his bet I knew he was obsessed by the being and her comings and goings. But I found nothing astonishing about disappearances and couldnay understand what all the fuss was about. Okay it made an interesting story but nay mair than that. These unusual Uhmerkin true-borns vanished constantly. Maist didnay return but some did, even eftir long stretches. Personally I did think she would reappear but I wouldnay have bet on it. I had never seen her myself. There were comrades in the section who knew people who knew people who had witnessed the being but there were too many differences of opinion on appearance for my liking. Apparently there were images of her captured on CCTV but nayn of the ordinary operatives had seen any. Maist of what I heard was fanciful conjecture. I dont exclude myself from that. My heid was beset by star-struck heiresses and this hypothesis explained the being's recent disappearance as well as any. Maybe she had been kidnapped and was lying bound and gagged in some godforsaken dusty vault located down by the creepy tunneled corridors, or else she had escaped and was on the run from uncaring heavy-handit father-figures, abusive father-figures, absolute shites of father-figures, humourless bas-tarn holy terrors of father-figures; these religious cunts who wantit to control their womenfolk and stop the spiritual and intellectual development of their young folk, domineering patriarchal no-gooders man they make your blood boil and they make my blood boil and I would never be like that with my ayn wee lassie, fucking bastards. My ayn father wasnay like that. Nor was Yasmin's who also died a long while ago. One of her uncles made up for it. He tried it with me one night, it was eftir the wee lassie was born. It was some faimly thing and the men were all sitting in the kitchen boozing and smoking. The craïc was no bad and I came in on a conversation; something basic, trying to keep my end up. But her uncle turned aside from me. But he knew I couldnay avoid hearing, and he muttered some keech about arrogant young whippersnappers and how once upon a time if the aulder generation was talking it was a case of When I speak let no dogs bark.

Oh yeh, fucking woof ya cunt.

With the state of the world as they left it for us? Whose generation was he talking about? Never mind relatives, infirm or healthy, a conversation is a conversation and if a newcomer to the faimly is trying to join in then surely he should be encouraged? no fucking smacked on the teeth. So what if ye were a whippersnapper, ye had to start somewhere. What the fuck is a whippersnapper man I dont even know, whippersnapper.

But I couldnay get the being out my heid. Me and the ex might be relaxing the gether eftir at long last managing to get the baby to sleep. Then for nay reason the trundle of tiny cart wheels and I would start yapping on again. Ower meals I was yapping about it. Yasmin was sunk under it. I even yapped on about it to the baby when I was gieing her a feed or changing her diaper. Once on my night off I was up gieing her a bottle in the middle of the night and Yasmin came in and there I was bouncing the wind out the wean and filling her heid with stupit fucking stories. And this was when ye werenay supposed to talk to babies at all like it was that time of night when ye were supposed to gie nay input, ye were to feed the wean in silence. Dont ask me why. The ex tried to explain it to me but I couldnay fucking grasp it. I wasnay supposed to talk to my daughter! So who was gauny talk to her? Naw, fuck that for a game.

But I wasnay the only yin with that stuff on my mind. I knew it from the conversations on the bus to and from the airport. Once I may have come close to seeing the being myself. I was on my way to the Patriot Holding Center to uplift a package for delivery to the terminal Immigration and Assimilation Section. This was a weird night. One of wur ayn section had disappeared, a male compadré, he went for a quiet smoke and never returned. There was talk of bad relationships and so on, that he had made a dash for freedom. But he was a happily merrit man and my section didnay believe that explanation. A few thought he had strayed down an underground tunnel and by mistake had got carted into one of the compounds around the Patriot Holding Center. Blundering into these compounds was a perennial worry for the non-pink comrades. I mind one feller was grabbed by a Security squad inside the terminal building and locked in a safe room for 16 hours. They hadnay the decency even to smile when he telt them he was a third-generation citizen; they added "perjurer" to his file and inserted "suspected" when the truth was known. An immediate superior had to go across with the relevant paperwork.

Mair than a dozen of us were consigned to search for the disappeared comrade. We had good tracking dogs and handlers but they couldnay pick up a scent. We tried the lower boiler rooms and were prepared for the dogs to start barking at bare walls and under carpets. It didnay happen. My patrolmate here was Billy Zannu who knew the guy who disappeared. Billy hailed from Kentucky; his faimly ran a second-generation kebab and pizza joint. Me and him wound up the gether on many occasions. It wasnay a buddy-buddy relationship. I dont think he liked furnirs much and seemed to resent the composition of wur section. He definitely resented me because in his estimation I got the mair interesting jobs, the deliveries and stuff that took me into the heart of the airport terminal. Billy, I says, it is a racist country, ye know that. I'm a pink fucker and you arenay. He mumbled something that was unintelligible. Cheer up, I says, patting him on the heid. Here's a wee stick of big rock candy, that's a good boy.

Sorry, that was a fantasy conversation. Billy and me werenay so much enemies as mutually indifferent. We never spoke much except maybe if it was about the patrol dogs. He was aye sighing and making these wee groaning and moaning sounds. He did have an interest in weapons and sometimes had the energy to question me on the Skarrisch hand-to-hand combat tradition. I telt him that before battle the Celtic warriors recitit their personal genealogies like a prayer, my name is Ruraidh Short Legs, son of Ruraidh Short Legs, son of Ruraidh Red Beard, son of the son of Big Fine Ruraidh, son of Ruraidh Nay Nose, and so on, and that interested Billy so much I had to repeat it each time we partnered.

Besides the shillelagh sticks and knuckle-dusters we carried ankle bracelets with modified cutting-edge drop-loops; heavy fuckers. Some developed a method of wielding them like spiked throwing weapons, the kind used by some of the auld horsemen warriors, maybe Gauchos. The ankle bracelets carried a wee "Made in Scotland" logo. I avoided telling Billy although I would have gone up in his estimation. He was aye first to these militia-technology journals the agency ordered.

On patrol the food-breaks were staggered. It came time for ours and he returned to one of the offices. I didnay go with him. I had forgotten to make up my sandwiches before leaving for work and couldnay be bothered sitting watching him eat. I went outside for a smoke then the call came in and I had to go to the Patriot Holding Center and get the package. I left that building and crossed into another, intending to head down into the lower-level pathways but there was this sensation washed ower me and there it was man the rattle of the cart wheels. It was. And I knew, I just knew, that the being was somewhere close. And as soon as I had the thought I felt like it had come on the back of a much deeper thought I had had earlier that day without its having manifested.

I stopped and christ there definitely was a shift in the atmosphere. Yet I further knew that the cause of this sensation wasnay here but elsewhere, so I left that building and headed to an area farther out. The dog hadnay picked up on anything strange. It wasnay Buster; this was a different yin. He seemed close to retiral age; a few of the beasts we got were auld, maist were mongrels. Look one way and he was a rottweiler, look the other and he was a labrador. He gied me the occasional glance as if trying to remember was I friend or foe. Some dogs didnay live very long eftir we got a haud of them. Big-chestit dogs; I suppose their lungs were fukt. Comrades at the kennels were trying to organize a home where the craturs could spend their last days rolling about the floor getting their belly tickled. What a prospect! Can we all go! Some of them were cantankerous auld girny bastards but their teeth werenay made of plastic; they could still rip yer haun aff at the wrist. We werenay allowed them inside the terminal building, only for patrols on the outer sections.

But this was the dead of night and the lighting was poor, and I kept along by the wall, allowing the dog plenty lead; we passed a long row of 12-seater wagons. Up ahead I smelled smoke, tobacco. I was expecting to find a few down-and-out bodies gathered but instead two comrade gals were concealed behind the corner pillars and staring at the exit. It was Suzanne and Miss Perpetua. They had stopped for a quiet smoke. The dogs were alert but lying with their heids on their paws. They watched my approach. They were growlers. It didnay bother me or my dog; he threw them a look and sniffed, trotted to the side of the wall and lolled there in a peaceable manner.

Me and Suzanne were wary of one another. I was pleased when she acknowledged my existence. A misunderstanding had occurred between us a while back. I hadnay regarded what happened as a "fault" although she acted like it was one of mine. It had been a genuine misunderstanding and it was up to her how she took it. But now it seemed forgotten. They were baith excited. Maist of Miss Perpetua's heid and face were concealed beneath a veil but her eyes were wide and she gestured in the direction of the far exit. Yeh, whispered Suzanne, also gesturing. He just disappeared through there, one moment he was there the next gone.

Bodies dont disappear through exits, I whispered, they exit through exits. Ye're talking like the being is a ghost or something, an ethereal creature. Sorry Suzanne but to me that's a misuse of language and why daft rumours can arise and errors of judgment ensue; folk start believing ordinary events are irrational phenomena.

Suzanne gied me a look like I had said something preposterously stupit. She took a last puff on her cigarette and dropped it beneath the heel of her boot.

Okay . . . I pointed to the exit. Ye're telling me the being just pushed the grocery cart through the doorway there and disappeared?

No mister, she whispered, I'm talking about before ever he reached that point, before ever he reached to there, we was attempting to halt his progress by standing foursquare with the dogs here in front of his like cart, me and Peppy here. We was unsure what else to do and a snappy decision was required; you know the manual. And when that being guy is pushing that cart he wont stop for nothing.

Aw, so the being is a guy?

Sure he's a guy. He wont stop for nothing and nobody. And no dogs, he dont stop for dogs, he goes over the top of dogs. Dogs dont like him, they know something is wrong with him, they know it. Animals are wise, hey Peppy?

Miss Perpetua nodded.

That was some weird thing how he appeared mister it was so goddam precipitate, like myself and herself, we were there and suddenly you got them tiny ol cart wheels turning and there he is. So he's got to walk along here between them like 12-seaters and them there trucks, it's the only way he can go. So me and Peppy what do we do, we just like step right in front of his dang grocery cart, yeh and the dogs, we just stand there like what is he going to walk over the top of us!

Christ, I whispered, that's brave.

Suzanne frowned.

Naw, I said, I dont mean it in a sexist way if that's what ye're thinking. I wouldnay have eh christ almighty I would have used the word "brave" even if ye were a feller for god sake, the two of yez, honest, I'm no being sexist at all, I mean I just, christ ye know me by now surely. I aint no goddam sexist christ, Suzanne, ye know that.

She and Miss Perpetua were looking at me. Silence was a better policy. I hadnay been in the slightest sexist but to continue the conversation would prove disastrous. It was a typical male-to-female misunderstanding and should have been left at that. If there was a battle it was one I could only lose. And I was sick of losing battles. A lot of it was needless shite, brought on by nonsense, by circumstances, my ayn foolishness, the usual. I had so much to learn. Okay, I whispered, the truth is it was sexist.

Miss Perpetua breathed in sharply.

Yeh, I said, I take it back, it was stupit and ach, of course it was sexist. At the same time but anybody that confronts the being is exhibiting the opposite of cowardice as far I'm concerned and yous two did just that.

Suzanne pursed her lips.

The two of yez, I said and smiled at Miss Perpetua.

Suzanne brought out her cigarettes and handed one to her, then offered the pack to me. Okay, she whispered, here is what happened when that being guy rumbled into here

How ye mean rumbled?

The sound he made, them wheels on his grocery cart. Me and her now we managed to get round the front of him and we stood motionless, barring his route, them dogs in the middle. But that guy did not flinch mister, on he came pushing the cart, pushing it towards us. But now when he reached to us he kind of paused there like he moved from one foot to the other like marching time is what he was doing it was uncanny and scary, hey Peppy?

Miss Perpetua nodded. I was about to speak but thought better of it.

We could not move, we just could not move, whispered Suzanne, you know like they say? well that happened to us. What the hell was it? We didnt know. It was just so dang weird. Now you got the being guy he is marking time right in front of us, continuing to mark time right there in front of us he is like a marine top sergeant marching on the spot but with them little steps he was taking mister like dainty steps, it was not a natural thing but that now we noticed an unusual odour pervading the space, contiguous to its having come to pass that the being guy and cart now they had accomplished a form of transcendent transmigration and damn damn damn so now we hears the rumbling noise to the rear, yet still we could not move like we was rooted mister, rooted to the spot, and them poor dogs now we dont know what happened to them except they was slithering on the ground like on their belly mister, snakes on ice.

Suzanne wagged her finger at me. That was the weirdest thing, and it is not explicable. That being guy was not now in front of us but damn, he was behind us, yeh and so was that ol cart, rickety cart. Now listen to this also, and you recall how Peppy and myself we was so close to the being guy, almost we could reach out and touch him.

I nodded.

Suzanne had glanced from her comrade to myself, and her eyes were just so beautiful, what else to say, she was a beautiful-looking woman and I dont know what to say about that, but I dropped my ayn gaze to the ground and just smoked the cigarette she had gien me.

Yeh, whispered Suzanne, we could have touched him. If we had wanted to touch him we could have. She glanced to Miss Perpetua who nodded then raised her eyebrows significantly. Her eyes were like out a painting, beautiful eyes, ye were feart to look into them. Yeh, said Suzanne, and we could not bring ourselves to look and see but mister that is a fact and I am ashamed to report it, we just could not look and see.

Look and see what?

Suzanne hesitated. Miss Perpetua studied her boots self-consciously. Suzanne muttered something I couldnay hear, her haun footering with her silk scarf, then she gazed at me with what I thought was a lingering look, but it couldnay have been. She shrugged and stared away, but was I dreaming or was that a smile?

Now Miss Perpetua raised her heid and glanced at me slyly – I thought slyly. But it was like it was her eyes also, they were like that fucking painting by the artist where ye see one eye straight on and one in profile and like nay nose and how ye think fucking hell man there aint a damn thing ye could ever hide from this lady, she knows everything. Thank fuck she wore the veil otherwise wow! I was a total goner! Even as it was but sex was into and permeating my brain and there was nay chance of concentrating the way my heid was, as if the two female comrades had other business on their mind and I was the man they was looking for. Who knows who knows. But what total ego-centred male-centred nonsensical crazy nonsense man fucking stupit shite yet when Miss Perpetua hesitated with a fresh cigarette from her pack I had an erection. And she trembled when her fingers touched that cigarette. I know they did. I would swear to that in an open court, in front of god, king and hallelujah man what is an open court? I would swear in it. And what of Suzanne there, she too like what she was doing, standing there staring at me. I also had the trembles. What else is an erection but the biggest tremble of all, that is what an erection is, a major tremble. I thought my teeth were gauny start chittering. What the hell was happening? Even Suzanne – who always had these beautiful kind of silk scarves; that was what she wore beneath her uniform and sometimes held them around her chin, and she did it while she was in the office, changing jackets, she wore these silk scarves then and ye wondered if was okay for her so to do or was it against the rules or regulations, the Security precepts? christ.

I heard an engine revving. Down below an empty bus was backing into the carpark entrance. It would have come from depositing another load of furnir bodies at the compound. The driver would take a food-break. I had a delivery, a package to uplift and I would do it, I would do it; it was worthless but it was fucking worthless. What was gauny happen to me? My life wasnay worth a damn. I was a pathetic fool. What right did I have to be a father? Nayn.

What did I do? I let people down.

Suzanne was in straight eye-to-eye contact with me, and

Miss Perpetua also. One of the dogs shifted now, a low growl from the back of its throat. A squeaking sound came from their other dog. I wantit away from them. Suzanne had relaxed. She smiled, exhaling smoke peacefully out the side of her mouth. Then she whispered: It was sooo weird . . . It was like time got lost someplace, if it was trapped. Let me tell you we just could not move, we was rooted to that spot. We could not look and see, hey Peppy could we look and see?

No maam, murmured Miss Perpetua, snatching a glance at me, wondering if I had heard her voice which was a wondrous instrument of aural beauty. She smiled and knew me intimately, smiled again and I nodded, adjusting my stance and putting my right hand into my trouser pocket to avoid social dishonor. I rarely engaged in whimsical sexual fantasies but something was going on here and yet again and yet again I am saying yet again I was experiencing the stark pulsatory desire for baith of these comrade females and manifold variations flitted through my mind till it seemed like my knee joints were beginning to weaken. They were snapping. How to explain the sensation; sound and physicality, but that is the nearest I ever get – snapping. My knee joints were snapping. No I wasnay proud of myself but what had pride to do with it it was lust. And that lust was healthy healthy healthy. Of course it was. And entering my mind two sets of different possibilities, neither born in language but owing much to trumpet fanfares and streaks of dull red and amber. And Suzanne was staring at me, blowing cigarette smoke away from us. Hey mister, what is your life amounting to? What is it amounting to? This is what she was thinking. I smiled, trod the cigarette out on the ground.

I had something to say but before I could say it she leaned to touch my arm. You dont have no religion, she whispered.

No.

So if I have religion and you dont, why be sarcastic to me? Hey Peppy, why should he be sarcastic to me? why should he insult the religions of people?

I dont, I whispered.

You got a kid now, yeh? You showed me photographs. You give religion to her?

Her mother does.

You aint married, and you got the Class III. Why do folks get that Class III mister? Because what, your grandparents come from someplace?

My grandparents are deid and buried.

Suzanne inhaled on her cigarette. She turned to me again, What you think of this being guy? Where he goes, you ever think of that?

Sure.

You ever see the being guy's face?

No maam.

You think he is a devil?

No maam.

You dont think there are devils?

No maam.

You think his face got a beard?

Cleanshaven, she is cleanshaven.

Pardon me?

She is cleanshaven.

Oh, is a woman, this being?

I sniffed.

Suzanne smiled to Miss Perpetua. This guy knows about women. Hey mister, what you think you know about women?

Nothing.

Nothing is right, she whispered. You got bearded women, regular women, it dont prove a thing; gender is a complicated thing, hey Peppy?

Miss Perpetua raised her eyebrows then gied a humorous wee frown.

Yeh okay, I whispered, but let me say this: a body can be masculine and no male, or can be male and no masculine, but a body cannay be male and no be male.

Which body you talking about?

I aint talking about any body, no in particular, the being could have a full-length beard for all I know. I havenay looked upon her face and maybe I never will. I dont want to tempt the fates.

Oh you think there are fates? You got no religion but you think there are fates?

I smiled.

Suzanne also smiled. Hey, she whispered, you want to trail the being guy? Why dont you?

I intend to.

Oh you do?

Sure I do, yeh.

You think anybody can trail him? You think it's your job to trail him?

Pardon me?

Suzanne shook her heid, smiling. Miss Perpetua shrugged and gestured at her wristwatch, unwound the leashes. The dogs were already on their feet. Suzanne nodded. It is time for us, we go back to the kennels now. We make the report. Hey mister, she whispered, you are the first person we saw since.

What?

First person, since we saw the being guy. She smiled. Hey Peppy, for us it is the kennels, nice girls, they keep us there. Suzanne glanced at me again then smiled at Miss Perpetua and they strolled off, allowing slack on the leashes, the dogs moving well. I gied them a wave but they didnay acknowledge it. I lit another cigarette, had a slow puff before leaving.

The idea of me as the first person following the being. On the one hand good the other bad. Fuck it. I was already late from the call and they would be expecting me at the gate of the Patriot Holding Center.

But in future when I did deliveries or messages that allowed it I used the pathways down in the lower-basement boilerrooms. Security operatives from my section were wary because of the rumours but I felt okay about them and being a pink fucker I was less likely to experience problems.

It was exciting down there and there was aye the chance I would stumble across something of interest. Tunneled corridors were said to extend beneath the lower-basement boilerrooms. There were strategically placed trapdoors and disguised walls with secret buttons that might reveal descending corridors into cavernous dungeons, making use of ancient mine-workings that stretched for miles. If these could be found they led ye into the holding compounds, providing a direct link to the heart of the airport terminal and had concealed exits to within half a mile of the nearest interstate intersection, rendering the entire country available for mass transportation. Salty dawgs spoke of an underground road network that linked hundreds of miles, from the gold fields nor-west of the 98° line to a point south-west of Ciudad Juarez where an overground section ignored the border and extended west to the Californian coast. Here it was known as the silver trail, because of an auld trading connection between Mexico, China and the US State.

This network was developed for emergency purposes by the federal authorities during the early railroad navigation and track-laying period. At a time of government–corporate anxiety it was strengthened for the mass movement of men and arms around the turn of last century and further strengthened prior to the stock market crash of 1929. If I had known any of this when me and Haydar were doing the jazz, women and poker excursions then I would have tried to follow some of these trails. The way east led to the gold road, the one that went from the Florida coast to South America, and conveyed all the treasures thieved by the conquistador fuckers, these christian fascist fanatic imperialist genocidal maniacs who tortured, raped and murdered an entire fucking civilization in the name of god and the Zpanch monarcquy.

When ye considered some of the weird happenings that took place around the outer carpark areas a case might be made for underground tunnels as a logical necessity. Certain phenomena demanded their existence, including the disappearances. There were down-and-outs who believed that their colleagues were not disappearing under their ayn steam but were made to disappear by a special division of airport Security, known in the industry as "pest control". Every so often scare stories featuring "paedophiliac criminalist panhandlers" swept the airport and were picked up by the local media. Vagrants were perpetrating vile violations on the larger airport community. They were the scum of the earth, no-good cheats who preyed on hardworking Uhmerkins and were known to make a highly-lucrative income and send their kids to the best schools in the land. The nefarious practices of these "criminalist panhandlers" had a far-reaching catastrophic effect on the airport economy and had a causal effect on furnir tourism. Who was gauny fly into the nation if only to get terrorized by organized squads of villainous miscreants. Airport terminals were no longer safe havens for people with dough. Once upon a time elites could have exhibited their wealth freely. No now.

As soon as these "anti true-born" rumours occurred I kept my eyes open for signs of "pest control" purges. These might have happened in the terminal itself but no in the outer carpark areas, no that I heard and I would have heard. But many down-and-outs were feart of us. So ye wondered if they believed the "pest control" rumours. Maybe they were just wary of uniforms.

But it was the last straw when the grocery-cart pusher reappeared inside the airport terminal itself, and was witnessed by entirely appropriate sources. In the name of all that is holy, what an insolent fucker! Nay wonder high-up bodies get nonplussed. Nay wonder even mair a-girning and a-grumbling came about. Early reports had downplayed reality. Not only had the culprit appeared inside the terminal building s/he materialized in the presence of higher-level dignitaries, right inside the goddam VIP suite, the one nearest the fast-track check-in area reserved for executive-class flights to DC. And further, that s/he materialized amid some kind of conflagration or "dancing inferno", as it was termed.

Pardon me?

Yeh.

Hell, aint these people got a sense of propriety! Nay wonder the finer susceptibilities of higher-up folks get offended.

This heralded a system heading out of control. It was likely to undo all the good work achieved by the airline industry since the advent of "survive v. perish" insurance betting.

Later reports confirmed that the entire contents of the being's grocery cart had exploded into flames, including piles and piles of lottery tickets, auld betting receipts and scratch-cards. One junior diplomat had collapsed with a suspected heart attack. Suddenly weapons had been drawn and battle stations entered between the furnir diplomats' bodyguard battalion and upper-level airport Security. A stand-off developed. People ran for cover. Everybody was talking into their cell phones in a confined, restricted space.

Soon airport control was on the alert for significant pocket increases in static electricity and other causes of atmospheric interference.

It became very tense and could have degenerated into a shoot-out, both sides wanting to assert control. Shadowy official persons made it down to sort out the bother. Much to the surprise of the authorities the cause of the evil mischief had vanished. Vanished? Yeh, right in front of thirty or more upper-level Security operatives. They were staring straight at this figure one instant, the next they werenay. The cart was an inferno of flames leaping angrily skywards, and the being was just standing there "like a charioteer from the very bowels of the earth", according to one eyewitness account that was used by the newspapers.

How the hell could somebody just vanish like that?

Who knows, but s/he had, leaving behind one smouldering grocery cart. Throughout this period the collapsed diplomat had been left lying. Now he was rushed to emergency services. I never heard what happened to him. Airport Security operatives were discouraged from follow-up enquiries concerning the health and well-being of clients and customers.

But this diplomat incident created ructions. In the VIP lounge it had been a select grouping of indigenous politicos and their overseas guests who were representing a clandestine caucus from within the OPEC countries. They had been using the executive-class flights from DC for purposes of personal amusement or relaxation: sex, dope and rock & roll; the odd game of chemin de fer, a poker tournament or three, the occasional massage. Following a straight 36-hour session in casino town their sensibilities were down. That further applied to the battalion of bodyguards who had managed to snatch some free time and were licking their wounds, having spent it in pursuit of like pleasures. The last image they wantit was of a possible future, and when they gazed upon the grocery-cart pusher some saw a vision of themselves in years to come, or even months.

The airport authorities received complaints from crucially important persons. These politicos and their overseas guests were official bodies who needit a bit of relaxation. And could they get it at this airport? could they fuck man it was a goddam disgrace. Frequently these poor auld diplomats felt as though they were running a morality gauntlet just getting in and out the carpark area with all these lines of desperate-looking vagrant craturs staring them down.

Even without that these diplomats were a nervous set of cunts. It was suggested they be provided with a helicopter but it was negatory to that, helicopters having become mair of a survival hazard than cheap-deal lower-level flights in the days before the "persian bet".

Many people didnay like helicopters at all. It was said on strong authority that they brought bad luck. Whenever a helicopter was seen or heard the mair impressionable ped-estrians had taken to ducking their heids. The nation's weans were to blame. It began with a banal advertising gimmick to boost helicopter flight sales: "Dont Come a Cropper, Fly by Chopper". The campaign had about petered out when a school caretaker in Wisconsin noticed that weans were flinging them-selves on the playground whenever "the angry big bird" flut-tered into hearing range. The school caretaker texted his colleagues throughout the county, then the state.

The phenomenon was widespread. Race, nationality, eth-nicity, the religious persuasion of their parents; nayn of that shite mattered; weans across the land were walking in trepida-tion. Soon the adults startit paying attention to these infant human beings and their natural-born instincts. After all, nay-body wants to become a cropper. No even diplomats and members of the United Nations.

Obviously airport bookies were wary of executive-class flights used by targets and diplomats and politicians can be targets, another reason why they were so jumpy, so nervy. These dignitaries couldnay stand still or sit still and their bodyguards were aye remonstrating with indigenous Security operatives, wanting them to check out every empty cigarette pack or potato-chip bag for secreted items, items whose invisibility was nay guarantee of nonexistence. Their dealings with us in the Alien and Alien-Extraction Section took place around the carpark areas and were peremptory. My compadrés werenay to go into the main terminal building unless necessary and were to keep out the way of the DC check-ins. If dispatches or messages needit delivery the immediate superior checked to see if such as myself was free. Some of my fellers werenay pleased, further evidence of infiltratory malpractice from yours truly.

Agh well, fuck them.

But this minor notoriety fitted where my heid was in the private-eye story. Circumstances had me a loner in real life, and it suited me to have that wee bit extra freedom now. If there was a hypocritical element in my position that was all it was, an element. We arenay always in control. Sure I had my ayn ideas about things; that was logical, I came from another culture. But that was an aid to judgment. Maybe it helped me see things yer average person missed. For example, if the Security bosses had gien the Alien Section free rein on the "being problem" I was convinced we could have resolved it. Although the problem was common to the entire airport it was wur ayn section had maist involvement; down-and-out folks rarely inveigled their way inside the terminal buildings.

Us in the Alien Section could have telt the authorities there was nothing unique in such a disappearance. Down-and-out folks were aye doing it. But to no avail: already the manifestation had taken on an otherworldly aspect and believer-type bodies were coming up with some extravagant explanations for the manner in which the being could enter in and out of existence, apparently at will. During the next few days clerics, officers and robed administrators of the more popular religious organizations could be spotted at the scene of conflagration, hands behind their backs and nodding sagely, soberly, serenely, sagaciously.

Where did these perambulating persons go? They were vanishing into "thin air". Could it be they were in hospital, having collapsed in the street from malnutrition? Had their heids been battered in by teenage sadists on their way to corporate stardom? Or was it like a vagrant's vacation, a bizarre form of sabbatical? Maybe there was a seaside town where they gathered for their ayn wee offbeat conventions. It became a media topic. The level of public interest had grown in these unusual true-born citizens eftir the advent of the "persian bet". One of the weirder discussions I heard on radio featured a typical panel of sociologists, psychologists, religious chiefs and politicians. By the time I had lit a smoke and sat down with a beer the talk centred around a cranky multibillionaire with a heart of gold who insisted on anonymity and was a master of disguise. I thought I had missed something. We are talking here about some sentimentalized fiction straight out a 1930s movie and starring what-d'ye-call-him, that tall pink fucker with the amiable manner, Mister Middle America, him with the quiet voice (but dont get him riled boy dont get him riled). The existence of this philanthropic character was being linked to the numbers of down-and-outs disappearing from the airport. One panelist thought the doings of such an individual as "sagacious an explanation as any". Another scoffed at this "absurd postulate" and irritated her co-panelists by describing unusual true-borns as "domestic refugees" and "seekers of domestic asylum".

According to reports what this multibillionaire hero cunt

did, having retired from an exhausting time of it screwing the world out of untold riches, he had shipped a huge medieval castle across from Inklin and papped it slapdang in the middle of the Arizony desert, hired a hundred of them loveable upperclass good ol boy Inkliz butlers and a hundred of the best damn cooks in the world, all specializing in choice Tehano-Mehicano and Goanese fish dishes. The cranky multibillionaire also hired west-coast experts on dietary deficiency and tailors who knew how to darn socks and patch a guy's semmit and drawers. He brought in a genyoooine state-of-the-art laundromat that leaves yer clothes cleaner than when they went in and doesnay fuck everything up with strange, evil-smelling fluids and oose quiffs of unknown origin. This laundromat was a warm welcoming place, opening 24/7 and serving free coffee, good coffee, coffee thick as a bowl of broth, and fresh bagels man good fucking bagels, plus a decent wee library of paperbacks to pass the time, e.g. those auld Signets, Mentors and Image Books from years and years ago, featuring the usual great titles; *The Harmony of Capital and the Christian Church*; *Monarcquy and Systematized Religion*; *Kings of Earth and Heaven*; *The Inviolability of Privilege*; *Rape, Pillage and the Assault on Learning*; *Philosophy of Greed: The Age of Abuse*; *Two Thousand Years of Hypocrisy*. What a treat! Then too there was a good auld-fashioned cobbler on the premises, one who remembered how to mend the boots of parties whose soles were flapping and whose heels had all but dropped off.

Every bit of the essential detail we need to bulk out a fantasy, all of it was there. Some believed that he and the grocery-cart pusher were one and the same feller, one whose boyhood passions were good deeds, conjuring tricks and treading hot cinders. But no matter his identity that good ol anonymous multibillionaire WASP philanthropist fucker with the amiable manner had thought of everything and bought everything, he hadnay left nothing to chance. He was like the king of amiable multibillionaires. He was a god, he made them all sit up and listen; including the unusual Uhmerkin true-born citizens many of whom had been disillusioned sir they had been cynical, they had been no-gooders, but now, christ almighty, these impoverished individuals had turned the other cheek and dang one's britches did they no take to worshipping the same multi-billionaire, yes boss may it please yer majesty why shorely they did and he had to explain he wasnay God but just an instrument here on earth man it was fucking heartwarming. And once he had done all of that, one of the grateful auld salty dawg down-and-outs bestowed upon the castle a name and with his last dying breath he breathed that name into the ear of the multibillionaire: Mom's Applepie Honky Tonk Hideaway for Hobos and Ramblers, says he.

Now word spread that suchlike parties were not only wel-come in the state of Arizony but that this yere Honky Tonk Hideaway was a palace built for them and them alone. Not everybody was pleased, as the panelists on the radio program reminded the Chairperson, countless Uhmerkins work entire lifetimes and never once get no dang sabbatical leave like them dang commie welfare fucking hobo bums. We are talking here hardworking, honest and uprightly decent and respectable indigenous citizens. Maybe no too indigenous. We dont want no native warrior varmints in the neighborhood.

In senior diplomatic circles the episode with the being and the combustible grocery cart caused a furore; town and state hospitality was the subject of many a horselaugh. But the serious Security clampdown had begun from this point. Nothing like it must happen again. The airport authorities didnay care how it was to not happen just that it didnay, and *ASAfuckingP*. All operatives were called into the Security lounge for an emergency seminar. Each Security agency was having similar seminars and meetings. From now on sentimentality was barred. Naybody was to feel sorry for these down-and-out bodies. They were criminalist panhandlers with not one shred of decency between them. No exceptions to the rule, skint insurance bookies and corporate bankrupts notwithstanding. The merest whiff of sympathy and ye were out the job. And as for that grocery-cart pusher – the so-called being – he or she or whatever the fuck was to be a-vanished from the premises altogether. Enhanced contracts lay in store for the successful agency, amazing kudos for the successful operative. According to another rumour "amazing kudos" might lead to adult wages. Some of my alienigenae comrades were romantic fuckers and fell for that one.

One solution was to palm the being a winning ticket on a lower-end airplane seat to Labrador City or Santiago. Us lower-rung Security operatives thought that too straightforward. No unless "somebody" was there "to meet" the being at the destination, otherwise s/he might return. When it came to a-vanishings alien operatives were in agreement with certain authorities, the only true removal is from the face of the earth.

But this was a busy time aw the gether and how was a feller to cope. With the constant nightshift I hardly saw Yasmin. I saw mair of my baby daughter than I did of her. Eftir she resumed work she cleaned offices on a part-time basis. When she was leaving the house I was arriving – five minutes at the maist.

Och man, sometimes it was a great five minutes; superb clinches and cuddles and stroking and softness and warmth.

Okay.

If I was late I had to collect the baby from an apartment along the corridor, from an elderly couple we knew. The man had been in Security himself, worked for a spell as night watchman. I got on fine with him. I stayed with the wee lassie for a couple of hours then wheeled her along to one of the cousins. Sometimes I fell asleep with her on my lap, woke up with the two of us in the same position, me sitting on the feed-bottle. It was dangerous and I tried no to let it happen, but happen it did. I was tired all the time and when ye are tired the defences are down, intellectual and otherwise. It was eftir midday by the time I got to bed. (I had to be back for the airport bus at 5.30 pm.) Yet still I couldnay sleep. All sorts of fantasies choked my brain; scary scenarios featuring ghoulish craturs who emerged from the sulphurous depths of disused mineshafts. Some of it was enmeshed in the private-eye story where I had an idea about the central character getting in tow with the runaway partner of a Broadway producer who was the daughter of a big Californ̄an landowner or maybe an Arizony yin. And she had slipped and banged her heid on the ground thereby rendering her unconscious and eventually losing her memory which to me was a blatantly obvious possibility. And maybe to challenge her and confront her would somehow awaken her from a nightmare mental slumber that I might rescue her and lead her back to her ayn kith and kin; visions of covering her with a warm blanket, getting her to sip a drop of brandy, flinging her into a fast car and driving her hame to the sparse south-west territories, into the warm embrace of a relieved and eternally grateful faimly. And if her father did own vineyards along the Mexican border or some-place else in the region maybe he needed an overseer. I would have been a good boss, rough as fuck but with a heart of gold; not only would I bestow affection on the afflicted peon I would fucking crack the whip and carry the shotgun on folded arm. And a personal irony lurked somewhere: these selfsame vine-yards were the original destination of my namesake ancestor when he set out on the Santa Fe trail, but took the wrang turning and wound up a fucking christian, or so the sorry tale tells us.

But the job at the airport was definitely interfering with my life. Like booze or gambling, when that happens, ye have to consider yer position. Add traveling time to the 12-hour shifts and it was far far too long. The actual journey to and from the airport was a grind. The bus dropped me downtown and from there I needit other public transport, whether to the ex's apartment or to my ayn place, the en suite cupboard which I still kept and frequently used. The main reason why I still kept it and frequently used it was because me and Yasmin were not living together on a permanent basis. She had not fucking invited me to come and do so. But she couldnay anyway because her cousin continued to occupy the spare room. The apartment belonged to the baith of them. The only way out was us to move into another place. But for that we needit money, money money money. It was me that needit it. And I had to get it. But how the hell would I get it? The wage they paid me was just a fucking joke. How could people earn so little for so much? These are the questions that floor a body.

Being a messenger did break the monotony but it could backfire and the uniforms didnay help matters. Different agencies had different styles, cuts and colours. In my section males and females would have been as colourful as any if allowed and that enforced insipidity didnay suit us. Mind you, individuals are aye inventive and accessory items were favoured; especially scarves, cravats, ties, belts and footwear separates; and, obviously, bracelets, bangles, brooches and earrings, bodypiercings and other jewelry; also some of us wore unusual laces or ornate belt-buckles; some had jaggy spikes on their fancy-heeled, tall-stepping boots. But even then, amid all that sartorial fucking innovation, dignitaries and higher-authority figures continually mistook us for chauffeurs and servants, and started shouting and bawling orders at us to go fetch their gameboy-laptops and pornomag-carriers.

Naybody liked dealing with these people. In the days following the diplomat scare I had to go messages three, four or five times a shift. These messages came from the Patriot Holding Center or else were bound for there eventually. I carried them in and out the terminal. One night I passed the usual plainclothes Security and gied them a nod, a friendly nod as I thought. It turned out the pair werenay "the usual" at all, having just been transferred in to help cope with the "recent emergency". They stepped in front of me so I halted. They wantit to know if that was a uniform I was wearing, and if so what sort of vehicle was I driving and where was it parked, did I know the regulations governing airport usage? I telt them I wasnay a fucking chauffeur. I telt them I was on my way across to Interior Immigration Section Eleven with a package. They checked the package externally, which was fair enough but they were still annoyed at me for seeing through their Uncle Joe public disguise. Being annoyed at themselves would have been understandable; why take it out on me?

Look, I says, with respect to yez and nothing against the job yez do but when I saw through yer plainclothes disguise I was merely recognizing fellow professionals. Yez are my comrades, my fucking comrades, I says, pardon the language, surely I'm gauny notice ye? Okay yez arenay wearing any uniforms but naybody is gauny mistake yez for Uncle Joe public.

They didnay like that one. But they had yet to identify themselves and I was in a quirky mood. Everybody knew a crucial part of training for the plainclothes operative centred on the need to remain calm and collected in sensitive circumstances. But I knew they had intended the chauffeur remark as derogatory. The domestic Defense industry has its ayn hierarchy and in certain company chauffeurs dont get a foot on the ladder. The Alien and Alien-Extraction Section might have been a lowly outfit but at least the ladder had been reached, and that was something.

These plainclothes strangers had never seen operatives from any Alien Section before and didnay believe an entire Security section could exist that was composed of me and my compañeros. I telt them it wasnay a big section and one of these days it would get even smaller.

You got any ID?

Sure, I says, have you?

They didnay smile but displayed theirs. I displayed mine. They took mine and kept theirs. The concept "Red Card" interested them; the manner in which they were studying it suggested they hadnay seen many, no outside textbooks and training manuals. The one hauding it frowned and gripped me by the shoodir. When I flinched he says: Hey now buddy settle down. It says here you're a atheist socialist from Skallin and I wanted to touch you, begging your pardon, an aged ancestor of my family came from your country.

Well aint that something, I said with a cheery grin, noticing his comrade had his haun inside his jacket in such a way it had to be resting on the butt of a firearm, unless his galluses had bust and he was hauding one strap up. But it was neither of those. It was a cell phone. He was already dialing a number and moved outwith hearing range before speaking. I said to the other feller, Tell me this: is the only genuine removal disappearance from the face of the earth?

You want to explain that?

Sure, I hear on good authority that certain individuals may be persona non grata in this airport and greater airport territory. At least one such individual has been designated. The person is to be removed. There have been discussions among my comrade operatives and it is their belief, based on experience, that the only true removal is disappearance.

You want to explain that?

I thought I just had.

Pardon me?

I hoped you might explain it to me.

Oh you did?

Yeh.

So where you from buddy, you say Skallin I think not, I think you are a Turk, maybe from Hungary. Heh, you Hungary for a Turkey?

No sir.

So where exactly?

Glasgow.

Not Montana?

No sir.

The other one had put away the phone and returned. He stared at me then took the Red Card from his comrade and looked like he required another dimension to gie it the complete inspection. He glanced at me, then back to the ID, then at me, then the ID.

Okay, I says, ye wondering how come an inkliz-talking pink guy lands in the Alien and Alien-Extraction Section?

He proffered the ID but I was beaten to it by his comrade who was wanting to gie it yet another read and when he did so he frowned at my legs. What the fuck was that about? I glanced downwards in case there was something wrong. Maybe he was seeing if my right-leg trouser was rolled up, if I belonged to the Order of Venerable Set Squares. Maybe they would relax if I whistled the second movement of Mozart's clarinet concerto, the section used as a code by particular lodges in stressful situations.

So where do you guys go? he said.

Pardon me?

That a secret you keep?

Aint nothing wrong with secrets, said his comrade. Mister Brown, you want to keep a secret you keep a secret, you got freedom in this country of ours that provides succour for those who seek refuge and will lead them into its warm and tender bosom if granted mete dominion. And so, now, well, I got to tell you, you asked us a question and here is the answer: there are people who belong to an extraordinary group of individuals. You got that?

Yes sir.

Well now that group of extraordinary individuals may only go away. They are outside of all officialdom and they are beyond all authority. They are so far gone there aint even a bell they can carry to warn ol Joe public of their impending appearance, you know what I'm saying?

Sure.

So Jeremiah, if that indeed be your name, the other guy smiled, why dont you fellers wear that turban headdress or them fehzeeeezehz then we could recognize you and no mistake. Or like you know that skirt you got and them pipes? why dont you wear them?

Thanks, I says, and you can put on the auld loincloths and the bow and arrows, your feather headdresses, the fancy moccasins.

He gave me a playful punch that numbed my upper arm for five or so seconds.

Aow, I replied. Except we aint allowed wur ayn cultural clothing ... I was still rubbing my arm. They gie us these nonpartisan uniforms in the interests of the integratit assimilatory majority.

You bet, he says.

Hey, said the other yin, you know this aint personal.

Of course, I says, ye dont see me as an individual at all, it's just a general situation that might have happened to anybody.

And I dont mind yez acting in the authoritative manner and I aint a-gauny blame yez for it. No because I'm no a churlish guy but because acting in the authoritative manner is what you boys get paid for.

You bet.

Sure, I said, and about these disappearances, what I believe – and it is based on my ayn direct experience – I believe that certain beings exist in a purely transitory condition, it is like they live a life on wheels, and sometimes if they're up a hill the wheels start turning and they pick up momentum, and they dont stop when they reach the bottom, no sir, no at first, cause the bottom bottoms out so to speak, and these wheels trundle on, and on, and on.

The feller who had tapped me on the upper arm smiled. I stopped talking. You move around on the delivery run? he said.

Yes sir.

So you seen this grocery-cart being recently?

No sir.

When d'you last see him?

Well I havenay.

He frowned.

I've just heard people talking.

You aint ever seen him?

No sir.

What d'you mean then with "direct experience", what you talking about there.

It was a metaphor.

Oh okay. The feller proffered the Red Card and I raised my hand as though to take it. He moved it towards me and I moved my hand towards it; then he gied me the fucking thing and, stepping back, performed a wee one-fingered salute, but dragging the forefinger to angle it at his right temple. It was then

I knew this guy was gauny commit suicide, and he was gauny do it at some point soon.

Ye married? I says.

Huh?

You got kids?

He stared at me. I've got one.

That's nice.

Yeh.

I got one too.

He smiled.

I stuck the ID back in my pocket. Hey, I said, yous guys entered the lottery yet? Our section has a big thing gaun on the being's age, name and gender; you have to take into account the guiding star from his or her horoscope, what were the planets in the exchelsis at the time of his or her birth, then you got parents, what religion, proclivities and politics they got; all of that's mixed in on the bet, their likes and dislikes and then the grannie and grandpa, the ancestors, what about them and their star signs and aw that el shitero mein herr I was never into horoscopes myself, just too much information to take in at once, I aye preferred a clean-cut even-money shot; all-in run or not, spin that wheel and throw that ball, chinko chinko there we go but fate is aye involved in this and I dont know if yez are into fate. Myself? no, I like to control my ayn destiny.

Hey, other folks in your section, they seen this character also?

Well now sir I dont know about that because fact aye gets mixed with fantasy, folk are fooled even by middling phenomena. I think maybe some have in my ayn section because of where we're stationed, on the peripheries, and that's where the being turns up except for infrequent particulars like the recent diplomat scare. Here is a singular occurrence but, and it is consistent within the reports, that ye can see the being and it just goes right out yer heid. Imagine it! Ye stand there gazing upon the person till moments later ye come to and it's like wow, where did she or he go! It is like this being's face is so nondescript, I says, so nondescript one's eyes cannay linger on it for long. And yea though we may want to figure out the nature of this conundrum such that it may help us engineer his or her disappearance, why sir it am too late, too late because that ol bumpkins being has a-vanished right from under one's nostrils. Then ye got the other weird yin where ye see that ol being bumpkins and ye cant hardly remember it like you see it and the next moment it is gone from yore mind, it isnay even a memory, like somebody has pulled a switch and dang if that illumination aint gone sir. For all I know I saw the being ten minutes ago.

One of the pair was staring hard at me, typical dangerous cunt. A wee whack on the heid would sort him out. His partner said, Okay bud where d'ya say you were headed?

Interior Immigration Section Eleven, I says, holding the package firmly. I realized they were wanting its contents described. Authorized business, I says, I got to go.

They watched me.

See you fellers later, I said and strolled off; only about twenty metres though, then I paused as though to examine my shoelaces. One of them was staring eftir me. The other had the phone back to his ear and was nodding. I gied them a wave but they made no show of recognition. I was annoyed at myself and couldnay figure why. It hadnay been a good experience but I couldnay blame myself for that. How else could I have handled it?

Now that I was down on my hunkers I thought to redo my shoes properly. Yasmin had gied me a new pair of chequered laces the other day but they were far too fucking long for the round socket things, the eyelets or whatever ye call them. And so the bows I made hung ower the sides of the shoes and went all straggly in wet weather. I was forever stepping on them and nearly falling on my face. Now I undid them. But right at that moment there was this infant ran up and stood watching me. A wee boy. How ye doing son! I says. He must have been two to two and a half years of age. I looked about but there were nay adults. He was frowning at my shoes and the unusual laces. Where's yer mammy? I says. He didnay reply, except now he gied that weird look infants can gie, a kind of non-reflective but fearful scepticism. Who knows what goes on in their minds. Recently I noticed my ayn wee lassie gieing the same look to a neighbor. She wasnay a year auld at the time. I was seeing it as a sign she was maturing healthily, gaining an increased innerlife subjectivity or something.

The wee boy was also studying my hat like either he was expecting me to gie him it or else produce an ice-cream cone from the place occupied by my heid. The hat was maybe the most nondescript part of the entire uniform. It had a steel wire rim inside to keep the outer shape permanent. To combat this my comrades had extracted and mangled the wire then bashed the hats into mair interesting shapes. The wee boy was frowning now and appeared quite anxious. Is yer mammy no here son? I says, Eh? where's yer mammy?

He gied me a look of horror.

What about yer daddy? I says, Is yer daddy here?

Now he was back to gawking at my shoes, these long trailing laces, one of which I still hadnay tied.

There were many people in the vicinity but I couldnay see any parenting-style adults with worried expressions. The "lost wean" part of Security work didnay much happen for my section because we spent 99 per cent of the time outside the terminal building. If it did happen it would be serious business. But for indoor operatives lost weans were a daily occurrence.

I reached for his arm but he backed off. Dont worry son, come on, I says, gie me yer hand. But he kept backing off and I saw he was set to bolt so I reached and caught him by the elbow, and he screamed. What's up wee man? I says, Heh, dont cry.

I was onto my feet now and hoisted him in the air. Heh, here, here, sshh sshhh. But he started kicking. Ssshhh ssshhh ssshhhh. But he wouldnay ssshhh and his screaming got louder and louder. Heh wee man, dont worry dont worry, heh dont worry . . .

People were looking across now and nay wonder with the wean, he was gaun fucking dementit; shrieking and kicking at me and pushing out with his forearms and I was having to work to control him, he had some strength. He was like a goddam I dont know, no like a wean anyway, mair like a tiny wee weightlifter or boxer.

What's up buddy?

Two Security guys had moved in on me while I fought to calm him down. They had the top-level insignia on their caps and baith were fingering stun guns. A lost wean, I said.

What d'you say?

He's lost. I'm pacifying him. And now the wee boy startit lashing out with his feet again, just missing my heid. I raised him a bit higher.

Hey, said the other guy.

What?

He was holding his arms out to me. Give him here, he said. What do you not know how to hold a kid? You dont know how to hold a kid?

What?

Dont swing the kid like that.

Who's swinging him? I'm no swinging him, he's kicking.

Give him here.

What ye talking about . . .

Give me the boy.

Sure, I said, okay, here, and I passed him ower, his feet still kicking out, still shrieking. The operative held him to his shoodir and patted and rubbed his back. The shrieking had subsided into greeting. You aint ever held a baby before? he said. That's no way to hold a baby.

What . . .

You dont know how to hold a baby?

What! Fucking cheek, I says, ye kidding! I'm trying no to lose my temper here, I've got a wean of my ayn so dont talk to me about how I dont know how to haud weans, I'm used to hauding weans, gieing them a bath or else changing shitty diapers, whatever, I'm used to it, right, gieing them their fucking bottle man through the night and when I get hame in the morning, just about every fucking morning, I do all of that – what do ye think an alien cannay haud a wean man gie us a fucking break.

Pardon me?

Aw sorry, I says, am I too guttural? Then I smiled ironically.

Nah, I have to say that I didnay "smile ironically". And I didnay say nothing about being "too guttural".

Okay, and nayn of the angry outburst happened either. If it had they would have arrested me under Section 2 of the Extremist Outporings legislation, my use of Alien English deemed to produce terror among true-born true-breeds. What I really said was: Sorry mein herr.

Naw, I didnay say that either. I cannay mind what I fucking said, whether I managed to be ironic or what the fuck I dont know, except I was inordinately upset and wrathful and it was pretty darned close to the surface. Probably I was rendered speechless. It would have looked like I was cowed by authority, often the best means of escape.

He shook his heid at me and moved backwards and forwards

lulling the wean whose greeting had become a tearful whimpering. A few passers-by had stopped to spectate. They were nodding in appreciation of how the Security body handled the situation.

Obviously he knew what he was doing. I am no denying that. He probably had half a dozen weans of his ayn and bathed and fed them every night of the week. Nay doubt he breast-fed them, one of these new natural father bastards. Plus he was an authentic enforcer of the law and this fitted in with nationwide propaganda in praise of a people-focused Security industry whose only aim was to care for waifs and elderly personages of an infirm disposition. Whereas me, with my fucking voice and that stupit uniform what did I look like, I dont know what I looked like, no even a chauffeur, some kind of – I dont know.

The situation was hopeless. I was within a semicircle formed by tourist spectators. They stared at me. The other Security guy stepped aside to make a call on his phone. I noticed his concentration flicker between me and the package. I had lain it on the floor when I bent to tie my laces and it was now about six feet away. It wasnay that it was inappropriate for me to collect it and leave, just that if I had tried it, well, he might have used the fucking stun gun. Me and electricity have never got on the gether.

Now who should arrive on the scene but the plainclothes fuckers, with a woman at their elbow, the greeting wean's mother. A quiet conversation ensued between them and the other two operatives, their gaze straying to me. There was nothing I could do except act naturally. I was stranded in this totally horrible, totally awkward fucking situation like I was some clumsy kind of baby-snatcher. And I couldnay escape!

Escape is the wrang word.

Naw it isnay!

If I could have managed to shift things back to normality. If

I could somehow get everybody to relax. The wean wasnay lost and the mother was found and they were baith reunited and that was that and everything was happily ever eftir, end of story.

But it wasnay end of story: me and the package in the context of a lost child; it was like a detective-movie plot. The woman held the wean in her arms but he still wasnay pacified. Even with her hauding him he was girning and squirming. She looked at me. I smiled. She kept looking at me. Acute venom. Worse than that. Her son had just been saved from a horrible death and I was the paedophiliac murdering monster responsible. Fair enough. One gets these looks on a daily basis, one must proceed with one's life. Mistakes happen; these are no to be taken personally. Nay need for paranoia. One lands in the occasional predicament as a furnir body and one simply extricates oneself as best one can, ofttimes by flight, one can race down a street in order to outpace a baying mob, or perhaps by guile one may remove oneself, and here I stepped to the four Security bodies, reaching for the package. I lifted it. They watched me. Alright, I said, this is authorized, I better get on and deliver it.

Pause.

Ye know where I'm going, and ye know whence I've come.

One nodded. The others didnay respond. The mother of the greeting wean avoided looking at me.

I walked, the tourists and other spectators parting for me. I kept on, crossing the area, the package tucked under my elbow and upper arm, keeping my gaze to the ground and this time I didnay glance back ower my shoodir. I knew they were staring. Anything I did was suspect.

It was a bad situation and escaping intact was primary. And I had escaped. How many poor cunts would have failed in the attempt? Across at Interior Immigration I got the business done.

The operatives who received the package werenay familiar to me so I couldnay refer to the incident. I wanted it noted by somebody on my side because it certainly had been noted by the opposition. What had been noted by the opposition?

Whatever they fucking wantit. Nothing was something. It was another entry on my record. If any official hesitated ower my status this foolish nonsense could tilt the decision.

Fuck the terminal dispatches and deliveries, I wantit back to carpark patrol. This shite was just fucking too much man I just get sick of this forever having to fucking explain myself christ it gets ye down man it really gets ye down.

There was nothing to regret about how I had handled the incident but it weighed on me, of course it weighed on me; it wasnay one incident it was two. I thought maybe I could discuss it with Riçard Osoba and waited until he arrived but then I decided against. I just didnay talk to folk in that way. I didnay even know how to broach it. It would just embarrass us baith. Ye kept that kind of stuff out yer life, humiliations and fucking all that stuff, ye didnay keep on about it with each other because it was fucking humiliating for the two of yez. But what I did was a quick report and I sent it to an email address "of convenience". It wouldnay reach nay cunt because there was nay cunt to reach but what it did was get my statement recorded and read by whoever was patroling the computers.

I didnay tell the ex about what had happened. She would have laughed. New entry on the database: nay parenting skills. Elements of it were funny. Naw, nay elements of it were funny. Weans can be dangerous. Aliens dont get involved with weans. If ye see one in trouble ye look the other way.

Yasmin wondered if I had made some stupit joke against the Securitys, if I had antagonized them. I hadnay made nay fucking jokes. I was the joke.

Unless I had been sarcastic. I dont know, how the hell do I know, ye just do these things in conversation. I dont work it out. Maybe I had made some stupit comment. She was right. I did antagonize cunts. Sure I antagonized them. I meant to antagonize them. What does that mean, "antagonize"? These official fuckers antagonized me all the time. They just didnay know they did, that they had succeeded. I showed them nothing. But sometimes I raised. Once in a while ye have to. Ye go for it. It is the name of the game, no just bluff but a sensible appeal to the fates; ye have to check out that flop, see what yez hold in common, these bastards with their stupit pairs man ye have to strip them of all authority then see what they are made of. If that is grounds for guilt then I hang the heid, one has to hang the heid.

It was obvious that the reason I was gien messages between the Patriot Holding Center and the terminal was because naybody mistook me for an inmate. A guard yeh, no a prisoner. The job was supposed to improve my immigrant status, no act as a nail in the deportation coffin. Now I wondered how soon before I was on constant pooch patrol, or consigned to permanent office-work. These wee head-butts with authority draw attention to ye. When I worked in the booze trade I was anonymous. In a job like this just a twitch of the eyebrow gets ye noticed.

I should have got out there and then. With Yasmin and the wean; I could have grabbed the two of them and headed hame to dear auld bonné. But I didnay.

But I didnay have the fucking money, the money the money the money. I didnay have any. And my daughter was less than a year auld, too young for flying oceans, even if the ex had agreed. She didnay no agree because I didnay ask.

My mother would have been so glad to see us. But it wasnay to be and it didnay happen so so what, so fucking what.

Nay doubt it was my fault.

But it wasnay a time for self-pity I just needit to face the truth. What was the truth? Nothing in particular, I was aye a fucking I dont know. I had to learn to relax, quell one's passion.

Except one was on edge one was on edge, one required a cigarette, one had been a non-smoker of same for a lengthy period yet the torture only increased. One tried to cope; one lifted one's beer.

Perhaps a uisgué was in order, perhaps I could allow myself one in honor of my last night. There was a musty bottle of Glenmorangie on the shelf, I would buy it. For tomorrow I was certainly returning to the land of my birth and henceforth that fucking bottle of malt uisgué was the only ID I was gauny show any cunt man any fucking fascist cunt, fuck them, I was catching that flight hame tomorrow, oh mañana, and my ticket was bought, I had bought it man I had bought it, how many times had I studied it and checked it and it was like fine, fine, it was all fine, the auld el le billet, it was there in the motel room, all my documents, my dough, it was waiting for me. Christ when I got fucking out of here it would be by the skin of my teeth man I would be running along the tarmac, luggage in hand, the air stewardess keeping the cabin door open, the rope ladder dangling, the airplane already backing off, Jump for it Mister Brown jump for it! and all the passengers' heids at the cabin windows. Oh for fuck sake man here we go and I have to leap up for the damn thing, catch the rungs with one hand, the luggage swinging behind me, then steadying myself, pulling myself up, but I manage it I manage it and the air stewardess gies me this great big smile and helps me inside, shutting the door, her cheek brushing mine and her perfume, and then the pilot looks ower his shoodir and he is like: Well done Mister Brown, ye made it!

Jesus christ. Nay wonder ye get upset stomachs. Milk is what I needit, no beer. I was aye escaping by the skin of my teeth. That had to stop. I had to change my way of living. I was a father, a father for fuck sake man I had to settle down I couldnay settle down

put up with the shite, how do ye put up with the shite, how does one cope with the nonsense? In the job or out the job it all be the same sir that ol ruling authority son it done chokes the goldarn breath out ye, them fuckers, they dont gie a feller peace, peace.

christ, my kingdom for a smoke.

a bottle of milk for the stomach.

When did I last shave?

I noticed the time on my wristwatch. How come nayn was passing? How come it was so early? What fucking zone was I in! It felt like the wee sma oors, or else I had landed in one of these eerie sci-fi scripts where time has stopped and all the locals are tuned in the gether against the one stranger, a handsome young feller who blunders into town and his only escape is making common cause with an indigenous damsel of beauteous aspect. Sally. Fucking hell man where's the note-book. Some scenario but when ye think about it. Good movie material. Especially with interesting special effects. The locals turn into blood-sucking pagan monsters and they gie all these nasty knowing winks at each other when the feller isnay watching, and their eyeballs are blood veined. Enter the sheriff, some bible thumper with a chip on his shoodir because he thinks some no-good atheistical bum is sleeping with his missis.

And the only reason he got the sheriff job is because his wife's uncle is big politically, a dude with a shady past. The no-good drunken atheistical bum isnay really a no-good drunken atheistical bum man he used to be a US marshal but lost his nerve in a gunfight and hit the booze but the only person who thinks he isnay a worthless loser is yer woman, the sheriff's missis

who is the big sister of the luscious lassie, that indigenous damsel!

Fuck sake where be ma notebook! Then there is a town fire and the young hero feller bursts in and rescues all the women and weans and he dang nearly gets killed, in fact he dang does get killed and the whole town feels ashamed and guilty ever after but will we forgive the fuckers, danged if we will, no sir.

Some of these fantasies had potential. I worked out my ideas while patroling the airport carparks and tried to hold them in my brain till I got hame and could switch on the auld laptop. But when I did I had nay energy or else I forgot the ideas, or they turned out to be a load of nonsense; embarrassing shite, and halfway through writing them down I gied up, double-clicked on a game of patience. It was that Security job. It would be great for future reference but at the time, the actual time, when ye were working at it jesus christ it was hell on earth, I needit to get away. I startit taking days off and of all job-crimes this is the worst.

When the weather became warmer, coming off a shift, I would go straight to the ex's place. A couple of months eftir the wee lassie was born she got occasional out-of-town gigs and it was tricky with babyminders but when we got the chance we sat outside on the fire escape. Sometimes we had a wee drink, she was wary with the wean there but a couple was alright, a wee gin or even a fine black rum which we insisted on ruining with soft drinks. That rum should be treasured, according to her uncles and other auld yins. They liked it with ice and water, accompanied by vegetable pastries and salt fish, and a kind of what-do-ye-call-it, ratatooie, prepared by Yasmin's Auntie Doris, a great auld lady who had shaken the hand of somebody who had shaken the hand of somebody who knew somebody who had shaken the hand of Bob Marley. Bob Marley, I says, what about his ancestors? No sir. The ex had nay interest in hearing one single solitary fucking word about Bob Marley's ancestors and I wasnay to raise the matter within her wider faimly circle under any circumstances, no a whisper, no a peep, no a fucking whisper of a fucking peep. No under any kind of circumstances, nayn, nayn whatsoever. And that went for my book as well, she didnay like me talking about that any mair, no except to herself. She did listen and it is only prejudice that has me recall how her eyes glazed ower. She also became uncomfortable if I spoke about the airport and all the baggage that went with it, e.g. that "goddam being person", as she called her. Goddam being person!

So okay my dear, nay beings and nay ancestors and nay folk tradition of the Celtic peoples. So you're leaving me with sex, drugs and rock and roll! I laughed. Honey!

She raised her hands: Dont crush me!

I wont, I said, although I had wantit to gie her a big fucking cuddle. I aye got these rushes of blood. I took baith her hands in mine and kissed them, kissed her wrists and up the insides of her arms. She allowed it. I breathed in on her hair, the slight perfume. Yazzie, I said.

Yeh?

Nothing.

What?

Nothing.

She smiled. What you saying Jerry?

Nothing.

That aint like you.

Are ye kidding! Ye steal the words right out ma heid, ye steal them goddam words, ye just slither yer way in through the corpuscles of ma brain, the pores of ma skin, the minor orifices of one's entire fucking body. You are the woman,

275

Yasmin, here is to you, you are the lady, you are the one, let us clink glasses: sláinte, skol and bottoms up.

I didnay mention her eyes. She had these unusual eyes, they took in yer entire personhood. And the way she moved and held the mic and waggled her shoodirs when she was singing, elbows into her sides. When she strolled on I just smiled. She started singing, I just couldnay stop smiling. That first time I heard her sing, it was like one minute I had never heard her, never heard of her, never seen her, never knew a damn thing about her, and then there she was and it hit, washing ower me, all ower me; it is awesome when it hits ye, and this daft smile, it doesnay leave yer face man ye go for a piss and wash yer hands and ye see yer reflection in the mirror and there it is, the daft fucking smile gawking back at ye.

What a strange and enticing nightmare it all was. Relationships are extraordinary states of affairs. As a boy in Glasgow I must have discussed it with my mates. Of course I did. I couldnay have done otherwise. It was just so incredible. But maybe I didnay. *Because* it was so damn incredible. Maybe nayn of us could handle the idea of being married to a beautiful and luscious lassie and christ almighty can ye believe it, getting yer hole every day and night for the rest of yer life for fuck sake right till ye drapt deid! Such a thing is maybe beyond the collective adolescent comprehension. If one of us alluded to it the rest of us probably fell silent. Unless we never alluded to it. I dont remember ever alluding to it, ever discussing it with anybody; mates or doctors of psychology, big brother or feyther. Fucking nay cunt, I had naybody to talk to, it was just my ayn fantastic inner dramatics.

That never occurred to me before.

It was me wanting to manoeuvre her into marriage. She wasnay ready for that. No officially. So okay, I was talking about a semi-permanent relationship where one partner moves in with the other, where ye gie up yer ayn place and move into yer partner's. Permanent, or semi-permanent. It wasnay about "tomorrow". I never thought about tomorrow. It was nothing to do with that. It was today, it was the present moment, that was what I sought.

No sir, I never thought about tomorrow. No now, no ever.

No even tomorrow would I think about tomorrow. Ha ha.

Oblivion! Heh Sally, get me an oblivion, a large yin, on the rocks.

But I didnay have to catch the plane. I could hang up my traveling boots right here and now. I could stay where I was, forget all about the journey hame; ignore all thoughts of the ex except insofar as she was my ex, that that is all she was, mother of my wee girl and nothing more. I could stay here and who knows maybe get chatting to somebody in the bar, there were a couple of women around, just chat to somebody. One requires to escape one's head on occasion and the existence of other bodies is an aid to that. Not to mention a certain luscious lady behind the bar.

Just chatting to her for christ sake a conversation.

Then tomorrow morning I could apply for any job on offer, one that demanded I carry a faithful stick and knuckle-duster, stun-gun, ray-gun or gas canister, nailed club or broadsword, the trusty cuffs hanging from my belt; or what about one of these fashionable sub-machine scatter-guns the Security operatives carry on Saturday nights in most downtown areas, and all to protect Uncle Joe public. Yes sir, I could have applied for any job.

But no too far away. I didnay want to go back to the west coast. I didnay want to be too far from the wee yin. I was seeing her once a month and sometimes even twice. I didnay want to encroach, I didnay want to risk losing what I had, losing it aw the gether. But I had to get away, for my ayn heid man I had to get away.

But what about the wee yin's heid, would she have been better off no seeing me? Do camels swim, of course she would. No seeing me

spell it out. No seeing me was a good thing, he said, reaching for the smokes.

We are talking six months without a cigarette. That is a sign of something, some form of will power. I wasnay a total failure.

So this town where I now had landed – because I had struck a deal with a down-at-heel air-ticket salesperson who wanted to save me a petty few dollars, a middle-aged woman whom I liked; she had gumption, trying hard in an uncaring environment. Fine, let her get me a deal, and so she did, the deal of deals, so this town where now I had landed – a town-whose-name-escapes-me kind of town but one nevertheless

about this town

But what a pleasant surprise to find a decent bookshop. It made a burg like this a possibility, a place where ye could bring up a wean.

I checked my watch against the clock on the wall, it was 8:45 of the o'clock.

Quarter to nine? Surely that was what it was hauf an hour ago! Where does time go? Does time go anywhere?

There had been a certain wintry snap in the air. It wouldnay have surprised me if snaw lurked.

So, what to do? It was the decision I was considering. I had had six bottles of beer, or was it five, christ it might have been seven. There was that first pub I went to when I left the motel, the motel such-and-such, what was its monicker again? I had forgotten its fucking monicker. But lite beer it was, mighty short on the alcohol percentage, even had it been seven of them. It couldnay be eight. But the low alcohol was intentional, just a wee drink, no to get drunk; I needit the company. I just couldnay be in my ayn heid. No tonight. And nay nonsense, nay fucking stupit mental stupidity. I was a responsible feller nowadays. This was the new Jeremiah Brown. I had a bus and a plane to catch, and memories to dump; memories to dump. And passions to conceal.

My childhood wasnay full of music. My parents didnay listen to much at all. Music just wasnay part of my upbringing, it was all television, goggle goggle goggle, forced to watch a bunch of fucking middle-class bastards trying to be funny, haw haw haw, haw haw haw. How come people fall for that shite? My auld man just sat there. That was his fucking life. I do mind him singing stupit pop songs when I was a baby in the pram. I even mind being in the pram so what gets stated is attested and as it happened, a verbatim account from the one person that was there, aside from ma mammy.

I was an observant child. My ayn daughter was an observant child. Eftir the ex returned to her morning job I was in charge of the baby. I was on regular night shift. When I came hame Yasmin was leaving, so a wee peck at the door and off she went. What I discovered is I liked weans. That was what made it so ridiculous about the greeting wean incident at the airport.

Christ it was so goddam ironic! Me! I was like a wean expert; me with a kid of my ayn man I loved it, it was great, I loved it. I was a natural fucking father christ almighty. I loved them all, suffer the little children man the fucking lot of them. It started out with my ayn kid then spread out. Yasmin's cousin had weans and the neighbors had weans and I loved them, loved seeing them, how they got engrossed in their wee projects, all what they were up to, getting on with their lives, crawling about the flair with their toys; being with their ayn wee comrades, making up their ayn wee stories, creating their ayn myths. And for me, the likes of me, I felt great, it was like

I was a part of something, a regular community, being a part of it, coming up the stair and seeing somebody, Hullo. Christ. When I came hame from work I would be tense as fuck but as soon as Yasmin dumped the wean in my arms that tension was gone, that wee thing staring at me, gripping my finger in her hand, then her smile, hearing my voice, her eyes following the light, jesus christ, dont fucking talk to me.

The apartment overlooked the back alley and I held the wee yin on my lap; we watched what went on below. All of life was there. When she was a grown woman she would remember it and she would think of me and no matter, no matter what the hell or where the hell, where she was or I was, even if I was fucking deid! she would think of me and remember. Until the day she died herself christ almighty unless she suffered brain damage or something touch wood, ye dont even want to think about it. But that wee wean would be with me, we couldnay be separated, it wasnay possible. She knew me and she knew I loved her and she loved me. And she should have been gaun hame with me to see my maw, her grannie, that is what should have been happening. And the ex too, she never knew my mother never mind my auld man before he died. Imagine that. And it would have been good. She would have liked Glasgow, Glasgow would have liked her, and then when she sang.

Agh.

Fucking money, money money money. My last bad gambling day was a while ago but it was a sair yin; it wiped me out with interest. I had had a couple of minor escapades since then but that was a big one and it was a real sickener. Everything about it. Just fucking mental crazy guaranteed to explode yer brains and ye cannay dwell on such an event, because these type of things, they are no just sent to try us they are sent to

Close yer eyes and count to ten. Nah, keep the fucking eyes open.

For days eftir that last beating – and that was what it was, a beating, fucking beating – for days I sat there. Talk about depression; I just sat in my room and stared at the walls. I didnay have the energy to look out the window never mind turn on the television. The computer was out the question; things like stories and books were childish shite. Ye make up a wee story and then expect somebody to read it. It wasnay so much boring, it was goddam presumptuous; that was what it was. I was a presumptuous bastard. We all have stories, the whole world; humankind in its entirety, each and every individual. Who is gauny read them all? We arenay expected to read them all. Even good yins! A lot of stories are fucking crap but some arenay, some are fine. My ayn would be fine if it didnay keep going off at tangents. The guy goes on this long trip down south and then heads across Arizona way and there was gauny be immigrant workers and corrupt politics near the Mexican border and then he encounters this lassie who is incognito, working in the booze trade, some juke joint where life is wild and the music sweet. The guy has a pal; Bill, a caretaker in an apartment block, an aulder guy with a big faimly. These two get on well, good conversations, sometimes meet for a beer in the local tavern then Bill takes him hame for his dinner. Bill's wife likes Jamie and makes him feel like one of the faimly. Nay illicit affairs or nothing like that. She is a woman auld enough to be – maybe no his mother but his auntie. But what a fucking cook! Big pots of soup and home-made stews, plain fare; herrings in oatmeal and ketchup, the occasional kipper or Aberdeen finnan, fucking wholesome.

Even where they live, a nice comfy apartment, good space, plenty books and cds, and cushions and carpets, fucking comfortable, and clean, aye clean, good big windows, plenty light, great. Then the auldest daughter, a lassie of just about sixteen or something, beautiful smiles and innocent, she listens agog to what Jamie says, doesnay believe everything but just enjoys the craïc. Her mother calls him a loveable rogue but the lassie thinks he is great because he has this dangerous job where he has to kill baddies and sort out rights and wrongs, she even likes his name, Jamie. It all makes her look at her dad in a new light. Although Bill is a lowly caretaker he has interesting friends like Jamie so maybe he isnay dull and boring eftir all, maybe it is cool to be a caretaker and now she can walk tall at school where she was having difficulties because of these stuck-up fucking kids in her class, little upper-class WASP bastards. It isnay so much she was being bullied because she has a mind of her ayn, a strong-willed lassie as well, real depth, and no so much beautiful but at the same time good-looking, nice breasts, maybe mair like 18 than 16, a developed body. But Jamie would never have sex with her although sometimes he sees a certain gleam in her eyes – wistful or something – but he doesnay look at her in that way at all. To him she is like a wee sister and Bill is his mate and his wife is just brilliant, a great woman, hospitable, so why fuck up people's lives? It isnay as if sex was absent from his life anyway. He was a personable sort of young feller and had friendly relations with a few women, a couple of whom he slept with but no in a horrible adulterous life-affecting way, it was just like a bit of fun for christ sake, healthy young animal sort of thing, and then as well there was a local woman who kept eftir him, aye gieing pretexts to try and drag him into bed when her man was away to his work, but he managed to avoid it although she was good looking but in a kind of blowsy way and a couple of years aulder than him and maybe even she was a bit unstable mentally otherwise

Otherwise nothing.

I sneezed.

Somebody was smoking behind me and I sneezed again, the

smoke gaun right into my nostrils, thank christ, but up the wrang fucking pipe! How many pipes do we have in these protuberances anyway?

Fortunate was I that I carried a bunch of napkins for emergencies.

Naw but I was thinking that story of mine would make a better movie than a book. Ye saw a lot of movies where mine would fit. The book could come eftir the film premiere. By then the publicity would be out so everybody would want to buy it. The amazing thing is too ye can buy these books everywhere, but only once the movie is distributed. Then everybody has heard the publicity, all the celebrities have been on the television and in the Sunday supplements so then the public gets to know about the book, so they all want to buy it and you are already thinking about a follow-up, a sequel to the original, or else a prequel, about what happened before. So a couple of characters will be the same but other ones go, and obviously there are different lassies.

It was all there, it was there, just a question of getting it down. The problem was I couldnay get my heid into it, and nay wonder. How could ye concentrate on writing when yer napper was full of real stuff? Because when you and yer lady part you and yer wean part. Because that is what happens; man and woman split up means man and woman and wean split up cause ye cannay hauf a wean in two. Then yer everyday working life, how does that affect ye? does it affect ye? Everything affects me. Plus my concentration was fukt. So I sat in ma room.

I just sat there. Gieing the heid a rest.

What else?

Nothing. Just bleak, life was bleak.

If I had had the energy I would have gathered the goods and chattels and headed south. I wasnay gaun back to the west coast. The bridges were burnt. The idea of heading right the way south had begun to appeal, down through Mexico. I knew I could get a job. There were theme bars everywhere, oirisch fucking molly maguire bars; they would hire me in a minute; they never knew the difference anyway. Then I would join with the revolutionaries. Gradually the locals would trust me. Gaining their confidence would be a slow process but I would gain it. Eventually a couple of them would sidle up and suggest they took me to their leader, who would spot immediately I could be useful, maybe if I had the knack of dynamiting bridges. But first I needit to learn the language. But I would learn it, it was a case of application.

My life.

That sums it up.

But concentration wasnay always there and couldnay always be there and it wasnay always a person's fault, it wasnay my fault, I just fucking I dont know, sometimes I heard her songs.

Funny how that happens. The soundtrack in this music bar wasnay put on for my benefit and yet the songs playing were songs she might have selected. "That Ol Devil Called Love". The ex would have smiled when she heard it. It was a smile she gied, just a smile, if somebody in the company put on certain music. Once when she gied me that smile I tried to cuddle her; she resisted strongly, pushing me away. She resented the intrusion. I could be presumptuous. It was a fault of mine. But some presumption is natural. When ye enter a relationship ye arenay expecting yer partner to keep bits of herself out of bounds. Or are ye?

I dont fucking know. My ideas were all to fuck where relationships go. Another reason for gaun hame. I was blowing the last of my fast car savings on this trip. I had lifted the goddam lot bar two hundred dollars. I left the two hundred to keep the account alive. Never close a bank account. No in this country, the original fucking bureaucratic nightmare. The hollywood adverts never tell ye that.

But how many times in the past have I been saving dough for one purpose or another, and then gone and blown it. I am like one of these insects that has to keep rolling its ball of shite

Wrang metaphor.

I needit a car when the ex started doing the out of town work. She landed a regular spot twice a month but it was miles away and transportation was difficult. She could have had the gig on a mair regular footing but twice a month suited her. It was a distance from where we lived and the traveling got her down.

One of the fellers playing with her had an auld van and everything piled into it; them and the equipment, the PA and all sorts. It was a ramshackle auld effort but he had access to expertise as well as mechanical equipment and kept it roadworthy. But some nights it was scary gaun through long tunnels. Two or three fellers acted as roadies but they werenay reliable and it was aye the same yin did the driving, a musician; some nights he was out on concentration; who knows, too much booze or dope or something. I felt sorry for him and offered my driving services but Yasmin said no, she didnay want me involved. She didnay want me involved. All I was proposing was a turn at the wheel now and again, if I was going to a gig then why no do a bit of driving? why no help out if I could?

It was out the question.

I suppose they might have come to rely on me. It isnay as if I went all the time, only when it coincided with my nights off. If I had been able I would have gone mair often, if I could have exchanged shifts with a Security comrade, if it had been possible, but it wasnay, even when I was back in the booze trade, it just wasnay straightforward, my hours were her hours, plus we had to have babysitters, her cousins.

Ach but the musicians never made me too welcome. There was nay need to take it personally because it was a total squeeze in the jalopy, scarcely room for them never mind bodies with nay function. I was either on the floor at Yasmin's knees or stuffed in at the rear with the speakers and amps.

I did get myself a car but it was a fucking dismal fucking goddam heap, a sack of clapped-out mechanical bones, like one of them efforts Laurel and Hardy used to drive; that one where everything collapses, craziest thing ye ever saw, the doors fall off and the fucking

I needit a proper machine, one that purred and didnay crackle and rumble and go bang every ten minutes. I needit something reliable, trustworthy and healthy; one that didnay keep breaking down or depend on spare-part surgery. These weekly trips to the knacker's yard for fabricatit organs man I was sick of wading knee-deep in grease and shite in a search doomed to failure. It was alright if I had had the proper contacts but I didnay. Let me rephrase that, through the ex I had access to contacts, they just werenay accessed on my behalf. It was all down to me, most especially the artisanary skill base. One of my comrades at the airport was an excellent mechanic. I just needit to take the vehicle in to him. But that was what constituted the problem, the vehicle couldnay get taken anywhere because it couldnay move from the fucking spot unless pushed, dragged or hit by a bomb.

I needit to get my money sorted out. And my materials. All my bits and pieces. Sometimes I felt like my only belongings were a tongue, a nose and two ears. I hadnay been near a woman since me and her split. I just kept gaun at my work. Ye get into routines. Time passes and ye dont even know it. I hung about because what else was there. And the wee yin was closeby.

Promotion was a joke. Some folk have to be awarded stripes but they usually get awarded them before they start. People began at the top with this agency. If I could have stuck the job for a couple of years it would have gone in my favour as far as the immigration status went. Christ, the idea of a Green Card! I would have been happy with that. Fuck sake I would have been overjoyed. There is nay question promotion would have helped. Maybe they tried to gie me it and it just hadnay worked. They put me in the office but it was so boring and really man it was terrible and all one could do was whatever one fucking did. Maybe I didnay fit in to the agency's perspective. The dispatches and the deliveries were fine while they lasted but for some reason there was aye some stupit misunderstanding. Ach but promotion wasnay part of my plans anyway, no really, it was aye a bit of a joke. It would have operated against my basic sensibility.

But it wasnay a case of wants, needs or choices. Other bodies make decisions in this world. We learn that and leave adolescence.

There are few opportunities in life to impress so when one comes along you grab it. I just failed. Sometimes ye do fail. Other times ye dont recognize an "impressing opportunity" until eftirwards, by then it is too late too late too late was the cry. And then there are occasions ye could impress if allowed. And these other fucking stupit occasions when ye impress and there is nay cunt there to bear witness. And that happened to me a lot. So much of what went on in my life was cloaked in the veil of anonymity, shrouded in the midst of obscurity, and so on. Fuck success. Who wants to be one of these multibillionaire bastards. I would fucking shoot the fucking lot of them man.

Once hame in dear auld bonné I would consider the future. From my maw's neighbourhood I needit a bus to reach the countryside but there were local parks, plenty grass and stuff, wee swingparks and roundabouts, good places for weans. My wee yin would love Glasgow, and people would love her, my faimly. I would take her walks, pushing the pram. Other people would want to, my maw, maybe my sister or her kids. But I would do it myself. It would help get my heid straight. I had to sort out the rights and wrongs. Okay I would go for a few beers, see if anybody remembered me. A couple of the auld pubs I went to years ago, if they hadnay been knocked down, yeh. So what if they had, there would be new yins. Except how would I meet up with the auld faces? But I wasnay that bothered anywey. I was wanting to lick my wounds; I would be happy sitting about the huis, getting to know my maw again. And my sister and brother. Nay doubt they were good bodies and it was me. I was the original teenage nightmare. And I hadnay improved. Except for the occasional phone call to my maw, I never contacted my faimly. And when I did it was always out the blue and at some weird hour, so she nearly collapsed on the flair. It was the time zones, I was aye out with them, four hours behind, five or is it six, or eight christ ye never knew. At least I never knew. I was just a fucking idiot. Nay wonder Yasmin called a halt. I dont blame her for anything. I read someplace the emigrants werenay the best people, the best people steyed at hame.

But buddy we aint always got a choice, either we get burnt off the land or we burn the goddam boat. And why do that, why burn the fucker if it is the only hope? Fucking suicidal manoeuvres.

I had to smile, my attention attracted to a couple of bodies at a table nearby, male and female. She had whispered something to him and he grinned. And they hadnay spoken for the previous quarter of an hour. They werenay much aulder than me, late thirties or something.

In six years time I would be forty.

Hey mister, what is your life amounting to?

A woman once said that to me. I met her in Tahoe, me and Haydar – Haydar! Who knows where he was. He just upped and disappeared man he a-vanished. But everybody vanishes, that is what life is, unresolved business.

The people I have known who disappeared, their names would fill a book.

Hey buddy, talking about them good ol physical characteristics and ma lil ol good ol worldé associations. If I didnay have all that I wouldnay have felt so settled in this music bar. There wasnay that much cultural diversity. Raise a kid in this burg, she would get the wrang idea about the world.

But it was real comfortable, warm and smoky. Nay question that my poor auld lungs were appreciating the tobacco smoke; passive was better than absence.

Christ and the music, sometimes I missed that music.

Okay, I was staying for the music. But no longer than half an hour. Surely to fuck they would have started in half an hour. If not

agh relax, relax.

The layout in this bar wasnay great, a kind of L-shaped room, yer view of the stage was restricted. But there were nay better positions, maist of the tables were taken. Christ they all were taken. Customers had filtered in while I wasnay looking. I had the urge to get up and serve them. They could have done with mair help. If my work history was known I would be offered a job. Even scabby prick the manager, he would have asked me to come on board.

But if I was gauny stay I could find a better position. Of course no having such made it easier to leave. If it was owerly strong on the jazz I would do just that. In the past I landit in situations where I was obliged to stay and listen to god-awful shite music because I didnay want to affect the sensibility of the musicians, or indeed hurt their fucking feelings. Musicians can be "hurt", even jazz musicians. Some of the ex's gigs were a nightmare from that perspective. I wound up in bother. Even somebody getting up to go to the bathroom, ye took it as an affront if she was singing. Heh you ya arsehole scabby cunt ye that is ma lady up there, stay in yer seat or I'll batter yer fucking heid in.

Okay a customer is entitled to leave. But why do it during the song? A wee bit of common sense is to be exercised. Manners! wait for the applause man wait for the applause. Singers can put themselves on the line. Yasmin wasnay acting a part it was her up there and some of these cunts could have treated her better. I couldnay have done what she done. Unless there was silence, complete and fucking total silence, if folk shut the fuck up man stop fucking talking, just stop it, stop it. And clinking their bottles and glasses and scrunching their tables and chairs. And then laughing, screeching! They start fucking screeching! The musician is playing some all-time great tear-jerking ballad and some prick guffaws at the back of the fucking room man ye want to batter them, if it was me singing man I would have jumped off the stage and got a grip of their fucking throat. It got so I couldnay sit there.

Her cousin was good, she calmed me down, she laughed at me.

But nay wonder. It is just that lack of respect. Why is there such a lack of respect? It meant I was on tenterhooks from the moment she adjusted that mic, when she smiled at the band. My entire body, the nerves were jumping. I just had to calm down. Her cousin was good, she sometimes took my haun and gied it a squeeze or else sometimes she held it, my breathing got better.

I thought the band should begin with something fast and furious, just go right into it, nay introductions or fuck all. Make that opening number the introduction, grab that audience, fucking grab them, dont gie them nay escape, just right into something absolutely immediate. They can talk all they want: if they can! That sets the tone and the mood; it dictates the gig and wins the proper attention; the proper attention only comes from respect. Fucking bastards.

Who?

I dont know, I dont know.

Sally was also a musician. There was nay question. The evidence may be adduced as follows: 1) the bar here where she worked, 2) the swing of the hips, 3) her relaxed manner with the band, 4) her relaxed manner with me. Which could mean anything. I was hopeless at reading the signs. Every time I chatted to a woman it was misunderstandings and miscalculations. It could bring a feller down.

She was not in view.

One mair hour. Then I really needit to get back to the motel – fucking motel man what was its name? I had forgotten its name. What if I couldnay find the goddam place!

What if I missed the flight? I would just go back to from where I came and get a job, earn a dollar. Naw, I wouldnay, I would head south-east, plenty booze-trade work in Florida for Celtic blokes of average bearing. Or else New Orleans. An airport comrade of mine had returned to Louisiana. Maybe I would bump into her. She was beautiful. No that that was a reason; she was a woman I liked. Although it wasnay reciprocated. Well she didnay no like me, she was just eh

I dont fucking know.

But sometimes I thought she did like me. Maybe under different circumstances. If I just turned up as like an ordinary guy.

The point is I could go where I wantit to go, any damn place. I was free. Free! Yes sir. In the nick of time he leapt to his feet and ran as fast as he could go, three steps in a row, stepping three at a time.

Everything I had in the world was either in my pockets or else back in the motel room. I was taking hame everything. I chucked my job and gied up my lodgings. And I had dough. I wasnay gaun hame skint. So nay worries. Unless they were holding poker games on the airplane. Mind you, it wasnay a bad idea.

Christ I was hungry. There was nothing in the motel. Nay restaurant nay room service nay nothing; it wasnay that kind of place. It was a cheapo man that was the kind of place, one in a mile-long string of cheapos out on the highway. I would get a cab back. Maybe I could fluke the guy from Ghana, he knew the general direction. Take me to motel mile and drive slowly, I would say, and I would recognize mine when I saw it. Who needs a name. Fortunate was I that the means to hire a cab

christ I had been here before.

I had been here before.

Was there a wee river in this damn burg? Of course there was. I saw it earlier. Ever since arriving I had this sense of no quite déjà vu but

the time I was remembering, it was me and the ex christ almighty we were on wur way to Denver!

On wur way out of Denver, we were heading for Rapid City. So it couldnay have been too far from here. Nay wonder I was getting these feelings. No especially good feelings. Where had we been? Omaha or someplace, starting out from Twin Cities and then returning to there for the second night. The Benefit Night! Fuck! Whenever I hear that phrase I want to run a mile. The thing startit because she landit two good gigs, one in Denver and one in Twin Cities.

It was herself landit them, no her manager. It was through an out-of-towner being in the audience at a venue she was playing, and appreciating what she did. Whoever it was – we never found out – it was them spoke for her. The invitation came from an independent brewer. That was how she landed the two gigs. It was nothing to do with her manager. We were just to pretend it was him "fixed the tour". Did he fuck "fix the tour". It was me he fixed, her and me.

That manager conman bastard, what he did, he got her a third gig. This third gig was a so-called Benefit Night: she worked for nothing and was treated like shite.

The ex didnay like hearing the facts. When I raised the truth she shut me up.

When the brewer's invitation came what the so-called manager did was scratch his heid, pick up a map and study it to locate the destinations. Maps were one of the countless administrative aspects of business that the clown couldnay handle. Twin Cities was a major problem for him being as how it wasnay one city but two cities that sit side by side. Once he solved the mystery he brought out his address book, set it beside the map and spent another two days fixing his fucking "mini tour".

When folks in the entertainment business do these out-of-town shows with spaces in between they try to find local gigs to make the trip pay for itself. I have nay quarrel with that. This is what Mister Ratbag the manager was reckoned to have done.

Why do women believe obnoxious conman arseholes? This yin was blatant. All he needit was white spats and a chalk-striped suit, black shirt and a white necktie. He already had the machine gun. This so-called manager had only been out of the big city twice in his entire life. He boasted about that. The silly prick boasted about it. So there he was peering at the map, figuring out which way up it got held and if there was anything between Twin Cities and Denver. Aha! A big dot called Omaha! Omaha . . . mmm . . . familiar ring about that.

So he studies the map again. Omaha is only a couple of inches to the south left en route to Denver. Okay. And out of Denver he found another big dot, Rapid City. Yeh, fucking ideal. So he checks the address book again. Eureka! Rapid City and Omaha! Two brothers own music bars in baith towns. Why these are the finest goddam music bars in the country, these guys are true jazz aficionados. Out west they call them the Jazz Brothers. Why, didnt Dinah Washington and Ella Fitzgerald no play there in the days of blubarbrhubarb, and what about Aretha and auld Nina herself, were they no . . . ? That so-called manager would have had her doing a double-shift on the pony express if I hadnay been there.

This Benefit Night thing was connected to an educational institute. It was a worthwhile cause. Nay criticism possible. The manager said it would be good for her career to be seen supporting liberal programs. Although there was nay dough it was a prestigious thing and could lead to bigger stuff. Yasmin thought I would be pleased. Apparently there was "a politics". I asked for mair details. These right-wing fascist think-tanks were located on campuses all ower Uhmerka, disguised as centres of intellectual integrity, and it wouldnay have surprised me if the Benefit Night was being organized to fund a new Weapons for Peace initiative.

She checked it out with her manager. I would have checked it with him myself but the prick wouldnay talk to me. From the wee snippet of information he dealt Yasmin I got onto the web to trace who or what the "Night" was to benefit, who was to profit by the deal. I discovered it was to raise dough for a project that appeared to lie within the statutory duties of the city and/or state itself. I wasnay great at research but, as

I understood it, responsibility for this damn project lay with a local authority. So how come concerned citizen bodies were raising dough to do it themselves? Here was a classic case of a public campaign whose only raison d'être is to bail out an arm of government. Support yer local politicians! Bail out yer fucking local authority structures!

What a con! I had to button the lip when she telt me. Anyhow, it wasnay me gieing the time and energy. Although in a wey I was because I was gaun with her.

No matter what anybody said I was gaun with her.

I had to do deals with immediate superiors to get the time off. Vacations dont come easy in the Security business. I kind of hoped they would hand me an ultimatum and then, when I stuck to my guns, have no option but to sever wur relationship. Come what may I was gaun on the goddam mini tour.

Yasmin's cousin and sister-in-law looked eftir the baby. The sister-in-law was okay but kind of lukewarm towards myself. She had three weans and Yasmin was wary of asking her. One night was fine, two was stretching it. But five! five and a half nights! Nah. We hired a friend with a kid of her ayn. We paid the dough. Sure it was a lot to take on but this was special. For a mother to be away from her wean for this length of time it had to be. It was extra-special, crucial and career-changing. No a stupit wee five and dime thing. People's career moves are important. Yasmin's career was all important. No just for her but for everybody; me and the wean, her cousins, all the faimly. Even though I thought this so-called mini tour a bad move I didnay say it. Personally I thought it was wrong. But my word went for fuck all when that manager bastard was around. He was Mister Socrates, Mister Aristotle, he was Mister fucking Superbrain.

Of course it was Yasmin doing the goddam gigs, no me. Fine. She had developed the necessary mental state, she could switch off. It was me that found it hard. I did. I found it hard being with her and suffering goddam it I did not find it easy. I should have stayed at hame. Of course, she says, so why the hell did you come?

Why the hell did I come, because I want to be with you, why else, christ almighty. I am coming with you and that is that.

But there is no need, says she.

Ye dont want me to come? says I.

Jerry, she says.

What? I says.

Yeh, she says, there is no need, that is what I am saying.

Honey, dont even think it, I dont even know what needs are. If I dont come I'll explode; that is the reality. I want to go with ye, I need to go with ye, I need to be with ye, I need to look eftir ye in the midst of all this one-night stand malarkey trying to run a home and bring up a kid. They are ripping ye off for christ sake, all these rag, tag and bobtail management fuckers, if I'm no there it will be worse, ye know, it will be worse. Plus I am looking forward to it. Nothing is a problem. I can get a change of shift and days off. I need a break, I need it, and I shall get it; there is an immediate superior owes me a favour, he owes me two favours. He shall fix it, I need to get out this goddam uniform. I am going crazy.

I would have gone to every last gig the ex played. That was what she couldnay understand. But it wasnay possible to go more than twice a month because of the constant nightshifts. This was our first real jaunt the gether of any description.

She cut two cds in advance. A couple of local radio stations were gauny pick up on her visit. Her albums were great. People had to buy the two to get a proper feel for her music. She had that voice. On one album she did covers of traditional jazz stuff and on the other she did her ayn compositions, just her and two guys on drums and bass. I hardly spoke to the drummer; usually he went into a stupor. But the bass and me, we didnay hit it off. At first we did but later on we didnay. Yazzie played rhythm guitar herself. But christ, what an album that was, really fucking beautiful. The other yin was fine, the traditional jazz stuff and she used musicians she knew from the 3rd Street bar.

But on this wee mini tour it was her alone. She was picking up local guys at each venue but playing the Benefit Night herself. It was one reason why these kind of nights were of value. Apart from her ayn commitment to whatever political and social shenanigans were happening, they gied her the chance to play her ayn stuff, just her and the auld geetar.

So there was a lot at stake. Yasmin didnay go on about it but I knew she had high hopes and big dreams, exotic imaginings.

Me too.

All it required was one track off the albums to get picked up by a radio station. All I wantit was a proper place to live. If we got that I could move in properly. She had to earn money. The cleaning job paid peanuts and the gigs she done were dependent on tips. So it was me, I was chief earner. I had cut out the mental gambling. I still looked in on Ranjit when I stayed at my ayn place. The monthly game with his people was tempting but any night off I spent at the ex's. If she was doing a gig I usually stayed hame and looked eftir the wean. I enjoyed looking eftir the wean. I telt her stories and played wee games, the usual father stuff.

But I was saving dough!

I was aye amazed at the money ye made when ye werenay gambling. It was like a new life or something. It made me look at folk differently. All these people walking about with money in their pocket. Christ.

And if she could earn a bit through her music. Fuck!

But really, we would have been fine. We could rent wur ayn place, a proper place, one with two good rooms. I could get on with the writing, get the laptop on the table, maybe get myself a faster machine, get the fucking book wrote.

I could do it, I knew I could do it. Some of the stories I read were total keech; ye just couldnay believe bodies got paid for writing them. Fucking preposterous shite man and yet there they were, suffocating the shelves in the airport mall, the bus station bookstore, the railway station bookstore, yer fucking neighborhood fucking secondhand bookstore. Army stories and secret-agent stories, fucking love stories, medieval knights and wicked sorcerers, stacked to the gunnels with outright propaganda on behalf of the US Defense industry, homiletic so-called fictions towards the glorious creation of fuck knows what, the worst ye can think of. And these writer cunts got paid big bucks. How come they didnay write them in uniform? military uniform; stars and stripes on their fucking underpants.

Jesus christ, ye felt like never opening another book in yer life. So why write another yin?

Because mine was gauny be different. No great but different.

I had to get away from that airport job, I really had to, it was just like things crowding in on me and I felt sometimes I wasnay coping, I wasnay coping and like deportation, that was an acceptable price to pay, if it had to be it had to be. There were restrictions on my Class III Red Card: I was required to walk straight into another job. My alternative was to disappear. I quite enjoyed disappearing. And now I couldnay, because of my new commitments. That was true, I was a faimly man now. A faimly man. I was. Yes sir. Cleanliving. A cleanliving fucker.

There was a feller in her manager's entourage said he could get me a job in a bar, he could speak for me. I thought the idea of the bar was fine but no him speaking for me. Yasmin said I was prejudiced. I wasnay prejudiced. What she didnay understand was that a guy like me cannay put himself into hock with these hood bastards. Too much to lose. Why take the chance. Different if they had a politics but they didnay have a politics. If they did I never observed it. Unless if they were fervent idealists when I wasnay there, okay, anything is possible.

No sir, I didnay want nothing to do with them. Even if I did I couldnay. It was too goddam risky with all these pentagon immigration bastards creeping about. Association with known baddies wasnay a good entry on one's database. The first chance they got and I was on that plane.

I needit a new job but I would get it myself. I was back to carrying the essential paperwork and employment details on my person. Who knows? Ye pass by someplace and a phil-anthropist steps out from a street corner. Hey buddy, want to earn some dough? I got a great job for you.

Here are ma papers sir here are ma papers.

If I didnay find a new job I was gauny have to disappear. But I couldnay I couldnay I couldnay.

I had to clear my heid. This mini tour was just the right thing at the right time.

So there we were preparing everything when at the last minute Mr Fuckface the manager pulled out. He said he couldnay make it. There were things gaun on he had to attend to. He had thought it would be okay but now it wasnay and he couldnay be in two places at once. Now that I was gaun with Yasmin that was fine, it allowed him to do the other thing.

What a shite. I knew precisely what was happening. It was a variation on the Cincinnati deal. Him or me. This was the ultimatum and I was supposed to back off. But did I fuck back off. For that ratbag? Fuck him. I was glad.

The ex wasnay glad. She wasnay glad at all. What would she have preferred her manager to me? Yeh, of course.

Agh that is unfair, she didnay think that at all. She just kind of didnay say nothing about it, she left it for me; if I thought I could handle it then okay, she was relying on me. She relied on me to make the correct decision. So I did the best I could.

I couldnay gie up that trip. It was the biggest thing, the biggest thing for us, I had to be with her christ almighty she was my woman, mother of my child.

Okay so I wasnay her manager but I reserved the right to condemn the cunt that was. How could I do otherwise? Yasmin was my lady, I wasnay gauny let him walk ower the top of her. So yeh, I condemned him. So she backed him up.

Why do women fall for these fuckster hucksters man I dont know. I am no talking about their personality but the spiel they gie. It was obvious he fancied her too. I wouldnay blame him for that but surely she could spot a conman. This yin was a dealer; soup to nuts, dope to corpses; this was his business, mister fucking rentacrime. He knows what he is doing, she said, what she always said.

But when he went so did his car, and mine was a wreck. I hoped to borrow one but I couldnay, and hiring was out the question. So it was public transport.

Three bags and a guitar. That was her traveling light. Then the cds; we hauled piles of them; they were a hunner per cent essential. No matter what a sane person might think, carting these cd albums from gig to gig was the one true route to fame and fortune. They all done it, all the stars. They took their albums from gig to gig. Fucking hell, if she believed that she believed anything. But what did I know. Except I was the body would carry the fuckers, would collect the money from sales, keep track of all the transactions.

We went by train and would return by train. All the in-between travel was done by bus, starting from the morning eftir the Benefit when we left for Denver. Five nights later we were back in Twin Cities for the proper gig, the one where she got paid.

The manager booked us the train return for the first part of the tour, the east coast to Twin Cities. All the bus travel we arranged wurselves. I did it. Money would be returned to us from diverse sources; from the people in Denver then the Jazz Brothers would see to things for the Omaha and Rapid City gigs. And for the opening night, that good ol Benefit Night? Why, we were to see the Treasurer for the reimbursement of "genuine expenses". This Treasurer would be expecting us.

We werenay looking for no fucking fee, only help with the goddam fares and subsistence. Was that too much to ask? Sure is buddy.

And accommodation. Where was the accommodation? Had it even been arranged? Okay the manager "knew" it would be okay but me and Yasmin didnay. There was nay money for motels and stuff. Where were we gauny sleep, out on the fucking back porch? These northern towns are like Greenland's icy mountains. Without adequate expenses we were in trouble.

We were aye in trouble. Me and the ex man we had nay chance. We never had a penny; never nay fucking dough. In all the time we had the gether we were broke. We chased here and we chased there.

Benefit Gigs. They were all fucking benefit gigs. That first night in Twin Cities I was trying to find the Treasurer and I couldnay. So I waited beside the box office figuring he would come past there sooner or later. Unless he saw me first and tried to hide. That was what Treasurers did. Of course if they went looking for you it was a different story; they were like the fucking mounties these cunts. I was getting sick of it. Here was the first night and I didnay even know where we were sleeping. Yasmin saw me. She came up and took me by the hand. She must have seen the smoke issuing from my ears and thought to adjust the lid on one's heid. Hey Jerry, how's it going? she kissed my ear and chuckled.

Naw it wasnay a chuckle it was a chortle man that lassie chortled, and she chortled before I could reply to the question so I knew something was up. Sure enough: We aint sleeping together. She grinned.

I also grinned. What?

No, she says, you in one house I in another, friends of the Organizers.

Flummoxed.

One night, she says, grinning, trying to make a joke of it. She gripped me by the elbow then kissed the side of my face, put her arm round my waist.

Ah well, I says, we willnay be in bed long enough to worry about it.

She sighed. Then she frowned. Huh?

Now it was my turn to smile.

Jerry, she says, what time for our bus? What time we got to be there at the bus station?

0620 hours. Twenty past six.

My God.

It was either that or later.

Well why didnt you get later?

I thought this one was best, so we could get into Omaha early, see the sights, check out what's what.

What you talking about Jerry?

There's a lot in Omaha, I checked it on the web. So what about yer stuff? bags and all that? are they gaun with you or are they gaun with me? How do we meet up in the morning? Will somebody drive us to the bus station or do we have to take a cab?

I dont know.

Well christ sake Yazzie I mean we're here doing them a favour surely to fuck they can gie us a drive to the bus station. Eh?

She shrugged.

It isnay a lot to ask.

Jerry, she says, that is your work. You take care of it. It is what the manager does for me, if you want to talk to them talk to them, you want to ask them something go ask them, it is what you are to do.

Sure, I says, I know that, that's how I'm standing here trying to find the Treasurer. Plus I need to organize the cds, and no let them get stuck in a corner where buyers cannay see them.

Yeh, yeh. She smiled.

I shrugged. She gied me a kiss. Eftir she went back into the main concert hall I managed to have a word with one of the Organizers. But the first thing he did was try to sell me a "worthy cause" raffle ticket! These yins were ten bucks apiece, extra donations always welcome.

I smiled, I thought he was joking. I telt him again who I was so now he tried to sell me a "worthy cause" lotto card. I held my hands aloft. Pardon me, I says, but I telt ye already, I am with the performers.

Oh you are! Hey, he grinned.

I explained about the cds whereupon he pointed me along a corridor where I would find a stall designed to that very purpose; he pushed me towards it. When I turned back to him he had vanished. I collected a carton of cds and I took it through, then returned to the concert hall. The ex was sitting at the Performers Only table. I joined her, had a laugh with her about the demon ticket-seller. These things are always the same, she said.

We held hands. She could be relaxed before a gig, or gied

that impression. But it reminded me of myself before a poker game where she lacked concentration and became absent-minded. It was hard to talk to her and she never remembered what she had said a minute ago. I felt jumpy myself. I asked if she wantit to go outside for a smoke, but she didnay.

Dont worry, she said, I'll be fine.

Aw I know ye will, you'll be great, that's because you are great, you are just different class, wait till they hear ye!

Do you need a smoke?

Who me? naw, I was thinking of you.

Oh I'm okay.

Great.

Maist people hadnay turned up so there were plenty of seats. A kindly body asked if we had noticed the sign. What sign? I winked at Yasmin. Performers Only. Yeh, says I, I'm a musician and she does a stand-up routine. Yasmin chuckled.

Oh I'm sorry, said the kindly body, it's only like it'll be busy here very soon, I'm sorry.

Fuck off, I said but not aloud. The table next to this had the sign Organizing Committee. Soon others had come to sit and I walked with Yasmin to a side door for Performers Only; she was heading backstage to tune the geetar and prepare herself. She was fine, in fighting mode; she was wearing one of these very loose unbuttoned tops with a kind of tee-shirt thing in one of these strange materials that are like who knows, liquefied leather or something, and a pair of what d'ya call them man leggings, real skintight, and kind of sequins. But it wasnay her best outfit by far. That was the thing here, she was keeping her best for other gigs. This was her relaxed, doing her ayn thing, just her and the ol geetar, like she was just gauny be up there alone, that was her, she would walk out, everybody staring, christ, Yazzie.

What? she looked at me.

I grabbed her, squeezed her too tightly. Oh fuck I was fighting back the tears. Fucking hell man I was fighting back the tears, jesus christ almighty how could I be fighting back the tears! I held her, clung onto her. She patted me on the back and whispered into my ear. She gied me another squeeze then exited backstage, the door clicking shut behind her.

Jesus christ.

I needit a smoke so vacated the premises, as was necessary, it being a non-smoking venue! When I tried to get back later I had to explain to the woman at the entrance who I was and why I was there. Her attention was only half on me and I had to repeat myself a hundred and thirty-seven times.

By now the Performers Only table had filled up. I should have left my jacket draped ower the back of Yasmin's chair to safeguard it.

I went for a beer. A queue had formed at the bar. Through an open door I saw the demon ticket-seller talking to somebody and from a whisper in the queue I gathered that he was the Treasurer. The Treasurer! I had forgotten about the Treasurer. So it was him! Yeh, it made sense. I thought to nab him while the going was good so I walked along. But when I arrived he had disappeared. So back to the bar which now had mair people in the queue and it was askance looks when I tried to reclaim my place.

I just thought Fuck it, and joined the end. Life is too short. And what do you know, two minutes later the Treasurer popped up again. This time I did grab him. He startit blethering. I had to listen hard. He surely wasnay hinting that a portion of the expenses money would be a powerful donation to a very "worthy cause". Then he brought out another pocketful of betting cards and flourished them at a group of passing bodies. When he returned his attention to me I said slowly and clearly: My girlfriend is the next singer up there. She is back stage right now. Mair than fifteen hunner goddam miles we've traveled to get here, and we cannay even get a seat the gether and now ye're wanting me to buy a gross of yer "worthy cause" lottery tickets! Gie me a break. I've bought three of the fuckers already out my ayn goddam money.

Oh man, he says, I apologize I really do, where you from? You Swedish? Neat, yeh, it's just so damn busy. I dont know who's performers and who's audience. We werent expecting so many people. They said we would be like lucky to get an audience at all, they said we could not like pull it off but man, did we pull it off! We have worked our butts off. We got this thing up and running clear in advance and like we never saw daylight man we did that old publicity thing, using all channels of communication, and the response has been awesome, truly it has. But we worked so hard man, so hard.

Well done, I says, and meant it.

We got a good team, he says, we got the best.

Yeh, great, that's it when ye've got a good team, I says, well done, well done again.

Then it dawned on me I was getting hit by one of these apologies whereby ye wind up congratulating the culprit. He was supposed to be saying sorry to me but here was I gieing the prick compliments. Before I could say anything about Yasmin's expenses he patted me on the shoodir and off he went. For some reason I smiled, it must have been in acknowledgment of his performance. He was probably on the IMF payroll.

Back at the bar I joined the end of the queue. But I had let the bastard annoy me. I do confess. On the one hand I admired his performance on the other it was against me it was directed. So it was like contempt, he was treating me with contempt. I had a cigarette in my mouth and fumbling for a lighter when a guy goes, Hey bud, and points to the smokin verboten sign.

Yeh, thanks, I said, baring my teeth.

Back outside for a smoke. Back to the back of the queue. When at last I had my beer and returned to the main concert area Yasmin was already on stage, she was singing "Only a Wish" which meant it was near the end of her set.

It *was* the end of her set. She had prepared for forty minutes and they had gied her fifteen. Fifteen minutes. One and a half thousand fucking miles.

A few bodies were loud in their applause; others continued chatting.

What the hell

I just stared. I couldnay believe what I was seeing. Fifteen minutes. One and a half thousand fucking miles. She was already offstage now and girls came on wearing fancy traditional outfits and they did some fancy traditional dancing.

There was mair attention gied to them than the music. They were about 14 years of age and of course they had these nice figures lassies have and plenty springing up on their toes, fingers tight against their thighs: christian-style anti-sex dancing except the lassies transformed it and ye were aware that the church couldnay stop them growing up no matter how they tried, dried-up bastards.

I hung about waiting for Yasmin's return. It was half an hour before she did. She just treated the 15-minute set as a joke. I went with her to the table and lo and behold there was an empty seat.

It was amazing how many folk spent their time chatting at these concerts. They didnay listen to fuck all. At the Organizers table they only listened to one another. While we watched the next performer a woman arrived and hovered beside us. Her agitation became evident. It was her chair! Yasmin exchanged glances with me. I got up and gied her it, crouched down beside Yasmin.

The performance was good; a guy, a singer. But it was difficult to hear with these Organizer pricks all laughing like fuck every ten seconds. They resembled business consultants and university professors; Mister Dickie Bow and his department of geopological wankers. Haw haw haw haw, haw haw haw haw. That was them all the way through the performances, except for a couple who kept gawking at Yasmin. And she wasnay wearing her performance outfit, she had changed clothes. They didnay listen to one single act all night, excluding the MC clown who did the intimations and announcements in between. He kept talking about "housekeeping". I have some "housekeeping" information, he kept saying. Then he recited these long lists of individuals and groups who had contributed so much to the evening's success. They got mair time than the performers. But the Organizers were attentive as fuck then they all applauded and roared encouragement. Later he sat at their table pretending he was shaking like a leaf, wanting to know if his "contribution" had been "passable", did he say the appropriate things. Fucking idiot, I would have ate him up man, spat him fucking right out. Nay wonder my teeth were on edge. But if I had been allowed to sit beside Yasmin I would have made her nervous. Eftir a show she needed time to herself, in company she could sit for an hour and say nothing.

The whole goddam event was inefficient in relation to the needs of individual human beings. The attitude of the Treasurer summed it up. I tried to approach him again but he was engrossed in other company. When he paused to speak to one of the Organizers I stared at him and he made no sign of recognition. He was avoiding us. Yasmin disagreed. But it was obvious. How arrogant these semi-official bodies are. They must think the rest of us are dumplings. Ye felt like grabbing him and gieing him a shake. Yasmin put her hand on my wrist.

She hated upsetting scenes between individyou-ells, unlike me who loved even saying the words. Does it never occur to them parties that we might lose wur temper and get physical. They rely on us having these eternal so-called rational conversations. It was my fault for no bringing the shillelagh baseball bat. I could have gied him a wee dunt on the skull in remembrance of the eternal verities. I had meant to bring it. I just fucking forgot. Yasmin was smiling at me, she was wanting me to relax. She had finished her set and was exhausted. Now I was filling her space with nonsense. Could I no take a break from the worry. Sorry, I said. It's just how can ye relax when people treat ye this way?

She patted my wrist.

Another annoying thing was the lack of hospitality. They didnay even offer us a coffee never mind a sandwich. All we got was a closet to dump wur goods and chattels. As it happens we had eaten but they didnay know that. So either they were stingy as fuck or they had nay regard for their guest performers. When they put her on early christ hauf the fucking audience hadnay even turned up. And they hadnay prepared a proper schedule; it was a case of when somebody arrives stick them on. This is what happened to Yasmin. It was our fault for being early. If we had been arrogant fuckers and arrived late ye would have had a better spot. Fucking typical. Folk that do things correct get victimized, they get victimized.

Jerry . . .

What?

Ssh.

Okay.

Did you make the call?

I had forgotten to make the call. It was to check everything was okay with the wee yin. Yasmin did it while I got the drinks. Mair people were at the Performers Table when I returned.

There was nay space and there was a guy talking to her. I recognized him from his performance. I gied Yasmin her drink then went to find a spare seat but had to take one at the other end of the hall. I was gauny carry it back but then I sat down for a minute, draping my jacket ower the back. At a nearby table there was a crowd of students or some other bunch of stalwarts. The conversation would have drove ye batty; world politics and the postmodern economy; Jesse James and the guy who shot Billy the Kid; the function of Lee Harvey Oswald in contemporary politics with reference to hollywood law-and-order movies.

Everywhere people were talking their way through the performances. I noticed Yasmin glancing around. The guy who had been talking to her had gone. I stood to gie her a wave. Then I walked across. She smiled, nibbled at a rough edge of skin on her lower lip. She also bit her fingernails and chewed the skin at the edge until sometimes blood came. Except for these nervy expressions she rarely showed tension and when she spoke she was calm and matter-of-fact. A band was the next act on. They played blues, supposedly; it sounded mair like a group of christian glee-club singers doing an advert for milk and apples. I recognized the keyboard player as the guy who had been sitting with Yasmin. He was a harmless enough looking cunt, except he was a keyboard player. The woman now occupying his seat reminded me of something. The airport! She had the demeanour of an undercover Security operative. Probably she was one, here to check out the running-dog liberals. She said she worked in television. Maybe it was that gied her the right to a chair at the Performers Table. I said to Yasmin: Hey, fancy a dance later? I gied her a wink and she smiled. Want a drink?

Yeh, she said.

The female operative was frowning at me for some reason.

Would you like something to drink as well? I said, my sarcasm so subtle it was lost completely.

Well yeh, it's very kind of you; you think they'll have a gin?

Sure. What do ye want a large one?

With lemon? Could you put in some ice.

One lump or two?

Yasmin was watching me. I gied her another wink and got to fuck at once.

The queue at the bar was enormous. Two harassed-looking bodies served the multitudes. Amateurs, even the way they looked below the counter for empty plastic containers. But so what, we have to learn sometime. I had to stop being so critical. The trouble is I was nervy, that was the fucking problem, nerves. I think it was this assumption of the managerial role. Seriously but I didnay want to let her down. There were things to remember. I had bought the bus tickets and we had the overnight accommodation. It was an early rise tomorrow and I would have to book a cab if naybody offered to gie us a lift. I would rather organize it myself anyway, I would rather just be the one. Even if somebody offered man I would tell them naw, thanks but no thanks. *If* somebody offered. I couldnay imagine it. But even if they did.

Then christ, right under my nose: two bastards waltzed up and spoke to somebody at the head of the queue, taking care to meet naybody's gaze, while worming their way in. Fucking unbelievable. The rest of us pretended indifference! A little shuffling of feet occasioned. The guy in front of me stared at the floor but I saw from the twitch at the side of his ear that he was restraining himself. I frowned and glared and smiled and thought of one's loving partner. I transformed myself into a smileful being. They could rattle their fucking cart wheels for all I cared, I was rising to no bait, the veritable soul of assimilation. The two bastards continued blethering.

I wouldnay say a word, I would just fucking breathe in and breathe out and think of churches. Continue with one's existence. Not collapse a raving fucking lunatic with a fucking massive stroke oblique heart attack, rude fucking bastards man one cannot for the life of one grasp why in the name of gods teeth they get away with it, yet they do they do they do, they certainly do.

Why worry: in the long run everybody's heart fails.

At length I was next in line to be served and having these fantastic interiorized conversations: Sorry sir the bar's closed

what do ye mean the bar's closed

it aint our fault sir; this side of the county line we got them licensing laws

what licensing laws

I aint at liberty to divulge that information

because I have a strange accent?

no comment

I take it ye want my fucking ID because I'm a alien

And then I was at the bar and being served. Needless to say I forgot the ice for the female operative. I was gauny return but the queue was too formeedablih mishoor and I knew I wouldnay cope with it.

Down at the Performers Table another feller was chatting up Yasmin. Fair enough. Hi, I said.

Oh hi, he said, proffering his hand as if to shake. I ignored him, pretending to have difficulty laying down the drinks. The female operative thanked me for hers.

They ran out of ice, I said, sorry. But what a queue!

Yasmin tells me you're a writer? said the feller, a broad smile on his fucking greasy chops. So what is it you write? he said, a slimy smile on his unsubtle fizzfuckingog. Is it poems, articles, stories . . . ?

Ye've got me there, said I.

Yasmin touched my wrist. I thought it better to place my beer on their table, lie fully stretched on the floor and gaze upwards, allowing the electric lights to mesmerize me. Please would somebody tickle my belly please.

Strange how women talk to certain males. If I was a woman I would just fucking ignore them completely. I smiled at him in comradely fashion. Hey, I said, what's your name?

His name's Bob, said Yasmin quickly.

I nodded, checked my watch, lifted my beer.

You bringing your chair across? she said.

Well it's Performers Only here, I said.

It wont matter.

Oh, I said, okay. Okay.

The basic question had taken root in my skull: how come a man goes up to a woman and says, Hullo? Are we supposed to accept this as informal social behaviour, an unambiguous end-in-itself activity? Not at all. It is the usual male-to-female affair and it amazes me that women fall for it even now, after how many hundreds of thousands of years. What the hell DNA is about I do not fucking know, what sort of information are we talking about here, what the fuck gets transmitted down one's goddam genes. What did auld Jeremiah send to me? a poor sense of direction and a feel for the domestic Security industry?

Yasmin was watching me. She looked away. I shrugged and took one of her cigarettes. Mine were in my jacket. I glanced to the back of the room and saw some imbecile sitting on my chair, his back against the jacket collar, crushing whatever tailored lines existed. To hell with it. I walked across. Hey, I said, that's my jacket ye're crushing.

Pardon me?

The jacket, I says, ye're crushing it.

The jacket?

Yeh, I says, the jacket, fuck.

He leaned forwards so I could snatch it out from under him. He shook his heid at a couple of folk at the adjacent table, including the lassie sitting nearest him. He had shifted the chair to be part of that company. I raised the jacket to examine it for cigarette-burns; checked the lining for rips and lastly went through the pockets, inside and out. Him and the lassie were watching me. I noticed a badge on the feller's lapel.

Hi, how's it gaun, I said, I'm in the Security trade myself, pleased to meet ye. I extended my hand then tugged the lobe of my ear.

What did you say?

I shrugged. This was actually my chair, I said. That was how I left my jacket draped ower the back, so people would see it was taken.

Well it was vacant when we came in.

Except for the jacket.

He frowned. The lassie glared at me. Hey, you want the chair? she said. Take mine.

Thanks. I put my hand out. Her face went pink. Sorry, I said, I thought ye were gieing me yer chair.

The guy smiled. Okay man you want the fucking chair you take the fucking chair!

No, said the lassie, these chairs are not reserved.

Ah, so that's the issue, whether or not the chairs are reserved.

What the hell do you want? she said, and now she brought in other members of the company. She pointed at me. Can you believe this guy?

They obviously could. They looked me up and down and figured pound for pound I was outmatched. I slipped the jacket on and balanced myself on the balls of my feet. I managed to avoid flicking my wrists in the manner of James Cagney.

Why dont you leave us, said the guy, gesturing with his thumb. I stared at him then jerked suddenly forwards with my right shoodir. His head jerked sideways. I grinned. He tried for a nonchalant shrug and failed.

Amigo, I said, why dont ye just fucking apologize, save all this hassle. You ees in the wrong for taking my chair.

Hey can you leave now? said the lassie.

Ye talking to me or him?

I'm talking to you.

Okay, snap yer fingers, I'm about to vanish. I gied the two a salute and walked on outa there. While in earshot I distinguished the terms "power" and "humiliation". Aint it amazing how strangers reach to the root of one's veriest deep-down innermost essence. Fuck them.

No, it was me, it was me to blame.

Madness is a short step from the deathwish. It is my opinion that the progression from madness leads to the selfsame point as when the world takes on a clarity such that no sane person would desire an escape. I rejoined the smokers.

But I was sick of "rejoining the smokers".

It was time to stop this way of living aw the gether. It was cold outside. I made the smoke a quick yin.

I heard the music; folk protest stuff but it sounded no bad. The next time somebody exited the main hall I peered in. The Treasurer was at the Performers Table. He was speaking generally. Yasmin was amongst the listeners. She would have it sortit. She would get the dough and accommodation information. There would be no hassle. She would be handed the cash in dollar bills. All of these affairs of business would be accomplished, with minimum fuss.

I was of no service to her. I was a fucking dumpling. If I hadnay insisted on going on the road with her then the manager would have been there, he would have had his nice big car, a bit of luxury, good music, a placid but enjoyable ride, passing through these nice little burgs with the downhome diners, stopping wherever the hell they wantit.

I sat against a radiator nearby the stall selling emblazoned tee-shirts, music, badges, books and other printed matter, much of it free and of a propaganda turn. At least they were trying. The other stall had stacks of cds from all the night's performers. A couple of Yasmin's looked to have gone; sold or stolen. No doubt there would be problems when I checked the sums later.

Why did I have nay dough? The truth of the matter is I was a failure.

But what does success mean?

I was aware of a stream issuing from one of my nostrils but I was not anxious. Maybe the stallholder sold paper tissues. What an error if he didnay. They could have been produced with embossed campaign slogans and customers could read them while using them. And eftir they dumped them not only would they purchase new yins, there was an outside possibility that a third party might peruse the slogans on the auld yin. It could be marketed as a poster tissue. These brainstorms can make a man a million. Fur-lined cart wheels, that was another yin

Of course the job depressed me. But sooner or later all jobs depress ye. I was a no-good neer-do-well. Nay wonder but I mean who the fuck wants to work for cunts. No me. Nor anybody else of sound mind. Work work work, the world was gripped by a psychotic masochism. It didnay matter where or what. The last job I had was driving a delivery truck and there too it was all sorts of hours but bodies looked at ye if ye complained; one has to take one's licks; be a man buddy, you wanna earn some moneeee go suck a dick. I was in favour of a universal strike, an eternal strike. All those in favour! Aye! Aye. The ayes have it Mister President. I should have emigrated to Tahiti. Or dear auld Canaday; I sometimes wondered why I didnay move to Labrador City.

This break from the airport gied me a chance to think. It was so good being away. Better if we had been able to bring the wean, except she was gaun through a greeting and windy stage; it was hard getting a sleep, then when she had her bottle she was spitting out the milk and even she was vomiting man it was a worry. Yasmin wasnay getting a sleep at all, coming hame eftir maybe doing a late-night gig someplace and her cousin would have been taking care of the wean, so when Yasmin came hame she had to take her and then it was like the next two hours just holding her and winding her, christ it was hard, nay question, and when I came in later in the morning, it was just like holding her, petting her, seeing she was okay, letting Yasmin shoot off to her cleaning job. What a fucking life man. Nay wonder we failed. What fucking chance ye got.

So this was a real break, for the two of us. If I had had a decent car that would have helped. But I fucking didnay have a decent car. Nothing, I had nothing. Grocery carts were too good for the likes of me.

Nay dreams. Reality. I had a job that took me nowhere, that became mair difficult by the night. It was like I was separated from things. I couldnay get close to any of my comrades. I seemed to be out of step, like I approached subjects from the wrong angle. I seemed to annoy folk at an early stage and couldnay recover.

Somebody exited the main hall. I had another smoke, lurked the corridors for another few minutes then returned to crouch by her feet.

It turned out we were staying the night together eftir all. Yasmin had indeed met fruitfully with the Treasurer. She also mentioned how early a start we had to another member of the Organizing Committee who passed the word. An aulder woman volunteered to take us in. We left early. She was cheery and interested in us and wantit to know what I thought of her country. She made us a tasty supper and played nice music. It was like heaven. Even a television in wur room. We were welcome to enjoy a late-night movie, except it was roundabout five hundred miles to Omaha and Yasmin was tired. So was I man so was I.

The bus we were on traveled up hill and down dale. I dozed some of the time. For all I know we crossed mighty rapids, still waters, some great grand dams and forests of antiquity the girths of whose trees were mighty. Entire hours it lasted, with breaks in small bus stations, other passengers coming and going. Nay doubt there was an express service we could have got.

But it was good being able to no speak. We had had an argument earlier. She took one position, I the other. Generally she didnay criticize me outright, just let me carry on thinking whatever I wantit, meanwhile she was thinking whatever she was thinking. This time naw. But I didnay blame her. How could I? Why had she landed herself with me? What the hell did I gie to her?

Bother, problems, headaches, pain, misery.

Her heid was turned into me. She was dozing again. I breathed in on her hair. It was a beautiful smell, this whatever – fragrance, fragrance is the word. She gied me so much. Really. No woman no cry. Fucking hell man just being with her! When I took my arm from her shoodirs she opened her eyes and gied me a funny look then turned to stare out the window. A moment later she chuckled and slapped my chest. Hey Jerry look!

Jesus christ.

Snaw was on the mountains. What a country for weather;

one minute it is heatwaves the next it is floods and Arctic storms; typhoons, fucking blizzards. Hey, I says, see before I met you, I used to sit for hours in front of the weather channel. It is the best drama they have on the tube. And I dont mean that as an insult to my chivalrous hosts. Where I come from the television is even worse, so too is the weather, the weather is like a nightmare. We stared out for a while. I put my arm round her shoodirs again, and sang, Put your sweet lips, a little closer to the fohohmm, let's pretend that we're together all alone.

It's phone, she said.

I know it's phone.

So why d'you say foam, you always say foam, it drives me crazy.

I was about to retort but I noticed a girl on the seat across the aisle staring at me with unbridled disgust. Ten minutes later Yasmin's head rested on my shoodir. It is strange about women how ye have these fights all the time yet they turn around and do something like put their head on yer shoulder cant you see they love ya babeee, unlike for example me, I just stop communicating, it is terrible, plus it is unloveable. Let me attempt an analysis, I am talking about women, their relationship to men, how it aye goes bad, everything.

And before too long that lady was sleeping again. A city lady. The countryside may be starkly vunderbar in these yere parts but like them lil ol urban dwelling gals find it all rather boring. Drag yerself beyond the initial incredulity at miraculous nature and ye are into a world of nay stores, nay high streets, nay bistros, nay coffee shops, nay backstreet bargains, nay end-of-season sales, nay malls, nay fucking pre-owned second-hand used clothing end-of-range la bargeñas señorita that world of utter landscape wasnay for the likes of this luscious lassie and soon she was deeply asleep; her hair and heid dampened and creasing my shirt and her wrist lay on my thigh and there was something altogether good about it.

Why does a woman like Yasmin even look at a guy like me never mind date me never mind fucking sleep with me, have a kid with me. I was aye a foolish fucker.

The wee girl gazed at Yasmin then at me again. Above her head and the head of her mother I saw the villain drop down from the luggage rack, a long thin knife clenched between closed teeth, but I had my shotgun beneath my folded elbow, I was prepared, I would rise to the occasion, little did this all-knowing sardonic young lass realize I would wind up saving her from certain death.

The next time anybody spoke about birthday presents I would tell them to get me something useful, like a goddam shotgun. Yasmin would know how. With her contacts anything was possible. Weird fuckers hang about the music industry, especially if one is la femme, especially if one is la bonné-looking la femme.

The ex was half an inch taller than me but that was nay problem. I wished it was a half a yard taller, nestling into her beautiful breasts. There are interesting ways in which bodies can jingle jangle and that would have been a most fascinating experience. I mentioned it to her but she denied height difference had anything to do with fascinating experiences, that was not how it worked. By the time I figured out what she meant by "how it worked" she had lifted a book and was engrossed. We were then in bed. That was a while ago.

Some truly ridiculous conversations took place in her bed. And it was only four feet six inches wide. I lay closer into her till finally she laid the book down on her pillow, turned and gied me a withering look, then smiled and opened her arms, and said – and I quote – "You are a vexation."

The Omaha gig went okay. I keep saying Omaha but it

wasnay Omaha it was a town west of there, just a music bar but with an enthusiastic wee crowd and we sold the same number of cds as we sold at the Benefit Night: two! But the ex enjoyed it. What was great about it was the overnight accommodation. Eftir the gig she was exhausted and didnay want to stay behind drinking. If I wantit to stay I was welcome but she was looking forward to her bed. There were a few people around interested in talking to her. Who knows who they were, which contacts they might have had. If her manager had been around maybe he would have got to talking with them properly. But fair enough, she was tired out and they had nay interest in talking to me. I tried to pursue it at one stage but it was embarrassing.

The club owner's huis was one of these three-story buildings with an enormous basement, a typical wooden structure and beautiful. We never met the guy. His brother owned the venue in Rapid City. It was the manager of the club drove us there and spent the night along with us. It was a big auld-style place like in the movie *To Kill a Mockingbird*. Who couldnay like it? For the ex it was a dream. She was agog for the six or seven hours we spent there and referred to it for weeks eftirwards. If ever we got the dough then that was it, that was the one. It had real wide decking and a beautiful auld garden with thick vegetation, maybe weeds; weird flying-saucer-looking plant life which I had never seen before and cannay describe properly.

An aged maternal ancestor of the owner called it home. She was the great-great-grannie's cousin or something. She still lived there and had reached the age of 157. This woman was a wonder to behold. So was the club owner, according to his manager, he was the best dang employer in the entire state. Had I ever met him before? Naw. Had Yasmin ever met him before? Naw. Then how did she get the goddam gig? Bla bla bla. Did we know how lucky she was! Bla bla bla. The guy would have sat up blethering the rest of the night if I hadnay telt him to fuck off in the name of art. He kept looking at me with these stupid shakes of the heid till I felt like yanking that selfsame heid aff its shoodirs and sticking it on top of the town fucking flagpole. I knew what the looks were about. I got them all the goddam time. How come a prick like me had got off with a woman like Yasmin.

The Denver venue was big but she was one of four acts and only down for a 30-minute set which I found disappointing. She sang the traditional stuff but introduced a couple of her ayn songs. She was wearing her "blues" outfit. She was great. As soon as she walked out, ye knew she was the real stuff. Obviously I was proud. Of course I was proud. I sold six cds. What did it matter. One of the roadies with another act telt me six was good: it might have been six different heads of six different mega music corporations. That was the sort of positive outlook I had to acquire. His band was from Portland and they played down California occasionally. I knew two of their venues. The roadie thought Yasmin was "strong". That was his word. He took her address in case something ever came up.

Ye never know. She just needit a break. She deserved it. Ex girlfriend of mine, ex partner, ex lover; mother of my child; my beautiful wee lassie, that I saw on rare occasions, rare occasions. The last time she was wearing a sharp wee dress, pale blue and fluffy shoulder sleeves, her wee white socks. Four years of age and she had style. It wasnay biased of me to say so. I had my wallet in my pocket and could prove it. I had two photos of her. She beamed into the camera. Another one with her and Yasmin, Yasmin in a long skirt and blouse tied at the midriff man that style I love. It was me took the photos. The three of us jumped a train to be by the sea and walk carefree on the sand, yeh, and when we strolled along the boardwalk the heel of her shoe got stuck in some strange way and she tripped, grabbing onto my arm and me carrying the wean on my shoodirs, all laughing. That was a time.

One day off a week from that fucking airport man ye were knackered, ye didnay want to go anywhere. Nay wonder things didnay work out. We would have had to be fucking geniuses to make a go of that relationship.

Agh.

A father should be allowed to take his child back to the ancestral home. Just to see the damn place. I have my people and these people are my daughter's people. Firsthand relatives. Whether these are terrorist aleyun communist muslim hindu atheist running-dog catholic jewish proddy antifuckingcapitalist jazz or country music loving pure anarchists, so what. So what? Ye get sick of cunts telling ye what to do all the time.

There was nay beer left in the bottle and my haun was shaking and my other had just appeared from my pocket. Hullo haun, why are you empty? Cigarettes there are nayn.

My fingers were looking worn. Each one lined and creased with worry. Wee scars and nicks, fibrous patches that were about four layers of skin behind the rest, and toty wee circles. Yeh. What the hell were they at all? Maybe a blood problem, circulation. I held them out, palms up, stretched them so that the lines became more delineated. These palms of mine were like paddles. How come a woman ever let them near her body, especially items as sensitive as nipples. Nipples are wondrous creations. But for manual workers nipples are a trial. One has to sandpaper the hauns before going to bed with one's woman. Or else practice using the backs of them; the area around my veins was soft and I used this method. But the backs of my hauns could be highly sensitive and sometimes tickled to the extent I giggled against my will. In the early days it put me off. I soon gave up on the construction work and settled for driving jobs but they produced hard skin as well. So I was left with the booze trade. The booze trade suited me. But my hauns again were suffering. And they remained in bad condition no matter what, until eventually I realized it wasnay manual work responsible; the condition of my hands was an effect of bad cards. Every time I lifted a shite fucking hand at poker my fingers suffered a physical relapse. I couldnay remember the last time I won through to a semi-final never mind won a final. No just cards, every damn thing.

The last pool tournament I entered wasnay long before I booked the flight to Glasgow. I made it through to the round before the semi-final. It was twelve bucks entry and side-bets each and every round. About eighty players had entered so no a bad turn to the winner: 9-ball was the game, and it is the 7th and decider frame and I pot the fucking 3 and my cue ball cannons the 9 ower a pocket. I had to play the 4-ball safe; it was all I could do. Nay other shot was on. I had to leave it safe, tight on the bottom bank and run for cover. So I did.

I played that shot well. It was a good goddam shot man except this crazy fucker I am playing, Chicano feller, he gies me a smile and a shrug of the shoodirs, a deprecatory smile and a deprecatory shrug of the shoodirs, then *nominates two corner pockets* christ and just mair or less shuts his eyes and bangs the table with the butt end of the cue to the first corner and a nod of the heid at the 9-ball hanging ower the other yin and then he opens his eyes and he looks up to the ceiling like he is praying to the auld gods and steps forward and gies it va va voom, batter batter fucking thump all round the table, zoom eftir zoom it banks once twice three times right into the nominated corner pockets por favor oh lord genuflexion was always beyond me heavenly one and the 9-ball of course, yeh, the cue ball manages to nudge it also and it drops, pillonk into the other corner pocket.

For some reason I examined my cue; I kept my heid lowered. In the physical presence of spiritual beings ye have to.

He gied me a few moments' peace before shaking my hand. Cheers amigo, he says.

What's the name of yer church? I says.

A few beers later I was still staring into space until noticing him and his pals, grinning, pointing at me. La cuenta señor, gracias. I paid the tab and fuckt off. I was there with a couple of bodies from the warehouse I worked. My heid was gone but and I forgot about them. They were drinking beer near the slot machines. I forgot I was with them, I just left.

That Chicano guy but, eftir he beat me that was him into the final so he had to be a good player. Ye had to be lucky to win but ye also had to be good, quite good anyway, at least no bad.

Ach but my luck scunnered me. The bad variety had lasted for so long. There is no doubt it hastened my decision to go hame. I would be there for a month. Then back here, if they would let me. The idea of staying in Skallin christ it was unthinkable. Years ago my maw sent the occasional newspaper so I could keep in touch but later that was that, and ye never heard any news at all about the ol bonné place. If it wasnay for early morning screenings of *Braveheart* and *Graveyard Bobby* and that other yin where the ghostly wee town comes out the mist every hunner years then that would be that. In my last job the immediate superior was another of them that think Skallin is a wee town somewhere in mainland Europe, perhaps to the "left side" of Poland.

Sally passed, holding a tray of drinks. I couldnay recall if a ring encircled her wedding finger. Whether she was merrit or no, she might have had a couple of kids to look eftir, and this was her having to work nights in a bar to pay the bills. And what were the tips like in here? I would lay odds this was the kind of dump where customers cling to their lukewarm dregs for hours. I had worked in a few music bars and that happened a lot. Music bars attract skint customers, especially lonely males who fantasize to a Miles Davis score about the story of their lives.

And musicians are aye skint. If they get any money they dont turn up for their fucking gig. That was what happened to the ex eftir she put her band the gether. Quite a nice band but as soon as they landit a few dollars they were off. Once they were skint back they came like it was the most natural thing. How could she work with dicks like that? It would have driven me crazy. I got irritated with them, angry. So she got angry with me. No them. Me. She got angry with me for getting angry with them, these fucking cretins who let her down. They made me sick. The way they played as well ye know sometimes

Ach what do I know.

Sally was talking to one of them now, a musician fucker, he seemed to be the keyboard player the way he was tinkering about on the fucking thing, his fingers constantly moving, and Sally for christ sake was self-conscious. It was hard to believe a lassie like her would fall for that sort of stuff.

Never trust the keyboard player. Saxophonists are choirboys in comparison. Of course the guy who gave me that information was a saxophonist himself.

Saxophonist. What a fucking name. Why dont they just say saxophone player? Keyboardist.

Yeh, Sally was talking away to the guy. Maybe she liked him. Women have a habit of liking unlikely guys, unlikeable guys, guys that other guys know are to be avoided at all costs, guys that are total fucking arseholes. Yet women persist with them. They fucking persist with them man they fucking persist with them. What is it all about! That fucking stupit ex man she done that as well ye would see her with these guys, talking with them and laughing at their fucking stupit jokes, listening to their views on life and politics and the major things in the world, international events and affairs of state. Oh yeh and meanwhile aw they wantit was a quick screw round the back of the bar.

Fucking keyboard players. They think they are something. How come they dont read books! These bastards dont even read books. And yet they talk all night about the world and its fucking oysters. Total dicks. And nay fucking interests either. In life I am talking about. Nay interests. They cannay haud a conversation. Ask them about politics, they know fuck all. Yet still women christ almighty man they persist with them. Why do women persist with them? Maybe they see a lost soul or somefuckingthing. Poor feller, that mass murderer, he is a lost soul, I have to save him. So ower she goes, strokes the cunt's foreheid: now she lays him down to sleep, prays the lord his soul to keep.

Agh, one cannay even sigh.

Sally but, she seemed like the mccoy. Yeh, ye could tell by looking at her. A worker too. Worth her weight in gold and there was nay doubt about that. Even a crap job like this; she did it properly. Plus no doubt she had a dayjob, worked in an office or cleaned a school or something. This could even have been her third job; you got to labour in this man's country, hard labour. And no matter the number of jobs still she had to be up at the crack of dawn to feed the weans and wash them and clothe them and get them off to school. Probably her lazy bastard of a husband had fukt off and left her or else he stayed in bed all day and let her get on with it, reared in a religious culture: men are men and women do all the work.

How come I aye assumed what suited me. The place was busy now and there was definitely a buzz like something was about to happen. It was a good time to leave, just drink up and leave. A couple had entered and Sally went to take their order. I dont know if she looked at me, then or previously. What was I hoping? What was I sensing? I was sensing something. Or was it wishful thinking?

There was definitely a spark. No matter how dull a spark can have life breathed into it. I could breathe life into it. She was a beautiful-looking woman. So how come she was working in a joint like this in a town like this? the which gambit would have had me thrown out, sine died.

But she had the shape, she surely did, that sense of style, sense of herself, her movement, an ease – what do they call it in women, grace, grace. How do we equate it? With what? If such a feature does inhere would it have distinguished her from the ex? If no was she a clone? Not at all, the ex was brown-skinned, brown-eyed, dark-brown-nippled in maist lights but sometimes rust-coloured – rust-coloured! what the fuck does that mean? Red; a reddish hint. And me. What were my nipples?

Fucking hell. A pinky kind of light brown or something. Sounds quite sexy. But see when ye see them! Oh fuck naw, sexy isnay the word. What do women see in men. She called me a white ghost, and when she discovered my neck went red in the sun man the original red neck, that was heeelarious. I was too skinny but and my knees werenay even hilarious, just ugly. How can knees be ugly? Deformity was a word she used one time. She was joking but it preyed on me. I never regarded myself as a male beauty. I wasnay a soulful kind of guy although I smoked and worked a nightshift. I aye associated "soulful" with being in a smoky atmosphere at 4 o'clock in the morning but no when ye were sitting in a carpark office.

Okay, I wasnay cool. I didnay play the fucking cornet, sax or trombone. But who wants to be cool, like the advertising industry says, it isnay cool to be cool; to be uncool man that is fucking cool, that is real cool.

Lite beer is tastier than people gie it credit.

But deformity! So what? Is that a fact or a value? All bodies are beautiful. If ye are lying with another body then it is beautiful. Ye want to pore ower every detail and touch every spot with yer fingertips and yer tongue and the tip of yer penis and also yer nipples some people say but speaking personally my nipples are kind of dreary, naybody has ever been turned on by them, no even myself and sometimes personal matters took a turn for the worse.

But my feet were sensitive. Everybody that has feet are sentient beings. These most sensitive parts of the body, this is what I am talking about. Feet can be neglected in these discussions, especially if the company is male. But women know.

But if ye stroke a woman's body with yer feet then ye wind up in bizarre postures, arse in the air and having to take the weight of yer entire body no on yer elbows but yer hands and wrists; first thing to control is yer wind; it is all worth the effort but because ye master the art of midway-levitation, and without midway-levitation it is impossible to engage in the deeper erotic practices. And this is what women want, so they say.

So who says? Women? Psychologists? Women psychologists?

How the fuck do I know. Think of the very top gymnasts. They can do that special levitation given that most of them have yet to experience proper sexual intimacy because when they do they are fukt, their lust for gymnastics is at an end, given that their interest in the gymnasium may or may not continue and one thinks of women with beautiful tits, larger-sized breasts as one may term it, but for the likes of the Olympic Games naw, finito, if it isnay lust forget it, for baith sexes, that is how come these elderly athletes aye look like they need treatment of some kind. If ye look into art ye can discover similar truths. I used to go to a couple of galleries near the last bar I worked on the east coast. One specialized in sculpture and there I saw a fine exhibition by a woman whose stuff I thought was real good. It featured an unusual combination of spokes, limbs and non-mechanical spanners. She was influenced by Egyptian art, I have no doubt about that, something to do with

Forget it.

The ex was beautiful. The first time I went with her to a gig she wore her first-choice stage outfit; skintight leather slacks and a wee skimpy top, scarlet with ruffles, very low cut; if she flung her heid back ye expected her tits to jump out, and her shoodirs bare, beautiful shoodirs – athletic too when the light outlined the muscles. Nay wonder the audience were glued to her. If it was a traditional all-jazz night she had another outfit, a long skirt. She asked me about it and appreciated my opinion. I telt her what to me is the truth: men like short skirts, medium skirts, long skirts and nay skirts. We like everything. It doesnay fucking matter. It is all to do with how. How do ye wear it honey, how do ye slink around. Let them fucking hips waggle. I say that in light of full and impartial consideration. But in another way all bodies are something else. And if she was so obviously beautiful how come I wasnay handsome. If we were a couple. I had no objection to being called beautiful if she wantit to call me beautiful. Okay it is a term for females but I wouldnay have cared about that. She called me a white ghost, a skinny white ghost. I had to remind her I was pink and a couple of her cousins were skinnier than me but she said, I dont sleep with them. It wasnay particularly funny but I laughed. It was to do with possession. At the time of that comment she was pregnant. The skinny pink non-integratit furnir with the deformed fucking non-integratit knees had impregnated her. Say it again. It was me that done it. Me. It made me smile, especially when I was in amongst an audience. Pride.

Pride! It comes before a fall.

Fuck sake, I might have known.

Amid all these bastards who sat there gawking at her when she was singing, kidding on they were into the music and it was just fucking horny man they were just horny; at least tell the truth, ye know, instead of the fucking hell with it christ nay wonder people's hauns start shaking, people's tickers start gaun nineteen to the fucking dozen, sitting there, me just sitting there. It got me down but. They just sat there gawking at her. Okay, listening, they listened to her. Some did listen. But she had mair passion in her wee fucking pinkie

fuck it

That big guy at the bar was looking at me again. A third cunt was with him now, chatting to trucker five-bellies, another refugee from the Shooters and Horses emporium. The bar-tender had probably sent him across the street to check if I was here. The Curse of the Alien Stranger starring Corey Parker, boy detective and baseball superhero. Yeh I was here, I was fucking here alright, exercising my rights as a card-carrying Red Card carrier. The right to be alive is what I was really exercising, cause that was the right they were trying to fucking deny me, fucking religious maniac capitalist bastards.

One occasionally got angry, occasionally snapped. I was the wrang person to carry a gun and any of my true-born compañeros could have walked into any true-born pawnshop and bought me one. I would have got masel a good yin for self-defence purposes. Imagine getting attacked by a bunch of good ol pentagon pricks in their ivy-league clobber and frank sinatra wigs, all set to drag ye off to the nearest yardarm, knotting the noose on the rope as they go, when suddenly ye produce yer high-powered high-tech pistol and hold them all off, lousy cowardly fucks now the odds are evened. No sir, them fellers only hunt in packs. Us in the Alien Section had to learn the unarmed-combat stuff, how to fight with nay weapons. Y'all got the right to self defence but ya cant have no fucking armoury, no sir.

Some of my comrade aliens were good at the phizzicue stuff. I wasnay in their league but I had learned a couple of tricks. We wur required to figure it out for wurselves because the agency assumed it was less expensive that way. But was it? What it did was disseminate information arbitrarily amongst employees and nay powerbase should regard that favourably. I thought it bad practice and the economic advantages un-proven. Why not organize self-defence workshops operated for and by the section? I wrote my thoughts into a wee report on the computer in the back office. I did it ower a period of maybe three weeks and I thought it good enough to send to an academic journal devoted to alternative hand-to-hand combat. I whiled away the weary hours by writing some mair stuff. It wasnay as good as the first yin and reminded me of these angry letters ye get in newspapers. Some of it I transferred to my home laptop for future reference. My texts werenay tampered with or modified but I knew they were "noticed". This was confirmed one morning at the end of a shift when I was in the back office preparing to go hame. Earlier I had written up notes on the economics of combat, singular and combined which I intended revising into another report. An immediate superior came around to oversee the shift change-over and he entered the room and peered about the walls at things of interest. I waited. He had something to say and would say it. But then man I nearly laughed in his face, it was the word "combination": he was interested in my varied use of it.

The only thesaurus available on computer was a version of

the updated *All-American Book of Words* and it didnay contain the term. If ye were referring to "combination" ye had to work by negation: "not not plural, not singular, not sole, not single, not unique, not only, not lone, not only-begotten, not without a second, first and last, not unitary, not univocal, not unilateral", and so on. I did a quick printout and discussed with him the particular context, bodies working the gether on tactics designed to keep them alive, the existence of communities. My immediate superior sighed. Ye're wary of an implied politics? I says.

No son, he says, it aint that. Hey, okay if I keep your printout?

Naw, I'll take it as a compliment. I'll photocopy it first but, plus I'll shove in the date and we can both sign it.

By the lord, he says, you surely are a cautious feller.

Thanks, I said.

But us of the alienigenae were lucky and between us held valuable shared experience. I wantit to teach them the headbutt for busting noses, mouths and eyes but maist of the compañeros knew it. And from other cultures were angled variations, one from the South African townships that left brain damage on anyone taller than 5' 11". These were crucial refinements for class warfare and ye had to respect that stuff.

A few of the squad had faimly experience that included hideous tortures, rapes and lucky escapes from certain death, and survival techniques had been passed down. One of the second-generation lassies could distinguish dormant – "secret" she called them – pressure-points on the human back. She could stun somebody by applying force by finger and to demonstrate put a feller "to sleep" for a few minutes. According to her the information was transmitted on the maternal line. Her people hailed from South America. An interesting matter arose here; during that demonstration another operative "awoke as from slumber" and could proceed with the same demonstration. His maternal grandparents had arrived from the eastern Bangladesh region. That to me was fascinating for a number of reasons and I jotted down notes. I related it to a short story I read in a Wide World anthology; its writer was anonymous but from a people whose present defence culture contains combative elements of known antiquity.

I was good with the stick. I had the knack. I reckon this too was in the blood, us Celts knew how to twirl a baton. I got attached to mine and gied it a name which embarrasses me to recall never mind divulge, and which I aint a-gauny divulge. I sought excuses to bring it out and examine it. It had a finely-wrought knuckle-duster handle. I would love to have carried it on a few off-duty occasions.

When me and the Security agency parted company I was required to haun the stick back. That wasnay justice, we had become firm friends. I could have acquired one privately but it wouldnay have been the same, there was only one Buster, the finest stick known to man.

Christ I divulged the name! Never mind.

I aye liked the name "Buster". I called my dog Buster as well. If I had had a wee boy instead of a wee lassie I would have called him Buster too. Even if the ex didnay allow it. So what? I was a tough cunt. I would have called him Buster behind her back. When in doubt lie through yer fucking teeth man that is the story of relationships.

Ach I was definitely hitting the road, I was getting out of here. First I was gaun hame to Skallin.

So I couldnay hit the road till eftir my return.

Then it would be a fast car, I would save like crazy, nay nonsense, just get the money the gether. Maybe head down Florida. Naw, fuck it, I was crossing the border. So save save save, I needit to save. I would get lost in Mexico or anyplace they dont speak Inkliz because I was just fucking sick of it. Bodies I knew said Monterey was the place for me, that I would get a job in the booze trade. A Skarrisch gringo fucker, le socialiste. I would be a tourist attraction. Only thing, would I don el kilto? Sure. I hadnay donned el kilto since I was a boy but now was the time.

But I needit that fokn motor. This is a sizeable country and it isnay as if ye can hop a freight train or hitch a lift with impunity. Maybe in the auld days ye could, if ye had the build and savvy of guys like Lee Marvin, Humphrey Bogart or Steve McQueen. Or ye wore a 12-inch miniskirt, cut-off jeans and looked like Audrey Hepburn. No sir, I wasnay too keen on hitching a ride across lil ol mean ol. Furin fuckers dont take these kind of risks, hombré meester eees too fokn dangerous. The mounties, managers and military, all the cops and gun carriers; the fucking inhumanoids, the shooters and horsemen, the true-born authenticks: they all hate that kind of unfettered stuff.

Also, me and the ex were having wur ayn wee difference relationship. Ye had to be careful walking down the street lest pop, some pentagon greysuit cunt pulled out a shotgun and whacked ye. It happens. Then they got promoted. In the land of the free ye were aye on guard. Yazzie had watched her back since the day she staggered out the pram. Sometimes being in the pram was a problem; ye heard terror stories about these racist bastards attacking wee weans. Ye had to fucking really watch it. It was alright in her ayn neighborhood but in one of these suburban mister jones places with the manicured lawn or else outside the city, ye had to safeguard the wee lassie. Plus yerself. Then the paranoia: ye were aye prepared for when it strikes. Ye can only fight yer way through that, and preferably with knowledgeable bodies in the company.

The airport terminal had a rash of these extreme paranoias

and rooms were sectioned off for the immediate use of both workforce and air passengers. Eftir sixteen hours incapacitated customers were transferred to a protected wing within the holding camps. We only ever had a couple of these cases in the Alien Section because for us the condition is an everyday experience. I mentioned in one of my wee reports how the Alien and Alien-Extraction Section contained a general experience in psychological disorder that would be useful in managing the problem. We were known for wur paranoiac tendencies and were constantly dealing with the grounds for paranoia personally, or else we fucking suffered paranoia, to whatever extent. Ye get sick of cunts staring at ye just because ye speak different. Try sticking on a kilt and a turban and walking into yer average sports bar. Nay wonder we all sit talking to wurselves. All these cunts looking for ye and watching for ye and listening for ye and preparing for ye man they want to smash ye, they dont like ye much at all. Wur nurse, Miss Liu Lee, had been commandeered to solve the paranoia problem and been put in charge of her ayn battalion.

Some musicians the ex played with, if I was traveling with them, they didnay welcome me because of the Celtic origins. My presence vexed them and they couldnay be at ease having to watch out for me, so they said. In the jalopy and passing though some neighborhoods they telt me to hide down on the floor.

Being a musician would have suited me. Naw it wouldnay. How do ye cope with all the side stuff that goes on. These managers and bar owners, cheats and card-sharp conmen managerial fucking dead-beat hangers-on, I would have shot the bastards. That was the problem when I accompanied her.

Let me rephrase that: I was the problem when I accompanied her. My absence was the preferred option. On that goddam mini tour nothing I did helped the situation. I didnay seem to know how to talk to people. I used to know how to talk to people. Now I didnay. Or when I spoke naybody heard me. That was fucking weird. I would be at a table with her and the musicians, maybe the guys that ran the club, and I would say something, and naybody would reply, they would just go off on a tangent. It was her they spoke to. She was doing her ayn business. I was just a fucking I dont know, nothing. We discussed it eftir the Denver gig. The next day was Sunday and it was a free night. Until Monday morning we could enjoy wandering the city, I was wanting to check out that group of streets with the Skarrisch names. Maybe there was a local museum. I thought it would have been good the two of us gaun for a wander. Instead of that the ill feeling set in and the discussion we had became a bad argument, then silence. She did one of her legendary vanishing acts when I was having a bath. Those had mair or less stopped eftir the baby was born. This was the first I had noticed for a wee while. That doesnay mean she wasnay doing it, it just means I didnay notice her absence.

And that bath, I didnay even want a fucking bath. We only had one room and there was naywhere else to go. I went so she didnay have to keep breathing the same oxygen as me. I was aye sensitive to the needs of my lady.

She was gone when I came out. I had stayed in too long, kept the water too hot and was dehydratit. I lay flat out on the bed and dozed off, a not uncommon event. And she still hadnay returned when I awoke, shivering. One and a half hours had elapsed. Where the hell did she go for one and a half hours? Did she go to the bar, did she go for a walk, for a hamburger, did she climb aboard the broomstick and fly out the window to land in the arms of some scabby bastarn keyboard fucker? How the hell do I know. It was a taboo subject. Personal business. Dont attack the sanctity of the inner life. And what gied me the right to criticize her? Had I no vanished when she was doing her Benefit Night performance! Sure I had, I left her on stage alone. She didnay have a friend in the entire place. She looked for me and couldnay see me. I had explained to her I was searching for the goddam Treasurer, I explained it all.

And what gied her the right to attack me? Where was her show of loyalty when I gied up my seat at the Performers Table? How come she hadnay left in protest? She just looked at me like I was foolish. I couldnay figure it. How come she had sat on at that table knowing I couldnay? If it had been me: naw, if she couldnay sit there then I couldnay sit there. And if she had went with me to the back of the hall I wouldnay have wound up in a stupit argument with the dick that stole my chair. She had heard about that. Fucking unbelievable what people have to talk about. Somebody had referred to it at the Organizers Table and her ears caught the word "Skarrisch". Nay doubt the female operative from television land also heard and nay doubt she also texted the information to the appropriate authorities.

How come they hadnay deportit me already? Maybe they used me as a living example. Of what? Who knows. But I could imagine them studying me. They might have implanted one of these toty wee electronic devices in my napper. And some poor Security comrade was employed on my case 24/7. Hell mend the bastard for taking the job in the first place. But imagine meeting him! Ye go to a bar one night and get chatting to this guy and he turns out to be yer ayn personal surveillance body. Imagine if everybody had one? That includes themselves, the bodies doing the surveillance, each of them had their ayn surveillance. That would be like

Fuck.

Then it was my turn to vanish. She could vanish so could I. I was a fucking past master at that game. Oh yeh. We were on the long haul to Rapid City from early Monday morning when the bus pulled into some little burg north of Cheyenne. There were definite similarities to this place. What I recall is the number of antique and bric-a-brac stores. We stopped for an hour and a half. The ex was asleep, or pretending to be. I left the bus for a smoke and a wee walk. It would gie her peace and gie myself peace. I needed to simmer down. There had been nay communication since Denver but that doesnay mean we were calm and relaxed. Maybe she was. My heid was nipping. All kinds of nonsense. I had my notebook and intended writing wee snippets for my story but I drifted from there into meditations centred on the domestic Security industry and I started to figure how matters might be improved on the efficiency front at a federal level. That struck me as the key. Since Omaha I had been aware how close I was to the route taken by my namesake ancestor eftir his blunder off the Santa Fe trail. Maybe he passed through this very town. Christ, I sensed a benign presence. It was him! Maybe he was my guardian angel. Maybe the fates held something in store. I was aye open to offers and who knows, the idea of landing in some little burg and being made so extra welcome ye realize it is like a preordained thing, it is like ye have come hame. Maybe I would find a telltale sign. Maybe I would be sitting in the local diner and suddenly be struck by an overwhelming faimly resemblance between myself and the guy flipping the burgers. That happened in life. I could check the local phone directory for the name "Brown". Years ago I used to wonder how the fuck I landed in Sacramento and it maybe made sense because of the auld cowboy trails and I saw something significant there in relation to my ancestor but I couldnay unravel what it was.

Anyhow, I had an hour and a half break from the bus, or so I thought. The bus station was shite; two benches against a wall and the drinks machine was bust. I went for a walk and of course missed the departure. Yes sir, that ol bus, it done gaun man it fucking left without me. Nay search party was sent. A tearful and distraught Yasmin wasnay picked up by the cops as she hunted high and low for my emaciated corpse.

The stopover hadnay been for one hour and a half, it was for one half hour: thirty minutes.

A piss-stop, says the clerk at the bus station when I made my enquiry.

Mair like a piss-take, says I, but he didnay get it. Instead he squinted at me then pointed at a certain blue-bordered notice on the wall. I produced the ID instantly my good fellow, there you are.

Thank you, he said.

You bet, I said.

Then he added, Pardon me sir, and left with the card to a back office. When he returned he passed me it without a word, heid lowered, no meeting my gaze.

Hey man dont worry, I said, I aint no spiritual manifestation.

I looked about the vicinity of the bus station in case the ex was there but she wasnay. She had stayed on the bus. Obviously the show must go on. Good luck to her. But it was fucking hours I had to wait for the next damn bus. It was a disgrace; freezing cauld and with a hell of a wind. All I had was a stupit jacket that was fine for southern cities but no for these parts. I wandered about avoiding the bars, looking for a place to get a coffee. I realized there were nay bars to avoid.

I beg yer pardon?

Nay bars! I wasnay avoiding the fuckers, they didnay exist.

Nay bookstore. Any pool halls? Nay fucking pool halls! What did a guy do in this yere burg. I checked out the antique stores. Wagon wheels and rusted chassis; kitchen, farm and hunting implements, plaques and wall pictures; carved toys, cribs and mangers; arrowheads, ripped moccasins and beaded materials, other stuff. They were of interest. I could imagine auld Jeremiah coming this way and no mistake. Now and again I called in at the bus station to confirm the schedule, then christ I blundered off the two main streets. How the hell did I manage that. I fucking did but and got lost in rows and rows of neatly ordered huising with uniform lawn gardens and the smell of dandelions everywhere. The rows of huises seemed to move up to the summits of wee hills at either end, yet it was like a weird illusion and ye couldnay see beyond a mental dip in the middle of the road, it was very fucking weird. I checked the cigarettes I was smoking and managed no to panic about being strandit there forever and ever, my wasted decayed corpse a stark reminder of pioneering days, instead I trudged to and fro and let the sky guide me; whereupon a cop parked his car slap dang to the front of me and his comrade opened the door and climbed out. Hey buddy, can I help you?

Of course ye can, I said, you're the very man. I kept the hauns where he could see them and he ushered me into the backseat of the patrol car where we had a pleasant conversation. I gied them the kernel of my story. Nay damn embellishments. Those have been my downfall. I had to tell them I was also a Security operative. And blubarbrhubarb. Kindly they returned me to the local bus station and kindly they waited until the bus trundled in. Fortunate was I there were plenty seats to spare. He bade me farewell. Without further ado I reached Rapid City mid evening, still in time for the gig. I asked a female bus station worker if she knew the location of the venue. No, she says then called in a comrade who telt me it wasnay in Rapid City at all, no sir, it was a wee town north of there. Nay bother, I wasnay in the mood for dejection. I jumped the first stagecoach and hastened slowly in time for the tail end of the first session.

In the bar I hung about the entrance and listened. It

wouldnay have been fair to show myself. The audience was fine, they werenay noisy but receptive. The band sounded real good. The bit I heard veered mair to rock from blues than blues to jazz; mair like auld Etta James than anybody. As soon as the applause died down and she stepped away from the mic I gied her a wave. Hey, she said but neither smiled nor frowned. Then she dropped her gaze and strolled past me, straight on to the ladies' room and didnay return for twenty minutes. I waited by the door for a word in private. I had misjudged the situation. I thought she would have been relieved. She wasnay, she was furious. We moved down to the rear entrance, stepped out the back. It was mair than "furious". Fuming? Naw, fucking worse than that. What I didnay like was it was controled. But beneath the control she was a mass of quivers. She must have thought about this conversation right the way through from when the bus left without me; maybe right until an hour before, when she stepped up to the mic here in this club. It was the idea I missed the bus intentionally in order to fuck her. This was just, it was too much, too much. She couldnay believe I would do that to her. This was just like the very worst. Couldnt I even have phoned?

Naw, I had nay fucking phone; she knew that, it was impossible.

Naw it wasnay "it" that was impossible it was me that was impossible I was the fucking

me, I was impossible.

It was like an onslaught she gied me. I was taken aback christ totally unprepared. I had been expecting I dont know she would have been worried, worried; and she would be glad to see me. Something like that. But now she was like whatever relationship we had man that was it finished, if ever I wantit to show her it was finished I had succeeded, but what a lousy way to do it.

What was she talking about?

Now she walked past me, just left me there outside the rear exit.

It hadnay been lousy what I did it was an accident for christ sake, it was a stupit fucking hearing problem; the driver said one half hour and I heard an hour a half. It wasnay even my hearing problem there was a lot of crackle in the bus sound system. So it wasnay all my fault either. The very idea I would miss the bus intentionally, it was plain ludicrous. How could she figure such a thing, christ almighty. But that was what she did figure. She didnay believe what I said, reckoned it another excuse for me to mess up her life. I says, If it was intentional how come I didnay take my bag with me?

Why, she says, because you wanted to leave it for me, she says, you knew I got three bags you wanted to make it four. And then on top of that, she says, I got the fucking guitar, you knew I got the fucking guitar.

Yeh but ye never let me carry the fucking guitar. No at any time!

Sometimes she didnay even like me holding the damn thing because once I banged into a door with it. Once, one time. "Pass me the guitar Jerry" and I would pass her it. That was fucking that. So what had guitars got to do with it, except it was in addition.

How am I to carry it all, Jerry, it aint fair to me; you're supposed to carry the damn bags.

I know that, I says, and I'm sorry. Honest, I'm sorry. I do want to carry the bags, because that is my function to carry the bags cause I aint a goddam artiste, and who wants to be a goddam arrrrtiste, fucking artiste, I says, I'm just yer man.

Silence.

I'm just trying to look eftir ye.

I dont need looking after Jerry.

Naybody says ye need looking eftir.

Huh! you just did.

Yeh but no like that christ ye know what I'm talking about, I'm trying to take care of things. I havenay done it before, I'm learning, learning as I go. It doesnay help matters with these crazy gigs I mean fucking hell, could he no have made things a bit easier? I'm talking about yer manager, so-called.

You dont like it you stay home. Dont come and fuck up, you're fucking up, she says, fighting with me; all the while Jerry that's what you are doing. I cant take it. I have to go on there and sing, how can I do that? You just god Jerry you just embarrassed me here, you were coming then didnt show, you didn't show, and the people here are like they dont know we had a fight, they dont know you left the goddam bus, they dont know nothing. They dont know none of that stuff. All they see is me there with four goddam bags and a guitar. You didnt call me, you didnt call me.

I've lost my fucking cell phone, ye know that, it was impossible.

She just stared at me. It was my second in two months. I wasnay buying another yin, no yet. Plus I was sick of carrying it everywhere. It was just another thing to lose, like yer lighter or yer smokes and these personal belongings ye have that aye disappear from under yer nose.

She returned to the bar. I followed her. She moved quickly. A few people were smiling to her and making like they would applaud her to her seat, wherever she was sitting. Then a couple were like "Who the fuck's that!" – looking at me.

There was a seat for her at the musicians' table and I pulled one across to sit next to her. One of the bartenders was coming ower. He had a huge smile on his face. Obviously he loved her music. He was about the same age as myself. He had a coffee and a drink for her – a rum and sprite plenty ice, which is what she enjoyed during the show. And if it was me mixing the thing I would have looked for a sprig of mint, you want a nice drink maam you try that, guaranteed.

She introduced me to the company by name but said nothing else. But her voice was better; what would ye say, softer, it was maybe softer. I passed her a cigarette and she took it. I laid my haun on her shoodir, a moment later she leaned away from me.

The owner was there, a big guy with an enormous chin and a stetson hat – a leather yin with wee studs round it – the other half of the Jazz Brothers. Him and his wife were hosting us overnight. He kept scowling across the table as though he hadnay been prepared for nay boyfriend. But he knew I was coming. Unless he hoped I had vanished forever. Maybe he thought I was freeloading. And I wasnay even a musician! Musicians drank booze but them that returned the hospitality could be counted on the fingers of one haun.

I caught him staring at me again, then glancing at Yasmin. He had his ayn wife for christ sake did he need everybody else's? What was the law on polygamy in this state? I saw him whisper to the bartender who soon arrived with a pint of ale, and wouldnay take my money. He indicated the owner and I raised my glass to him. He nodded in reply. He reminded me of somebody. Desperate Dan! the kid's cartoon character! He was the spitting image. The drummer and bass had returned to their place, the second session was beginning. I placed my hand on her upper arm. Yazzie, I whispered, all the best. She squeezed my wrist and closed her eyes. All the best, I whispered, and she squeezed my wrist again. I tried to put my arm round her waist but she was up and walking to the mic.

Friends of the owner had arrived, including his wife, and a couple of tables were shifted the gether, chairs dragged across, but although these tables were wide it was still a crush. The atmosphere was relaxed and people were there to listen. It was enjoyable and for me emotional. I settled to listen but she startit with traditional jazz numbers that I found empty shite, if it hadnay been her singing them. I think I would have dozed off. One thing about this mini tour thing, it was sorting my heid about small towns. Sometimes I thought it would be good living in one; other times naw, ye couldnay be anonymous. Then yer politics. Ye couldnay even talk politics never mind get involved. Then if they knew ye didnay gie a fuck for the supernatural and aw that stuff. Plus if ye were an alien; forget it if ye were an alien. Just nay place to hide. Naw, I was a city boy, born and bred. Her as well. It was just money money money all the time money. She was earning and being a mother and I was earning and being a father. But at what cost, sometimes I wondered.

Any extra money I saved towards a night with Ranjit and the hold 'em squad. But I never found it easy in the company. The last time there one of his uncles took a hand, a crazy auld fucker who bet like there was no tomorrow. And when the cards went wrong he shrieked these weird diatribes, waving at the ceiling. Maybe they werenay weird, just they were in Urdu and I didnay know nay Urdu and he aye seemed to gape at me when he was shrieking, was I demon or deity, to be conciliated by offerings or stuck with a dagger. No sir, they werenay great players and a couple were hopeless which is why nothing ye done worked because they didnay have the brains to know what ye were up to! They didnay watch the cards! They just fucking laughed and threw in the dough! I wantit to gie them a shake and teach them how to play the goddam game. It wasnay just me. John Wong felt the same. How the fuck could you win in this company. Okay it was the friendliest game in town but in another way it was the deadliest. When ye bluffed them they should have folded but they didnay. Because they didnay know what ye were fucking representing because they didnay read the fucking cards; they didnay even look at the cards man when the flop happened they were too busy yapping about the ways of the world. How could these bodies throw in their dough and no know what the fuck was going on! Ranjit shrugged. John Wong was irritated. The guys are fucking dicks, says he.

Naw they're no, says I, they are mad fucking mental bastards and they dont deserve to leave that room with one damn copper coin in their pockets. The next time I come here man I aint gauny fucking relax, I aint gauny play like I'm in the school bastarn playground or playing some no-dough game with my aunties and uncles round the fireside on New Year's Day man with mammy's steak pie basting gently in the goddam oven. No sir.

But what did it matter the way I played. Everything I touched turned to dust; every hand I turned was no-stay no-stay no fucking stay no fucking hope go hame go hame go hame; that was what like it was. At the same time I knew I could hit it eventually; patience boy patience. And the knowing when, when to lay it down. Anybody can gamble, but to gamble the correct way?

What is the correct way? I never found out nay correct way. I aye got beat. Nay wonder my brains were pugglit.

But it wasnay all my fault. I played well and I done the right moves, it was just that auld devil moon man these fucking fates it was that what do ye call it man luck it was fucking luck, my luck was shite, and if yer luck is shite

dont leave the huis, if yer luck is shite, pull the clothes ower yer heid man go back to bed.

And how do you play if you aint got no money? Easy, you dont. And when do the good hands come round?

When you aint playing.

My life was a joke. It was my ayn fault. Nay wonder the ex couldnay cope. If I could just concentrate on the writing. If I could just get down to it. I could see it becoming a movie or even just staying as a book, I could imagine folk reading it. It was just a case of doing it. And those occasions when me and her were the gether, the baby in the cot, her doing the music and me my writing; her composing and me composing, she was doing her music and I was doing my story, and between the two of us we had made a real live human being, a wee lassie who was perfect, a wee lassie who

Gie us a break.

Also the smoking, the two of us were trying to stop the smoking, because of the wean. Whenever we wantit a smoke we went outside or else kept it for wur ayn room and opened the window. Plus I was saving for a decent jalopy. A lot of this crap would never have happened if I had had a decent jalopy, a roadworthy effort, sleek as fuck. All this shite about missing buses, it would never have happened; these fights with Yasmin. It was avoidable garbage. Nay wonder she wouldnay talk to me.

It was hard to watch her on stage. The first set would have suited me better. When she finished the encore session she left the room and the band played another couple by themselves. She headed for the bathroom. I saw her leave. She gied me a kind of smile. She was gone a long time. I thought to go wait for her but figured she was needing her ayn space.

Eftir their second number the band finished but remained on stage, sipping beer, chuckling ower who did what and who was out of step, who came in too soon and who was an ego-centred bastard and so on.

There was a rise in noise. Conversations were many and loud. Another pint of beer had arrived in front of me courtesy of who else but the Jazz Brother. Somebody next to me had got up for some reason and now the owner's wife was sitting next to me. Lindy was her name. Me, her and another couple of bodies were talking together. I had been saying how Yasmin's musical preference included blues and funkier stuff than that traditional jazz stuff. Obviously my ayn prejudice had come through and a wee auld guy to my left took umbrage, but in good humour. I explained I wasnay a musician. What do you do? he says.

Well, I says, generally speaking I work in bars. Yasmin sings the blues and I sling the booze.

He laughed and repeated it to his neighbors. Naybody seemed to have heard it before. Remarkable. Maybe it was be-polite-to-strangers week.

We carried on chatting. I telt them I was working in airport Security. The wee guy's attention lapsed but Lindy found it interesting. She knew all about survive-or-perish insurance deals. Emergencies were common in mountainous regions and her faimly hailed from Wyoming. Relations of hers had been on a plane that crash-landed once. She wondered if it bothered me working so close to human tragedy. I beg yer pardon? I says. She repeated the question. Her interest was genuine and the conversation moved forwards. I listened and said nothing. She also chatted about the trials and tribulations of being merrit to people in the entertainment business. Apparently her man played keyboard and played professionally before opening the music clubs with his brother. Lindy said it was bad enough being merrit to a musician never mind a club owner and all what that entailed. We carried on blethering. I have to confess I was enjoying it. Then the amazing thing happened, she was an actual writer! It was her passion. She wrote short stories and poetry and attended a group where bodies met and bleth-ered about the different aspects. They read their work to one another and discussed it critically. They further discussed the finer points; choosing what publisher to go to and dealing with screen rights and optional arrangements, whether you should get yourself an agent or what. She had the names of agents and said I should write to them when I had my story finished. I told her it was a novel and she asked me about it. Her ayn stories were mair from true-life as she called it, true life experiences, "life writing". She wantit to know my favourite authors and did I like poetry. It was a great conversation and the first yin I ever had. Really. I cannay mind ever having one like it before. And I dont regret a fucking single thing. She knew all the ins and outs, stuff like "marketing". Christ. She even wantit to know about my laptop, what kind I worked with and nayn of the auld cliché jokes about if we had computers in Skallin. I said that to her and she laughed. It was ten minutes later I saw Yasmin had returned. She was sitting across from me, two bodies away from Desperate Dan who I noticed staring at me.

Well well, pistols at dawn.

I lit another cigarette and sipped his beer, then got my Red Card ID into position. The prick was gauny ask for it. When he did I was gauny reach up to his heid and abracadabra it from behind his ear, right from under the brim of his stetson fucking hat. Next to Yasmin another guy was talking but I knew she wouldnay be listening. Sure enough she glanced across and we exchanged looks. It was one of these occasions where in a packed room everybody is bawling and laughing yet you and yer partner are alone in yer ayn space.

Maist of us were crushed the gether now. Lindy was talking to the person on the other side of her and had kind of backed into me. She said something but I never caught it because of the wee auld feller who kept shouting funny remarks to a guy on the other side of her. I made a jokey comment myself and they laughed. Then I regaled them with the one about me missing the bus and the patrolcar cops taking me to the station. Fucking hilarious! Desperate Dan scowled at me. How else to describe it. One of the major mysteries of South Dakota was how Lindy put up with him. I gied him a wee wave and raised the pint he had bought me: sláinte. It attracted Yasmin's attention. We exchanged looks again. She held the look.

Maybe I should have moved to her side of the table but there was nay room. Nay room anywhere. Maybe Yasmin thought me and Lindy were too close the gether. I tried to edge clear but it was a squeeze and I was aware of her against me christ it was a real squeeze; the type where usually ye gie up trying to keep yer distance and just relax at the touch of the other person but though we kept it civilized wur upper thighs were the gether, sure they were, it was impossible for it to have been otherwise. I think I was smoking, stubbed it out and had another slug of beer but it was so much a squeeze I had to leave my haun on the table or else put it behind me, and that meant around the back of Lindy's chair and of course I wasnay gauny do that, and she was still talking to a woman now on the other side of her. Meanwhile the wee auld guy was talking to somebody else. I nudged him on the shoodir and says, Hey pardon me, how far is it from here to Minneapolis?

Oh Minneapolis? How far from here? why now it must be a thousand miles.

Christ, that's a long way. Where I come from that is a long way, that is a real long way man that is a distance.

He nodded and returned to his neighbor. And time went on and who was talking and what the fuck they were talking about I dont know because I was too aware of the body pressed against me it was like being in a cocoon the two of us, I was wondering about her underwear for christ sake, what was I wondering about her underwear, I cannay remember, how the hell – I just had this image of something shockingly taut and stretched and maybe silky self-coloured see-through-coloured something, skimpiness or something, naw, much thinner than that keeping breaking into my concentration, I was trying to listen but I think trembling, having to exercise will-power, when was the last time I entered a church or sang a hymn or a psalm or something a prayer it must have been years ago definitely man a hardon was the last thing I required and the crucial test would come as soon as somebody got up and left the table; when that happened would we separate? Yeh and what about Yasmin, and that thought got me to look across the table. And for fuck sake she turned at that exact moment and looked at me.

How the hell does that happen? Ye cannay tell me there isnay a physical side to the spiritual. Telekinesis, what is telekinesis? The body puts out some mysterious wafting substance, an ether that is not odour-free, an ether that contains samples of a body's heat and that which occasions the heat; I am talking about blood and flesh, sinew and muscle, and that in combination is what reaches the senses of the Other; static electrical currents, and that Other cannot help but respond. The ex and me knew each other's bodies and it was like every time I got an erection she experienced a wee twinge, nay matter how far apart we were. So this was nothing, she was only one wide table-width from me. Christ she was looking awful tired, a couple of streaks around her cheek bones maybe a little sweat or something. Yeh she looked tired and she was tired. This was her fourth gig in five nights; tomorrow was free but only because the goddam trip back to Twin Cities took so long. We wouldnay be hame for another three days. So far it hadnay been great. No quite a disaster but fucking hell it was a disaster and I was responsible for it. If I hadnay wantit to come then the manager would have come and he would have had his ayn car and the trip would have gone smoothly. He would have looked eftir her and he wouldnay have fukt up. He might have done other stuff as well – promoted her.

"Promoted" her.

What does it even mean! There had been talk of radio-station interviews before the trip but nayn during it, nay sign of any radio-station interviewers. What the hell happened to them? There was the band from Portland whose roadie I talked to in Denver; maybe I could have firmed something with his outfit. Maybe he could have gied me crucial information on venues and the rest of it. Or else they could have invited her to do a guest spot. Or maybe suitable venues in Portland, then up in Seattle. Between the two of them. I had been to a couple in Seattle and they would have suited Yasmin. The problem was the travel. And she wouldnay fly. They were out the question. So really, there was fuck all, fuck all I could have done. Somebody else might have. Her manager. Sure. I couldnay.

Sometimes I felt the west coast was the place to be as a base. If Yasmin could be persuaded in that direction I reckoned she would do well. She could play up and down that coast, then too there was Nevada, there was plenty places there for her kind of act. Haydar's address book would be stowed out with the names of music bars and clubs. If he ever resurfaced I could borrow it. Maybe he had. Maybe he hadnay disappeared. Sometimes it is you that disappears. Ye think it is other people but it isnay. Even me gaun hame to dear auld bonné, I might meet a lassie and stay a while, who knows, get offered a good job or maybe I suppose my maw might no be well and needing regular support from a close faimly member so I stay on an extra few months. Then when I get back to the States I meet some auld acquaintance, Hey where ya been man aint seen ya for a fucking blue moon, where you been? Well sir I aint been nowhere; danged if I can shuck off this yere skin of mine, I'm marooned inside ma body sir.

Yasmin had gone. Where the fuck was she! The john. There was a sudden rattling noise christ sake I glanced round, it was the bartender, fuck, who was I expecting! the fucking being! It is strange how we react to stimuli. I noticed the crush of bodies had eased. Lindy was chatting to the person on the other side of her and no longer pressing in on me.

I felt sensible, signaled the bartender and ordered another round of drinks for the immediate company. I shouted across to the owner: You wanting a drink yerself? He stared back at me then gestured at his ear, pretending he couldnay hear me properly. It was a brusque gesture and if he had hit his ear by mistake it would have been quite a sting. I asked Lindy if her husband would like a drink. Sure, she said.

The bartender helped me work out the order. It came to a few dollars. Just as well the ex was out the room when I paid the dough. When he returned and set the drinks down hardly anybody noticed it was myself paid the bill. That irritates me. Ye buy strangers a drink and they drink it down and dont even know it was you bought the fucker. Next time Desperate Dan looked across I was gauny raise the glass to him. The wee auld feller had lifted his beer, he said, Thank you sir.

You're welcome.

So you Skarrisch?

Yeh.

I knew a guy was Skarrisch. What was it now? Was there some princess of Inklin thing?

Yeh.

The wee feller chuckled.

There's the queen of Inklin, said Lindy.

That's another of them gals, I said, we got plenty of them

back there, yeh and all these other crazy yourpeen places, and they got them elsewhere too, their sheiks, popes and princes in the name of all that's holy can ye believe it, in this day and age? What would happen if we ever made contact with space aliens from a different galaxy and they all turned out to be either religious potentates or king and queen monarchs? Imagine it, everybody from Mars was like goddam royalty and ye had to bow and scrape and curtsey to the bastards, even wur ayn monarchs and potentates, they also had to bow and scrape to these sovereign alien beings and we all had to tell lies to wur children about them being god's lieutenants here on planet earth, them and their ten thousand pairs of shoes. Seriously but we would all have to emigrate, find a new fucking world all the gether pardon the language, a new universe I mean, excuse the language.

I was blethering and it was fine to rise and leave the company. But what to do and where to go, there warnt no place no how no sir. Ye find that: the world is a foreshortened arena, there aint enough spaces on the planet, ye wind up climbing a tree or a mountain, then ye get to the top and ye breathe out: Aaah, freedom, and then ye fall off the fucker.

Mind you with my luck

Fuck my luck.

But going hame was less than appealing, except of course my mother, it was her made the difference. What else was there? Then came the hassle of returning to the States. Once they slam shut the gate it gets rusty and reopens with reluctance. Imagine being trapped in the UK forever!!

And what about the wee lassie, what about her? I would phone her regularly, every second night. I wasnay gauny vanish. My daughter had a daddy and I was that daddy.

I still hadnay made up my mind to go. Still time to call the whole deal off. Even if they didnay reimburse me for the auld le billet so what, it was just a loss, ye take yer licks. And also, that loss would have value. In that sense it wouldnay be a loss. It would be a purchase. I would purchase my freedom.

At the wall to the left side of my napper was a group study of blues musicians from 1952 taken from an auld-style boardwalk outside the bar. And to the fore was a middle-aged woman with a ukulele, or was it a mandolin. The men were all smiling but she was not smiling although she had been asked so to do. There was that sense about it, that somebody had asked her to smile. But a smile was impossible. Even making an attempt didnay occur to her. She was the focus of the photographer but also the male musicians. She was the one. She had resigned herself to it.

Yasmin kept picture albums of these auld blues singers, their signatures scrawled across the photograph. Unfortunately, that could obscure things, and it was beautiful work so that was a shame. Nay mention of the one who took these photographs. Somebody had to call the shots. The poor auld artist, doomed to obscurity. Probably s/he had lived round the corner from this very bar and they called him or her in when they needed the job done. Maybe s/he was still alive. And drank in the Shooters and Horses!

Here was Sally at long last. She returned my look immediately. Very interesting. A minute later ower she came. Could I have a uisghé please? Naw, I said, make it a bourbon, a small yin.

I thought you were going home? she said.

Flying home, yeh. Tomorrow.

Flying, oh. She frowned. So where's home, Skallin?

You got it.

She gave me a look and a twitch of the head. Both of these actions signified something kind of nice. Whiskey? she said.

Bourbon, yeh. And a glass of water with a little bit of ice.

You bet. You want to run a tab?

I thought I was already?

No, she said, lifting the empty bottle by the neck, gripping it by the knuckles of her right index and middle fingers, holding it slackly but no so she would let it fall. I asked you before . . . She shrugged.

I have a memory like a hen.

You ever kept hens?

Kept hens?

Yeh.

No.

She had pursed her lips but didnay smile, then left my table. Kept hens. Naw I never kept hens. What does that mean? to keep a hen. In order to sort through the ambiguity I would require to know what the fuck she was talking about, the full terms of reference: the complete elemental constituents. She was behind the bar now but no acquiring the drink; nay doubt she had passed the order onto scabby prick, the guy who spent his time talking to the musicians. I watched him for a moment. His form of maleness was an embarrassment. A jumped-up show-off braggart who spent his life yapping at folk who couldnay afford no to listen, wasting everybody's time. Women never bragged like that. How come they couldnay accept what they were? fucking bartenders. What was so wrong with that that he had to carry forth this nonsense, aligning himself with the band, that he was only a virtual bartender, the "real him" was Meester ultra cool, jazz-blowing hombré, leader of the Drifting Cowboys Bluesband, yehhhh. I saw it when I worked in pubs with music. It was cool to be a bartender but no once el musicos had arrived for the session. Yez were baith working. But whereas you were pouring pints they were picking tunes, making people listen, forcing the intensity. I saw it with the ex. Bodies can be sitting talking the gether then slowly but surely the conversation ceases and they shift on their chairs. It is fucking rapture man that is what music can bring.

And some barstaff cannay handle that, they have to put on the cynical attitude. They cannay cope with what happens to customers when the music herds them in. They stare at the audience and cannay believe it. They see it as a sort of con or else the audience are a bunch of gullible fuckers. So they sneer at the women in the audience and treat the men with contempt. But they alternate with the musicians, either they kowtow or it is like false camaraderie, they treat them as successful conmen.

No sir, serving a drink and making music are two different activities. I saw it from baith sides. Sometimes I went to gigs with the ex and saw some feller serving drinks to a table with that smug look on his face and I thought Fuck!!! that used to be me! Even when the music was hot! What a dick!

But it was the bar gied the musicians the gig. It was the bar helped the band earn a dollar. The bar bought them a meal and a few drinks, made them feel at hame, let them strut about, treated them like artistes, like fucking aria-yodelers; all they needit were the evening gowns and fucking penguin suits man who cares.

My heid was aye full of irrelevancies. Get rid of the irrelevancies and I would be okay. These irrelevancies preoccupied me. I used to sit at the corner.

What corner?

Any fucking corner. Corner of the bar, corner of the booth, corner of the table. I was on the periphery is what I am saying. The perennial eavesdropper man I was a voyeur. But that was fine because I read someplace this is how writers operate; no all writers but some, they go about collecting vital informational data concerning the movements and behavioural patterns of the human species. They say nothing and hear everything. Of course some writers are supposed to yap all the time so no doubt they hear nothing. I enter both categories. Sometimes I talk sometimes I listen. Sometimes I listen to myself, he grinned. But I was acutely self-conscious, and not only that,

forget the "not only that".

Kept hens.

The larger feller at the bar, the guy who thought I had been staring at him, he was now speaking covertly to another of like mien. There was nay doubt about it, this pair had walked straight out of the Shooters and Horses.

Who gies a fuck.

So what about a plate of ribs and some mashed spuds? Dont mind if I do. Some gravy and good bread? Or was it only greasy fries available. What about if a chap wanted to be healthy, without necessarily going down the whole vegetarian highway? Some fish, herrings or something, caplin, catfish or cod tongues. There was a wee menu at the far end of the table. I browsed through it to pass the time.

I was glad I had left the motel. Although I could have bedded down for the night; purchased a couple of sandwiches and a six pack, goggled the tube until conking out. Yeh, I should have stayed at the motel. This was a time for caution; a tricky period in one's life. And if the sensory perceptors acted in a dysfunctional manner, misunderstandings would occur that judgments might not be acted upon at once lest something or other, that they arrived too hastily, that

Kept hens. That was a good yin. Nay doubt Sally did keep hens, or her parents did, or had. If her parents were still alive. But why ever not? She looked about thirty, under thirty; twenty-five or twenty-six; maybe even twenty-seven – ages were complicated. Never the same thing twice, like water passed in the night

But uisghé remains the same and I was gauny purchase one and it would be more than tasty, and with a dash of water which I took with most everything except beer and wine. And Sally was by my side. Is the food on? I said.

No. She placed a little whiskey in front of me, a glass of water alongside.

I was gieing her a look of mild bewilderment.

You saw me with food earlier?

I did.

Yeh, she said. It was for the band. She lifted the menu from my hand and pointed to the front page where the times for food were marked: until 8 p.m.

Fair enough.

We had it prepared from early. The guys drove a long way.

New York?

Not New York, no. She frowned, thinking I had been sarcastic. There's a bar just along the street, she said, they'll do you food right until late.

Thanks, I'll get something later . . .

It should have been significant the way I tailed off the sentence but perhaps she missed it. I smiled bravely. Now she was leaving. I meant to ask if she was sitting in with the band, doing a guest spot maybe. I was pleased I didnay ask. At last I was learning sense. My life had been plagued by stupidity. When it came to ill judgment, inferior calculating-strategy, woeful situation-assessment, overall bad decision-making

Some thoughts are unfinishable.

I lifted the glass of water and dashed some into my tumbler of bourbon, it sloshed over the sides, sloshed over the sides. I stared at the puddle. The bourbon had been so damn toty. It was my ayn fault.

So what was I to do now? lick it off the table surface? Perhaps if skin could perform the blotting-pad function. But no such luck. It wasnay an utter tragedy, there still was a wee drop left. I soaked up the spilt stuff with a napkin and thrust it into my pocket to be wrung out back at the motel.

Spectators! A man and woman had arrived at my table; an aulder couple, in their fifties or sixties. They didnay check with me if the chairs were free, just sat themselves down; probably they had taken one look at the shenanigans with the whiskey tumbler and assumed I was slightly drunk. It couldnay be anything else. It wasnay as if I was smelly. I had picked up good habits ower the years and nowadays changed my socks daily; the same went for my underwear, he coughed delicately; and only a light stubble graced my chin. And my outer garments were real fine; sharp trousers, shirt and jumper with an interesting anorak. Plus I had a fair stake stashed in the motel safe. Also my jewelry was non-imitation. My two rings, the bracelet, the watch. All were fucking classy objects bought to thwart bankruptcy. Gamblers need to buy good jewelry for those swift but random visits to the pawnbrokers. I reeked of class. If anything I was too classy. In joints like this I was a stand-out, nay wonder Sally was showing interest.

!!

Sally was not showing nay interest.

Better.

The woman at my table, she brought a pack of cigarettes from her bag, glanced at me then lighted one. When the first puff of smoke blasted in my direction I entered a sneezing fit. Out of my pockets I brought a few used napkins. I stocked these because I aye forgot to buy tissues. Neither the woman nor the man looked at me. If I had been in their position I would have wished me well if not apologized. If this was Japan I could have had them arrested for pollution offences.

Moments later I was still sneezing, then doing that action where ye nip shut the nostrils and try to breathe regularly and shallowly through the mouth. I took my fingers away. My nose dripped. I held it ower the whiskey.

Only kidding!

But mine was a surprising constitution; one had quit the smoking several months ago, yet this nose and sneeze debacle continued. I would ask the woman for a cigarette. The fates were tempting me. They knew I had quit. It was them forced me to quit, or so they thought. I would soon show them. Cheeky bastards. Had they never heard of the free will debate.

The bar was now busy and there was a definite buzz of anticipation. Occasionally I heard somebody tuning the guitar, checking the mouthpiece for auld saliva. The average age of the clientele was about thirty-five, forty. In the next booth sat five males having a good laugh at life. Boys' night out, here for the craïc, the music was a bonus. Nothing wrang with that. I saw two tables with females. The bar didnay have the feel of a meeting place but no doubt it was. And why not? 'Twas surely the ideal spot for lovers' trysts and dalliances, the which trysts and dalliances might progress toward the sanctity of the wedding vow, the state authorization of wur participation in the propagation of wur illustrious species.

The guitarist had been twanging away softly, and now the drummer tapped on the metal edge of a drum. And lo and behold somebody gied a toot on a trombone. I couldnay believe my luck. It was my favourite instrument ever since I was a wee lad and had a fixation on a great auld ska trombonist, with his music in my ear I danced that road to school. A toot from the clarinet and soon they would all be playing. I took a toty wee sip of the whiskey and discovered I had relaxed, and it was good. It was the same when she was singing. She would stand there at the mic, head inclined, the band starting, running her haun down her belly, and when she smiled and launched into that first song the woes of the world had dissipated.

A cigarette would have been a bonus but nay point talking about cigarettes. And soon I would return to the motel. And there was nay room service, even if I could have afforded it. Of course I could have afforded it, at least a sandwich. But I would resist unless having partaken of too much alcohol in which case anything was possible. I would maybe pick up something at the all-night convenience store.

Wait a minute!

Yes sir! Thank you lord!

Again thank you lord thank you.

I pulled the paperbag out from my anorak pocket. The man and woman stared at me. I was flourishing it like a conjuror. Allez oop! I said: presenting the Great Gusto ladles and jelly-spoons, le Gusto el Magnifique!

But neither smiled. It's a sandwich, I said sheepishly. I opened the bag and took out the muffin. Then I took out the sandwich and showed them. I shrugged. It's a few hours since I ate; I forgot I had them.

Oh. They smiled. The woman puffed on the cigarette. Obviously they were hoping I would leave. I hadnay done nothing either, apart from remind them of the side effects smoking can produce in the sinuses of an innocent third party.

How come they were sitting without a drink? They were waiting for Sally of course. Eventually she would come. Maybe there would be eye contact between us. But maybe no. She would avoid me all the gether. And who could blame her, a nice lassie like that, probably merrit with a young faimly, her man also out working. Maybe he drove a truck or was employed in the construction industry, grafting so hard they barely saw one another; when he came hame she was gaun out, and vice a versa; that auld scenario, they had my sympathy.

It was plain the auld couple disliked me on sight. This happens. I have one of those faces that irritate people, especially women. Maybe they consider me a desperate rascal. I certainly do not consider myself a desperate rascal. I could have taken out my wallet and flashed the photographs of my wee lassie. But to hell with them, they didnay deserve it, that wee beauty of mine, the spitting image of the ex but if ye looked sideways in a certain light why then she was me through and through. I gloated over that. Every time she saw her wee daughter she would see me! How petty can ye get.

The woman was studying me surreptitiously! To hell with it. Hi, I said, my name's Jerry, I'm from Skallin, I'm flying home tomorrow and I'm just here for a couple of beers, well, and this wee uisghé. I noticed they had a nice one there on the gantry so for auld time's sake . . . I shrugged. I havenay been hame for a long time.

Did you say Skallin? said the man, cupping his hand to his ear and leaning forwards to hear more clearly.

Yeh. By the way, I was just sitting here by myself so it's nice ye've sat down. Sometimes when it becomes hard to communicate with folk in the immediate vicinity what I do is grab 'em by the lapel, in a manner of speaking. Ye dont mind?

I sure dont, said the man, that strikes me as commonsensical. He turned and nodded to the woman. My wife Rita, I'm Norman.

I'm Jerry, short for Jeremiah.

I had a schoolteacher named Jeremiah, said Rita.

Oh you did?

Yeh.

Was he Skarrisch?

I dont know.

Small world.

So you're going home? said Norman.

Yeh, mañana. I was thinking of my wife and kid there so it is better to take myself out of that.

Oh, said Rita.

They're ower on the east coast. Agh but I'm glad to be gaun hame. No for good of course, I'll be coming back again. Will ye no come back again, sure I'm coming back again. But no to the east coast. And know something else, no the west coast either. I'm sick of the two of them. I quite like that 98-degree line. I reckon I'll just travel up and down it.

Rita squinted at me. Her husband wasnay even listening, he was trying to attract somebody's attention – Sally's attention, he was wanting a goddam drink. Sally was a luscious lassie but no the fastest, and that wasnay to be critical, being a bar worker myself my standards were the highest. Yeh, I said, the place is getting busy.

Yeh, said Norman swiveling on the seat to get me into proper focus. He had these heavy lenses on his spectacles, failing eyesight and bad hearing. But he had a heid of white hair. It was to that I could look forward. At least he was with a woman, a good woman, quirky. I liked quirky women. Norman said, You live around here Jerry?

He's living on the west coast, said Rita.

That's right, I said.

She took out a fresh cigarette and held the pack to me. Dear Lord. I shook my heid fervently, stared upwards to the dull ceiling which was full of bulges and cracks, damp streaks. Was it gauny collapse on us? Who knows. I had expected wooden beams and rafters. Rita was watching me. I said, The problem is I gied up the smoking but tonight I'm finding it excruciatingly difficult.

Well I apologize, she said and laid the pack on the table. It's there if you want to change your mind.

I appreciate that. Maybe just blow yer smoke in my direction.

You're encouraging him, said Norman.

You bet.

Well that aint helpful.

Rita nodded. I know how tough it is to quit.

So do I, said Norman.

You quit twenty years ago.

Sure I did.

Well you did.

Norman smiled. So what is it you do son? What kind of work do you do?

Anything and everything.

Huh? Oh, yeh. Me also, I been a jack-of-all-trades . . . He looked at his wife and shrugged.

What I really want to do is write books. I startit one about a private eye. That was what I was thinking would be good. People like to read private-eye stories, they're popular.

I like them, said Rita. Nowadays you got some real good private-eye stories and it's women, they are the detectives and they do it every bit as smart as the men.

Female gumshoes, said Norman.

Sure, said Rita, she winked at me.

What do you think of female gumshoes son?

I think they're grand. The mair the merrier. I'm trying to make the one in my book different. For a start he reads a lot and is into philosophy and r & b music. It's weird though, we all write these stories about private eyes and gumshoes, all sorts of undercover detectives, and we've never met any. It's pure crazy! I mean have yous ever met one cause I havenay, no in my entire life. Mind you, on the personal front, I worked for a while in the Security business

Oh you did? said Norman.

Yeh so I do have that wee bit of background experience.

That's important, said Rita,

Norman frowned. Hey son, you saying you worked as a Security agent?

Yeh.

Well good for you. So what's your book about?

It's about a private eye, I said, but he's a different kind of private eye. He isnay typical. Then as well as him there's the other characters.

The bad guys?

Yeh. But no just the bad guys. Ordinary folks as well, males and females. Maybe even kids, I like kids in a story.

You got any kids? said Rita.

A wee girl.

So do you draw your characters from real life?

Yeh, I think that's best.

So do I.

For instance a crookit politician from Arizona has a crucial role, also his good-looking but precocious daughter who falls for the central male character, the young Skarrisch guy who has only been waiting for the right dame to come along.

Ever been to Arizona?

Yeh.

They glanced at each other then back to me. Up at the bar I saw the big guy watching out the corner of his eye although he appeared to be listening to his cronies. Maybe they knew this couple. Christ of course they would, it was a wee town. Nay doubt it was a set-up and they were accomplices, and I would have to hightail it outa here. Ye could imagine the shite that ran the joint texting the local coven, get yer white sheets out the drawer.

We been to Arizona. We liked it fine.

Me too although I didnay spend enough time to see it properly so I'm just like inventing I suppose ye would call it. I dont know how you two see it but for me Arizona is a passing-through kind of state and that aint being derogatory.

Well we stayed there son and we enjoyed it.

Sure we did, said Rita, it was pleasant, nice food and plenty to see.

Yeh, I said, some bodies regard it as like an entire arts centre in itself, so I hear. The feller in my book, he's gauny be based on somebody I met once in a diner, it was in Flagstaff.

Flagstaff, yeh. You take the road south from there son that gets you to Phoenix.

That's right, said Rita. We been to Flagstaff and we liked it, the folks there are fine.

Yeh, well this feller I met he was a crookit politician.

Crooked politician? said Norman, pursing his lips. The woman raised her eyebrows.

Yeh, I said, it was one of these occasions when the auld Skarrisch tongue turns up trumps. I'm talking about my accent. It would have got me a job if I had wantit, and much mair besides. I'm talking about a wife. Yes maam. See me and a couple of pals had been moseying down a road through the mountains, looking to reach the auld historic Route 66. We picked that up way south of a burg named eftir some ancestors of mine then headed east to Albuquerque to get a feel for it properly; then back to Flagstaff via Gallup, stopping on the outskirts for some food, the evening meal to be precise. It was me doing the driving and the other two fellers used the time to get a few beers, and then of course they were insisting on nay moose steaks and wanting to lay me a bet on nay moose steaks, 20 to 1 against moose steaks which isnay unreasonable if ye think of the Canadian export trade.

Well now there were nay moose steaks to be had and they drank that beer till it came right out their ears. I ordered ordinary steaks and lied to them it was moose steaks but they didnay believe me. But they were real good steaks, and then they drank a lot of wine, had a few uisghés too, then they lapsed into a stupor. I sat there having a smoke. I was smoking then Rita, I was enjoying life; in fact it was like a natural pastime. So I was sipping my coffee, fine coffee, mighty fine coffee. It was then I noticed a body watching us, aulder middle-aged kind of guy, dressed in western claes, leather stetson, johnny cash coat but polished-looking.

What age was he? said Norman.

Eh, forty-five?

Forty-five! That aint so middle-aged. Forty-five! Why son that aint old at all!

Rita grinned.

Of course not, sorry. I smiled at Rita. So anyway, we were the only folks in the place and the crookit politician, he is staring at us with suppressed antagonism. I thought it expedient to offer him a steak and salad. He declined the grub but acted like it was an invitation to sit at wur table. He was quaffing tequila and that Meheekin beer with the Aztec name, con mucha la sal y sucking limes. So how did I know he was a politician never mind a crookit one?

Yeh, said Rita, puffing out a cloud of smoke.

Easy, I said. What is more he traded in illegal immigrants, a cause close to my heart.

Pardon me?

Illegal immigrants.

Is that in your story? she said.

Naw, that was in another story, they made it into a movie years ago. It's reality I'm talking about, the guy I met in Flagstaff.

It's a fine little town, said Norman.

Yeh, well, that was where I met him, we were passing through. It wasnay even in Flagstaff it was on the outskirts; in a wee diner, stagecoach country. Illegal immigrants was his business. From that fiscal source was formed the bulk of his income. He telt me so himself. He figured me being Skarrisch

I was into purity and mother countries. He looked at my two sleeping partners and asked if they was Skarrisch also? No sir, I says, Californians.

From Frisco? says he.

Naw, says I.

They sure look like they's from Frisco, he says.

How come? I says.

It aint hard to figure, he says. Then he looks at me for a while. Y'all heard of the "chequered funnel"? he says.

No sir, is that a motor-racing thing?

He just sniffed and took a sip of his tequila. Son, he says, and then he took me into his confidence. Just like that! He did. I dont know why he did but he did, took me right into his confidence. I think he liked the looks of me and thought well of my heritage. And then too he wondered if I was single. He had three daughters roundabout my ayn age so maybe he figured he had found some guid auld-country breeding stock. He even spoke about something called brangus, brangus beef, a sturdy mix of Highland cattle and Texas longhorns.

Wow! said Norman, glancing at his missis.

Yeh. So then he explains to me that once the illegal immigrants crossed the border they came up through this what-d'ye-call-it "chequered funnel". The reason he divulged such sensitive information was because my two compañeros, whom he wouldnay have trusted an inch, were in a booze-induced trance. He wouldnay trust them, cause no matter what I says to him he figured them from Frisco and he didnay like Frisco folks, all whores and homosexyoualls, lesbian anarchists and pinko commie liberals. But you Skarrisch folks, he says, yous are of the auld persuasion, he says, but what about them two? he says with a pained expression.

I telt him for the tenth time that my two buddies werenay from Frisco then I carried on listening in evident passivity. Ye see he was a large feller and carrying weight, but some of that was muscle and definitely he was packing iron.

Huh? said Norman. You knew that for sure?

I figured it. Yes sir, that was the kind of body he was. What tilted the balance in my favour was how he had a soft spot for the folks back hame. His ancestors were Highland chieftains in the style of auld William Wallace, as he thought, Aryan to the hilt of their claymores.

No thanks, I said to Rita who had just gestured at me with her cigarette pack. Some commentators do suggest William Wallace was Aryan to the hilt of his claymores but others say he was a member of the Gaeltach. Whereas me, I dont gie a fuck, pardon the language, sorry, sorry about that. But that ol crookit politician, he just squints his eye at me and says, Hey, yous folks, you got the ol rites, you got them good ol rites . . . drawling out the words, he was a slow-talking type of individual. Masonic rites is what he was talking about. Aw aye, I says, the PKK.

Huh? said Norman.

Sorry, the KKK. He was pointing at my buddies, they aint Skarrisch?

No sir.

They from Frisco?

No, I says.

Well, he says, if I was you I would dump them.

Sound advice, says I, and then

Can we buy you a drink son?

Pardon me?

You want a drink? It was Norman doing the asking. He had risen from his seat and was gesturing at my bourbon and beer.

Okay, thanks.

Skatch?

Nah eh, I'll just have a beer eh, it's just a lite. Thanks. I shrugged

You bet. Norman glanced at his wife and her empty glass. They exchanged nods. At the bar he stood by the large fellers. The pentagon guy glanced at him nonchalantly and nodded a greeting. Norman nodded in reply.

I said to Rita. Do you and Norman come here often?

We like it.

Do most people who come here come often? Or is it just eh passing trade or what?

They get a mixture.

Mm. What about the Shooters and Horses Sports Bar, do people go there?

Sure. Rita smiled.

I reached for my beer and sipped, sipped again.

Agh, for some reason my heart was sair.

But I liked her and Norman. Her cigarette pack lay close to my fingers but there was nay chance of me taking one. Excuse me for changing the subject, I said, but have you ever heard of these Domestic Retraining Camps down along the border?

Pardon me?

I was looking at an auld map back there and I reckoned they might be someplace off the beaten track, maybe between Yuma and Nogales. It comes into this book I'm writing about the private eye and the crookit politician.

I havent heard about that, said Rita. Domestic Retraining Camps?

Maybe it's another state. I do a lot of reading and sometimes get mixed up.

Okay. She frowned and inhaled on her cigarette.

I opened my food package and took a mouthful of the muffin.

You dont eat enough, said Rita, and when you do it's the

wrong things. You are thin. I didnt look at you before but you are, you're skinny. I see it now. Your mother must worry about you back in Skallin, does she?

She does.

She must worry if ever you're going to make it back home.

Yeh.

She up in years?

Yes maam.

But you keep in touch? You phone I guess. You got email back home?

Yeh, we got all the technologies, but I'm no sure if my mother uses them much. She's getting on in years. I was a young son ye see, the baby boy. She's near seventy.

Well that aint Methuselah, what age do you think I am?

You?

Rita smiled.

I dont know.

What about him? She nodded in the direction of the bar where Norman was now in conversation with the pentagon fucker and the beef-eating trucker.

I'm nay good at ages, I said, gieing Norman a wave when he glanced across at us. He didnay notice my wave, he shook his heid at something the trucker said then turned from him.

We watched him return to the table, followed by Sally with the drinks on a tray. Rita tapped me on the wrist: Ask him about the Training Camps.

Huh? said Norman.

I heard they were between Yuma and Nogales, I said, maybe even farther east, they're Retraining Camps. Domestic Retraining Camps.

How far east you talking son?

El Paso?

You're a little out there now El Paso aint in Arizona.

It's in Texas, said Rita. Maybe you misread what you were reading. Maybe it was someplace else.

Maybe, I said. One thing I learned as a wean, a child, and this is for sure: never comment to strangers except on particular issues. I looked from Rita to Norman. You two ever hear that?

I did, said Norman.

I dont know, said Rita, you hear so much.

My boss at the Security agency used to say something along the same lines, I said. General conclusions are de rigueur in Security operations, that was what he telt me. Universal blethers lead to moral imperatives and naybody wants into that sort of stuff, especially in uniform. He said it with his ayn accent.

He from Arizona?

D.C.

D.C.! So these guys got an accent? said Rita.

Everybody's got an accent, said Norman and he winked at me. So this guy, your boss, was that in Security operations?

Yeh.

What kind of Security operations?

Och anything and everything; domestic, regional, federal. We were expected to bash the heads of demonstrating peace persons and attend high-risk pre-preemptive-strike areas, often on the same day; then if it was Mardi Gras we could be rounding up highschool terrorists, plastic bullets obligatory, or else bodyguarding worldbank pickets at the entrances to anarchist conferences, and of course inside the local immigration complex we were herding and strip searching bunches of pregnant ladies with full internal explorations. And that's just the white people.

What kind of ladies?

Mothers usually.

And this was out on the east coast? said Rita.

Yeh.

Well some people got it tough, that is for sure.

Ye're dead right Rita. And there it could be terrifying. They put me to work in the area to the left of the mid north-east where the usual partnerships were selling entire infrastructures to enclaves of energetic entrepreneurs and government-sponsored financiers, shifting their funds into furin territory "futures" in a welcome surge of patriotic endeavour.

How long ago? said Rita.

Oh, no that long.

What administration? said Norman.

I'm talking a couple of years ago, coming to the end of the airplane-insurance deals.

Silence.

We dont like talking about that, said Rita.

Well, said Norman, it aint so much we dont like to talk about it, it's just now the old "persian bet" thing is history so what is the point? On television it used to be day in day out. You want to complain but who to? Our airplanes are as good as any, some say we got the best.

Exactly, I said, some say we got only the best, some say we got all the best; I respect what people say and I respect why they say it.

So you got a bone of contention? said Norman.

No sir.

I thought you had.

No sir. I swallied some beer. In the Alien Section wur central problem was ammunition because nayn was available. Teams of us operatives were transported out to indigenous airports whose names I never discovered. Some of us went long long distances.

Down south? said Rita.

And midwest. Usually we discovered wur whereabouts

when the masks were taken off. They put them on us at the start of the trips. We had to guess, they telt us nothing. They thought because we wur seekers of succour that we wouldnay guess the topography. How wrong can ye be. Take me for instance, I'm a walker, I walk everywhere. This great country of yours, I have walked from one end to the other, lowlands to highlands, plains and forests, dusty deserts, grand canyons, the lot. I've paddled canoes on white water. Also I've skied, I like the skiing.

Too cold for me, said Rita.

Rita prefers the warmer climates, said Norman.

I was brought up on torrential downpours, I said, if I dont get one for a while I get edgy. It's just the real cauld, snaw and ice, the Arctic and Antarctic, I'm no keen on that. Mind you if ye have the proper clothes as my auld mother used to say. So where was I? Yeh so that crookit politician, he calls me to one side where this great German shepherd dog was bouncing about with a studded collar, and a chauffeur was reining it in and he telt me the dog was a bitch whose name was Queenie, named in respect of the brrisch monarcquy, an admirable thought and one that must consolidate the friendship between baith wur nations, bearing in mind wur respective histories. He ushered me into a tiny cloistered area to the rear of the diner, no far from one of the smaller compounds where he gied me some individual questions. I knew they were designed for potential high flyers cause I have to say, and I hope it doesnay sound like a boast, but in some jobs I've done in recent years the immediate superiors saw me as a potential high flyer.

How come? said Norman.

Easy, I said, blatantly easy.

Norman frowned at Rita and attempted to conceal the frown by raising his glass of beer as though for a sip.

So the politician asked if I had developed any strategies for these kinds of assignments and if I got the job would it be all my ayn work or would I base it on procedural manoeuvres as outlined in the appropriate manuals? Would I truck with these local officials if I had to? And dog phobias, you got any dog phobias? he says. No, I says. Okay, he says.

I didnt think you would have a dog phobia, said Rita.

Well to be honest, I could have telt him a couple of childhood sob stories but he interrupted me. What he was wanting to know was if I would come and do that kind of work for his company, morally unsound work. My company right here, he says, and down along the border. If necessary, I says, sure, I says. You use weapons? he says. Yeh, I says. What kind? he says. Sticks and stones, I says, sticks and stones.

You said that to him? said Rita.

I did, yeh.

Were you being humorous? said Norman.

Yeh, we only have the one life.

Rita smiled and shook her head, tapped her cigarette into the ashtray and inhaled on her fine cigarette. Sticks and stones, she said, exhaling smoke. She gestured with the pack but I declined though the good smell of death was again entering one's nostrils. Rita said, Jerry you impressed that guy. So he wanted you to come work for him.

He sure did. Son, he says, you can work for me any time, day or night, I trust you, he says. But you got to keep them ears open, and your eyes. He tapped the side of his temple. And keep yer trap shut, he says.

Not very polite, said Norman.

No sir, a bit of a rough diamond. It was at this stage I decided to ask him the all-important question: Do ye have a daughter? Yeh, he says, I got a daughter. Yeh, he says, I got three, three daughters. Three daughters? I says. Lovely gals, he says, beautiful gals, he says, you want to meet one of them? She's outside loading the truck. So, well, I have to confess I went out and met the lassie and man was she beautiful she sure was beautiful, I just have to say that Rita excuse me. But then what happened to her, she just disappeared, one day she was there and the next she was gone and the poor auld parents and wider faimly circle – yeh and include the politician in that, crookit or no, a man's a man for aw that for heaven sake we are talking about the guy's daughter. So this lassie, she just upped and disappeared into thin air, where did she go and what did she do? who knows. Some say she formed an alliance with a shady club owner and then hit the skids when he had had his evil way with her. Others say she gied up the christian faith and joined an eastern commune. Myself, I reckon that young lady donned a new persona. But new personas can be a psychologically damaging experience, as us aliens know to wur cost, and that same lassie ended up on the streets, she just had no place else to go, she was at her wits' end, trying to eke out a living, wheeling that ol grocery cart from one indigenous food dump to the next, and it be a mad uncaring world out there as well we know.

Mm. Rita nodded.

What you dont think so? I said.

Rita smiled.

So you and the young lady, you got together? said Norman.

Pardon me?

You marry the young lady?

Rita shook her head, closed her eyes. Norman glanced at her, he frowned and reached for his beer, then he frowned at me and said: The guy from Arizona, he your father-in-law?

Not at all. If he was I wouldnay be in this mess. I never met my father-in-law, ex father-in-law, although I did meet his brother, a strange auld buzzard, but they said he resembled him, my wife's father. She is a musician by the way. Ex wife

I should say, she's from the east coast. Well, I call her my wife but we never got merrit, we were just eh what ye call partners, she was my girlfriend and I was her boyfriend.

Oh you dont have to worry about us, said Rita.

I nodded. We were close and we lived together, we loved one another, it was a love-match; or so I thought. But if the feller from Arizona had been her daddy I would have got a proper ID, a respectable ID, one of them Green or Blue Cards, no this stupit Red thing that sends god-fearing folks into a tizzy.

Huh? said Rita.

You got the Red Card? said Norman. I heard of them.

Yeh, want to see it? I showed it already to them behind the bar. Mine is Class III. It says I aint ashamed of being an un-assimilatit unintegratit alien socialist but object strongly to getting called a decadent post-christian secularist with agnostic leanings.

Okay, said Norman.

I know yous are christians, I said, but what I believe is tolerance for one and tolerance for the other.

Sure thing, said Rita.

Thanks, I said, well now . . . Blow some of that tobacco poison in my direction would ye! What was I saying now . . .

You carry shotguns in Security? said Norman.

Naw, they dont gie us them in case we launch a fucking mutiny!

Tch, haaaa.

Sorry, pardon the language, sorry, sorry Rita, pardon the language.

It kind of jars son.

Sorry.

So, you dont get weapons?

Sorry. Naw.

Norman pursed his lips and raised his eyebrows.

What yous'll be thinking is if we aint got weapons how can we do wur job? Well what I say is there are weapons and weapons. If ye look at me ye'll think who is this weasel? Why this young feller aint nothing but skin and bone, he is like a weed man he just aint a physical specimen. Am I right?

I know ye willnay want to insult me but if something is a fact then why no state it, that is what facts are, things to be stated and if for example I was to go to the men's room right now the fact is, and dont take this the wrang way, but if I was to go to the men's room right now, then yous would want to talk about me when I was gone and yez would discuss this that and the next thing about my private business, my wee daughter and my ex wife; and how he – me I mean, I'm talking about myself, "I", but yous wouldnay, yous would be saying "he", "he this" and "he that": how *he* could land in a situation where danger lurked, where a lack of control existed, where *he* was aware that *he* lacked control but that he wished to combat these forces which aye were abroad and with a mind and a will of their ayn, *he* whose commitment and engagement could be taken for granted, yet still ye wonder how can that be, this young feller with the Red Card, this self-avowed anarchist, unassimilatit socialist and atheist with a hatred of ruling bodies everywhere; religious, monarquic, political, corporate or financial, who gies a fuck, pardon the language, sorry, yet here he is at this very moment in time – sorry about that, I do apologize – why he is so close to ye, is sitting so close, so close ye could reach out yer hand and stroke his face, this seeker of sanctuary within, so close ye could close yer eyes and sense his breath on yer face this furin stranger varmint, congenital member of the evil undead.

I sipped at my beer, then raised my tumbler of uisghé. This was a uisghé sure enough. Uisghé makes me talk. Other folk fight. Sorry about that. But what I will say is this, tonight is my last on this soil. Fortunate am I that my flight is scheduled for tomorrow. And this yere uisghé – I think you bought me a sneaky one there Norman – so good health to yez. Sláinte. Rita was watching me. I slapped myself on the chest. Mind you, I said, holding the tumbler aloft; sometimes with another yin of these I wanna howl at the moon!

Rita smiled, tapped ash into the ashtray. If you were ten years older!

Hey ho! Norman winked at me and raised his beer in that same salute.

One thing about jazz, ye cannay dance for god sake know what I mean, music is the food of love, how can ye have music and no have a dance, when the music's playing ye're feet are tapping. Mine are anyway. I think I was spoilt on the west coast because of the dancing; a lot of that nice southern sound, speedy accordions and brass, hearty high yohs, smart rhythm sections with these brilliant drummers. Excellent, ye were aye strutting yer stuff.

Okay, said Norman, and he slapped the table to bring me to order.

I smiled and winked at Rita.

I want to say this to you now son before we strike off in another direction; what am I thinking I'm thinking if you aint got the weapons, what you gonna do? You're no middleweight boxer but what about pound for pound?

Flummoxed.

I reckon you box your weight, am I correct?

Norman boxed, said Rita.

Oh you did?

Yeh. Norman shrugged. But you know I was too tall son I was too dang thin, what they call cruiser, like a light heavy? You got guys my size and build, coat hangers, or you got littler guys, them little flies and bantams.

Packed solid with muscle, said Rita.

They sure were. These little boys could fight.

So could you fight Norman you could fight.

But some of these real little ones now Rita they get in below your guard and why they can fight, they surely can, their thick little arms, they can bust your nose, they did that with us bigger boys. Norman smiled, his fists had clenched and his shoodirs moved one way then the other. He shook his heid. Well we called them *catch weigh contests*. And when we fought them we thought why we must beat them we're so big. Well now!

But didnt they come from all over? said Rita.

Sure did; eastern places, way south, down over the ocean. Norman smiled. But son I look at you and what springs to my mind, you are a pound for pound young feller, I can see it.

He's too thin, said Rita.

Well honey you said I was too thin.

You werent too thin you were rangy.

Rangy, sure but now you take old Carl there . . . He was pointing at the pentagon fucker. You see him Jerry?

Yeh, I said.

Norman nodded. Now you come on a big feller like Carl and you might get a strange feeling right in your gut there and I know that feeling myself, I got to tell you, one time it was a real big feller, black feller, he was in my platoon. What it is now you want to tackle him, you think to yourself Why he aint so big, he's just full of fries, fries fries and more fries.

And the beer, said Rita.

Yeh, and the beer. He is blubber you think, let's him and me go outside for a fair fight, a stand-up honest-to-god fight, just me and him. You ever think of that son? You get him out there and you'll wear him down; he wont land a punch, you'll dance your way roundabout son why you'll just wear him down, and then when the time is right why you'll whack him, you'll whack old Carl there, right where it hurts. You ever think like that son?

Who me, naw, speaking personally, at least no nowadays, maybe when I was younger; it reeks of self-congratulatory posturing, hollywood macho nonsense, teenage dreams; I hope I've passed that stage. Mind you if I've had a couple of beers on a Saturday night then it's like the whole world belongs to me and my heid gets crammed full of fantasies, fantasy upon fantasy. I jump up and get my writer's notebook.

Good for you, said Rita.

I dont reach for the boxing gloves.

Okay, said Norman.

But an auld relative of mine was a boxer; he came to this country many years ago, back someplace on my father's line. But I didnay hear much about my father's line; he never spoke about his faimly; maybe he didnay like them. So all we got are these basic facts: here was a man, he was a boxer, he went to the States. For all we know he fought at Madison Square Gardens. But that was him, he disappeared. Maybe he changed his name and became a multibillionaire and all that money is just lying there waiting for the first bona fide claimant, or else the lawyers stole it already. Yeh, they probably stole it. What lawyers do, they gie it to each other; they take yer money and like what they do, they distribute it among their ayn profession. Absolute rascals, they just dont care about human beings its money money money, gie us the money; what you want a phone call? two hundred dollars? what you want an email? two hundred dollars.

Yeh but son your relative would have his own family, he would have left his will.

Maybe not, said Rita, some folks are messy.

Messy? I said.

They dont live in a regular way.

Not everybody wants to do that, said Norman.

Well sometimes I wish they would, said Rita.

It's their prerogative honey.

It's having some thought for their neighbors.

Yeh but that goes two ways now surely?

Rita raised her eyebrows, lit another cigarette.

Hey ho, said Norman.

Rita looked to me.

Well, I said, personally speaking I dont want to mix fantasy with real life. I dont like stories that do that as if it was like a diary, ye're keeping a diary instead of writing yer ayn book. Entry: Tonight I met this big guy, plain clothes, worked for a secret government agency, Charlie was his name, espionage the game; this guy was a bum, he was a no-gooder, he was out to do mischief to the hero, the young private-eye feller who is trying to correct the world of all its woes, watch yer back! I chuckled.

Wow! Norman shook his heid.

Rita inhaled on her cigarette and glanced at him. I used to keep a diary.

You still do, he said.

Only if something happens, like we go someplace for the weekend. Or his sister drops by. Or if something unusual happens.

Unusual, like what? I said.

Well it can be anything, just if it strikes a chord.

What about me? Will ye put me in yer diary? I grinned.

We'll just have to see now Jerry wont we! Rita reached to slap me on the wrist.

I laughed.

Norman smiled. Dont you worry, he said.

I wont!

So what time is your plane tomorrow?

Ah, crucial question, I cannay quite remember. Check in around 14, 1500 hours I think. I've got to get into Rapid City tomorrow. I noted the bus times in my notebook – which I bought in yer local bookstore as a matter of fact.

Kitty Perkins's place.

That's right, I said.

Norman smiled. I realized he had been watching me. So you been through our town before? he said.

Naw.

Huh? I thought you had.

Maybe I passed through, but I never got off the bus.

I must have picked you up wrong then son.

Yeh. What I might have said was how it reminded me of a place I once passed through, which was near here but it wasnay this one. I'm sure I would have remembered. Mind you my memory is hopeless, worse than hopeless, and when it comes to traveling, I've been on the road now for years. It gets like ye cannay distinguish one place from another; and I dont mean nay disrespect. Respect is an important thing in your country and I dont mess with that, I hope I've as much respect as the next person. Also I like this town, I would've remembered it, a couple of good bars plus a neat wee bookstore, then you got the river and the bowling and it aint all fastfood shit and motels, you still got the auld downtown.

There's been a lot of construction Jerry, they've been building homes. It's changed.

Yeh? I thought I saw some places earlier on. You got a college here by the river?

Sure but it's a ways away, you got to go find it.

Right.

Norman leaned closer to me. Son, he said, you dont mind me asking, how come you passed this way?

I dont mind ye asking at all. I was here with my ex wife, my girlfriend, she's a singer, I think I telt ye. She was doing some gigs around here and I missed out on one of them because I missed the dang bus, got involved in this game, stupit dang thing, crazy. Wait a minute, I may be mixing that up now, there was another time . . . a beautiful time . . . The one I'm thinking about wasnay so beautiful

With your wife?

Well ye know we never got merrit Rita I have to say that. Naw, this yin was just stupit. Ye get these stupit times in yer life. I dont know about yous two but it's like they can follow ye around.

Son, didnt you say you got involved in a game?

I did yeh, in a manner of speaking, some games are like they arenay games at all, it's like the auld song ye know "The Devil's Gonna Git You", who's that now, like sometimes my ex sang that yin, depending, she knew I liked it.

So now it's personal business?

Yeh, to be honest.

Rita nodded.

See it was one of these times like I'm saying, they haunt ye, I was slap dang in the middle of one of them, the whole damn thing, it's like when ye've got a kid yer life changes and ye dont get the time any mair, yez dont see each other so if ye get the chance then ye grab it so me and her, we had a few days so we went for it but what also happens things go wrong and this time every last thing went wrong, last gig on the road and she's disappeared, she's away to the john or something who knows, who knows where she went. Sometimes she did that. It wasnay too unusual, she done it even when we lived the gether. She wasnay gaun with other men like a few might have thought. I didnay think it. She just needit space, like when she finished a gig. And this time she had just finished a gig.

And we had been fighting before that, fighting then we made it up. Now here we were in this little town and there was this guy, he was watching her all the time and then watching me, he didnay like me man this guy wantit to hurt me. Ye get so ye recognize it. And I was gauny defend myself. I'm no just talking about fighting. Okay. So then I overhears this feller talking about a game; him and the musicians, a couple of other bodies, they're heading for the back room; it's a game of cards.

Where was this?

I cannay remember, that's what I'm saying. It wasnay here but. The guy I'm talking about that owned the place, he was gaun with them, he was playing, and I saw him watching me, he was aye watching me, I know what his problem was, he didnay like me being with Yasmin, a lot of them didnay, they didnay fucking like it. So that gets to me also and I'm like wanting to push it. Sorry.

I was cut out from the game ye see, sorry, naybody asked me if I wantit a hand at cards. Was that no classic bad manners? So that was what I thought, teach them a lesson. Yeh, teach them a lesson. City dude and the small-town bodies. So I says if Yasmin could get a hand. Can Yasmin play? I says. The band played for her at the gig so could she get a hand, wasnt she one of the musicians? Of course, they says, of course Yasmin can get a hand. So good, I says, that's great, I says, but she doesnay play cards but I do so what about me? I do the card-playing in our relationship. Can I sit in in her place? Well they coughs and clears their throat but then they says, Okay, because they couldnay find nay reason to say naw and I saw the owner, he was looking at me. What was his name? Daniel something. Daniel . . .

But christ that guy hated me, it must have been one of these instant dislikes. I saw him smiling. Yes sir, the thought of my impending bankruptcy brought a smile to his greasy chops. So what was the game, draw poker. These bodies played rules I hadnay seen since schooldays man it was just such dang nonsense. Draw poker; the favoured game of nincompoops and bumpkins, its popularity a byword in the very bowels of the earth's bubbling cauldron. Yes sir the dang dealer takes four. Ever heard anything like it! We would have been as well playing three-card brag, deuces wild, plus threes and fours. Why no make it the entire 52 wild. Then we can all sit with the top haun, this is Uhmerka.

I cannay win at these kind of childs' games. There is just about nay skill involved. They demand luck and money, neither of which I ever held in abundance. And I'm no pleading for sympathy here. Yez are probably wondering why I didnay change the game? Good question. I couldnay. It was what they wantit to play and it was what Mister Big wantit to play, that dang owner rascal. And I was a guest-stranger, so I was being polite to the home company; that is my style, if I act in that appropriate way maybe things will move in my favour.

It is a peculiar thing to say, and I'm beginning to see this mair, speaking as somebody who likes to gamble, but I've aye been an unlucky body. Incredibly so. It isnay that my opponents carry good luck man it is me that carries bad. All my life I've been battling against the odds and the worst and most prolonged struggle has been against the fates. What d'ye make of that? The fates! If it comes to a showdown I aye get beat. Yet I do the right thing, the appropriate thing. And I still get beat.

And all I wantit was to impress her. I wantit to surprise her. Us men, that is what we do, we surprise the women. The surprise we gie is good news. That was the plan. I wouldnay have played just for the hell of it. It was for her benefit. But ye see that dang owner arsehole – sorry about that – what was I saying, I was saying about the guy that owned the bar and wantit to beat me up, I couldnay figure out his problem, maybe it was my very existence, who knows what. Then somebody telt the ex about the game. Imagine that! Some grassing bastard. While I was playing. Somebody actually telt her! That's hard to believe. So she didnay come in to see me she just dang – away, away she went. Her and the owner's wife. The owner's wife was there, she took Yasmin back to their house. So I'm left with Daniel, he of the sacred harp man I'm left with him, and I got wiped out, wiped clean out, every damn cent at that stupit stupit crazy mental fucking game man it was just sorry, sorry.

Norman sighed again. It's a little hard on the ears.

I do apologize.

You get excited, said Rita.

Ye're right, I do.

People use that language in Skallin? said Norman.

Naw, it's just me, I get carried away. The problem is I'm flying hame the morrow and it is making me nervy, nervy. I keep waiting for this music to start but there aint no music or else who knows, but the thing about me, if I'm too long away from music ye know I get nervy, like for me it's a narcotic. When people talk about music and like it doesnay happen man that gets to me ye see. It doesnay affect everybody the same, ye think of that dang rascal like when the game is ower, I'm standing there, I dont know, I'm waiting to go to the place we're staying, it is his place but he makes out he didnay know they were putting me up.

Huh? said Rita.

Yes maam, that owner rascal, how the hell would he expect to put up somebody's wife and no the somebody? That is what I couldnay understand and that was what made me think of ulterior motives. So me and him, we had an argument about that, I thought he was gauny dump me out the car and leave me to rot. He didnay talk to me the whole ride and it was about five miles out of town. His huis was one of these 19th-century five-story buildings, typical auld wooden structure, mair like a sailing ship than a huis. It was the hame of the feller's aged ancestor, his great-great-grandfather's place, a mean ol Ebenezer Scrooge type of body. Naw, he wasnay, he was mair like the auld skinflint uncle in what-d'ye-call-it, the one by him that lived in Frisco. I visited his huis, it was high on the hill, just up from a nice wee diner that opened 24/7. I went there a lot, maybe he did as well if it was still a diner back then – he wrote *Doctor Jekyll* and that other great yin for kids where the wee guy goes searching for buried treasure and goes mad, scrambles ower the sand dunes and refers to himself in the third person all the time, who the hell was that? Billy Bones or something, what a name.

You read a lot Jerry? said Rita.

Quite a lot, I used to. Because I had nay money. People with nay money do read a lot. Secondhand bookstores, they're good. So I was talking about, what was I talking about . . . That guy, christ ye know he pretended no to believe I was with Yasmin, he acted like I was an interloper and pardon me when I say this Rita but I telt Yasmin, I telt her, I says he's only trying to get his haun up yer skirt honey that's all he's doing, pardon me Rita but that was like fucking hell man – sorry, sorry.

I'm sorry. Yeh but that was what lay at the back of the whole sordid carry-on but she didnay believe me. It is all in your mind, she says. All in my mind, I says, oh aye, anything sordid always is. You bet, she says. Danged cheek. Anything sordid is in my mind. Yeh, she says, You heard me, what did I say, did you see my lips move?

Oh! said Rita. She said that to you?

She sure did maam, of course when she called me Jeremiah like that sometimes it meant things werenay as bad as one might have hazarded. Ye know how it is with relationships, ye get things mixed up but if she speaks yer name to ye ye know things arenay as bad as they might have been, it's when ye get the silent treatment and she never says it man that is when things are no good, that is when things are no good.

You bet, said Norman.

Rita smiled. We girls need a weapon.

You got plenty, he said.

I'll drink to that, I said, lifting my beer, a fresh bottle, standing next to an aulder yin. Ever notice, I said, when ye're close to people ye can have these beautiful times? And then all at once ye get the complete opposite. But did yez ever notice how there's nay opposite for beautiful?

What about ugly? said Norman.

Hideous, said Rita, hideously ugly.

Horrible, said Norman.

Odious, said Rita, and she lit another cigarette. There's a lot of words got that meaning.

Right, yeh.

Rita puffed on the cigarette. Hey, maybe your head's only got room for beautiful things.

Hey ho. Norman smiled.

What d'ye mean? I said.

Oh I dont know. She smiled.

Hey I was thinking of a last drink, afore I go. Yous two ready for a drink? I'll have one mair. Otherwise I'll be out all night then miss my connection!

Sure, said Norman.

Rita?

You bet.

It's good talking to yez. Ye dont always get the chance.

Well it's a conversation, said Norman.

Naw, I said, sometimes life can be beautiful. But sometimes

things are the opposite of that, if there is an opposite of that: being honest I dont think there is; just there can be bad times, we get these bad times. You says ugly there Rita, odious, stuff like that; but I'm no sure if they are opposites. To me beautiful is out there on its ayn like if it's there in yer life, if beautiful's there in yer life. Nothing can touch that. There isnay nothing else. What is there? nothing, it isnay something else it's just nothing. Excuse me, I said, and reached for the napkins, her cigarette smoke was knocking me out. I sniffed again, wiped my nose.

Cold out, be snow later. Norman nodded.

You think so? said Rita.

Yeh.

Well you know the weather.

Norman winked to me.

I have a photograph eh . . . of the wee lassie, my wee baby lassie, although she isnay a baby now, she's four. Then I smiled, caught my haun before it entered the wallet.

What the fucking hell was this all about, photographs, nay photographs man fuck that. What was I gauny tell them the story of my life! Strange, I said. Usually I'm a reticent type of body. I try to be. Mind you, people have expectations, chance acquaintances in bars, long-lost relations, man and wife; we each have these things we assume will happen.

They were baith looking at me. I nodded. Yeh, I said, she's a grown-up wee thing nowadays. I got two photos of her here. She beams into the camera. My god, anybody can see it, just that way she beams. What other word is there? Beams. That goes to the heart of it. I was wanting to take her hame with me, I'm talking about my wee lassie, but the ex wouldnay consider it. How no? How come the father isnay allowed to take his daughter back to the ancestral hame? I have my people back in Skallin and these people are my daughter's people, these are firsthand relatives, what's wrong with that?

Well there aint a thing wrong with that, said Norman.

Sure, said Rita.

You got children?

We were never blessed.

Aw. Aw sorry.

Rita puffed again on her cigarette.

You talk on, said Norman.

Right . . .

A man should see his daughter. Norman smiled.

Okay. I looked at him for a moment. Yeh, I said, but the folks back hame, they've got rights too, it's their granddaughter; my mother I'm thinking about. But ye know the law; nine-tenths is possession; who owns what like as if a human being is a chunk of gold.

It's hearts of gold, said Rita.

Yes maam but what I'm saying my faimly arenay allowed to see my wee lassie. It isnay fair. I dont think so anyway like I mean how long do people live? My mother's getting on, I was a late child. Ye go away for years and that's you. Ye've got nothing to show for it, ye're as well just staying away. Nothing, ye've got nothing. Nothing's the opposite of something. Ye cannay go hame with nothing. I've never met naybody yet who went hame with nothing, if we dont take something hame christ then what's the point of gaun hame? ye wouldnay want to go hame. No me anyway.

Norman was frowning.

I havenay been hame for twelve years, I said.

Twelve years? said Rita.

Yeh – well, eight, if we're being precise.

That's awful.

Yeh.

Your poor mother.

Yeh, my poor mother, sure. Well I've got a wean, I said, that's what I've got, so I've nothing to be ashamed about. I've got a wee daughter, a beautiful wee daughter. That's what I've got. I shrugged. I had the photographs in my haun. The wallet, I stuck it back into my hip pocket. I looked for the lassie that waited table but couldnay see her. She had disappeared. It was a thing about women. It was a mystery. There was this big woman I knew, worked in real estate, she liked me but she kept gieing me rows all the time. I used to say Hang on, I'm no here to get rows. I made her laugh. But when she got an idea into her heid man that idea could not be shifted, ye couldnay convince her of nothing; she was a survivor, women are survivors.

The place was quite busy. So that was that and time to go. Go. Yes sir. Norman was saying something. But I didnay want to hear it! I needit out of here fast boy fast. How come I left the motel in the first place? That was just stupit, that was just typical.

But I had said about the drink. The auld couple had bought me one and I wantit to get them one back. Nice auld couple and nay mair to be said. I gied them the story of my life. An ordinary auld couple, just living their life and getting out and about, no stuck in front of that television all the time. They were talking about something and I was trying no to hear, they were talking to me and kept looking at me. But I didnay want to look at them. I smiled at them but I couldnay meet their eye. It was weird but it was like I couldnay listen to them any longer. I didnay want to see them either. That can happen when people see yer photographs.

Jazz music, Rita was saying something about jazz music. To do with big bands, how they liked the big band sound, big jazz orchestras. Well I got to say that to me it just seemed ridiculous. Forty musicians on stage. Who the fuck pays their wages? Do they earn a living? What do they get forty musicians into a dang music bar! The whole thing was ridiculous. Yeh, put out the jar, let's get some tips for them bodies in the band man all forty of the fuckers. It was pure exploitation. I felt like laughing but managed just to smile. But it was comical. The girl behind the bar, I said, what is her name. Sally?

Huh? said Rita.

She says to me an hour ago the music was starting, and one sees and hears the occasional instrument being tweaked, but apart from that it's no nay never.

Music takes time, said Norman.

Well it can do, I said, it can do. Like much in this world it depends. Ever notice how contingency rules, if you do something then I can do something, if you dont do it then I cannay, even if I wantit to.

And these boys are good players, said Norman. We aint heard them yet but they got that reputation.

I think we have heard them, said Rita.

Oh we have?

I think so.

I laughed.

Norman glanced at me.

Sorry, I said. What I was thinking but there is a word gets used in this country, Uhmerkin people use it. And ye know something? I dont know what the dang word means? Guess what it is? Ye dont know? "Goofy". What the hell does "goofy" mean? I been here twelve years man and I dont know what that word means! I thought once I get to use that word properly like if ever I can say it and get it sounding right then I'll put in for my Green Card, I'll write off to the Unassimilatit Furin Folks Department. "It sure was a goofy ol night last night" is what I shall state, clearly and unconditionally. So rush me a Green Card first thing in the morning yer honor.

I got to my feet, rubbed my hands the gether, lifted the anorak from the back of the chair. I looked again for Sally and this time saw her, she was there alongside the manager guy. I pulled on the anorak. Men's room, I said, that place is freezing; why dont they lay on some heaters in the back! I jerked my thumb in a northerly direction. Ye know the song, I said, if I had the wings of an eagle I'd fly o'er mountaintops, we would all do that. What is that for you Norman a beer?

You bet.

Ye want a wee uisghé?

No thanks.

And what is that you're drinking Rita? is that a rum and sprite?

It's a cointreau and soda. Some ice with it?

Okay, yeh. I walked to the bar. People were there. Plus the pentagon feller. Oh yeh. But mair besides him and the trucker guy, also the other yin.

I was gauny go straight to the lavatory. But thought to order the drinks first. I heard somebody mention snow. I was gauny comment but to hell with it. I kept to the side, no wanting to look like an eavesdropping bastard. Or else like I was trying to worm my way into their company or something in the name of fuck why anybody would want to do that I dont know. There was a vacant high stool. I settled myself onto that. It was a wobbly fucker. One of its lower rungs was missing. That made it difficult to perch. This is why it was vacant. Then too because it was high my feet couldnay rest on the floor, only the toe-tips of my shoes.

There was aye fucking something in this life. It doesnay matter where the fuck ye are or what the fuck ye are doing man there is aye fucking something. It brings ye down. I feel that myself. Ye try to kind of I dont know ye try to just – get ahead I suppose. I was never that bothered with the rags to riches scene, we can all be Andrew Carnegie. Who the fuck wants to be an inhumanoid multibillionaire strike-breaking cunt. I dont gie a fuck if he was Skarrisch. Gie us a real hero. Uhmerka's full of them, ye just cannay talk about them. One of Yasmin's neighbors was a New Yorker, an angry feller; him and his wife were right into social history and he says how New York had one of the all-time great radical traditions but the fucking Defense industry wiped it out man the soldiers and the cops, they done it for the men with money, them and the pentagon lickspittles, they destroyed it, all the welfare and human rights, infant mortality, the lot.

Agh fuck it, let us get hame.

The manager had his arm round Sally's waist.

How come life is so consistent.

Nay doubt they were a happily merrit twosome. Unless she had lost her memory or else gone mad. Christ that also fitted, it fitted exactly. These small towns man fucking incestuous shite. People go mad and they become a slur on the community; rather than treat them properly as patients the town elders fling them to the wolves. Never darken wur doorstep again they cry! Thus the poor auld outcast must wander, the cauld wind a-blowing and the torrential rain a-falling and still the outcast wanders on and wanders alone, spurned and rejected by a so-called caring society of whom more anon.

The two were to the side of the bar. I could see how it was. Sally had moved so her heid was against his shoodir, classic female-to-male posture, it made me smile, she was just so relaxed with him. How could ye no applaud that? What else was there? Ye just wantit her to relax, yer woman. That was me, that was all I ever wantit.

I saw Rita and Norman, Rita was saying something to him, he was nodding. Ye wondered about their life. It was an ambiguous thing. But that applied to everybody.

Hey there.

It was the pentagon fucker.

Hey, he said.

Who ye talking to me? I said.

Yeh.

Hullo, I said.

You're far from home.

Yeh. I glanced sideways. The two other guys in his company were listening to a woman calling to them from a nearby table.

Meanwhile Sally was serving booze. That was good. People go to bars they liked to get served booze. Scabby prick had strolled towards the band, he was talking as he went, talking to the saxophonist who was doing his best no to yawn. I recognized that yawn. But I couldnay recall its significance.

When I worked in the booze trade I made it a point of principle: serve the cunts! Back hame in dear auld bonné one experienced minor kerfuffles but one did get served. This place was a joke. If one failed to exercise caution one became psychologically damaged in the pursuance of the pettier experiential data i.e. mind-altering substances of a liquid substance. However, I was exercising caution. Caution and me were conmingled. Is that a word, conmingled?

So you're Skarrisch?

Skarrisch.

Neat.

You know the accent?

I got ancestors from your part of the world, they were in a clan, they would be chiefs, is that right?

Chefs?

Pardon me?

Well we got a few chefs.

He nodded. So you're in the Security business?

I looked at him. He had stubble on his chin, I had expected razor-smooth cheeks, chops and neck.

What is it you do?

Office-work, I said.

Oh really?

Yeh, I compile secret documents so I cannay talk about it. Do ye know any commissioning editors attached to radical journals? Sometimes I feel like doing an exposé of Secret State activities.

We sure could do with that, said his pal, the trucker.

Like Watergate? said the pentagon guy.

Yeh, he said.

Okay!

Watergate, said the trucker, now that was something. Hey that brought down a government, you people know about that?

Sure, I said.

Wasnt that something?

Yeh.

The trucker nodded. Enjoy our country.

Thanks, I said.

Him and the pentagon guy turned away. I got down from the stool. I got back onto it again and leaned my wrists on the bar, whistling for a moment. Ye have these conversations. Unfortunate was I that my bladder was bursting. Sally was smiling at me.

Naw she wasnay it was a damn figment of one's fevered musings. She was putting drinks on a nearby table and listening to the patter of the customers who were all laughing about something. So too the pentagon feller and the other two guys, they were laughing about something.

Maybe I was a laughable personage. I got down from the stool when Sally returned. Hey could I order a drink?

I'll bring it to you, she said.

Sure but I can order it here, two beers and a cointreau and soda?

Yeh.

So I ordered the drinks then strolled to the exit and along the corridor but when I got to the cludgé door there was a wooden stave through its open handle and one sign saying

BLOCKED PIPES – PLUMBER CALLED

and below it another one saying

DETOUR, MEN'S ROOM AHOY!

Fucking comedians everywhere. And christ it was cauld, strong draughts. I walked farther along the corridor; there was an immediate twist and another less sharp yin, and mair turns along the way. A big ARROW pointed me round a bend. Another DETOUR sign and I had to go along another corridor with mair twists and turns then a goddam door that was awkward to open but open it I did and there wasnay any fucking lights man what a nightmare, and I was dying for a piss too, the auld bladder was exploding.

Where the hell was I? It was like I had blundered into the lower basement of a huis, a real huis: one where faimlies might live, and the only door I found led me into a wee square, a roofed area, a sort of courtyard; all dark and gloomy and ye could hardly see fuck all. But there were nay icy blasts so that was something. Then a side staircase but nay direction signs.

So what next? Christ. Was I supposed to go up the damn steps. I could hardly see a thing, I felt about the wall for a light switch, but couldnay find it. I touched out with my feet but all I felt were mair wooden steps. A couple of deep breaths and up I went. Halfway there came a turn and a makeshift wall, but a little moonlight twinkled from somewhere and I saw wee flowerpots and ceramics; and on thin shelves on the wall were delicate-looking ornaments, probably made of bone china. And then the moonlight stopped, and ye couldnay see nothing and if ye werenay careful ye would knock a goddam vase flying.

What the fucking hell was it? Obviously I had blundered. But surely no into somebody's huis?

Slow down slow down. The men's room in the bar was out of commission so they were making use of a neighbor's. Surely no! The entire clan of male customers out of an entire goddam pub werenay being asked to tramp upstairs to a faimly's bathroom because a plumber was being called? Did naybody remember to tell the faimly? Ha ha. Nay doubt the owner of the place was some ask-questions-later maniac complete with kazalnikov.

No sir, I had blundered. It must have been along the corridors, I took the wrong turning, the wrong door. One had entered a stranger's huis by mistake. One had entered into the goddam huis because some imbecilic cratur had put up a faulty and misleading bastarn sign and was like who knows it was like it was designed to lead one towards the eve of destruction; some weird christian or other religious prank set up for the miscreant unbeliever. Because I ignored the path of righteousness I was being pushed, pulled and harried to my doom. At times like these I needed my guardian angel, my good auld great-great. Jeremiah! Jeremiah! Wherefore art thou! Arise and walk ye spirit of the mighty!

Seriously but. Heh! I need rescuing here, us International Workers of the World need reuniting. Heh Jeremiah!

Hick fucking towns and bars with nay cludgés. No sir. I had to get out of this joint fast, fast, get back to my motel room and lock all doors. I

careful careful careful, sshhhh,
careful

and I put my hand to the wall, still hoping to nudge a light switch but naw, even if it did, I couldnay take a chance in case it awoke sleeping bodies or else from the lounge maybe if they were in watching television. But naw, that just wasnay consistent here. I was aware of a queer atmospheric shift, like the carpets had thickened and the wallpaper also had thickened. And I smelled unfamiliar odours; herbs and dried flowers, candles, even horse shit, like I had gaun back in time. I never had nay rich auld fucking auntie but if I had then this place could have been hers – some auld woman, a hunner and fifty years of age and still able to waltz across Texas with you my love.

Maybe there were nay electric lights, just candles and oil-fired heaters. How could ye move about a strange huis without a light? It was fair enough if it was yer ayn huis and ye knew the layout or if ye hadnay much furniture but here was I a lonesome furin fucker, a stranger varmint, far from hame and burdened by sorrow, in search of a quick piss afore returning to a dreich motel.

Because now I knew I was gaun straight back to the motel. I wasnay gaun back to the bar, fuck them and their jazz music. Except the tab, I had a tab running, jesus christ, I would have to go back. Then there were the drinks I just ordered from Sally. No sir, I dont run out on a pal. But eftir that! Then I was hightailing it back to the what-d'ye-call-it, the Away Inn or Nip Inn or Stey Inn or Tuck Inn or Weigh Inn or Get Inn, fucking stupit fucking metaphors or something, anagrams, ye would need to be a crossword-puzzle expert to get a sleep in this yere burg.

The top of the staircase was also dark and gloomy and with quite a wide area, with doors off, and another staircase down and I chose this without hesitation. I needit outa here damn quick man fuck the bladder it was my heid I wantit to save.

I went slowly. This staircase was also full of stuff, all kinds of junk; huishold treasures, the sundry items gold prospectors and pioneer colonizers carried with them from the auld country. Their covered wagons were full of it; grandfather clocks and Possil ormolu, paraphernalia of Caltonian lineage, the finest pottery from Maryhill, Govan and Shettleston. It was a wonder these poor auld sowels ever made it west or even reached the start of the major trails. The Indian warriors must have got a shock when they first bartered with the cunts: Where's yer tools white-eyes?

Aw fuck sorry mate we've no got nay tools but here's a fancy bowl for yer fucking mantelpiece.

Jesus christ! shouts the Indian warriors. Nay wonder we're gaun on the warpath.

All that propaganda about pretty beads, it was because these early settlers hadnay brought fuck all else, the Indian warriors had nay choice; what could they swop with the cunts if they hadnay brought nothing useful? They couldnay tell them to fuck off back to Skallin and collect their tools and kitchen implements, their sharp knifes and hatchets, the auld scissors; forget the hand-knitted tea-towels and linen hampers.

It was good I was traveling light. If I had had the goods and chattels with me I would have been scattering bric-a-brac ornaments to the wind. That stuff was all back at the motel, along with my money. I hadnay much left in my pocket; once the tab was paid there would be just enough for a cab. And eftir hours these cunts charged ye a fortune. Unless I got the guy from Ghana. He would gie me a run hame. He knew I wasnay a fucking Immigration bastard, he knew I was just an honest cunt with a furnir accent, a worker, maybe naive politically, or so he thought, but I wouldnay con him, and if I was a few cents short of the final tally the guy knew he could trust me, that the full payment was back at the motel.

Yes sir.

I just had to be careful for christ sake careful. And breathe, breathe breathe breathe, dont forget to breathe, breathe, and quietly, quietly, without agitating oneself Jerry boy that is the last thing; one steps with caution, caution is a man's best friend; forget all that tension malarkey, that never did nay cunt nay good; just doon the fucking stairs slowly and surely, with caution, caution caution caution, caution is the root of all evil. Naw it isnay. Did I even know what caution was? Me! I was the caution! Sssh. Nay wonder one laughs. What else can one do but laugh. Life is just so fucking extraordinaire misoor, pardonnez mwah till I blaw my brains out, sshhh, christ, had I laughed out loud, surely no. My problem was that not only did I treat myself in a sadly ironic fashion I did it aloud and with fucking knobs on. Aye ssh, but if I cannay switch on a light and the moon isnay allowed to shine in the windows . . .

Shut up.

I just had to get down the stairs and through the lobbies and the corridor and stuff and that back alley where

what back alley we talking about here? I couldnay mind being in nay back alley. I dont think I ever left the building. I definitely could not remember an alley. Nay such entity existed, no in the real world. So if there was nay back alley in the real world then ergo I couldnay do a piss down it. So I was gauny fucking have to fucking improvise man one of they fucking flower pots or goddam vases man what choice did I have, nayn.

NO. NO.

That was the ex's voice! I could hear her! She was shouting into my lugs. She had come to my rescue. What a dame! I aye knew she loved me deep down. So it was her as my guardian angel, no auld Jeremiah.

Well well well, I might have fucking known.

But I would be careful. I would get out fast, fast, they werenay gauny kill me. No sir, ssshh.

So okay okay

But there was a courtyard. That is where I was gauny piss. Up against the wall. I wasnay looking for no goddam MEN'S ROOM AHOY.

And maybe that was it! Maybe the signs were directing us to that empty ground. Because that empty ground *was* the substitute cludgé. I had walked ower the top of it.

So there we had it. Then I had to get back to the bar. Good. And I was gauny take a smoke off Rita. Even gooder. I liked Rita. I was gauny take two smokes aff her. One for immediate purposes and one to get me across the road to the convenience store where I was gauny purchase two hundred of them thar coffin nails and blast the lot afore getting to the airport, if I ever got to the fucking airport, if ever I found my way out this goddam fucking huis on haunted fucking hill. Jesus but I needit a slash, this was a desperate situation and desperate measures

desperate measures.

Yazzie Yazzie Yazzie.

If she had been present I would have lain my hand on her shoodir. Sometimes she liked me touching her. Other times not at all and I could feel that tension, hostile tension, a freeze. Even when we didnay want each other a current charged between us.

Breathe in. I breathed in, moved my right foot forwards to the edge of the steps, and downwards, down the stairs I went. Soon I was back in a wee enclosed space with light coming in under – yeh, a door – and I opened it, and suddenly everything was white and freezing fucking cauld. I knew there was snaw in the air but this was like the end of a minor blizzard. It was lying quite deep. Jesus christ I hadnay the claes for this kind of weather. I was city folks man and this was pure country. Fucking hell. A practical joke. I turned back to the interior of the huis as if to catch them sniggering behind me but naybody was sniggering behind me and what else could I do but shake my heid and push my way out the front door, on down the outer steps one by one by one, gripping the handlebar thing in my left hand, kicking the snaw as I went. Christ it was cauld. Funny how ye aye feel it in yer chin. Once I hit the street I could turn the corner and head back down the main drag to the front entrance of the bar.

I stepped along the path towards the exit gate. The snaw really was deep. At least the wind had died. It was quite peaceful; that silence ye get with snaw, everything calmed; including my emotions although ye could sense there was mair to come.

Earlier it was the usual gale-force blowing straight from the Northwest Territories, probably the Mackenzie region; another of the ancestors, poor bastard, he froze to death inside a log cabin. That was where they found him; he hadnay eaten for weeks. So unlucky too: eftir having made it back from setting his traps, nearly getting eaten by bears and drowning down fast-flowing rapids, there he was, all set to make a nice pot of soup, a mug of coffee, when he discovered he had nay grub and nay matches, nay flint and powder; poor cunt, he fucking starved to death and was frozen alive at the same time. Some hand that the fates dealt him. The ace of spades with fucking knobs on. I aye wondered if they named the place eftir him instead of the guy they named the river eftir. Obviously they were cousins but at what remove man that was the question.

But by fuck and bejasus this was supposed to be the fall. Who could believe that. This wasnay nay fucking fall this was the goddam winter. And if the fall in these yere parts was winter why did the locals no call it winter? Surely they could relay such information to wayfaring strangers. No tourists. Places like this didnay get tourists they just got furnir card-carriers, absent-minded gold prospectors and pioneer bodies; them with sealskin trews, wellington boots and souwesters.

People should know the truth. Why do people no know the truth? Do they no want to know?

Yeh, in a word: No.

It wasnay my place so why complain.

Who is complaining?

No me, I was stating a fact. A fact buddy, ever heard tell of a fact? these little truth data that can masquerade as phenomena, depending on who does the recording. But this is Uhmerka buddy, land of the free, ifn ya dint notice; home from home for the dispossessed, the enslaved, the poor unfortunates; this is everybody's goddam country. My people were slaves as well. The ex found that hard to believe. The trouble is I couldnay remember my historical source. She wantit me to show her there and then.

When I reached the convenience store I was gauny splurge on a pack of the choicest tabac. Six months' struggle up in the air. But I didnay care. To hell with it. Fucking lungs man what did it matter, cancer of the sarsophigius or whatever they call it, these doctors and health people bastards. All these cigarettes Rita had offered me, I could have took them and just stuck them in my pocket for politeness' sake. Then I could have brought them out now and puffed to my heart's content. Except I had nay fucking lighter. Health gets thrust upon us.

I continued forwards, plunging ever deeper into the snaw.

Only kidding.

Seriously, it wasnay that bad. But I couldnay return to the huis because I had shut the door behind me. I glanced back and heard something scurrying under the decking; some animal, a snake maybe, one of them snawsnake sidewinders. I saw a National Zoological feature about them fuckers man how they speedily slither till they get their fangs into yer neck. I kept vowing never to watch these programs. No because the violence of Mother Nature does my heid in but because they are extraordinary right-wing propaganda tracts. Do these cunts think we are total zombie eejits aw the gether? Do they think we dont know what they are up to! Hey fellers, wur heids dont zip up the back.

Agh well, whatever happened now it was too late, that front door was closed and I couldnay return inside, no unless I rang the bell and woke up the owner. I tested the depth of the snaw. Get out the huskies and toboggans.

But I couldnay be bothered with cauld weather. I had become a soft-living sun-lover and wasnay ashamed to admit it.

Agh well.

Of course the ex smoked too but she gied up for the sake of the baby. It took me longer. I didnay manage it till eftir we split. Sometimes it was good between us. Sometimes she could relax. If I relaxed. If I relaxed she relaxed.

One is fascinated by the manner and frequency with which the present willnay let the past alone. But there were serious pressures on us. She wasnay the kind of woman that puts her trust in anybody, especially pink male fuckers, except maybe I was a furnir; that went in my favour.

Walk Jeremiah walk, walk you miserable cur.

I hated the snaw. Something bad aye happens when the snaw lies. Mind you, I had seen worse. But in this weather my boots were a joke, some sort of suede. Mair like bootees than boots. How the fuck I ever bought the bastards I dont know.

It was quite difficult walking but no too bad, and the snaw was dry. Naybody had been along this way since it startit so

I was plowing a lonely trail, the boots sinking in and the snaw going up one's jeans. At least I was wearing jeans. What if I had been wearing a kilt? I spoke this one out loud. What if I was wearing a kilt! I screamed to an uncaring moon. My bollocks would have dropped off.

I was about to sigh but stopped myself. Instead I flapped the snaw off my jeans. Already they were caked with the stuff. And my boots also. Suede and jean material are porous; ergo the snaw enters and clogs up the pores. In the auld days sealskin trews were the way forward.

Is that total bullshit? Sounds kind of genuine.

But where was I!

I stood a moment. It was just too stupit. One wondered about one's mental health. Behind me I saw the footprints receding. Yasmin had a funny wee pair of feet. They werenay that wee of course, no for a woman, but compared to mine they were midget-like if that is a word. Her boots werenay particularly narrow or pointit but they aye looked neat, very neat. Even her sandals and other types of footwear, there was that quality – neatness. And that was the ex: no too thin, no too thick. Thick! That isnay a word for women. Well I never like saying fat. Fat is fucking wrong man it is too fucking sexist a word. I am talking about the correct proportions. And her ayn woman. She was aye her ayn woman. I wouldnay have wantit her to be nothing else. Then of course she was a performer so there were aye these creepy cunts hanging around.

So what man ye fight them, all that shite, ye dont put up with it. Fuck them and their fucking stetson hats. Oh dear, a stetson hat! let me hightail it out of here, I'm a-feared for one's life. Fucking bastards.

I reached down and felt the snaw. Firm and crunchy but also dry and fluffy. Fucking hell man see life! extraordinaire, all things bright and beautiful; one felt like becoming a religious feller.

What was also interesting about the world the ex moved in was things like this very plight we were in. The music world was used to these traumatic moments of precariousnessosity. She could have phoned an acquaintance and telt them to come and pick us up man drive us to wherever, wherever we were gaun. Fuck the snaw, they would have come and got us. Unless it was me, then maybe they wouldnay have come.

Of course I never spotted that much solidarity among musicians. Occasionally the way they spoke and told stories the gether ye would have thought it was some great socialist movement, all gieing each other respect; share and share alike, telling each other the good gigs and the bad gigs; never keeping secrets and always telling the truth; saying their prayers before their three square meals. Yeh well, the trouble with somebody like me, I never met nay cunt that did what I did. Missis Desperate Dan was the only person I met in my entire life that wrote books. Well it was stories, short stories, she hadnay tried any actual books. She found it interesting I went straight to that rather than just stories. I hadnay even thought of stories, but it made sense. I reached down and scooped a handful of snaw, fixed it into a snawball. I had the snaw packed hard between my hauns. I took aim and fired at a electric light pole. It missed and sploshed onto the street. I was about to try another yin but a hundred yards on this tall guy appeared accompanied by a heavy-chestit canine cratur on a long lead, a big fucker; it looked like Buster, my four-leggit comrade from the auld Security days. But it wasnay. This was a pure rottweiler, shoulders thick as a bison buffalo.

Hey boy! Was firing snawballs at electric light poles an offence in these yere parts? Maybe they sent in the local militia order of the canine brotherhood. The lead was that long the baist was basically a free agent which surely was against all sorts of laws. It could have jumped up and tore yer heid aff. I attempted a smile but it came out an interesting shiver. The owner was reining in the "pet". He probably thought I had flung the snawball at him.

or else if I had flung it at the rottweiler!

How come anybody even thinks a thing like that, even in jest. I hated people that took liberties with four-leggit craturs, even monstrous carnivores that frothed at the upper gills when they see a human being, especially a defenceless one; and everybody's defenceless when it comes to rottweilers, unless ye happen to be packing a weapon, a shotgun preferably, which I wasnay. If I was I wouldnay have been in this situation because I would have hijacked a taxi and ordered the bastard to drive me to someplace fast, fast and at all costs. Preferably the east coast. Naw, fuck it, I would have ordered the cunt to drive me to Glesgu. And do step on the gas, there's a good chap. And if le chauffeur didnay know how to wing us across the ocean I would steer the craft myself. There was a steamship firm in South Carolina that offered a one-way package for vehicular machines: avast ye lubbers.

Meanwhile here come the dawg here come the dawg.

Fucking rottweilers; a couple of hunner pound of muscle, sinew and teeth. I was taking pains no to make any provocative movements, walking slowly and steadily. Le cratoeur was having difficulty controling its paws in the snaw and mister pet-owner was trying to guide it.

They entered hearing range. That beast was gauny get a wet arse. I couldnay care less what anybody said. Okay dawg on yer mark for a flier out the traps. The hare is on the move. Dear lord it had to be done.

Oh man why was I so damn predictable. Every damn thing I done was so predictable. Now I was talking garbage oh heavenly one what I said there was incomprehensible, the opposite of a tautology. Naw it wasnay. But why in the name of god's teeth was I about to fling a hard-packed snawball at a rottweiler's arse? Was that the action of a sane feller, a rational feller. But I was just so fucking irrational, fucking irrational, I was the most fucking irrational

I reached down and grabbed for a handful of snaw, then paused. Frankenstein was staring to the front while the baist stumbled along. He was wearing a lumberjacket and one of these hats with the built-in earmuffs. Superb efforts. On the west coast ye never saw nothing like it except in museums.

When wur paths crossed el doggero growled quietly, gieing me an inquisitive look. Bad weather for god's craturs, I said.

Frankenstein nodded vaguely and walked on a couple of paces, then stopped. I had turned to watch them go, he turned to watch me. Hey, he called. What did you say?

Bad weather for god's craturs.

He stared at me. He had spotted the snawball in my hand. I displayed it to him then chucked it ower my shoodir. I wiped my hands the gether.

He sniffed, turned and walked, stepping quite quickly, considering the heavy going. If this was a track they would call off the race, unless fitting the ponies with snawboots. My hands were tingling, so were my ears. I bent for another handful of snaw. But what was I gauny do: that was what I wantit to know? I was packing the fucking snaw and it looked like I would shortly be firing a missile at a killer baist. Jesus christ I was standing back and taking aim. Mister fucking Frankenstein and his fucking bigfoot outer yeti! ah well, here we go.

Jeremiah! spoke a voice.

What?

But without awaiting further hallucinatory stimuli I pulled

back my arm, raised my left foot, and with a whoooosh I hurled that dang no-good snawball fucker straight for the rottweiler's arse. Fortunate was I that it whizzed ower its skull and splattered near the middle of the sidewalk. Frankenstein spotted it and knew the score immediately: You crazy fuck, he shouted, You know what this dog is man this is a fucking rottweiler!

Dont threaten me with yer stupit fucking dog man I'll batter it's fucking heid in and have it with chips.

You stay away from me buddy!

Dont fucking worry.

I'll let this dog loose.

It's against the law to set rottweilers on human beings. Murder 2.

Yeh!

Fucking yeh ya fucking red neck stupit bastard. Ye probably feed it merr in a day than my faimly eat in a week!

Away back to scandinavia ya mad anarchist minnesota cunt! he shouted or something similar, I couldnay quite hear.

That's racism ya ku klux klan bastard, I shouted: Ye'll be talking about repatriation schemes next! Heh everybody, we've got a fascist here!

I was gauny fire another snawball but up at a window in a nearby huis a curtain was getting tweaked. A denizen of this fair state was watching the ruckus. Maybe it was a friendly soul. Frankenstein and the baist were well away. Good. I wasnay wanting into nasty arguments with the likes of yer man. But it must be said that I brooked no nonsense. The trusty auld shillelagh baseball bat wasnay tucked down my lower spine but I definitely wasnay powerless. I hadnay tackled a rottweiler before but so what man I would get down on the hunkers and stick the heid on the cunt. Mind you, even a rottweiler was a four-leggit friend. Maybe I was out of order, a bullying two-leggit bastard. I felt like rushing after the duo and apologizing profusely. Naw but it was true, them dogs was okay.

There had been nay need to go losing my temper and picking on the big guy, him and his canine comrade. All they done was come out for a walk and look what happened! harassed by an alien in their ayn domestic hinterland. Maybe the big yin had been dozing in front of the tube when his wife woke him. She had heard the dog yelping and telt him to take it for a walk. But it was snawing outside!

It didnay matter if it was snawing outside, she says, get that fucking dog outside this huis at once, before it shits the flair.

Fuck it, grumbled the big yin but gets oot the chair and collects the canine who is by this time moaning, bursting for the toilet and needs out to the back yard immediately. Because deep down a lot of these frothing caninical brutes are clean as fuck and would rather explode than soil a flair. But poor auld Frankenstein doesnay have a back yard, he lives in an apartment with an uncaring landlord. His relatives cast him out eftir his first wife died young. Nay wonder he was disgruntled with life's irrationalities. No that he ever regretted getting remarried. For all the hassle he would rather be a married man than a single solitary cunt, having to make do with books, wanks and the radio. Ever notice about single men, they never have proper
   jesus christ

But them big dogs – greyhounds, rottweilers, great danes, dobermenn, greater spaniels – have difficulty in getting their bladders and bowels to operate satisfactorily. It is due to the self-control they have to exercise; them being trained to bite and kill at the drop of a hat, they are aye in a state of tension which is bad for the intestines. It happens in war; before the troops fight, they all shite themselves. So I was telt, and one may adduce the evidence of one's ayn ears and peepers. Homer and Jethro explained it to me when I worked at the airport. They were army vets and had been through it all, the very worst, they says how some military hierarchy thought shite-sodden pants the worst of all offences. They wantit to make it capital, shoot the grunt cunts, that was what these military high-up elitist fuckers said.

I stopped to examine my boots. They were clogged with snaw. What I needed were those smallish types of tennis rackets they wear in Lapland, Siberia and the Northern Canadian wastes; so ye can slide ower the surface and the slush doesnay clog up yer socks.

I brushed off the snaw.

One time I stole a great dane. A Saturday morning in late spring, a sunny day, and there it was tied with a bit of rope to a lamp-post outside a massive carpark greeting its big ol eyes out. Ye know what like it is when ye hear something greeting be it a dumb animal or a child, it breaks yer heart. That is if ye are a genuine person. A lot of bodies arenay genuine persons aarh jack lad they be persons by proxy, they have trained themselves no to be genuine persons, their morality becomes a politics and the actual argument has to do with whether or no morality exists or whether or no an individual has an obligation to be moral. Yes sir. On the way hame from work I took pity on the great dane and thieved it. This was on the west coast. I was driving a wee pick-up. I gave the dog a bundle of caramel cookies which I borrowed from my deliveries. So what does he do, he gobbles up these caramel cookies like naybody's business, the whole works, a boxful of the bastards. So that proved to me it hadnay been cared for in a fitting manner by the previous owner or owners. It was a mangé auld baist as well, which is consistent with the master/slave-type lifestyle ye get between dog-owners and their so-called pets – because petting is the last thing the dumb craturs get. Surveys indicate maist pet-owners are control freaks. A master decides no to look eftir ye, ergo ye dont get looked eftir; ye are incapable of doing it yerself, ye are so used to no making decisions. Chicago economics. When I got hame the dog had to clop clop its way up all the flights of stairs to the apartment where I stayed, and its knotty paws kept sliding and slipping like it was gauny do the splits; fucking heartbreaking. I had to shove its arse up the last flight and it was all wet and caked with mud and fuck knows what else, dog's diarrhoea and vomit I suppose. If I had been a caring adult I would have shot the cratur. I would have. I would have opened fire, pow ya bastard, but that is the problem when ye dont own a shotgun, ye cannay be a kind and caring body, ye are unable to put a dumb baist out its misery.

Christ it was cauld, it was cauld. I hadnay realized how cauld it could be. It was weird. I had expected to turn a corner and land on the main street. But the one I was on just kept gaun like now I was wandering through a snaw-covered landscape.

Crazy. I pulled the anorak tighter round me. But what does that achieve? What is it that happens when one pulls a thing tighter? It doesnay make ye mair warm. That is an illusion. It probably makes ye less warm. Because it allows less air between you and the undergarments and I was shivering a bit now so I stepped up the pace, but the going was tough. I stopped to kick snaw out the instep of my boots.

Fucking cart wheels!!

Naw, a truck, it had appeared at a junction along the way. Two guys in the cabin watched me. Their engine was revving. Bruisers by the looks of them. I could fling a snowball at the bastards. With my luck it would hit the windscreen and their glove compartment would harbour weaponry. But I wantit to show them how some of us dont gie a fuck for macho posturing, which is what they were doing, sitting there staring at me. What did they think I was gauny run!

But where the hell was I? Maybe I could ask them. So what if they were watching me? What else had they to do, probably working a nightshift delivery-run, 10 or 12 hours of mind-numbing boredom. For what? Fucking pennies, the going rate in this country for working-class bodies. Ah well, be it on their ayn heids for staying here man they could have emigratit to Timbucktoo or Vladivostock, someplace nice and sunny; get away from this so-called fall which in reality was a bleak midwinter.

Oh god man tomorrow tomorrow tomorrow. Tomorrow I would be hame. Well no tomorrow. Once all the different flights were taken into consideration, it was the day eftir; I wouldnay be hame for another two days, or three. If I sat down on the snaw I could will myself there. For some bodies this wee suburb was hame. Unbelievable, these northern midwesterners; tough as auld boots, hunters and trappers, them and their huskies.

All one can do is walk.

I slowed to a stop by a garden fence and extricated my right foot from a snaw drift, leaned on a spike for balance, bent to scoop off the snaw but what a pointless exercise, reminding me of the present and how there was nay break for these adverts that whoosshhed ye hame to yer nice warm scratcher.

What? What was that? Fucking gobbledygook, unless maybe my life was a television farce with breaks for adverts.

Funny how the chin gets it, like I had been to the dentist and they gied me the needle and it went numb, the auld fucking chin. Then the cheeks, no so much the ears. It was my ayn fault for taking the hood off the anorak which I done a while ago in mair clement climes.

I got the laces loosened on my left boot, took off the sock, gied my foot a brisk massage. It was damp. Plus it was red.

Red meant blood. How come it was damp if it was red? A pure red foot with wee pinkish blotches like spider bites. The two of them were pinging. Soon they would go numb, lose the blood, the white hue indicative of that absence.

A way ahead there was a wee dot of a figure and I checked my watch. But who could it be? I had the urge to hide.

It wasnay my true love. I would wait for my true love.

But she wouldnay wait for me.

What can a man do except return life to its aching parts. When I walked from hereon I would stamp these feet down hard. Otherwise who knows, they might drap aff. There was a yarn from this neck of the woods about a wagon train coming to grief going ower the mountains. What happened then? They were all freezing to death so they formed a circle sitting on the ground with the spaces between them acting as a heat convector or something. A few survived to tell the tale, the others froze to death and were eaten by their comrades.

Only kidding.

I gied Yazzie a foot massage when she had the patience to let me. It was hard getting her to relax, especially if she was in a creative mood. Am I imagining things or did she have extra long legs? She wore jeans. They clung to her knees. She hated that. When she tugged them on she complained about her body. Even a pair of jeans, she said, she couldnay get a pair to fit her. Nonsense. I loved to watch her pull them up, the way she had to duck in her hips in that wee move. I thought she had great knees and said so. She disagreed. In her opinion they werenay great. I disagreed. I kept disagreeing. Compliments drove her crazy. According to her my knees were so deformed anything another person had seemed fine. Forget my knees, I says, it's your knees, your knees are wonderful. No, she says, they are not wonderful. But they are, I says. They arent, she says, I ironed my jeans an hour ago and now they're out of shape. Well if yer jeans are out of shape it isnay yer knees' fault, why blame yer knees.

Us males think such comments are thoughtful but they arenay; they reveal a sad ignorance of the female species.

I stopped, took my other boot off, gied the right foot a rubdown. It was sair. Anybody looking out a window would think I was lurking. Fuck them. But I pulled the sock and boot on fast and nearly cramped the instep, I stamped down hard.

That was the kind of folk small-towners were, selfish as fuck, totally into their ayn heids, their ayn bodily and psychological whatever-it-is, functioning or some fucking absolutely subjective state of being jees but it was hard going on the snaw, just this attempt at ordinary walking, due to this being a slope and for some reason my left foot kept sliding and it was like I was gauny do the splits. I caught the street name:

Dandelion Gate!

What was that some kind of mental downhome joke? Dandelion Gate! I am a city boy, I screamed to an uncaring moon. Nayn of this small-town nonsense!

There was a corner up ahead and according to my nose if I turned right and then along and then right again I should be on the main drag and then a couple of hundred yards on – and maybe directly across was the lil ol Shooters and Horsemen for fuck sake what a boon it would be to see the joint. There was bound to be a cab-hire nearby. Or else maybe there was an eccentric billionaire who drove around the place looking for luckless strangers. I would have paid double the fare. Even when they do ye a good turn these billionaire cunts want a wage. Treble I would pay. It wasnay beyond the realms of fantasy I had a few hunner planked in one of my anorak hidey-holes. I stuck money in pockets and forgot about it. Intentionally. When ye were fucking broke man it was plain common sense. When in my financial prime I was a walking bank. Other gamblers done it. Even a wee ten-dollar bill when ye were down and out, it gets ye a smoke and a coffee, a tasty burrito, all burning its way down, bringing warmth to the body. The auld anorak had pockets everywhere, pockets inside its pockets. Ye fucking need pockets, everywhere. That was how I chose it. This anorak even had a pocket in its hood, in the days when

What was I gibbering about man this was a nightmare. Where the goddam hell was I! I couldnay even bay to the moon. There wasnay a moon. That meant mair snaw. It was my ayn fault. How come I was such a fool. I called me fool to my face. Because I was!

So what? I would admit to foolishness. Maist people are foolish.

Fucking Dandelion Gate but, what was that about!

I reached the corner. Ahead lay unblemished snaw but to the left there were these almost obliterated footprints. I looked closely and saw them to have pointed toe sections and wee heels. Who else but a madwoman! Or a male with small feet and a taste for high-heel bootees.

Farther on were rows of neat huises with their lawns and skinny wee trees and bushes. If this was xmas they would all be lit up with fairy lights and fancy festive designs.

Tramp tramp tramp. I was into this odd psychological mode, saying tramp tramp tramp to myself on every second or third step, but during the ones in between I was shouting at myself to buck up man get a grip of yerself, dont succumb to the elements.

Then I saw her about 200 yards on. Yasmin! Yasmin . . . But she vanished round a corner.

There was nay need for that.

Hallucinations are better than nothing.

But I was bursting for a piss man I had to have a fucking

piss. Jesus. Okay. Okay. So snaw was now a-fluttering. With or without it these streets can look the same.

The only solution was to buckle down to reality; such is the better course of action when said situation is not of one's ayn manufacture. I had nay desire for silly games, if this is what the fates were up to, it was just annoying. They knew I was as unfamiliar with this crazy damn location as they were jesus christ almighty where the fucking hell was I anywey? Another corner. I walked to it. Nay footprints now. It was just a wee street leading to a T-junction. Okay.

Nay footprints. Nay pawprints. I thought Frankenstein and his rottweiler had passed thisaway. Their footprints could have been obliterated. Everything went in this weather. It was one of these end-of-the-world scenarios when time stood still. I looked left and right, crossed to the opposite pavement. Another face at a window. Neighborhood Watch man fucking sentry duty. I waved. Coohoo ya fucking idiot.

There was a long line of snaw-clad cars and a few trees with snaw-clad branches just waiting to be whacked by a naughty boy with a big stick. I could have been that naughty boy.

Right or left?

It had to be right.

I trudged. The hair on my head wet, melting snowflakes. My front was white; I hadnay realized it was coming down like that. Snaw is a stealthy substance. I gied myself a shake. At this rate

what?

I nearly caught myself gieing me a bit of advice. That made a change.

I was drifting farther and farther from downtown. I wasnay gauny find it ever again. Here we have a typical case of a mystical disappearance. Yes sir, in the heart of nor-midwest Uhmerka one had lost the train of thought man I was chittering chittering chittering, I was chittering now alright.

Christ I was

But they would remember me, the folk in the bar, and wonder about how I vanished, they would talk about it, the case of the vanishing Skarrisch cunt. Little did they know it was them had vanished, them and their town with no name, their entire downtown area. Funny how things drop in and out yer life. Especially bodies. One by one they come and one by one they go. Tonight it was a beautiful barlady by the name of Sally. Tomorrow night it would be

an air stewardess! And the night eftir that a Glesgu lassie would be serving me a pint. Ships that pass in the night. An auld cliché but convincingly appropriate because that was what like it was. Worse. Bodies flitted in through the torso's equivalent to the keyhole, had a good sniff about, decided against what they found, then fukt off. Some deal. Also, it was up to you to make them comfortable while they sniffed about, these ghostly personages, in the off chance they might want to hang around and fucking haunt ye. That was how it was for human beings, ye were a fucking salesperson, offering yer present and future to a bunch of ephemeral strangers.

Religion was aye a taboo subject between me and the ex. Nay wonder. One could spend hours in meaningless discussion, the whys and wherefores of utter nonsense. Ye wound up lost in a maze of snaw-clad isolatory objects. Gods are no so much good, no so much merciful as all-powerful. If ye dont pray thrice three five times daily then pardon me but not only yer feet shall be ennumbed, so too shall yer other bodily externalities, yer limbs and whatnots, nose and ears, yer bollocks fuck sake and yer dick, they can all drop off as far as we are concerned. We give nothing and we take everything; so there ye are, ye wantit a pronouncement, well there it is.

I sensed the rottweiler's presence. It was somewhere in the vicinity. If I could have captured it I would have put it to good use, manufactured a sled and had it pull me. It would have helped get me back to the motel. But how do ye capture a rottweiler? Trap it. Find a fucking cage and stick in the carcass of a cow, then wait for the cratur to get into sniffing range.

Ahead was a row of bizarre huises with funnels coming out the top and weird staircases, like the custom-built homes of ex sea-captains, but nevertheless these staircases led to warm bedrooms where bodies were abed dreaming and not dreaming, screwing and not screwing. Not a single one of them knew me. I might arm myself with snawballs and send them thudding into windows, scaring the fuckers into wake & watchfulness. Then I heard music. A piano? It sounded like one. This huis I was passing had a sign on it but snaw covered what the sign said. There was something familiar about it. The windows were dark except for one which looked like a candle was burning inside, or else a wee lamp of some microscopic wattage. Nay doubt my mind was playing tricks. It could never be trusted anyway. What an admittance for any human being, one couldnay trust one's mind! I gied ma heid a vigorous shake. It needit oxygen. Blood. What about a drop of rum I thought to myself with a hee-haw-like snigger that denoted pure and unadulterated self-laceration. Sarcasm, self-directed. How low could a guy sink. I shook mair of the snaw aff me. It was good the temperature hadnay got too low otherwise I would have been in a bad state. It was obviously below freezing point or whatever it takes to freeze the water that falls from the sky but the blood in my veins was hot and fresh. I shivered, but it wasnay to do with the weather.

I stared at the huis, the snaw draped from its roof and eaves, stacking up by the guttering and downpipes. It wouldnay have surprised me had people of my acquaintance been inside, playing possum. Once I was gone they would return to their snug peat fire, big piping hot toddies, rum & honey, and lemon with hot sugarollied water and somebody dispatched for a mega-plateful of ribs and home-made piping hot chilli out the enormous pot that bubbled away on the stove all night, and a plate of fresh samosas, fresh green chillies on the side, a nice lick of raita, two chapatis. That was what I felt like, two chapatis: better still, three – and homemade; soft and puffy, jesus christ, a mate of Ranjit's sometimes turned up for these card nights, we were aye glad to see him, what a cook he was! these lovely wee hot sausage-meat and vegetable pakora with folded pork pieces that he done himself in a marinade or so I was told though ye cannay believe everything ye hear, even by brilliant pastry chefs in the tradition of whatever, whatever it was. All my life I have been surrounded by remarkable characters. But ye hear about these popular bastards; every-where they go they get invitit to cunts' huises for mighty fine downhome cooking. These homely folks are aye glad to see these popular bastards, or so we are told. How come I was never a popular bastard? And they all seemed to be good home cooks too which is what I could never figure. Haydar of course he was the fucking obvious yin. People were aye glad to see him. Nay wonder but he was great at fucking everything. He could have got me out this mess. A fucking mountain man, these guys are used to snaw-laden landscapes. But that was his fucking ancestor! Haydar stayed in Caleeforña man he never saw nay goddam snaw although he could cook no a bad spaghetti with seafood, or was it a risotto. I think it was a risotto. Risottos are mighty fine in my estimation; various fresh sprigs, oregano and suchlike, delicate spices, plus who knows what ye might find hidden in the rice, a mussel or a dod of chicken, a king prawn, an ox's tail, a rabbit's heid, a cod's tongue, a bull's bollock, a pig's foot, a lamb's brain.

Strange how ye get bodies like that, bodies that other bodies are glad to see. Women love ye and males greet ye like a brother. The very opposite of a threat. Everybody wants to welcome ye into their lives. Without you their lives are that bit mair grey, a few shades the duller. Ye bring colour and light and radiance and spiritual music, that extra dimension, ye fill people's lives with cheerfulness, richness, breadth and diversity. If ye were a popular bastard ye could walk right up and chap some cunt's door even here in the bitter wilds of some small-town suburbia. Even in this goddam very weird situation a popular cunt would simply walk up a garden path, chap a door, say hullo and be offered shelter from the storm.

Because the ex had music she forgot how for others life was a mix of impoverishments, financial, spiritual and intellectual.

The idea of living in poverty wasnay a crippling kind of notion because most of my heroes were penurious lads and lassies anyway. I aye hated, nay, despised, these populist heroes who earned millions of bucks. Nayn of them seemed to have any politics worth a plugged nickel. They all toadied up to presidents, popes, politicians, mafia godfathers and priests, and any auld fucking monarch. Nah, no for me, sorry, I'll stick with the revolutionaries.

Sometimes we expect too much. Ye feel like folk should trust ye because ye are who ye are. It was disappointing that a certain trust was never gien to myself. People just dont see ye the way ye are. They dont try. They wont even think about who ye are, only about who they are and how you fit in with them.

Yasmin, light of my life, where the fucking hell are ye! Where was I if it comes to that. Dandelion fucking Gate, it was like a practical joke. The town council having a wee laugh at the tourists, the half a dozen they got every alternate year. Them and their Jim Bridger muskets.

Mind you it was my ayn fault I was in this predicament. Patience never came naturally to me and now I had lost direction altogether. Yesm ma en-tire laff, ma en-tire laff mboy, it done gone askew.

Maybe mmy end had come. Maybe ttonight was gauny be ththe night, mmmaybe that auld gguy with the long bbblack cloak and the ssscythe was a-gonna come lukkin fir me.

The more one thought of it the more convinced one became. If it wasnay me then it was somebody close, somebody damn close. The lord save us all. The guy with the scythe was out looking for us, ice dripping from his straggly yellowing beard. At times like these one thinks of uisghé uisghé good ol uisghé.

Imagine if I was doomed to die here but in this half-arsed burg with the no name. My daughter christ what a tragedy if they found her daddy stone-stiff and stretched out.

I sighed. But it was a nervous sigh. I definitely was freezing and for some reason the arse of my jeans was soaking. Maybe when I knelt down to check my boots the doup had nudged a snaw drift.

But it wasnay very good. The reality is I had messed things up. I didnay even know where I was. I had come out that goddam huis and blundered who knows where. Insteid of gaun left I went right and then maybe I went back to front from then on; because I thought I was on the other side I startit doing all the moves in reverse. So who know, who knows where the hell I was now. The fucking huises all looked the same in the snaw, people had their curtains drawn. The best thing was to go and ask somebody, go and knock somebody's door. But they would fucking shoot me for fuck sake this was lil ol mean ol man ye cannay walk on anybody's grun or it is fucking coitans man that is the law of the land. And if I hadnay been a cleanshaven pink fucker they would have put a bullet through me already.

If I could only find my way back to the main drag. It wasnay even late. Probably the music had just startit in the music bar. Naw! The music startit the minute I left the room. Nay doubt it was all a plot. As soon as they knew I was gaun for a piss they got out the "cludgé closed" sign and sent me on a wild-goose chase.

That sounded right.

They wantit rid of me. So here I was. Christ if they had just asked me to leave I would have left.

Rita and auld thingwi – what was her husband's name? They had acted friendly. Maybe it was part of the plot. The two guys in the truck I saw, maybe they had been sent out to check on my whereabouts. They were all in on it. Even the rottweiler who bore a resemblance to Buster, same maw different paw.

Fucking hell.

Nay moon either. A sky full of them auld clouds, snaw clouds. Nay Miles Davis score for my life, mair like Rudolph the Red-Nosed Reindeer man I was fukt, I was at a standstill. And it wasnay a time for thoughtful musings. I felt like fucking screaming. So that was a good sign. Nay reflection and nay thoughts, just action, action action action:

action! action!

The guy was a veritable hive of activity

I just had to get on top of things. I began by withdrawing my right haun from my jeans pocket. The wrist was raw-looking. The tightness of the pocket had impressed on my skin an inelegant set of circular lines. The other wrist was the same. And my fucking feet were fucking freezing. So cauld! It was a time good men cracked, they went rushing to a blessed saviour and fell on their knees a-weeping and a-begging for succour, asking only that it might be immediate. It wasnay too much to ask. Any god worth his or her salt wouldnay have to be especially merciful to grant such an enterprise freely and without the barter of thrice three prayers five times daily. It didnay matter the god, they were all bountiful bastards asking only that ye said yer prayers to them and them alone.

Even there of course they didnay, they didnay demand nay such thing. If ye did pray to the wrang god the right yins knew it was a genuine mistake. If ye were praying to some other god the real yin knew it was really him ye were praying to. Even if ye didnay know the difference yerself, it wasnay an eternity-style damnation go-to-the-big-fire problem.

There was the unfathomability issue, that had to be considered also. The gods knew all about unfathomability and the total absurdity of us humans thinking it was the right yin ye were praying to.

So ye aye landit lucky; pray to the general god and the real yin heard the prayer. So it didnay matter what religion it was. It was the same as the horses, if ye were a betting man, ye aye won, that is if ye were a bookie. Even if ye didnay know ye would win, ye always did, and that had nothing to do with fixing the result. Anybody could fix a race-result, especially the gods, and punters thought gods did fix the race-results. Yet these gods didnay. Immediate basics of any kind were never granted by them. I ask only for warm feet. No sir. Human enterprises were way beneath their ethereal machinations.

The big mystery about us gods is how we offer nothing and receive everything; that is the measure of wur unfathomability to all you atheists, and until ye accept it ye remain doomed to a life of bodily discomfort.

On the other hand I could see me converting. What if that millionaire taxi philanthropist chanced to be a religious person, first he does the good deed then insists on spaking the guid word. He willnay gie ye a ride in the car unless ye sing a fucking psalm. I would go along with it. And if I found religion then so be it. I just wantit out of here.

Poor auld Jeremiah but, imagine lapsing into christianity, he must have been at his wits' end.

Unless I bumped into the caninical bison buffalo and it fucking ett me. These things happen, people are notorious for getting ett by all kinds of baists, especially in cities like Thunder Bay and Spokane, Duluth, Bismarck, all these venices of the norths, moose and bears, fucking freezing places man I needit back to the west coast.

A window with a light.

I gathered my brains together, pushed open the garden gate. There was a drift of snaw here and no way round bar I fought through branches and big bushes with spiky talons and beaks. Once in there was no turning back. I continued on in the manner of a righteous person, pushed the intercom buzzer. A reply came; it was a woman's voice: Oh what is it now? she said as if I had been bothering her all night. If you dont leave immediately we shall call the police.

Dear oh dear, I said, that's me fukt.

I heard noises behind the door. Bodies were peeping through the spyhole. I smiled although no doubt the glass took the form that distortit yer features and I would have appeared a grinning maniac.

I returned down the garden path, collected some snaw, packed it hard and hurled it with full force at the window but missed the building altogether. It was an extraordinary failure from such a short distance. I stared at the building. There could have been irrational reasons why the failure occurred. At the same time ye have yer eyesight and all the appropriate parts of yer body and then yer brains to adjudicate on perception but here comes bad weather to impair the sense faculties, the act of perception getting impaired by snawy conditions.

The curtain moved at the window.

I was not pausing. I seemed to be taking five-metre steps.

I was getting aggrieved. Instead of showing it I tried to maintain ordinary discourse with the fates. I spoke to them as one rational being to another.

Of course the fucking anorak didnay help matters; as far as protection is afforded from inclement sources it was a no-no man a fucking no-no, it wasnay even like a real material, it was like cardboard. I would have been better with a big handkerchief wrapped round me for all the good it was doing.

And boots. From now on it shall be leather. Secondhand, thirdhand, who gies a fuck; whether or not we have a regard for the hide of dead animals, animals rendered dead in order that their hide may be available; let us call it skin.

oh fuck Jerry

–

It sounded like Yasmin. Yasmin in a bad mood – naw, in a sad mood.

Sad moods can be strange in people ye think ye know well. They enter into sad moods even as a result of mistakes they themselves make. Then they act like it was your fault, sparked off by what you their partner brings to the relationship. Here is a bad side of us, a sad side of us, and it wouldnay exist unless we were close to you ergo it is you to blame, something in your personality.

That is one of the strangest things about bad moods and sad moods.

With the ex it was difficult to know what she was thinking. She was a mystery.

No sir, people have to put trust in people, especially the nearest and dearest. She lacked trust in me.

My feet were sair and I was fucking tired of walking, I was just tired aw the gether, I needit a seat but there were nay seats. There was a small power box. I balanced on it, raised my right foot. I tried to unloosen the boot but the fucking laces were jammed the gether, the soaking wetness destroying any chance of unknotting the thing and I had to kick it and punch it and pull it, and eventually it eased somewhat and I could get it off, then the sock which was soaking wet. I wrung it out, my foot balanced above my left knee.

Just as well she wasnay with me.

What would happen if I collapsed from exhaustion? I would freeze to death.

Yet there was a cauldness about this place too, and it wasnay an earthly cauldness, mair an unnatural chill like death stalked abroad, the ghosts of all these 18th-century gothics. Who was that Uhmerkin guy that wrote the strange tales of mystery, darkly horrific experiences, out of the mind experiences.

Maybe it was the silence caused by the snawy wastes, the singularity of landscape. The snaw had stopped falling. It had done a while ago but without telling me. Ahead I could see a hill appearing out the night mist. Not a breathtaking hill. Nevertheless one could imagine a troika jingling in the distance, some doctor hightailing it out to a dying child, the parents in the candlelit gloom of the shadowed kitchen, listening to the strangled gurgles from their baby's breast, the slow monotonous sputter of the samovar, until the chigoinga chigoinga chigoinga, a darted look to the window, chigoinga chigoinga chigoinga – Sascha I hear the doctor! the little one yet may live!

Jesus christ what was that?

There was nobody apart from us two, the figure in the distance and me.

I sense these unnatural things. I aye had that ability.

Death choked the air, it was abroad this very night and I didnay fucking like it, I could sense its very core, a dull tick. Shut up about death, I said, you've always got to talk about that, that subject, and it is a pain in the neck, it really is, because ye always wake up alive alive oh.

So I do. Life is cheery after all.

I once convinced myself I was dying, and then of course I didnay die, it was amazing.

I telt Yasmin's cousin. Between me and you, I says, the doctor telt me I'll die young.

A stupit thing to say, I admit that readily. It was one night eftir a performance. The ex had been so damn good it made me just overjoyed, my heart palpitating. I kept looking round at the audience to see if they felt the same, I wanted to grab them by the scruff of the neck and shake it out them, ya bastards I hope yez are rightly appreciative. I was clapping away and it came to me I was gauny die quite soon. No suicide either which was a surprise; I kind of figured myself for a suicide.

But oh jesus when Yazzie found out! I had to confess on pain of her murderous assault on me. Why did I do it? Why! I told her cousin I was dying. It was outrageous. I knew I shouldnay have done it but I did. But why!

Well, sometimes it is appropriate to the occasion; it is a reminder about how beautiful life is, right at this very moment, designed for that, to allow people to recollect that this is no fucking rehearsal Yazzie, here we go acting like it is a rehearsal, we are on this planet one time and one time only, and if people dont want to act like human beings then fuck them, you might be gone tomorrow and then it will be too late, and they will have regrets. They will regret not having forked out this pathetic drop in the ocean, when either you are dead, or I am dead, and that might be sooner than anybody thinks, being honest about it I dont think I have long to go. So I aint got no goldarn je regrettes about fuck all.

I saw the police camera. I stopped and waved. It was perched up a pole at the corner of the street. Heh buddy, I called, I am skint! Gauny send me a chopper!

I did a quick semaphore and with big mouthings so they could lip-read.

I had stopped beneath it. I scraped snaw out the heel of my boot, just to let them gawp at the wintry conditions, what these actually mean to living individuals, when ye aint got the goddam apparel that pertains to said situation. I decided against taking off the socks aw the gether though it seemed a wise course of action; I could carry the items in one's front pockets and they would get warm and dry from the heat of my body; then I could return said fuckers onto said feet and they would be good and comforting.

The forces of law and order have to be reminded about life and its sanctity. Dont let the bastards off the hook. They try to act like we arenay real live human beings. They arenay trained in seeing us properly, us people I am talking about, these Security fuckers man it is trained out of them. I took off the boots. My feet felt good, they werenay cauld now they were just damp, with white patches where the blood had sallied forth. But still and all raring to go; these feet, with or without the fucking blood, they never let me down, my body dont need no fucking blood. What was blood to me? Fuck all. Nothing.

The bottoms of my jeans were stiff as a board; the snaw stuck to them, the hair showed at my ankles. At one time the hair would have covered my ankles, it would have covered the whole of the human body, human fur – just like the temperature of the groin, the genitalia interregnum, that would have been something like 45°C, back in the olden days, the ice age, nothing surer, the tadjer had to stay warm, had to stay hot, had to say ripe for progenyzisation. I wrung out the socks and put them into my pockets. There was a squeaking noise now;

my feet were slipping on the soles. Jees they were burning up. Fucking hell they were on fire! The friction. The life force. The living breathing blood-coursing life force, the very atom itself. That head to head collision. All these different parts of the body in constant engagement one to another, not only one another but with various outside parts of the material universe. Even the ears were affected, a steady hum through the branches of the trees, the vibrations colliding with the human ears, setting up this friction. That was why the auld monastics sought cells in the deeper recesses of the more inaccessible mountains, the farther away the better; not just from people but from the elements, they didnay want friction, they wantit no impingements to the Glory of the Lord which was always impending, so even the fucking sound of the fucking wind through rushes man that too was detrimental, acting against the impulse to meditation, the purity requisite for such spiritual trials man it fucking impinged on thought, it impinged on the very soul man its brave but foolhardy attempt at unity with God jesus christ people are amazing, they are amazing, they have been getting up to such mischief for 5 hundred thousand years.

Longer, it was a thing to check out, if one had one's fucking notebook but one never had one's fucking notebook one's notebook is always one step beyond thus the thought must await the morrow, but shall the morrow ever come? Do we want tomorrow to come? Can tomorrow be exploded into a thousand pieces? What is a piece of tomorrow?

Neighbors of the ex were creationists and whenever I was in their company they came out with the stuff. I was aye flummoxed, could never call to mind the arguments, so they wound up winning the battle, much to the ex's joy.

Strange how she wantit me beat by everybody, even although what I believed was what she believed. Life was a mad headlong rush for her, poor lassie, the very force itself was draining out her and she refused to accept the situation, she was fighting hard, clinging on, eking out each last gasp, it was amazing.

This was my last night on the planet. An alien starship would transport me across the universe. Who knows what the gods decree in their infinite leg-pulling, I was gauny be one of the great mysteries that dissolve into the preternatural twilight of time.

Suddenly I was reminded that inanimate objects cannay be cunning.

It would all be over soon. No matter what transpired, in an indefinite period from now there would have been a conclusion, there will have become a conclusion, and no matter the conclusion a form of consolation would arrive; conclusions bring forth consolation.

Then I was staring at an approaching shape. Who was this fucker? The shape was upon me. I could only smile and declare myself: Where I come from appearances like this are second nature, I says, and second nature implies intuitive forms of thought which arenay always trustworthy given their good intentions. When ye fall into the sea in the depth of winter ye are advised to don heavy clothes. This is farcical because the advice arrives concurrent to the minister or priest blessing the fleet, so their advice stops ye meeting yer maker 80 seconds sooner. As a non-swimmer I used to know precisely how long it took the average male to die of the cauld if he fell in the water – women last slightly longer.

The party coming towards me, he was gauny die. If I wantit to crack his heid I would crack it. I just needit a blunt instrument.

Now my foot got trapped in some peculiar twist of slush and awkward movement and I stumbled, slithered and sat down heavily on the snaw, the thump jarring all the way up

435

my spine and its effect on my neck was more than momentary. I sat there, I was getting my breath back. Mister cop gazed at me. I waved at him. Good morning, I said, I'm in the Security business myself, but the cheap end of the deal; see if I had your conditions . . . !

I wiped the snaw off the seat of my anorak and the legs of my jeans. Why did I no longer have my shillelagh baseball bat. That stick had its place in my existence. If I had the stick all would be vunderbar, given that the only problem carrying a weapon is the strong chance ye will use it.

Everybody has decisions to make. On the other hand

A heid appeared at a window, the curtain drawn aside. I gied whoever it was a beamer of a smile. All we do is prepare for various worsts; we get an idea of these various worsts, we posit them, and in the positing is our preparation.

The feet were numb. The boots had been a mistake. The decision to buy them was based on the foolish notion that wearing them might cast an interesting glow on a dull personality.

If we are discussing time: 'tis often at a standstill.

Excuse me, I said, eh excuse me! Is there a diner around here? Let's go for breakfast the gether.

The cop delivered me a deucedly odd look. He was a stolid sort of fellow with bushy eyebrows and on the whole it was best our relationship was at an end. But now I recognized the street. It was the very one! Unbelievable! Jees oh, I was off laughing, being reminded of a time I was about 15 years auld and slap dang in the middle of danger territory. Yes sir. Another gang's area and me and a couple of buddies had entered into it, just for the craïc, would we get hit by a bolt of lightning, and so on. Naw! Nothing happened. We walked up and down for two entire hours, whispering and giggling like fuck. What's Gaelic for "swaggered". One of the happiest experiences of my life. Doubtful I was ever happier. Someday I would set it down for eternity. Elated is mair apt than happy. Elation and happiness

But that was long ago. Now here was I a man.

It's just a suggestion, I said to the cop, fumbling for the good ol ID. Behind him I spotted his patrol car. How come I had missed it.

And now the snaw was falling. If I rose and dashed headlong I would fall flat on my face. I preferred to remain where I was. But soon the cauld was in through my skin and I was in a state beyond shivering. Ahead I saw a huddled group of persons. Who the fuck were they? If I rose and dashed headlong, down the streets up the streets, but without no fucking sidewalks, having to step on people's lawns, tricky stuff. In some states the lieges have the right to gun ye down for that transgression. All ye do is place a foot on their grass and bang. If they discover ye are a Red Card carrier then fine, nay cunt gets done for killing ye. Fortunate am I that my looks are regular. Some folks aint safe boy, no at first sight. This is no polemical diatribe against the evils of imperialism, colonialism, capitalism and all the rest of it. No sir, being a guest in the place I shall not abuse ma hosts, nor query the criteria relating to

quid bonum est

I forgot what was I gauny say

But being an outlaw is a serious affair. If anybody with a medical interest ever did a survey of these poor unfortunates it would reveal that the vast majority die of pulmonary diseases brought about by nervous disorders. Take Billy the Kid.

Yes sir.